STOIC

by Eliyang

HHB
HAO YIAN BOOKS

This book is intended for mature, adult audiences only and its not for the faint of heart. It contains explicit and detailed sexually graphic scenes, adult language, sexual assault, rape, and violence, which may be considered highly offensive by some readers. Discretion is advised. This book is strictly intended for those 18 years or older.

Editor and Proofreader: Darci Heikkinen
Front cover design created with Canva

First published in 2021
Hao Han Books LLC

ISBN-Hardcover: 978-1-956766-00-4
ISBN-Paperback: 978-1-956766-02-8
ISBN-EBook: 978-1-956766-04-2

Eliyang
eliyang.novels@gmail.com
https://linktr.ee/Eliyang
https://eliyangnovels.wixsite.com/my-site

To my husband for his unconditional love and support and to all of you who gave this new author a chance. I said the book would be an emotional rollercoaster, and you hopped in without hesitation.
Thanks for the leap of faith.

PROLOGUE

Their story takes place years after the continuous wars that rocked the world for decades ended. All nations and countries as people knew them dissolved, and most of the borders were erased. Maps were mostly big pieces of land, marking how the continents were shaped after the extreme change.

They were simple people like most people at this time. Their families weren't poor, but at the same time, they weren't rich. To be truthful, it was difficult to become rich or dirt poor in that place. There were no passports, no visas, just a universal law that applied to all humans, making them all equal, ensuring the distribution of all kinds of products evenly among everyone, and the fair contribution of all world citizens as well.

People then recognized that the only way to survive was together, so the whole world put aside their nationalities, religions, and ideologies and worked together to survive the catastrophe. The world had no prominent leaders, no powerful countries overseeing and meddling in everyone's business, and no big oppressors. There were laws and law enforcement, but it was enforced by villagers and designated officials.

After the big scare from the drastic climate change of the mid-forties, the disappearance of many coastal cities, and hundreds of millions of deaths, people moved to live in the center of their lands. The place their families called home was much like that.

Those who survived still had all past knowledge about technology and such, but since resources were so limited, most of them led very simple, minimalistic lives. People lived in plain, small homes, located in villages, with limited means for transportation. There were gravel roads, but most did not have vehicles. Not all settlements had schools, pharmacies, or big hospitals. The stores were small, and all non-essential products were scarce. Schooling was done mostly by parents at home, and people usually opted for teaching their kids their own professions.

Professionals and higher-education careers were pursued by those who truly loved what they were doing. Being a doctor had no higher reward than being able to save people's lives. You would have the same or slightly better commodities than everyone else. Scientists, engineers, and architects too. All these people made lives better for everyone. Whoever wanted a career like that just needed the motivation to go for it. All higher studies were free for all who were willing to serve their communities.

Everyone was required to work at least three hours a week farming in the fields, children included. The food was distributed to all. If there was too much food, they would exchange it with nearby villagers, and if the food was not enough, they would all ration it.

Since resources were so scarce, old professions like blacksmiths were in great demand. Melting and reusing metals was one of the first steps needed to stop mining. That was what their fathers did. Since all money systems were obsolete, their job was rewarded with the exchange of goods.

The system worked for everyone, but people had recently started talking about the rise of a tyrant in the north. A power-hungry shit of a person trying to control wealth and unite land for profit. Starving some of the population and enriching a very small group, himself included. They were all past that, and many were willing to fight for their way of life, hold the northern border, and stop those that sought to take their prosperity away from their hands. The vast majority lived their simple lives and trusted that the armed security forces would deal adequately with that situation.

As it was mandated for all males, at age 18, he was sent to the northern border for his military service, while for her, life was as simple as it could be.

Soon the countless words both failed to say out loud, empowered a destructive silence.

ONE

EMMERSON

Laughter, wine, food, and cheerfulness. Everybody here was happy, celebrating, completely unaware of my pain and misery. The warm summer breeze entered the house, swishing through the front door, cooling the room we occupied. This should have been a beautiful evening. The clear skies showed millions of blinking stars, and the moon shone on us like the queen she was, but I wasn't enjoying any of this. Jokes were being told, and memories from our childhood were being brought back to life. The stories that they all loved to listen to over and over again were being retold. I heard my name being called, and I saw their fingers point at me. I knew there had been questions asked, but I couldn't meet anyone's eyes–I couldn't speak.

Everyone was celebrating that my older brother Kenzo and his childhood friend, Stoic, had returned home safely after a nearly five-year-long deployment to the northern border. Glasses were being raised high, and the thundering sound of "cheers" invaded my mind.

My whole family was there. His whole family was there. He was there.

I had my sight solidly frozen to the floor, my nails digging into my arms and my knees trembling under the table. It took all my strength just to try and hide the pain and the discomfort between my legs from what had happened just a few hours before. I readjusted myself on the chair and felt a stabbing pain run across my core, my back, and my legs. My hand immediately grabbed my lower abdomen, as I hissed in pain. From across the table, I heard a low grunt, and then I heard him adjust his chair and lean further forward on the table. I could see him out of the corner of my eyes. He had his elbows on the table and hadn't for a second taken his gaze from me. I bet he was enjoying the sight, knowing that he had broken my body beyond repair, that there was nothing left of me but debris of my past self.

As dinner continued, laughter boomed and bounced off the thick wooden walls of my childhood home. I hadn't taken a single bite. I had been moving my food around the plate but never ate any. How could I? I could only feel disgusted. In my mind, his rough hands were still running over my body, his breath on my neck. No, I refused to think about it. I fixed my gaze on the floor and avoided closing my eyes for fear of seeing his face, like a nightmare that followed me and wouldn't let me go until I was shredded into a thousand pieces.

"Emmy, pass the vegetables." I heard my brother Ethan say, waking me up from my daze.

Picking up the bowl, I stretched my arm in front of me and waited for Ethan to grab it, when my eyes met Stoic's for a few short seconds. Great mistake. There he was, sitting right across the table, jaw clenched, brows frowned, squeezing a fork between his calloused hands, with pure anger in his eyes. Blue eyes silently demanded me to keep looking back at him, daring me, but I declined. I couldn't. As soon as Ethan took the bowl, my eyes dropped, and I felt the weight of his gaze all over me again. Like an overpowering darkness that slowly pulled the light out of my body.

I would rather be anywhere but here, hell included. The cold and darkness of Niflheim would be an escape from the burning flames of Stoic's deep blue devilish eyes. I would rather dine across from Hel herself than sit across from "The Dokken" for another minute.

Pulling my long sleeve up a little, I stared at my bruised wrist under the table. Rapid images of his monstrously big hands holding my wrist against the damp sand flashed through my mind. His heavy and wet body crushing me with his weight, holding me in place. His chest rocking back and forward over mine as he thrust hard inside me. The slapping sound of our skin as our bodies forcefully met. His thick rod mercilessly ripping my insides. The pain. The way he licked and bit my nipples and groped my breasts. His blue eyes staring down at me as his face became distorted with lust, his mouth hanging open. The animalistic grunts that escaped him as he used my smaller body for his own pleasure. The last hard thrust he gave before stillness took over his body and I felt him shudder, pouring his release inside me. The excruciating pain in my entrance, and the feeling of my blood and his seed running down my thighs as he pulled his softening member from me. His heavy breathing. The smell of it all. No, I had to avoid him. Once, I trusted in him. I always had. He was supposed to be like a brother, my friend, and not the perpetrator of my demise. I was reduced to nothing but a lifeless, empty shell.

I felt my right elbow being shaken, and my eyes landed on my mom. She had what seemed to be tears of joy in her eyes and a sweet smile on her face. She slowly pointed to the farthest right side of the table, where my father stood with a cup of wine in his hands.

"Emmerson, dear, did you hear what I just said?" my father said with his eyes full of love. He was a kind man, always caring for his family, always doing the right thing.

"What?" I asked, completely lost.

"As you have known your whole life, your hand in marriage has already been promised, and your mother and I couldn't be happier. After all these years, we have finally decided to tell you who your fiancé is. As we have always told you, your fiancé is an extraordinarily respected man, and no one is more worthy in my eyes of the great honor of becoming your husband. There's no one I'd be happier to call my son."

Why now?

I knew what that meant. At least I would be taken away from here and far away from Stoic. They said they would tell me who my fiancé was a month before the wedding. I immediately felt embarrassed. My husband would think I didn't wait for him.

How could I tell him that Stoic had stolen everything from me? Would he believe me?

My father coughed to get my attention back.

"With that said..." he extended his arm toward Stoic. "We are glad to announce that these two families will soon be officially united. Stoic, my son, the day has finally come when you can claim your wife, and in a month's time, you two will be jo..."

Silence...

I didn't hear anything else that was being said.

Those words felt like an ice-cold bucket of liquid shit had just hit my face. I was frozen in place, unable to move, unable to breathe, unable to think. Somebody had taken the ground from below my feet, and I felt like I was falling into a dark void. Reality came crashing down on me like the thunderous sound of that dreadful waterfall. I was promised to Stoic.

Mother. Fucking. Stoic.

Seconds must have passed by when I felt my mother excitedly shaking my arm. I heard cheers from my brothers, his parents, and our grandparents. I heard their voices, but I couldn't make out what they were saying.

Why were they celebrating this?

I couldn't fathom what had just happened, and tears started rolling down my face. I couldn't control them. I heard a round of "aws" coming from all parts of the room.

Fucking idiots, all of them.

They believed I was speechless out of surprise and happiness, but nothing was further from my horrible truth. I was terrified, holding on to my chair as if my life depended on it.

Stoic stood and started walking over to me. I could hear the hard sound of his heavy steps getting closer every second. As soon as he was close enough, he got on one knee and took my shaking hand in his, slowly putting a ring on my finger. When he let my hand go, it fell by my side, hanging lifelessly. I still refused to look at his eyes.

He stood and got so close to me that I could feel the heat coming from his big body. He leaned closer to my ear. His lips were so close that I could almost feel them move. With a deep but low voice that only I could hear, he said, "You are mine," sending chills down my spine. He tucked my hair behind my ear and left me there, drowning in my own tears. Soon, the space that his body occupied was filled with our family, all rushing to congratulate me.

All I could think was, how did all this come to be? Why was my family so brainwashed by him?

I only had one month.

How the fuck would I escape the devil?

TWO

EMMERSON

Emmerson 4
Stoic 10

~Fourteen years before the dinner~

I was a free spirit, a child of nature. I loved playing outdoors, getting my hands in the mud, rolling in the grass, and swimming in the river. We lived far away from the sea, surrounded by trees and nature, misty and mysterious, and a bit cold–but I loved it. I always wore hole-filled pants and a dirty T-shirt, with my dark brown super curly and tangled hair spreading in all possible directions, sweat on my forehead, and a big smile on my face. I spent my days climbing trees, chasing squirrels, and dancing to the sound of my father's hammer. My dad, along with his lifelong friend, Erik, were blacksmiths and ran a workshop down the main road.

My mother always struggled to teach me things. I didn't like taking my lessons. I had no idea of what I wanted to be when I grew up, and to be honest, I didn't care. Any time I could, I'd always run and hide from her.

"For the love of God, girl!" I heard my mom scream at me at the top of her lungs.

I was hiding behind a tree, a big grin on my face, trying hard to hold the laughter back.

"Emmerson Silva! Come here, right this instance!"

I kept quietly giggling.

"Come out, or I'm gonna tell Stoic!"

That did it.

She knew he scared the shit out of me. I would always do what he asked me to. I didn't want to get on his wrong side.

I ran straight into my mom's warm arms. She was truly beautiful. There was no one more beautiful than my mother in our village. My father was so lucky. She had the darkest shade of black skin I had ever seen. She shone! My father, on the other hand, came from a more Caucasian background–short blond hair, pale skin, green eyes, thick beard, funny looking, but strong and kind, as kind as a person could get.

I was the youngest in our family. Three kids, and my mom still looked like a model, flawless. My two older brothers, Kenzo and Ethan, and I would give her a run for her money. We all had light brown skin and wild, curly hair. My brothers' eyes were a very dark shade of brown like our mom's, just like a mirror, but not mine. I had light brown with green in them, like my father's. I really was Daddy's little girl.

Since my dad and his best friend had known each other ever since they were children, our families were very close. They lived so close we could see their house from ours. I always saw my Uncle Erik and Auntie Ida as my family. They wouldn't say it out loud, but I knew I was their favorite. They both were redheads and had fair skin, so of course, their son Stoic turned out to be a pale ginger.

Auntie Ida was a very beautiful woman too. Her long, wavy red hair was the envy of the village. She had freckles and pretty light blue eyes. Uncle Erik was a tall, hard man, very strong, like my dad. He was kind, too, but you could see he was also tough. He had long curly hair that reached his shoulders and was slowly turning white, a long beard, and many tattoos. His chest and arms were fully covered with them. He had some on his legs, too. My dad had some on his arms, neck, and chest, but not as many as Uncle Erik.

Stoic took after his father. He was the tallest child his age, over five feet tall. Strong as a bull, but stupid like a rock. Stoic was their only child, and he happened to be just three months younger than my older brother, Kenzo. No surprise, they were best friends. Ethan was only two years younger than them and would always tag along with them to play. The dynamic trio was the talk of the village.

As my mom started to wrap up the studies for the day, I closed my books and nervously started looking around our front yard. I knew what time it was. Kenzo and Stoic were about to be done with their training for the day, and Stoic would be at my house, staring at me with those scary blue eyes. He always sat next to me, making me feel smaller than I already was, looking down on me with that serious, expressionless, stupid face of his.

He didn't talk much, but when he did, he asked the most stupid questions and said the most ridiculous things. Stoic always tried to make gotcha questions to see if I had learned my lessons for the day. If I failed, he would look at me like I was a disgraceful bug. No matter what I did, I was always a disgraceful bug to him.

Every day was the same. He made me finish my homework and watched me eat my dinner with his angry blue eyes. He complained if I didn't finish my food and patted my head if I did. Like a dog. After dinner, he always complained about my appearance. He told me how little girls shouldn't be this dirty and roughly washed my face with his big hands. Stoic waited for me to be done showering, then pulled my brains out by "brushing my hair," calling it detangling, and scared the shit out of me with a Nordic tale before sending me off to sleep. Stoic liked Norse mythology, so he would always read to me about it. From the splendor of Asgard and Valhalla to the darkness and cold of Niflheim where Hel dwelt. He often babbled about this place.

He was a major pain, and everything was bad, according to him. He didn't like me playing outside by myself as he said it was dangerous. "Little girls shouldn't be climbing trees." He didn't like it when I played with my friends. "Little girls should be playing with other little girls." He hated seeing me full of mud and happiness. "Little girls are supposed to dress pretty, and they should be learning how to be a good woman for their future husband."

Stupid Stoic. He knew how to kill the fun in everything.

He treated me like a baby, not letting me do anything by myself. His nose all the time stuck deep in my business.

I hated him.

He even cut the food on my plate. "You need to chew smaller bites, or you'll get a tummy ache." He was so annoying!

I had always known that I was supposed to get married one day, but Stoic would always remind me. My parents said they had the perfect guy, but I could not care less. I was not supposed to get married until many years from now, so why worry now?

Stoic was the bothersome older brother that I never asked for. Thanks to him, I lost all my friends. He scared them all away with his stupid, ugly face. He was nothing but a bully. I lost count of how many of my friends he grabbed by the neck and tossed away like weightless potatoes. He was so cruel. My mom and dad loved him, though. I didn't know why.

He was always at my house. Auntie Ida was a nurse, and she was always busy since doctors and nurses had to travel to reach the patients. Ida usually returned home very late on weekdays, so Uncle Erik and Ugly Face would dine with us most days.

Tomorrow was my birthday, and Mom was gonna make me my favorite meal. I would be five, and Ethan said that I would love my presents this year. My family would usually get me very useful and pretty things like boots and books, but not Stoic.

His gift would not be a surprise to me. Stoic always brought me the ugliest, saddest-looking dolls you could imagine. He had awful taste. The things had mismatched arms and legs, odd colors, and heads that were too big for their bodies. Who knows what trash can he found them in. I already had four of them. The ugliest bunch of nightmare-worthy toys out there.

Stoic was so predictable. He would always get me ugly rags for my birthday, some weird-looking metal thing for the summer celebration, and something made out of wood for the fall harvest festival. Last summer, I got a weird-shaped metal he called "Jeg elsker deg" or something. He wrote the name on it, so I wouldn't forget it. He was so weird. For fall, he came home with a swing. He hung it from a nearby tree. Best present so far.

After dinner, I went to clean my hands and face with the devil behind me, watching my every step. He was like a shadow. After my shower, he sat me on the floor between his long legs and began torturing me with the comb.

Stupid Stoic.

My only comfort was that tomorrow, the weekend started. There were no lessons on the weekends. My whole family would do some farming work together in the morning. For the rest of the day, I would get lost in the woods and have fun digging rocks and finding frogs. In the afternoon, we would have my birthday dinner. It would be a great day.

As always, Stoic told me a story before bed. This time it was about how Odin, father of all gods, got wiser by drinking out of tree horns.

How could drinking out of a horn make you wiser? Stupid Stoic with his silly stories.

He covered my little body with my blanket and harshly patted my head. After he closed the door behind him, my room was finally filled with darkness. I closed my eyes and dreamed of the awesome day that awaited me tomorrow.

I couldn't wait!

THREE

EMMERSON

Stoic 10

~Day of Emmerson's Birthday~

"**D**on't go far, and remember to be back home early." I heard Daddy scream at me as I ran full speed into the woods. No one would stop me, not my brothers, not Stoic. I would climb all the trees I could and jump headfirst into the river.

As I arrived at my favorite spot, I saw my old friends playing. Noah, Mason, and Oliver used to play with me every day, but that was before Stupid Face got angry at me for not doing my homework and slammed down two of them on the ground at once. Now, they ran away every time they saw me.

I approached them with my hands up, "I come in peace."

The three of them stopped what they were doing, eyes landing on me and immediately after, desperately looking around and behind me. I knew what they were looking for, the devil's shadow.

"Can I play with you guys? Pretty please!"

"No, go away!" Oliver shouted.

"Yeah, go away, or Stoic will kill us," Mason added.

"He won't 'cause he doesn't know where I am. Please," I said, putting my hands together and begging.

"No way, I don't want to die," Noah said.

"No, I promise. He won't find us."

Why wouldn't they believe me?

"Yes, he will! The Dokken always finds you. No! No! And no!" Mason screamed in my face.

Well, that was not necessary.

"No, he won't," I screamed back at him, emphasizing every word. "The Dokken" sounded like a mythical monster's name. Pretty appropriate, I gave them that.

Noah raised a hand with a smirk on his face as if to say, "I got it!"

"Okay, we will let you play with us, but only if you accept our dare."

"OK, fair. Go ahead, tell me, what do I have to do?" Yes! I had a chance! I stood tall with my hands on my hips.

The three of them gathered in a circle and talked in a low voice. After a minute or so, Noah walked forward.

"We dare you to climb that tree and bring the sparrow's nest down with you." He pointed at the very top of the tallest tree.

"Done!" I said, full of confidence, not even looking up at my destination. I rolled my sleeves up and pushed my hair back, but it bounced back in my face. I could do this. Taking decisive steps, I walked my tiny feet to the tree.

"She's not gonna do it. She's scared. What a baby." The little jerks joked around.

Let's see who would be laughing after I got that nest.

Looking up, I didn't feel as confident anymore, but I wouldn't show them. I decided to do honor to my name and be brave.

I started climbing the tree and soon realized that the task was going to be more difficult than it seemed. It had rained in the morning, and the tree bark was damp and slippery. Refusing to give up, I kept climbing. After getting halfway up the tree, I lost all confidence, and now I was not even sure if I knew how to climb down.

"You're not gonna make it, you loser." They mocked me, and I knew they were right. I was stuck.

The three boys were so distracted laughing and making fun of me that they didn't notice Stoic getting closer to them.

Who was the loser now?

"Where the fuck is Emmerson?" his voice boomed. The three kids instantly shat their pants. They tried to run for it, but it was too late–there was no escaping him now. Before they could run, Stoic had one by the neck and the other two by their shirts.

He was angry. When I heard the harshness of his voice, I knew I was in for a whole lot of trouble. I looked down, and I saw my frightened friends trying to get out of The Dokken's claws.

My foot slipped, and I let out a high pitch scream as I held on for dear life.

"Emmerson," he said softly. Stoic dropped them all when he saw me. He didn't even look at them. As soon as they hit the ground, they all ran.

"Don't move. I'll get you. Don't move, Emmerson. Hold on."

It must have been just a matter of seconds before I felt Stoic's hand grab my arm.

How did he get up here so fast?

"Hold on to me, Emmerson." He pulled me toward him. And for the first time in years, I was so happy to see his stupid face that I hugged him. He hugged me back so hard it almost hurt.

"Hold on." He put me on his back, and I wrapped my arms around his neck. "Hold on tight."

I wrapped my legs around his torso.

"Don't be afraid, Emmy."

I wasn't.

Stoic climbed down the tree with me on his back. I could tell it was tricky, but he did it. I got to say, Stoic was strong and talented, but only for the physical stuff. Lucky him.

Once we were on the ground, he put me down, and I waited for the screams. I closed my eyes, flinched, and waited... but nothing. I opened one eye, but Stoic was just looking at me. Serious. Frowning. He pulled my right arm up and looked at it. He pulled my left arm up and looked at it. He dusted my pants and turned me around.

"Are you hurt?" He sounded angry, but once again, he always was.

Was he worried?

"No," I said softly.

"Good."

Silence.

Stoic just sat on the ground right in front of me. After what felt like minutes of silence, Stoic took a deep breath and stood up. I then saw the ugly red bleeding scratches he had on his arms. I felt bad.

"Come," he commanded, and I followed. No questions asked.

I thought Stoic would take me home and tell on me, but no, instead, he walked us to the river. Near our home, there was a beautiful river with a sandy beach and a waterfall. I loved the sound of the water falling hard against the rocks.

Stoic signaled for me to come closer. He started cleaning his arms in the river, and I carefully walked to him.

After two minutes of silence, I decided to speak, "Don't tell Dad."

"I won't."

"I'll never do it again."

He nodded his head and kept cleaning his arms.

I sat there looking around, completely absorbed by the scenery when I felt Stoic grabbing me and then throwing me in the water.

"That's what you get for not listening."

I jumped and gasped for air. Stoic was there at the rocks, looking at me with that serious face of his again. The cool water felt great. Ha, if he only knew! This was not a punishment for me. I'd been wanting to swim in the river for a long time now. I giggled, he was so dumb. I was like a literal fish in the water. I loved it!

Stoic sat on a rock, "Don't swim too far."

"What if I do?" I said with a bratty voice. I liked bothering him. Stupid Face got angry fast.

Stoic jumped in the water with me and made a huge splash. "Swim, Emmy, or I'll get you."

I squealed and started swimming as fast as I could. There was no way I would let the monster catch me. I screamed and swam even faster, and I was gaining some distance when Stoic caught me. He held me like a football and walked me back to the shore. I kicked and splashed the water with my arms and legs all along the way. I didn't want to go. Stupid Stoic always ruined the fun.

"We need to go back." He made me stand on the shore, squeezed my shirt a little, and tried to pull my hair back and off my face.

"Emmy, a hill or a valley?"

What? Another stupid question.

Stoic had the habit of making up nonsense questions, and he never explained why he asked them after I answered.

"A hill?" I said as a question more than an answer, and he nodded.

He put me on his back and carried me back home just in time for my birthday dinner. My mom helped me change my clothes, and once I was clean and dry, I joined my brothers in the backyard. The table was set, and Daddy and Uncle Erik were barbecuing.

Stoic arrived moments later with a box in his hands.

Oh no! Not another ugly monster doll.

He put the box down and went to play with Kenzo.

I ran after Ethan and played with him until Mom called us all to the table. Dad put a candle on a cornbread muffin, and everyone started singing "Happy Birthday" to me.

"Make a wish!" I heard Auntie Ida say.

I closed my eyes, thinking hard about what to wish for. There was only one thing I wanted, for Stoic's scars to heal. It was my fault, after all.

I opened my eyes, filled up my cheeks, and blew an exaggerated amount of air onto the candle. My family clapped, and Ethan rushed to me with three boxes

The first was from my uncle and auntie. They gave me a music box that had the most beautiful melody. I ran and hugged them both before returning to open the rest of my presents. The second gift was from my family, a fishing pole. I loved it! I couldn't wait to learn how to fish! I hugged the fishing pole and kissed it. The third was Stoic's.

I was ready to see an ugly doll, but instead, there was a dress inside the box. I lifted the thing with a confused expression on my face. The dress was green and simple. It looked more like a long sleeveless shirt than anything else.

"I don't want to wear a dress!"

"Emmerson! Don't be like that. Say thank you," my mom said, giving Stoic a reassuring nod.

"I don't want a dress. I want a sword!" I didn't want a sword, but that was beside the point. I didn't want to dress like a girl. Girls were boring.

"You need to start acting like a girl, Emmerson, not a savage little animal," Stoic said in a low voice.

What did that mean? Was he crazy? Had he lost it?

I shot my meanest glare at him.

How dare he?

"You're stupid," I said, stomping my feet.

"Dumb," he said in between his clenched teeth, but loud enough for all to hear. Stoic was not even looking my way; his eyes were fixed on the distance.

"And you're an ugly poop," I screamed, the worst insult I could think of.

"Clueless ignorant," he murmured, keeping his blue eyes away from mine, which made me angrier.

Dad coughed, "OK, kiddos, let's not fight."

"But I don't want to dress like a girl." I was not going to let this go.

"One day, you'll be a woman, Emmerson, and there are girl things you might want to learn," my father said. "Why not give it a try?" he asked.

With those cute, sweet green eyes of his, how could I say no?

I pretended to be thinking for a few seconds. "OK, I'll try, but if I don't like it, I'm not wearing a dress ever again in my life."

"Deal. Except for your wedding, OK?"

"OK."

You won, for now, Stoic.

FOUR

EMMERSON

Stoic 14

The dress thing wasn't that bad, but I wore it with pants. It was like having a very long shirt, and I liked it. I could still run and jump in it. The other three birthdays after that one, he got me dresses too. I guessed that from now on, he would be giving me dresses.

I remembered that during the summer, Stoic gave me a metal hoop as big as my head. He said that from that moment on, he would get me a hoop every summer, but that each one would be smaller than the last.

He was so stupid. Why would I want a collection of ugly hoops of different sizes? He was an idiot.

So far, I had four of them. They fit, one inside of the other perfectly. Some were thicker, some were thinner. Who knew why, though?

The wooden gifts for the harvest festival during the fall were always the best ones. Once, he brought me a small rocking chair. It was super simple, but it was just my size. He told me not to worry if I outgrew it, as he said we'd give it another use later.

Time passed, and I still had zero friends. Girls thought I was strange, boys were scared as chicken shit of Stoic, and wild animals were not the best company. I learned that the hard way. I must have got bitten twice before I realized that squirrels hated me.

Stoic would make me go to the river once a week to fish. Sometimes we caught big ones, and Mom would cook them for us. Stoic said that the fish I caught were his favorite meal, but then he made me fish for him as if I was his slave. Fishing took an excruciatingly long time. Boring, Stoic just sat on a rock as if he was among his family members and looked at the water. I got bored and talked non-stop. Each time I asked him about something, he would answer accurately. It didn't matter how specific and detailed the question was. I didn't know how he did it. Not even I could remember all the things I asked. Kenzo and Ethan would join us fishing, too, but they sucked at it and just swam in the river instead.

Stoic and Kenzo were changing fast, and they started to look very different. Stoic had been doing a lot of exercising with Kenzo. His shoulders were broader. He got taller, way taller, and his face was growing hair. Hair! Yuck! His face was changing, too, getting sharper. His jaw was super square now, and he looked hideous. The scariest thing was his voice–it had gotten so much deeper. At least I would have a laugh when it cracked and made him sound really ridiculous.

I didn't spend much of my time around girls, but I could hear them talking about him all the time. They were all idiots. I hated what they all said about Stoic. "Stoic is handsome," "Stoic is smart," "Stoic is so tall," "Stoic is so strong," "Stoic this," and "Stoic that." If they knew Stoic like I did, they would stay away from him. Some even pretended to be friends with me when he was around. I didn't care. I called them out right in front of Stoic's face, and they would all lose their shit. I liked how Stoic smirked when that happened.

Stoic didn't seem to be interested in girls, though. He ignored all of them. It seemed it was not just me; it looked like he hated all girls. Scratch that–I knew he hated girls. He looked at them like they were disgusting cockroaches. I knew many would try to talk to him, but he completely, absolutely, and painfully ignored them. I had even seen some of them cry over him.

My brother and other guys his age were utterly different. I didn't know why guys liked those fake-looking girls so much. I bet none of them would make it more than two hours in the wild without melting. Guys seemed to always be chasing them, but not Stoic. That rock only liked fishing. Maybe the only girl he could stomach being near was me, and because I was like his sister, he didn't have any other option.

It was mid-August, and Stoic's 14th birthday was today. I had the perfect prank in store for him. Uncle and Auntie were having a birthday dinner at their house for him later in the day. Since Stoic liked to fish so much, we decided to go fishing in the morning. Kenzo had a girlfriend now and had started acting stupid, so it was just Stoic and me again. It was the perfect time to put my plan into action.

I brought a little box wrapped with a red ribbon with me and told him it was a secret birthday present. The box was empty. I told him he could open it after he caught the first fish.

"Emmy, three or four?" There it was, the stupid question. I just started to answer with whatever came to my mind first.

"Four and a half."

He nodded and wrote it down. Weirdo. He had this notebook full of numbers. Who knew what wicked thing he was up to.

Before we knew it, the line was shaking, and Stoic reeled in the fish. It was huge. He put the fish in the bucket and extended his arm toward me.

"What?" I asked like I didn't know.

"My gift."

He was too tall, and for my plan to work, I had to be able to reach his stupid face. I walked backward, not losing sight of him. He had a strange look in his eyes. He might have known I was up to no good. He knew me too well.

He slowly sat down, and his eyes narrowed on me. Stoic knew for sure I was up to no good. I got the little box and stepped closer to him. I got closer than I needed to. He just sat and looked at me. I knew he didn't trust me. I gave him the box, and he hesitated.

"Open it," I sang.

He gave me another hard look and started pulling the ribbon. Stoic opened the box and found nothing.

"It's empty."

"What? No! Did it fall?" I mustered my best acting. I covered my mouth with my hands as if I were surprised and got closer to "look" into the box. He was caught off guard.

"What was it?" He looked around the ground.

By then, I was really, really close to him. He wouldn't be able to escape me. I internally had an evil villain laugh moment. *Wahahahaha.* He would be puking for a week.

"Oh, I think I see it!" I was a diva. I was standing really close to him, in between his legs.

"Where?"

"Here!" I grabbed his face in my hands, squeezed his cheeks, and pulled his face up. Once his face met mine, I kissed him. I gave him the wettest, biggest kiss I could. Ha, he was stupefied.

His eyes were wide open, and his face got tomato red. His lips were a little open from my squeezing, so I knew my saliva was in his mouth. I was enjoying my victory! Since Stoic was frozen in place, I just kept my lips tightly pressed against his, holding my laughter back. He didn't move. After a long while, Stoic still hadn't moved yet, and I started to think that this might not have been a great idea after all.

When I tried to pull away from Stoic, he put one hand behind my head, pulled my jaw down with the other one, and pressed me harder against him, slipping his tongue inside my mouth.

Yuck!

I tried to push him off, but he didn't flinch. He started licking my tongue with his, and his lips moved on mine.

Yuck, yuck, yuck, and yuck!

His eyes slowly closed, and he seemed like he wanted to eat me alive. The hand on my jaw slowly moved downward, touching over my chest and continuing lower. That felt wrong.

I was desperate. I didn't know what to do, so I kicked him in between his legs. My foot hit something hard, and Stoic fell on the ground, doubled over, and grunted.

"What the hell, Stoic? Yuck!" I started spitting and gagging, making as much noise as I could. The joke was on me. I would be the one puking for a week. Stupid fucking Stoic.

Stoic stayed there, all curled up on the ground, holding his pants. I couldn't even see his face, but his ears were red. I cleaned my mouth with the river water and spat many times. Minutes must have passed by, but Stoic stayed on the ground, face in the dirt until I started to get worried.

"Are you okay?" I looked at him like he was a strange thing I found on the floor and was about to poke with a stick.

"Turn around, Emmerson," he sounded embarrassed. The big old Dokken had been fallen by the foot of a tiny girl. I wished I could record this.

"Why, though?" I was going to give him a hard time.

"Because I said so. Just turn the fuck around, Emmerson."

"Make me!" I was a brat.

"Emmerson, turn around, or I'll kiss you again."

That did it! "OK, OK, you are so stupid." I turned around, and I heard Stoic move. I gave a little peek and saw him turning his back to me, getting in the water.

"What are you doing?"

Was he going for a swim?

"I'm going for a swim. Go, Emmerson. Take the fish with you. I want to be alone." He held onto his head as if it were about to fall off. He still had his back to me.

"No, I want to swim too." He always kicked me out of all the fun things.

"Fuckdammit, Emmerson. Leave!" he yelled at me. He was angry, and he looked desperate. I swear he was bipolar.

"OK, you ogre!" I picked the bucket up and stomped my way home. There still was a lot of time left before the dinner, so after leaving the fish with Auntie

When it was time, I went home, changed my clothes, and walked over to The Dokken's house with Mom.

During dinner, Stoic didn't look very animated, not that he ever was, but he looked more miserable than his usual self.

I'll be damned. My plan worked. Ha!

I must have taken a toll on his pride because Stoic still looked embarrassed during dinner.

Wahahaha!

He stood up, and his father followed him. I saw him talk briefly with his dad inside the house. From the look on their faces, it must have been something serious.

They came back when it was time for him to get his presents. He got an envelope from his father.

What did it have inside? I had no idea.

All I knew was that Stoic loved it. He gave his dad a tight hug, and his father patted his back many times before letting him go.

My family gave him some big odd-looking tools that looked like saws, some spiky things, and a shovel that my father made himself.

What did he need tools for?

I didn't know, but this was Stoic, so nothing made sense.

It was getting late, so we all started talking and joking around. Stoic remained silent–like always. Somehow my mom brought up the girlfriend topic, and Ethan immediately started making fun of Kenzo for his new "girlfriend." Kenzo swung his hand and slapped the back of Ethan's head so hard it echoed throughout the backyard. We all laughed, saying how come Ethan's head was empty enough to make that sound.

My mom jumped in and said that Riley was asking for Ethan that morning. Auntie let out a funny "weeeee" sound, bothering Ethan even further. We all laughed so hard that my belly started to hurt. Ethan tried to defend himself and said, "At least I have kissed a girl. Stoic runs away from them like they have the pest!" Kenzo chuckled at that comment, finding it completely hilarious.

I let out a big laugh and said, "Pfft, I kissed Stoic, and he was so embarrassed he rolled over and stayed on the ground, hiding his face for five minutes." I was laughing hysterically without noticing all the laughter around me had died, and I was the only one still laughing.

Suddenly, everyone's heads turned toward Stoic, and they were looking at him with disbelief in their eyes. His face was so red it almost looked purple.

I kept laughing, and my mom slapped my thigh. "Stop it"

"What? It's funny."

"Emmerson Silva, stop," she said, as in "zip it or else."

"Stoic, can I have a word with you?" My father's voice had never sounded deeper.

Stoic nodded, stood up fast, and walked into the house. My father stood up and walked right behind him.

"I'll join you two," my uncle said and followed them. Once they got inside, they closed the door.

Was he in trouble? I was the one that kissed him, though.

I heard a soft chuckle and looked to my left. Auntie Ida was covering her mouth, trying not to laugh too hard. I heard giggles to my right, and my mom was doing the same. Behind me, Kenzo and Ethan were laughing too.

"So, you kissed him?" Auntie asked, and I could hear more laughter.

What was happening?

"To bother him," I said, not sure I liked where this was going.

"Yeah, right," Ethan said.

Stupid, why else would I do it?

"I'm not lying! It was to bother him."

Oh, I'd be in trouble for this. Oh crap, they thought I liked the ugly face ginger.

"Yeah... bothering him. That's a good one, Emmy," Kenzo said, making quotation signs. I wanted to punch him in the face.

"Just remember, Stoic is not a little boy anymore, sweetheart," my mother said. He never was. He had always been tall as hell.

"One day, you'll get it," Auntie said, then patted my head.

FIVE

EMMERSON

Stoic 14

Two months had passed since the birthday debacle, and Stoic was barely speaking to me. I must have pissed him off. It looked like he was super busy, but he still came over at night for dinner, combed my hair, and put me to sleep. Luckily, that was pretty much the only time I saw him during the day.

He even stopped fishing. He said he didn't have time to fish with silly and immature little girls like me. It was not like I cared. I liked it better like that, anyway. With Stoic out of the picture, I was free to do whatever the hell I wanted without having The Dokken's shadow behind me.

I finally found a friend! A girl that was not girly, just like me. Amelia and I hated other girls, so we became friends fast. Amelia's skin was darker than mine, and her hair was afro like Mom's. Her mom always made pigtails for her. I thought she looked cute with them, so I asked my mom to make them for me, so I could look like Amelia too.

She was fun but weird, the good kind of weird. She had a thing for leaves, so she collected them. Since Amelia had a collection, I also wanted one. Not having much to choose from, I settled for collecting beetles. As you might imagine, my collection was a bit problematic for Amelia, but she didn't mind too much. So far, I had twenty-four beetles, but six died. I kept them anyway.

Since we spent so much time together, people started calling us twins. Some kids would call us names and try to bully us, but Amelia and I would throw rocks at them with our slingshots and make them sorry for even thinking about messing with us.

Amelia had an older brother, Landon. He was two years older than us and played with us sometimes. He was tall and athletic but not as tall as Stoic. No one was as tall as Stoic–he was a giant. Landon was a hugger. I was not very cuddly, so Landon did make me uncomfortable at first, but I thought I was getting used to it. Landon usually hugged me hello, goodbye, and pretty much anytime he felt like it without a reason.

It was fall, and that meant time to celebrate the harvest. I'd gone with Amelia's family to the fall festival. I had plans to meet my family later on for the concert. So far, we'd done the hayride, the corn maze, the rolling pumpkins, and we were on our way to the petting zoo. I was determined to hug every animal there. I guessed Landon's hugs were becoming contagious.

I had locked arms with Amelia and was skipping when I saw Stoic. He was a bit far, but I could tell he was holding something wrapped in a piece of fabric. I knew I was going to get my wow gift, so I pulled Amelia by the arm and ran toward Stoic.

Stoic saw me and just stood there waiting for me to reach him with his serious face on. Some things never changed. He looked at Amelia and raised an eyebrow.

"She's my best friend, Amelia." I knew what he was thinking. He didn't need to talk.

Stoic smiled at Amelia. Wow, that never happened. Maybe he was okay with her.

"Is that my gift?" I said, pointing to the fabric. I was excited. Don't blame me, I loved gifts.

Stoic nodded and gave it to me.

I eagerly unwrapped it, and what I found inside was something I wasn't expecting at all.

"A boomerang?" I asked. Don't get me wrong, I liked it, but it was just that it was not very Stoic-ish to give me something like this.

"It will always come back to you." He pointed at the boomerang.

Duh! Thank you, Captain Obvious.

I knew that–that was the whole idea of a boomerang, right? I turned it in my hands and noticed Stoic had put his name on it.

Narcissist.

"Thanks, I love it!" I really did. I smiled at him, and he smiled back. He must have been having a good day because he looked like he was in a really good mood.

"Emmy!" I heard Landon call me from not too far away.

Oh no! This was not good.

"Emmy, Amelia, I thought you guys were gonna be at the petting zoo," Landon said, putting his arm over my shoulder and pulling me close.

Oh crap!

I turned my face to see Stoic, and he had his eyes locked on Landon's arm, jaw clenched, and a big frown on his face. He looked pissed. Scratch that–he was pissed. He was about to breathe fire out of his nose and ears. I tried to laugh out loud to de-escalate the situation, but it sounded super fake. By then, I was really worried about Landon's life.

"We were on our way there when Emmy saw her friend. Look, a boomerang," Amelia said, completely unaware that her brother was about to die.

"Cool!" Landon took the boomerang from my hands, and I heard Stoic take a [illegible]

"Who's Stoic?" Landon asked.

I forgot Amelia's family was new to our village. There was no way on earth he knew about The Dokken, but he was about to find out the wrong way.

"Me," Stoic said with a deep, loud, monster voice. If looks could kill, Landon would be a goner.

Landon looked up and flinched when he saw Stoic's face. Stoic already had his hands forming fists and was stepping closer and closer.

I had to do something. I couldn't let Landon die in front of his family in the middle of the festival with all the children watching.

I pushed Landon's arm away from me and quickly stepped in between him and Stoic. I put my small hand on Stoic's belly and said, "Stop. Don't do it. They are my only friends, please!"

Stoic stopped and looked at me. By the way his eyes were moving, I could tell he was thinking about it. Good, there was hope.

He took a deep breath, stretched his arm over me, and harshly grabbed the boomerang from Landon's hands. He gave it back to me.

"It's for you and you only." His eyes locked on Landon as he spoke, but I didn't know if he was talking to the other boy or me.

Was he talking to Landon or me?

Stoic then leaned down and kissed the top of my head, still looking at Landon. Well, there was no blood. I counted that a victory.

I walked to Amelia and locked arms with her again. "Let's go! To the petting zoo!" I tried to sound cheerful.

We took a few steps, and Landon started following us. Before he could put his arm around me once again, Stoic grabbed his arm. By the look on Landon's face, Stoic was squeezing the life out of it.

"Don't touch her." That sounded more like a murderous promise than a command.

Landon tried to shake his arm off, but Stoic just held it tighter.

"Stoic! Let him go this instant!" I felt like I was talking to a dog. Bad Stoic!

He looked from Landon to me. "He touches you one more time, and I will fucking break his arm." He was not joking. He said that to me, but the message was for Landon. With that, Stoic dropped Landon's arm and stepped back.

"Hey, what the fuck is wrong with you?"

No, Landon, no.

That was definitely not the moment to get cocky. I barely saved your ass.

Stoic raised an eyebrow at Landon as if to say, "you fucking dare, you little shit." Stoic gave him the scariest, creepiest smile I had ever seen and stepped closer once again, making me fear the worst.

"Who the fuck do you think you are, huh? Acting like Emmerson is yours or something. You creep!"

Well... it was nice to meet you, Landon.

Stoic nodded, "Yes, Emmerson is mine, and I fucking hate it when a piece of shit like you touches her."

Landon opened his mouth to reply, but before he could say anything, Stoic's body shifted, and he gave Landon one solid punch right on his mouth, knocking the hell out of him. It was so fast that I didn't even see his fist moving forward.

After a loud cracking sound, Landon fell to the ground out cold and lay there, unconscious, with his mouth bloody. I thought Stoic broke one or two of his teeth. Definitely busted his jaw. Ew!

I got so angry. Furious, to say the least. All of a sudden, I remembered– Amelia! She was in shock with her hands covering her mouth, frozen in place. Oh no! I was about to lose my best friend ever because Stoic got all weird and violent again.

Fuck him!

"Fuck you, Stoic! You ruin everything! I hate your ass!" I screamed at him at the top of my lungs and kicked his legs as hard as I could. My attack did zero damage, which enraged me even further.

Stoic said nothing. He just took the boomerang, grabbed me by my hips, threw me over his shoulders, and walked away.

"Let me go, you huge asshole!" I kicked and screamed, but there was nothing I could do. He was calm, serious, like nothing had happened.

When Stoic got a few feet away from the scene, Kenzo tried to stop him by pulling his arm. "What the fuck, Stoic? What happened?" Kenzo said, looking back at Landon on the ground and the people gathering around him.

"Motherfucker had a death wish."

"Fuck, Stoic, I understand, but you can't keep doing this. We talked about it, dude." Kenzo started walking beside us.

"Had to." Stoic just kept walking.

"You're gonna get in trouble for this, man!" Kenzo was nervous.

"Don't give a fuck." He really looked like he didn't. Damn Stoic, he didn't care about anybody but himself.

"I hate you! I hate you, I hate you, I hate you." By then, I was crying, snot to want to talk to me ever again. All because of Stoic.

I kept kicking and hitting his back with my fists. I'd make him pay for this. I bit his back as hard as I could, and he spanked my butt hard.

"Stop that, Emmerson!"

I only stopped because I didn't want another spanking.

A few more minutes went by, and then we were home. He took me to my room, dropped me on my bed, and pointed to the floor. "Stay!"

I was not his pet! Like hell, I would!

I stood up and tried to walk to the door.

He pulled me up by the armpits and sat me on my bed again. "Stay, Emmerson, or you'll regret it."

I was angry, but I knew he wasn't lying. He had that scary "I'll destroy you" face on. I was too scared to fight him any further.

Stoic left, slamming the door behind him. I could hear Kenzo talking to him, and then Dad's voice joined in too. Soon there were a lot of people all talking at once, and I couldn't tell whose voice was whose.

I threw all the ugly dolls on the floor and stomped on their heads, pretending they were Stoic.

Evil jerk!

His only joy was to make my life miserable.

SIX

EMMERSON

Stoic 15

The joke was on him. Stoic got grounded. It was about time Uncle and Auntie put a leash on the wild dog. Stoic was grounded for about three months. Everyone tried to help fix what he had done. My mom made a nice dinner for Amelia's family as an apology. Uncle Erik gave them two free metalwork jobs as compensation that he made Stoic do by himself, and Auntie Ida helped Landon with the medical stuff. My dad didn't do anything. For some reason, he sided with Stoic, and so did Kenzo. But that was not a surprise–Kenzo and Stoic always had each other's backs.

Stoic did break two of Landon's teeth and his jaw. Landon looked funny without them for a while, but then Auntie Ida helped him get them replaced. He had a bandage wrapped around his head for a long time. With that said, Dickface was not allowed anywhere near Landon.

During the time he was grounded, Stoic picked up a new hobby. He was already good at making things out of wood, but this time, he was not making them for me but for exchanging. He started learning with an experienced carpenter and worked for him during the weekends. He was good. The furniture he made was surprisingly nice. Dad told me he was working on a new bed for me since I was growing so fast. I bet that would be my fall gift.

That winter was colder than usual. The snow covered everything, and we were stranded at home for most of it. Dad, Kenzo, Stoic, and Uncle Erik reinforced the roofs of both of our houses to make sure they would hold up for another strong winter like the last one. Ethan was not a muscle or hands-on kind of guy. Ethan has started to become more interested in studies, math, and books. I was sure he would be one of those people who would go for a long education and become a "professional," like an engineer or a doctor.

It was July, and Amelia's birthday was today. She was turning eleven. For some reason, Amelia decided to keep being my best friend. I was so happy she didn't abandon me. We were the best of friends, and we were growing closer and closer every day.

Her moms made a birthday lunch for her and invited us. Dad and Kenzo were busy helping Stoic and Uncle Erik do something, so it was just Mom, Ethan, and me.

For some reason, funny, silly Ethan was always super quiet when he was near my friend. Maybe he didn't like her. He never talked to her. Not even when she spoke to him. Nevertheless, he always tagged along with us. He was spending a lot of his time around us.

"Hey, Emmy!" I heard Landon call me with a big smile. I was glad he didn't hate me. He never put his arms around me again, though. I was kind of glad about that.

"Hey, you!" I ran to him, stopping abruptly once I was close enough. Ethan followed me. "Where's the birthday girl?" I couldn't wait to see her. I made her a gift all by myself, and I couldn't wait to give it to her.

"She's in the backyard. Come, I'll take you there." Landon pointed at the backyard, and Ethan and I walked behind him. Mom stayed behind and talked to Ana, one of Amelia's moms. Amelia's backyard was much like mine but with more trees. It was a hot sunny day, but the tall trees made the perfect amount of shade.

"Amelia!" I let out a squeal and ran to her. As soon as I got to her, we gave each other a huge, bone-crushing hug. "I got you something!" I sang, doing a little dance as I gave her the small box.

"What is it?" She shook the box with both hands.

"You'll have to open it to find out..." I sang it again. We chuckled, and she sat on the grass with the box.

Amelia opened the box and found my creation, my masterpiece. Mom had let me mend together some leftover fabrics, and I had made a small bag for Amelia. It was simple and mismatched, but it looked cool.

Amelia's eyes lit up, "I love it!" A smile spread across my face.

"I'm glad you like it. When I get better at it, I'll make you a better one."

"Nah, this one is perfect. Can't wait to use it!" She gave me another hug. I liked hugging her. She was the sister I always wanted.

She stood up, hung the bag on her shoulder, and pretended to model. "How do I look?" she said, pretending to flip her hair. It was funny because her afro hair didn't move. I laughed and stood next to her.

"Say, I believe you are absolutely spectacular," I said, trying to sound like a sophisticated middle-aged man. We laughed like idiots, and Amelia shifted to her side to look behind me.

"Hey, Ethan, I see you there!" Amelia screamed at him. I looked back and saw Ethan's reddened face. He tried to stay out of sight but failed. Ethan turned around and left, annoyed, like always. Amelia laughed, she liked bothering him. He might be her Stoic.

That evening we had dinner with the Dokkens like we always did. Auntie Ida lived with us this time. Mom had made so many biscuits that Ida and Erik took a dozen to go. I knew Stoic would eat most of them. He ate like a loose pig.

After everyone was done with dinner, I took a shower, and as always, Stoic sat with me on my bedroom floor to comb my hair.

"Emmy, a big window or sliding door?" The stupid question. He never stopped asking them.

He asked a stupid question, so I would give him a stupid answer. "A glass wall! A big one," I said, spreading my arms wide. Like always, he nodded.

"Emmy, are you OK?" he asked while combing my hair.

Why was he asking?

"Yep, why?"

"Emmy, there's something I want to talk with you about." He was talking slower than usual.

"Yeah?"

Well then, just spit it out.

"It's about... It's something important." He kept combing my hair. He was beating around the bush.

"Yeah..."

Any day now.

Stoic coughed, "I... well... you see. Guys, I mean boys and girls have some differences."

"Yes..."

"And, sometimes, when a boy and a girl get older, they–"

"Have sex?" I jumped in. Yep, my mom already taught me all about it. Super gross, if you asked me.

"No! I mean, yeah, but... um ..."

Hmm... he was mumbling. Interesting. "But what, Stoic?" I turned around to see his reddened face. I could see he was uncomfortable talking about sex. Being the little brat I was, I was going to give him a hard time.

"Yes, people get interested in sex as they get older. But not everyone is thinking about it the same way," he said faster than his usual talking speed while shaking his head. Pfft, he looked funny.

"Are you thinking about it?" I wanted to see how long he would last until he lost his patience and sent me to hell.

"That's... that's not the point I'm trying to make, Emmy."

"So, you are not?"

"Emmy, I... I'm not talking about me. I'm talking in general," he said, and I studied his face. Yep, he was super uncomfortable.

"Do you or do you not think about sex? It's a simple question, Stoic." I knew he was getting embarrassed. Stoic acted so maturely, but he was so easy to bother.

"Well, sometimes... Emm, the point is that some guys don't have good intentions, so you need to be careful." He wanted to wrap it up, but I wouldn't let him.

"What do you mean?" I put on my "I'm dumb. I don't get it" face.

"Well, sometimes girls want friendships, but guys are looking for something more...."

Oh, I knew what he wanted to say. Stay away from boys, little boys are the devil!

Nice try, Stoic.

He couldn't scare me out of having friends. My eyes narrowed on him. He was trying to manipulate me since he couldn't bully my friends anymore, or his ass would get grounded. He thought I was stupid. I was going to make the conversation impossible for him. I would make him pay for all he had done.

"What if the girl wants the same thing the boy wants, though?" I said, narrowing my eyes more. Got him. His eyes went from confused to angry.

"Emmy, you are too young!" That sounded like a warning.

"Who said we were talking about me? We're talking in general, right?" He stayed silent. Gotcha!

"We're not... Well, in part, we are... That's..." He facepalmed and harshly stroked his eyebrows.

You are in my claws now, Stoic.

"Girls like sex, too, you know..." I muttered matter-of-factly and gave my back to him. A smile was creeping onto my face, but he couldn't see it. I was going to spin it on him fast.

"I know, but that's for older girls only, OK?" I knew that.

"Yeah, I know. I'm so young. There's still so much I don't know..." I turned back to face him and gave him an innocent look with big puppy eyes. "But it's good I have you to answer any questions for me, right?"

Fall for it, fall for it, fall for it...

He thought about it for a few seconds. "Yeah," he said with a nod while pulling my hair once more. He fell for it! I gave my back to him again. Now I just needed to

"Great!" I said, rubbing my hands together like an evil villain.

"Now that we're talking about this, and I only ask because I really, really don't know," I said while thinking, trying to come up with something.

"How... big... is... a penis?" I said the word penis louder than I needed to. Stoic stopped combing my hair.

HA! Mission accomplished!

I looked back and saw his face fall to the ground.

Pick it up, Stoic. Pick it up.

He was extremely red now. He needed to learn not to get himself into this kind of a mess. I turned away from him, trying to hold back my laughter.

"Um... Emm, I don't think that's..." he paused, coughing, "why..." His brain was malfunctioning. I laughed internally.

Oh, Stoic!

There was no way around it. He was gonna have to give me an answer. "Because I don't know..." Again, I gave him the innocent face plus the "I don't know, I'm too dumb" look combo. I should have been an actress.

"Everyone is different, Emm," he said, scratching his neck. I nodded, and he breathed out in relief because he thought he was out of deep water, still combing my hair.

Not so fast, Stoic.

"I see. There's no way you would know. OK then, how big are you? You must know, right? I mean, it's attached to you." I pointed my fingers at his pants.

Stoic's face turned purple. "None of your fucking business!" He covered himself with both hands, forgetting the comb in my hair as if I could see it from here. Pfft!

"Is it that small that you got so embarrassed?" I knew guys were self-conscious about their size. Mom told me. Mom talked with me about everything.

"Emmerson, I'm anything but small." He was still purple, but he couldn't let me believe he was below average. Nope, he had to rectify that. Interestingly big, the size of his ego, I mean.

I made my innocent face again. "But how can you tell? It's not like you know how big everyone else is." I kept playing dumb. He gave me a look of disbelief. He should have known by then that I was messing with him.

"Trust me, Emmy. I'm big." Yep, a super big ego. Stupid boy. I gave him my "bullshit" face.

"Look, Emmerson, what's important is that you learn to recognize guys that present themselves as friends but instead have bad intentions. You need to be careful, Emmy. Do not let anyone touch you inappropriately, okay? OK!" He stood and left before I could say a word, leaving the comb hanging in my hair.

"Go to sleep!" he said from the door before he closed it.

A big evil smile spread across my face. Now that I knew that sex talk was Stoic's weakness, I'd use it against him. Who would have known that the fastest way to get rid of Dickface was to ask him about penises and vaginas?

Well... it wasn't that I'd use it often. Kenzo and Stoic were about to start their training camp for the militia, and I might not see them for weeks at a time. For some odd reason, they were assigned to a different base, one that was far from here. Mom said their training would be more challenging there.

Just what those two needed–more muscles and fewer brain cells.

Great!

SEVEN

EMMERSON

Stoic 18

My body was starting to change, and I was not sure I liked it.

I felt like I was getting taller by the minute. My chest was beginning to grow, and my nipples were very sensitive. All my clothes were starting to get shorter on me, and the new things my mom had been making for me were very... girly. I didn't like them. I was still the same, Amelia too–the non-girly girls. My hair was growing longer. Since Stoic was not around much, I learned how to comb and take care of it myself.

I got to see Kenzo and Stoic every other weekend. They went to a different village to train. I had no idea why, and to be honest, I didn't really care. Out of the three days he had free, Kenzo always spent one at home, and for the other two, he got lost. He didn't come back until late at night or early in the morning before their train left.

I had heard Dad lecturing him, but I guessed Kenzo always ended up doing what he wanted. Mom didn't like his behavior either. Ethan was so different. He never got himself in trouble like Kenzo. He was more into his studies and spent little to no time outside. When he did go out, he did it very secretly. I thought he had a secret girlfriend. He tried hard to hide it, but I knew better. I could read it on his face.

Stoic usually used most of his free time to follow me around. Gosh, did he love to bother me! At least I only had to put up with it for four days every month. There was always one day that he disappeared early in the morning and didn't return home until it was time for dinner.

Stoic didn't say much, just lingered around me like a creep and scared my friends away. He watched me play with Amelia and wrote things down in his notebook. Regardless of what he did during the day, he always did the same things during the evening that he used to do when I was little. Watched me eat, waited for me to be done with my shower, combed my hair, told me stories, and put me to bed. I thought he hadn't realized I was growing and didn't need help doing those things anymore.

Mom and I had been going to this new dance group a friend of hers started. I loved it. We danced to the rhythm of African drums. The dance was similar to my mom's culture, so she loved it too. I must have had it in my blood because swinging and moving my hips to the beats came very naturally to me.

Amelia joined us too. Once we got good enough, we would do performances and everything. I was super excited. Dancing was so much fun, and it filled my heart with happiness. Stoic hadn't seen me dance since we usually danced on Tuesdays and Thursdays, and he only came home on the weekends.

Other than dancing, Mom had also started to teach me some of our relatives' native language, Portuguese. I thought it would be difficult to learn, but I was getting the hang of it fast. I knew I'd be good at it very soon.

I was spending so much time with Mom that I was even learning to sew. It was sometimes tricky, but I was getting it. I didn't like making clothes, although I liked making other useful things like bags, backpacks, and quilts. So far, the things I had done were very simple. Amelia said I had a talent for it. Stoic noticed I was interested in sewing, and one day, he came back from the camp with a new sewing machine. My very own machine. I'd make something for him later. I didn't know how he got it, but I was glad he did.

Their training was ridiculously hard, but I thought they were doing good. Somehow, both Kenzo and Stoic got taller and more muscular. They were starting to look more like beasts than humans. Especially Stoic, he was intimidating. Mainly his dead-serious face.

The other day, I was talking with my friends, and as soon as they saw Stoic, they ran. Stoic always told me that I needed to stay away from boys and take care of my body. He said I needed to start thinking about my future husband, that he wouldn't like it if I started hanging around guys. I didn't know why he would care so much, but he did.

Mind your own business, Stoic!

It was winter, and the weather was impossibly cold. Since it was so cold, everything was canceled, including their training, so Kenzo and Stoic had been at home for about three weeks now. That was the longest they had stayed in the last two and a half years. Then, there was this massive storm two weeks ago with strong winds, snow, and freezing temperatures. An enormous tree fell over Uncle's house and smashed part of their roof.

Since it was stupid cold out. My dad asked the Dokkens to stay with us until the weather warmed enough for them to be able to make the repairs to the house. We moved their things and food to our house, and we all stayed there together.

Since my home only had three rooms, Mom gave mine to Uncle Erik and Auntie Ida. Stoic had made me a bigger bed, so it wasn't that uncomfortable for them there. We were a little cramped since our house was not that big anyway. Even with just the five of us, I sometimes felt like there was not enough space. At least it was fun because we played many games, and playing games was more

Since I had no room, I went to sleep with the boys. In Kenzo's and Ethan's room, there were two beds. Kenzo chose to sleep with Ethan, which left Stoic and me the other bed. It made sense, I guess. Kenzo and Stoic were too big to sleep in one bed, so was Ethan. To be honest, Stoic was just too big for our beds, period. He needed to sleep diagonally, and even then, his feet would hang off it.

For two weeks, I shared the bed with Stoic. He was a cuddler. I had to admit I liked sleeping next to him. He was like a warm blanket, which was sort of perfect in this cold weather. One of his arms was my pillow, and the other would be wrapped around me, holding me tight. I knew that there was zero chance of me falling off the bed. Most nights, he would pat me to sleep or rub my back. It was very comforting.

For some reason, he always put a pillow in between us–he called it personal space. I thought it was ridiculous since we were so close already, but if I had learned one thing about Stoic, it was that nothing he did made sense.

Today I woke up earlier than usual. The sun was barely up, and when I opened my eyes, I saw Kenzo on the other bed sleeping with his arm above his head and Ethan beside him, snoring softly. I looked down and saw Stoic's heavy arm over me. I liked sleeping in the fetal position, and he held me as if I was a little teddy bear. He was always the big spoon.

I turned around in his arms and studied Stoic's sleeping figure. He looked so much better sleeping than awake. He was kind of cute when he wasn't angry, which, unfortunately, was all the time. I let my fingers brush his eyebrows, and I softly touched his dark red eyelashes. They were so long. He would have been a pretty girl. His shirt was stretched, and I could see his neck and the strong muscles of his upper chest. I didn't know how his body could be hard and comfortable at the same time.

I touched his straight nose and then ran my finger along his sharp jaw. Even though he shaved recently, I could still feel the new hair growth. Yep, he would soon have a long beard like Uncle Erik and Dad. His face was hard and well-defined. Very... manly. I understood why girls had always found him so handsome. He sort of was.

Stoic still hadn't gotten himself a girlfriend. I was sort of glad about that. I didn't want stupid girls' dramas around us, around him. We had enough with Kenzo alone.

Stoic took a deep breath and held me tighter. He let out a low grunt and kissed my head. "Sleep, Emmy. It's early," he said with his eyes closed.

I didn't realize he was awake. I snuggled closer to him, wanting to get warmer. He smelled good. I put my head on his chest, and I could hear his heart beating hard.

"Stoic?"

"Hmm..."

"I'll make you a backpack. Do you want it black or green?" I whispered, so I wouldn't wake Kenzo and Ethan up.

"Surprise me," he whispered back. He put my hair behind my ear, and I nodded.

I would.

"Emmy, stone or wood?" he asked with his voice sleepy, his eyes still closed. More nonsense questions.

"Stones last longer than wood," I said in a low voice, and he nodded.

Stoic gave me more of the blanket and kissed my head once more.

I closed my eyes, and in between his slow breathing and mine, I fell asleep again.

EIGHT

EMMERSON

Emmerson 13

Stoic 18

My body was seriously changing. My breasts kept growing, and I had to start using a training bra. My hips were getting some curves to them, and my butt was getting rounder. Also, hair started growing in areas where I didn't want it. I was going to start shaving soon.

About three weeks ago, I got my first period. I was not expecting it to be so painful and messy.

Once, Stoic saw me lying around and in a lot of pain, and he got worried. He thought I was sick, so I had to tell him what was happening. But instead of getting grossed out and running away from me like I thought he would, he pulled me in for a big hug. Weirdo!

Stoic told me that he was sorry I was in pain but that this was a special thing we should be happy about. He said that one day I'd be able to create a life. Stoic sat me on his lap, held me in his arms, and hugged me for a long while. He rubbed my belly with his warm hands, and that sort of did make me feel better. He seemed oddly happy, and since I was in pain and tired, I didn't even question him. I just let him be. He did help me feel better, after all.

"East or north?" Another stupid question. He never stopped asking them.

"Northeast," I said while resting my head on his chest. Stoic rubbed my belly until I fell asleep, and then he took me to my room and left me there.

I knew he was busier than ever now that he and Kenzo were about to leave. Even though, Stoic still followed me around whenever he could, which was kind of annoying sometimes. I knew exactly how to get back at him and make him disappear. Whenever I wanted to talk to Amelia in private while Stoic was lingering around, all I had to do was start saying "my vagina" out loud, and he would get tomato red and get lost. Worked every time.

Yesterday, Kenzo and Stoic started to prepare to leave. They would leave and not come back for three years. I made them gifts. It took me a really long time to get them done as I had made backpacks. Kenzo's was green, and Stoic's was black. I made sure to put lots of pockets and zippers in them. I reinforced them and made them impermeable. Mom helped me. I hope they lasted for a long time. Inside Stoic's backpack, I put many tags with my name on them. If any girls saw it, they would know to stay away. Stoic wouldn't like any of them, anyway.

I packed snacks and essentials inside the backpack, too, like toothbrushes, matches, and a water can. I asked Dad and Uncle Erik for knives, so I could put them in, too, and they made them for me. I gave them a drawing of how I wanted the knives to look, and they tried their best to copy it. They turned out to be super cool. They were not that big, but they had an incredible curve to them. The handle of Kenzo's had his initials "K.S." Stoic's knife had ours, "S&E." Uncle Erik wrote "Góðr" on the other side of the handle, too, but I didn't know what it meant. Mom made them leather protective pockets, as they were very sharp.

The day before their departure, we all had dinner together. It was an odd dinner. Nobody really talked much. At times, I could see all the adults trying to be cheerful, but Kenzo and Stoic didn't look too excited about leaving. Especially Stoic, he looked miserable.

I gave them their backpacks, and they both loved them. I wanted to show all the things we had put inside, but as soon as Stoic saw the knife, he grabbed it and the backpack, stood up, and left the house before I could show him the rest of the things. Rude much! Uncle Erik, Kenzo, and Dad followed him, and they didn't return until more than half an hour later. By the time they were back, the rest of us were almost done with dessert.

Stoic decided to stay at home with us that night, so he could leave together with Kenzo in the morning. He slept with me in my bed. I didn't think he rested much because he looked like shit in the morning. His eyes were red, and he was even paler than his usual self.

We all walked them to the train station to say our goodbyes. Many other families were there as well. For some reason, everyone was overly sentimental.

Kenzo's eyes were glassy, and Mom and Dad cried while hugging him. Uncle Erik and Auntie Ida were crying and embracing Stoic too. I thought they were all overreacting. Leave it to the grownups to be the dramatic ones. Three years would pass fast, and before we knew it, they would be back.

As I saw it, the worst thing about the northern border was the cold. I had heard from some people who had come back that it was an incredibly boring and tedious job. Mostly guarding a fence with a walkie-talkie in the cold. Others said they moved boxes and stuff.

Kenzo pulled Ethan and me in for a big hug and told us to be good for Mom and Dad. He kissed us and put his backpack on his shoulders. I saw from over Kenzo's shoulder that Stoic was hugging my parents goodbye.

Once Kenzo stepped back, Stoic stood in front of us and pulled Ethan in for a hug. He said something to him that I couldn't hear, and Ethan nodded. In two years, it would be Ethan who would be leaving. He would start his training soon, but he wouldn't have to travel as Kenzo and Stoic did. He was to be in a regular camp, so he'd be at home. Once he was 18, he would go to the north just like [illegible]

Once he was done hugging Ethan, Ethan left, and everyone stepped far away from Stoic and me.

Stoic got down on one knee and hugged me tightly. I could feel his tears rolling down the side of my face.

"There, there. It's going to be okay. Time goes fast, you'll see." I patted his back and hugged him back.

What a big baby.

"Emmy, do you remember your boomerang?" He held my face in his hands and looked into my eyes. His eyes were still red.

"Yeah, why?"

"I'm like that boomerang, Emmy; I'll always come back to you, OK." Oh! I got it. I didn't know Stoic would give this much thought to anything. Was that a coincidence? That was kind of cool of him.

He kissed me hard on my head, stood up, grabbed his backpack with one hand, and walked away. He kept his back to me and got on the train without looking back, not even once. Kenzo stood at the train's entrance and waved bye to us. Soon the train doors closed, and the train started moving. We all stood there looking as it disappeared into the distance.

Just like that, they were gone.

I'd miss their stupid faces, but they would be back.

He'd always come back.

NINE

EMMERSON

Stoic 21

Life without my brothers was somewhat easier. No dramas, no fights, no crazy girls chasing after them. Yes, I was counting Stoic as my brother too. My brother from another mother.

It'd been three years, and they were finally coming back. But, for some reason, things didn't go as planned, so they would have to go back to the border in six months. At least they got a nice and well-deserved break.

I couldn't wait to see them! I hated to admit it, but I did miss them, all of them. I thought about them often, especially Stoic. He left me gifts with Uncle Erik, Auntie Ida, and Mom. Even when he wasn't here, I still always got my birthday dress, my summer hoop, and my wood gift for the fall. He carved a beautiful Yggdrasil on a round tree slab. I kept it in my bedroom next to the metal thing he gave me when I was little, the "Jeg elsker deg." That made me miss him even more.

I went with Amelia to wait for them at the station. We stood right in front of it, where the little shops were. Amelia wanted to eat pastries, so we were stuffing our faces before the train arrived.

Mom, Dad, Erik, and Ida were waiting for them inside. Ethan had left for the north last year, and I had made a backpack for him too.

Looking back these past three years, I had been so busy. I got really good at sewing bags and backpacks, and I was already making a lot of exchanges for my work. I recently got a wooden bow, and I'd give it to Stoic when he came back. He was going to like it. The dancing was going well, too. We had had many performances, and the crowds went wild when we danced. I learned Portuguese, and Mom and I spoke it all the time–mostly if we didn't want Dad knowing what we were talking about.

Ever since Stoic left, I had been spending a lot of time with Auntie Ida. I didn't want her to feel lonely. She taught me some of her and Stoic's favorite recipes, and we cooked them together three times a week. When Stoic came back, I might surprise him with a nice meal.

My body was completely different. I had to admit that I had grown up. I actually looked really pretty. I was way taller, my curly hair almost reached my lower back, my hips had curves, my breasts had grown to a nice comfortable size, and my butt was round and sort of big like Mom's. Since I did so much dancing, my legs were nice and toned.

I also changed the way I dressed, and I could say I had quite a style. Mom helped with that. All my clothes showed off my perfect curves, hugged me in all the right places, and enhanced all my enchantments.

I never stopped being a brat, so I walked the streets swinging my hips like the queen I knew I was. Guys hit on me all the time. I got whistles and stupid pick-up lines everywhere I went. Amelia called me the microwave–I heated them up but never ate them. Amelia grew to be astonishingly beautiful with a killer body. We could drop them all dead! Who would have believed that the least girly girls turned out to be the cutest of them all? Ha! I had zero shame. I didn't mind kicking my own butt every now and then. I was beautiful, and I knew it.

I didn't care much about guys, though, as none of them were interesting or cute enough for me. Amelia said I was picky, but the truth was that I tended to compare them a lot. None of them were tall enough or handsome enough or strong enough for me. They always lacked something. I was not looking for perfection, but they were definitely not what I wanted. Some of them even got frustrated because I didn't even give them the time of day. My "old friend" Noah was one of them.

It was funny that when the cats were away, the mice relaxed and thought they could come out to play. I was sure that as soon as Kenzo and Stoic came back, all these idiots would have to swallow their own tongues. One catcall in front of Stoic, and heads would roll. Landon's knockout would look like a children's game compared to the massacre that awaited them.

Noah must have asked me out like twenty times already. I ran out of ways to say no. He had the habit of showing up everywhere I went.

"Sup, Emmy?" Talk about the devil...

"Sup?"

"Not much, just hanging around. What are you two ladies up to?" Noah said, trying to sound cool but failing. Oh, he was not going to like it.

"We? Not much, just waiting for Kenzo and Stoic to arrive." I said in a very disinterested manner, pointing between Amelia and me. His eyes grew double their size.

"Stoic?"

"Yeah, Stoic, and Kenzo," I said, giving my cheese danish a big bite.

"Stoic fucking Dokken is coming back today?"

Game over, dude.

"Yep," I popped the 'p' at the end. Amelia couldn't hold back her laugh and started chuckling in between her teeth.

"Fuck me!" he said and pulled his hair.

Ewww, no thanks.

"You know what, I don't fucking care. I'm not that small child he used to toss around all the time. I won't let that asshat intimidate me anymore." I nodded. Interesting, he was going to try his luck. Cute.

"OK, good luck!" I waved my hand at him, turned around, locked my arm with Amelia's, and started to walk away from him.

"You must be happy, right, Emmerson?" Noah said, and I turned to look at him. His ridiculous face looked pissed.

"What?" I said with my mouth full.

"Your boyfriend is coming back."

"You mean my brothers," I said after swallowing.

"Nah, you heard me–your brother and your long-time boyfriend."

What? Who the fuck did he think he was? The nerves!

"Don't be stupid, Noah; jealousy doesn't look good on anybody. Stop making shit up." I turned again and started walking.

"Nobody but Stoic, right?"

What was he talking about?

"Stoic is nothing but an overprotective brother." He, more than anyone, should have known that.

"He wants you, Emmy, he always did. He wants to give it to you hard, and you don't even fucking notice it."

What?

This moron was delusional. That was it. I was done with him. "Not every guy out here is a pig like you. Stoic is like my brother. Just admit it, you're angry because you know you ain't got no chance with me. Piece of advice, move the fuck on, Noah."

"You can say whatever you want, Emmerson, but in his eyes, you are his woman," Noah said as he turned and started to walk away from us.

"Oh, fuck off, you cunt," I screamed at him.

"OK! Come on, let's go." Amelia pulled me away before I decided to take my shoe off and do some damage. Noah left, fuming.

Trip and die, Noah. Trip and die.

"What the fuck is wrong with him?" I said, eating my pastry. Amelia gave me the "you know" look.

"What?" My mouth was full again.

"Emmy, I don't think Noah is completely wrong," she said hesitantly.

Her too?

"Oh, come on, not you too." I was tired of people giving me that ridiculous argument.

"Just saying..." she said, shrugging.

"Trust me, that's a hard no. OK?"

"OK... If you say so..." She still didn't believe me, but I was not going to argue about that stupid topic anymore.

After we finished eating, I brushed the crumbs off my shirt. I looked at my reflection in one of the shop's glass windows, made a turn, and gave myself a wink and two thumbs up. I looked good. I was wearing a tight white sleeveless short, crocheted shirt that ended at my ribs and high waist loose shorts that adjusted to my waist and accentuated my curves–they ended mid-thigh and flowed with the wind. They actually looked more like a skirt. I had my white tennis shoes on, my hair was up in a messy bun, and my tanned skin was glowing under the summer sun.

"We should head back. I see people coming out, so I think they must have arrived already," Amelia said. I agreed.

We walked back, and as soon as we passed through the station's entrance, I saw him. He was very far, but his red hair towered way over the crowd. He was back. I took some steps forward, and my heartbeat got faster.

Why was my heart beating so fast?

He was looking around, desperate, his blue eyes searching the crowd. He must be looking for me. Kenzo was standing next to him, talking to Dad. They both looked so different. A good kind of different, though.

A smile spread across my face, and all of a sudden, a sea of emotions consumed me. I screamed his name, and his eyes landed on me. His eyebrows frowned, and I knew he barely recognized me.

For that moment, the world stopped, and my mind blocked out anything else that wasn't him. I laughed and ran to him. I ran as fast as I could between all the moving bodies–they were nothing but a blur. All I could see was Stoic. My heart was racing, and I bumped into at least four different people on my way to him. He stood there, a smile on his face and his blue eyes shining like stars. I saw Kenzo lean over and tell him something, and he nodded without taking his eyes away from me, not even for a second.

My messy bun fell, my hair scattering in all directions, but I didn't care. I kept running to him and screaming his name. As soon as I got closer, he dropped his black backpack on the floor and opened his arms. I jumped into his arms, and he caught me. My arms immediately wrapped around his neck and my legs around his waist. He wrapped his arms around me and hugged me tightly.

"You're back!" I felt like crying. Why did I feel like crying? I hugged him so tight.

"I'm back, baby." His voice. I missed his deep voice. I didn't realize I had missed him this much.

I pulled back a little and looked into his eyes, smiling like a small child. He had changed a lot. He had a beard now with an arm covered in tattoos, but it was him. He was built like a beast too. I bet he could rip a log apart with his bare hands.

Had he always been this handsome?

"Emmy..." He was studying me. His eyes traveled down and then back up. I was not the little girl he left behind three years ago.

"Stoic!" I squealed and gave him another hug. He buried his face in my neck and took a deep breath.

"Don't worry about your real brother here. I'm fine, by all means... Just hug Stoic. I'm fine," Kenzo said, but we ignored him. He just picked up Stoic's backpack and walked away, mumbling something. I couldn't stop smiling. Kenzo was being overdramatic.

"I missed you so much," he said and squeezed me harder.

"I know you did. There's no other like me in this world." My inner brat.

He chuckled, "You are right." See, that was a smart answer.

"I don't want to let you go! I'm gonna hang on to you for the rest of the day," I said.

Stoic laughed. I was not kidding. I could hug him for hours.

"I could hang on to you for the rest of the month," he said, and we both laughed.

He moved his hands from my waist to my thighs to help hold my weight. As soon as his warm hands touched my skin, I felt goosebumps. My eyes traveled to his hands and then back to his face. He was staring into my eyes with an expression I had never seen on him. What was it? It made me excited but nervous at the same time.

He raised an eyebrow at my expression and smirked. This was my Stoic, but at the same time, he was different. We just stood there, looking into each other's eyes for the longest time.

"Do you two want to go back home with us, or are you going somewhere else?" my mom asked, interrupting us.

"Go ahead. We'll catch you later," Stoic said without breaking eye contact with me.

"OK... Dinner is at six. Don't be late," my mom said and walked away.

"See you at home, son." My dad patted his arm and followed Mom.

"Emmy! I... Oh! I... I gotta go. My moms must be looking for me. Let's talk later, OK?" That was Amelia. I didn't answer her or move my eyes from Stoic's. It was like a staring contest. My eyes remained fixed on his like a magnet.

"Do you want to go for a walk?" he asked me after everyone left. All I could do was nod my head like an idiot. I couldn't stop the smile that was spreading across my face.

"Come on. Get on my back." He put me down, turned, and got on one knee. I didn't think twice before hopping back on him, wrapping my arms around his neck and my legs around his torso. He held onto my legs and started walking.

We walked out of the station and down the road toward the park. I gotta say, the world looked different from up here. That was a long way down.

Was this what it felt like to be six-eight?

Every time he readjusted me, I hugged him tighter. There were a million things I wanted to ask him and talk about, but nothing came out. I just held on to him, enjoying the way it felt having him this close.

His hair had grown. He had it tied in a bun, and I wondered how long it actually was. I wanted to run my fingers through it so badly. His back was wide, and his muscles felt hard. He had always been strong, but now he resembled a god more than anything else. Even when he was just wearing a simple black T-shirt, jeans, and boots, he looked like he had just walked right through Bifrost and out of Asgard. None of his clothes were tight on him, but you could still see he was absolutely shredded underneath them. Stoic was hotter than the freaking sun, and I felt like I was slowly melting over him.

Oh crap! Noah and Amelia might have been right.

He got us to the playground and sat me on a swing bench. We were under a big maple tree, and the shadow it made over us kept us cool and comfortable on this warm day. He sat next to me and pulled me closer. Stoic put my hair behind my ear and kissed my head. The place was mostly empty, only a few little kids running in the distance.

"You have grown a lot. You look so different I barely recognized you." His thumb caressed my face.

"You changed too." I gently touched his beard, and he smiled. I pointed at his tattoos. "When did all this happen?"

He started to think as if he was going to measure his words. "Many of them, I always wanted to have. I guess the time was right to get them."

Damn it, he looked hella good with them.

"Are you sure it was not to impress the ladies?" I lifted and dropped my eyebrows in a comical way.

Oh wait, were there any ladies?

There must be. He was too handsome. Girls his age must be falling head over heels for him. Begging on their knees.

"Nah, there's no one to impress there."

Bullshit. I call bullshit!

"So, you're telling me no girls are running after you in the North as you have them here?" I said, my eyes searching his deep blues.

He fixed his eyes on mine. A shy smile appeared, and he shook his head. "Nah. I mean, yes. There are girls, but..." He patted my head, "I've never been interested in any of them."

Horseshit!

"So... are you telling me you don't like girls? I mean, that's okay–"

"I fucking like girls, Emmy." He stopped me before I could finish my thought. Almost forgot how easy it was to get him angry.

"Oh, I thought–"

"I'm saving myself for the right one." Oh, wow! I didn't think Stoic was this romantic. That's way better than being a man-whore like Kenzo.

"Good! I like that. Keep up the good work!" I said, giving him a thumbs up.

"I don't think I'll be able to for much longer," he said, looking at the ground.

What did that mean?

"What?" I started.

"Let's go back," he interrupted me. He stood up fast and kneeled. I hopped on his back again, and we headed home.

Stoic took the long way back home. Instead of the road, we went through the woods. He stayed silent for a while, then asked me one of his famous dumb questions.

"Emmerson, a hammock or a swing bench?"

What the hell? That was random.

"A swinging daybed!" I chuckled, and so did he.

After that, he stayed quiet, but I couldn't stand it and broke the silence.

"Stoic, what were you actually doing there?" He stiffened a little and readjusted me.

"Not much. Just guarding the fence. It was pretty boring."

Why does he need to be so strong just to guard a fence?

Maybe he was like this because he had nothing else to do but exercise. "I missed it here. I missed this," he told me.

He must be talking about quietness and nature.

"Is the north as boring as the girls that live there?" I was not dropping the topic. I really wanted to know. I didn't think I would be able to sleep well if I didn't find out for sure. He must have had a girl back there.

"Emmerson, the girl I like is here, not there."

So, there was someone. Oh no!

"Oh! So... you have a secret girlfriend?"

Please say no, please say no.

"Sort of. I'm taken if that's what you're asking." I stayed quiet. I didn't like that. I didn't know why, but I didn't fucking like that.

Stoic belonged to someone?

"And so are you, right?" he asked with a cheery voice.

Was he happy about that?

I had never given much thought to my future husband, but right now, for some reason, it didn't feel right. "Yeah..." I tried to not sound depressed but failed. "Do I have to marry him?"

"Yes." That sounded like a definitive answer. Leave it to Stoic to cut a conversation short.

"What if I don't like him?" I might not want this wedding after all.

"You'll learn to." Another definite answer. He was not leaving any room for argument.

"What if he doesn't like me?" I was just searching for excuses now.

"That's not possible. You're drop-dead gorgeous, Emmy."

Did he really think I was gorgeous?

Well, thank you for the ego boost. "Do you think so?" He couldn't see it, but I was biting my lip.

"Yes."

"Well... you are not alone there." I laughed, thinking about all the guys that had confessed their love for me.

"What do you mean?" His voice got serious.

"I'm quite popular. Little old messy me grew up to be steamy hot," I said in my sexy voice, and he stopped walking. He might not believe how stupidly narcissistic I was acting. I bet this girl he liked was not even half as pretty as I was.

"Are guys hitting on you?" There! That was the Stoic I remembered.

Hello, my old friend.

"Pfft, of course. All the time," I said, laughing.

"Who?"

"Why do you want to know that? So you can go on a murder rampage? Don't be silly, Stoic. You'll have to kill half the village." I laughed some more, but he didn't seem to find it as funny as I did.

"Have you dated anyone?" he asked, his voice dropping. Yep, he was angry. Oh, I was gonna push his buttons.

"Uhm... Let's see... What counts as dating?" I pretended I was thinking.

Stoic put me down and turned around. He looked angry. I forgot how easy it was to bother him. I bit my lip and held my laughter back.

"Has anyone kissed you?" His hands were forming fists. The only person I had kissed was him. Long ago, on his birthday. I remembered how his tongue entered my mouth, how I kicked him, and how he couldn't stand up after. I couldn't help but smile.

"Has anyone fucking kissed you, Emmerson?"

You did, you moron.

"Well... I can't say no to that." He cracked his neck and got closer to me. He was pissed, so I stepped back. He gave one step forward, and I gave one backward.

"Are you still a virgin?" he asked, looking up and down at my body.

What the fuck? How? I mean, why would he ask that? That was super personal.

"That's none of your business, Stoic." Another step.

"It's a yes or no question, Emmerson." And I didn't want to answer it. Another step.

"What if I'm not?" His eyes widened. Oh, he was furious.

"Don't fucking joke around, Emmerson. Answer." Another step, and I hit a tree behind me. Uh oh!

"I don't have to tell you shit, Stoic," I said in my sassy voice. Big mistake.

He took another step, and his body was so close to me I could feel his heat. Stoic looked down at me, put his hand over my pussy, and caressed my mound with his thumb.

"Tell me now, Emmerson, or I'll pull these cute little pants down, spread your legs open, and check it myself." His voice was deep and dark.

I gasped loudly. I was petrified. I felt my heart abruptly stop. I couldn't breathe. My eyes got wide, and my mouth dropped open. Heat spread all over my body, and I knew I must be blushing. No one had ever spoken to me like that or touched me there.

"I... I... am," I said softly. I was afraid he'd do what he said he would.

"You what, Emmy? Use your words." He kept brushing his fingers over me. His face was close to my neck, and I felt his breath on me. Oh gosh, I was getting wet.

Why was I getting wet?

"I am still a virgin," I said quickly, pressing myself further against the tree. He nodded, and his hand slowly moved up. He moved it very slowly, the back of his fingers just brushing over my breast until he reached my neck and jaw.

"Have you let anyone touch your body?"

"No," I said softly. My pussy clenched, and I felt more wetness.

"Good girl."

Oh, God!

His hand moved down again. This time, instead of brushing with his fingers, he had his whole hand moving softly over me, putting a little pressure when he moved over my tit. I was definitely soaking now.

"I would have fucking hated it if anyone had touched you." His hand moved further down my body. He held my hip and moved his hand behind me, grabbing my ass.

"Nobody else can have this body." His voice sounded so sexy. I started breathing hard.

What was going on?

He lowered his hands and touched my thighs and then moved his hands up, sliding his fingers under the loose fabric of my pants. I flinched and covered my

What the actual fuck?

"Have you been a good girl, Emmerson? Hm?" His lips were so close to my neck that I could feel them move when he talked. He moved his hand incredibly slowly up my leg. I didn't know what to say to that.

What did he mean?

"Have you touched yourself, baby?" His hands were getting higher.

Oh, fucking hell!

He put his other hand on the tree and caged me in. "Have you played with this tight little pussy?" His voice was full of desire.

"No." I shook my head. That's the truth. I knew other girls my age masturbated, but I never really felt like doing it. I had never been interested in sex. However, I had the feeling that was about to change.

His hand reached my damp underwear, and he slightly brushed them with the back of his fingers.

"Are you getting wet, Emmy?" His voice got lower somehow, but he stayed calm.

"I... I..." I couldn't make words come out of my mouth. Stoic took his hand out from under my pants and put it on my waist. Immediately, I realized what he was doing. Stoic pulled the zipper at the side of my shorts open. He slipped his hand inside my pants and underwear, slowly moving them down on me.

Holy fuck!

I grabbed his hand with mine, but he kept moving down. My eyes were fixed on his hand, my breathing ragged. Finally, his hand reached my mound, and he softly passed his middle and index fingers over me. His middle finger was right over my slit, with his index sliding along my lip. He trailed them slowly down my mound. Once his finger was low enough, he added a little bit of pressure and slipped his middle finger inside my lips. He softly circled my entrance and then moved it back up, ever so slowly.

I squeezed his hand as hard as I could, not knowing if I wanted him to stop or keep going. It felt good.

"Fuck, Emmerson, you are so fucking wet." He let out a low grunt and pressed his hips to my body. Stoic reached my clit and rubbed little circles around it.

"Uuhh!" I moaned, my head falling back.

Stoic kept rubbing circles with his warm fingers, and I held onto his hands as if my life depended on it. His eyes locked on mine.

"Uuhh! Uuhh! Uuhh!..." I moaned softly, my mouth open and my lips trembling. He knew how much this affected me, and he bit his lip.

Stoic stopped rubbing my clit. He slid his hand up and down my pussy multiple times, making all his fingers slick with my juices. He gave me a little tap on my pussy that made me jump, and then he pulled his hand out.

I saw how he put two fingers in his mouth and tasted them, his eyes on mine. "Mmm," he said, licking his lips after.

Oh, fuck!

I was embarrassed. I wanted the earth to open and swallow me whole.

Stoic zipped up my pants, pulled me away from the tree, and dusted my clothes. Taking a few steps back, he said, "Little girls shouldn't be walking around with their underwear soaked, Emmerson. Let's go home. You need to wipe yourself clean and change. Everyone is waiting." I saw him rub his mid-thigh as he said that. When I gave it a better look, it was not his thigh that he was rubbing. His dick was hard, and fuck, it must be huge if it was hanging that low.

Stoic turned around when he saw me staring at his tented pants. "Move, Emmerson," he said, giving his back to me. Then, he started walking away, and I quietly followed him.

What the fuck just happened?

TEN

EMMERSON

Stoic 22

After the way he touched me the day he arrived home about four months ago, I thought Stoic was definitely sexually attracted to me–but he wasn't. I was so fucking confused. Stupid Stoic must have been playing with me when he did that. Maybe that was payback for the river kiss I gave him on his birthday years ago.

We went home that day, and he acted as if nothing had ever happened. The rest of the time, he acted the same, no funny looks, no insinuations, no touching. Nothing. I couldn't fucking read him. He was so... impossible! Ever since that time, I would get super, almost embarrassingly, wet when I was near him, secretly wishing he'd put his hands inside my panties once again.

I guess he really had his mind set on another girl. He had zero interest in me. Of course, he must have seen me as a sister. I was so stupid. It was so awkward.

Why would he lead me on, though?

The day after he arrived home, Stoic was already busy. I didn't see him much or at all for the first two months. He would have dinner with us most days, but that was it. His dad, mine, and Kenzo disappeared with him sometimes. I had no idea what that ball of bearded machos was doing.

I was busy too. Our dance group had a presentation, and a lot of people came over to see us. Stoic saw me dance for the first time. We practiced for that show for months, and it was a complete success. Well, for the most part.

At the beginning of the dance, I wasn't nervous at all, just really excited. I had invited my whole family, and I knew they'd love it. When the music started playing the rhythm of African drums, everyone started to cheer. As we started dancing, I was full of confidence, like always. Looking at the crowd, I found Stoic's tall figure and danced while looking at him. Got to say, moving my hips that way while looking at him did make me wet. He just stood there, arms crossed, leaning on a column with a soft smile on his face. I could tell he was enjoying it.

The beats got faster, and we danced in unison with a combination of hip rolls, chest movements, hand gestures, and feet shuffling. We turned our backs to the audience and sensually made round hip movements, slowly turning. We had our feet slightly separated, leaning a little to our right, and our hips rolled more as we all bent down. Our hands hit the floor hard before we popped back up sensually and continued dancing. The crowd cheered. Guys started to whistle and yell out compliments.

I was happy until I saw Stoic's face. He was furious. His face held a touch of pink, and his fists closed, eyebrows frowned, and jaw clenched. Obviously annoyed with all the guys, but not once had he stopped looking at me. There was a fire in his eyes, and to my surprise, there was something else. That same thing I saw in his eyes the day he touched me. Desire.

He made me distracted. I missed like four steps before I got back in rhythm. No matter what I did, my eyes were locked on his. I had never felt so nervous while dancing. I could feel his eyes eating me up. I was getting so wet that I was worried that it might show on my tight pants. This wasn't right.

As soon as the dance ended, I ran off the stage. Amelia followed me.

"Emmy, what happened?" she asked, panting like I was.

"Amelia!" I pulled her hand and took her to a place backstage where no one could see us.

"Can you see anything?" I was so embarrassed. I turned and pointed at my butt.

"What?" she said, leaning over to see better. "Are you on your period? I see nothing."

"Oh, thank goodness. I have to go to the nearest restroom!"

"What? What happened? Stop, Emmy! Talk to me!" She had no idea...

"I... I think I... Forget it!" I turned around.

"No, tell me what happened?" Amelia insisted.

"I have to talk to you, in private," I said that last thing quietly. "But I need to stop by the restroom first."

"OK... let's go."

After using the restroom, I sneaked out with Amelia and went to a quiet part of the park. We sat on the grass behind a couple of bushes, and I felt like I wanted to be eaten by a giant bear and disappear.

She noticed I wasn't talking, so she went ahead and asked, "It's Stoic, isn't it?"

Wow, right on the target. "Yes... Oh gosh, I'm so confused!"

"Confused or horny?" she said, and I slapped her arm.

"Amelia!"

She laughed. "What? It's normal. That man is a living god!"

She wasn't wrong. "It's driving me crazy. All this feels so wrong!" I shouldn't be feeling this way!

"Why?" Oh, come on, don't act stupid."

"He's like a brother to me." I facepalmed.

"Emmy, he ain't your brother, and I believe that's clear to everyone but you. He looks at you like a delicious piece of candy he's about to devour." She laughed in my face. I was going through an existential crisis, and this fucker laughed.

Have friends, they said. They'd have your back, they said.

I crossed my arms, looking miserable.

"There's not much to think about, Emmy. The guy is hot. Go for it. I bet he has a deliciously big, hard dick you could bounce on for hours. Why hold yourself back? Besides, you'll be the envy of almost every girl in this village." She winked at me.

"Amelia!" I gasped and hit her arm again. Twice.

"Come on, Emmerson! You're not a little girl anymore. All kids our age have already started doing it."

"Ha! Not all kids. We haven't."

Silence. Amelia nodded and looked away.

I pulled her to me and made her face me. "We haven't, right?" No answer. Motherfucker! I couldn't believe her.

"Emmerson, I didn't want to tell you because it's sort of awkward."

I'll be damned! Amelia was smashing?

"Who, though?" Why didn't I notice it? I had never seen her with anyone.

"Um... I... It might be better if I don't tell you."

"Why? What's going on, Amelia?"

"Because it was supposed to be a secret. I wanted to talk to you all about it, but to be honest, it's awkward."

"But you and I have always shared everything with each other." She gave it a thought.

"Okay, Emmy, I'll tell you, but you have to promise you won't tell anyone. He doesn't want his family to know about us. That's the main reason why I didn't say anything to you before."

"What do you mean?"

"I've sort of been secretly dating Ethan for years now. We did it right before he left to the north."

WHAT?

"Ethan? As in my brother, Ethan?"

She nodded. "As you can see, me talking about the details of your brother's sex life just doesn't sound like the kind of conversation you would love to have with me."

"Holy shit! Ethan! That motherfucker. I'm gonna fucking kill him."

"Emmy, no! We really like each other. We are serious about this. He wants to get a career first, though."

"Holy shit, do you think he'll marry you?"

"That's the long-term plan. Are you okay with it?"

"Am I OK? Amelia, we're going to be real sisters!" I jumped on her and gave her a big hug and repeatedly kissed her cheeks. I pulled back and looked into her eyes. "Was he good?" She bit her lip, trying not to laugh out loud.

"He fucked me so good!" She let out a squeal and hid her face.

True, it was uncomfortable knowing what my brother did with his dangling meat, but I wanted to be a good friend and be there for her.

We sat there behind that bush talking about sex for about an hour. After that, we went back to the now-empty hall, grabbed our things, and changed our clothes.

I wore a tight gray dress. It had a high neckline and long sleeves. It was calf-length, made from a thin, stretchy fabric that hugged all my curves. I left my hair loose to flow with the wind. I put on my combat boots and headed out with Amelia.

"Let's go to the river! It's too early to go home." I didn't want to face an angry

Stoic now.

"Alright then, come on." She put her arm around me. We took the short trail there and arrived in less than twenty minutes.

Once we got there, we found Kenzo and Stoic sitting shirtless on a rock, all wet and laughing like little kids about to do something naughty.

There were other people there too. Some of their friends were swimming and talking, and some girls were eyeing the boys from the water. Fuck! I didn't freaking like that.

Bunch of idiots. Why swimming, though? It must have been freezing cold.

"Kenzo!" I called out to my brother, and both of them looked back. Kenzo smiled at me and patted Stoic's back before he stood and walked over to us. He was ripped. You could tell all the girls were eating him up with their eyes.

"That was quite the show, Emmy," he said, playfully punching my belly. He was cold.

"Did you like it?"

good work!" Kenzo patted me and walked into the water. There he grabbed this pretty blond girl by her hips and kissed her. I recognized her. It was Ava, his first girlfriend. I guess they were back together then.

Amelia poked my arm and pointed at Stoic. He was still sitting on the rock, looking into the distance.

"Go get him, tiger!" She slapped my butt hard and ran away before I could convince her not to leave me here all by myself.

Taking a deep breath, I shyly walked over and sat next to him. "Hey..." I said so low I thought he wouldn't be able to hear me.

He continued staring out into the distance.

OK, maybe this was not a good idea. I was about to slowly disappear before he noticed my sad attempt when I heard his voice.

"You looked beautiful dancing. Like a fucking goddess. Did you have fun?" He was serious, still not looking at me.

"Yeah, I did. Did you like it?" I thought this was going to be the part when he told me to stop dancing. I waited for him to lecture me, but nothing. He nodded. Nothing else, just a nod. OK then...

"Dark wood or light wood?" A stupid question. I was glad to know that some things never changed.

"Dark, because why the hell not!" I laughed, and he glanced at me and laughed too.

We saw Kenzo swimming across the river with Ava and disappearing into the woods shortly after. Stoic shook his head. My eyes landed on him, and I couldn't help but examine his body.

He was a walking piece of art.

Now that his shirt was off, I could clearly see all the tattoos he had. There were so many. "These are cool," I said and pointed at his right arm that was covered entirely with them.

He had an ax wrapped around a snake-looking thing and knots that ran from his shoulder to mid-arm. At the shoulder, it blended with a raven with its wings spread toward his chest. On his forearm, the image of a harsh bearded, braided old dude with a blind eye and a Viking helmet blended with the knots on his ax. The details on the beard were mesmerizing. That was Odin, for sure. The whole thing looked like one big tattoo instead of many woven together.

He looked at his arm and said after pointing at the ax, "A tool for building or a weapon to destroy." He leaned forward, resting his weight on his elbow perched on his thigh. He opened his hands and looked at them before closing them and letting them hang. Hmm... Ok.

"Oh! What about this one?" I pointed at a weird shape of three interlocking cones on his left shoulder.

"The triple horn of Odin."

"Oh, I remember that one! Wisdom, right?"

"Yes."

"And this? I think I have seen this somewhere else." I pointed at a word written on the left side of his chest. It was under the wings of another raven. The raven's wings extended all the way to his neck. The two ravens were in different positions.

"Góðr, it means brave." He patted his chest softly twice. "Right over my heart where it belongs."

"Braveheart? I like it. It goes well with you." I gave him a shy smile. He just stared at me.

He raised his left hand and used his fingers to comb his hair back, and I saw another one on the inside of his arm.

"What does that say?" I pulled his arm to me and read the words written down his inner arm in English. "Brave woods?" I asked.

His eyes were fixed on mine. My hands held his arm, a finger running over the words. He was cold too. He said nothing, just nodded. Stoic tilted his head a little, and a red curl fell over his face.

"Let me do it!" I said, moving behind him. "You combed my hair a thousand times, so it's my turn now." He didn't object.

I undid his bun and ran my fingers through his hair. It hung a little past his neck. It was soft and a vibrant deep shade of red, like Auntie Ida's. My hands caressed his hair, and I ran my fingers deeper into it, touching his scalp, detangling it. I loved the feeling of his silky hair moving in between my fingers. Finally, I got all of his long curls in my hands and gently twisted them into a bun, tying a band around them.

"Done!" I cheerfully said.

Instead of moving away, I hugged him from behind, putting my face next to his face and my arms around his wide shoulders. Maybe I could warm him a little. While on my knees, I leaned on him, and my chest pressed against his back.

One of his hands went to my arm, and he gently brushed his thumb over it. Stoic started humming softly, an old song with his baritone voice. I immediately recognized it, "Misty Mountains." He used to sing it to me when I couldn't sleep. He learned it from a book he liked to read when he was little.

We stayed like that for the longest time, simply feeling each other, taking in the scenery right in front of us. There was laughter coming from his friends playing in the river, but it all became background noise. Birds were chirping, squirrels jumping from tree to tree, and the blinding reflections of light bouncing from the still river's water. This felt right. Hugging Stoic like that felt right.

ELEVEN

EMMERSON

Stoic 22

That night, I couldn't sleep. It was getting late into the morning, and I was still awake. I had turned and rolled in bed, thinking about him all night. My mind went to his strong chest, all his tattoos, his defined arms, his thick beard, and his deep voice. Everything about him made me get a massive lady boner. I remembered the way his skin felt on my fingers, his hand slowly moving down inside my underwear, and his finger slipping in between my pussy lips.

"Ahh! I can't hold it anymore!" I muffled a scream into my pillow. I was determined to do it. I had never done it before, but I had to try. I could rub my bean and please myself.

How difficult could it be?

I pulled my blanket over myself and let my hand drift inside my soaked panties, finding my clit. I spread my legs open and thought about how he did it, and I rubbed circles around it. More wetness spread over my fingers.

I was overly sensitive, and it started to feel really good. I let my body relax and threw my head back onto my pillow. I thought about the way Stoic smelled, the way he rubbed his hard dick over his jeans that last time. I imagined how it would feel to have his tongue inside my mouth, to have his kisses run down my body. "Uhh!"

Fuck, that felt good.

I was so immersed in that delicious new feeling that I didn't notice my bedroom door had opened. "Uuh! Uuh! Uuh!" I was moaning softly as my fingers went faster. I was enjoying myself.

"Emmerson." I heard Stoic's low voice.

Holy Fuck!

It couldn't be. I jumped up, uncovered my face, and confirmed it. The worst thing that could have happened right at that moment. He was here, with his angry eyes on me. He stepped into my room and closed the door behind him.

Oh, no! Did he know what I was doing?

"Stoic..." I said, feeling myself close to freaking out. My heart felt tight in my chest.

"What were you doing, Emmerson?" He spoke in a low voice, and I was glad because I didn't want my parents to find out I was pleasuring myself.

"Nothing." I held onto my blanket tighter as he walked over and sat next to me.

"Nothing?" he said, raising his brow. I didn't think he'd buy it.

"Yeah, nothing!" I tried to sound confident but failed. Yep, he was not buying it. He pulled back my blanket and revealed my current state. I had on a white shirt, but since I wasn't wearing a bra, I was sure he could see my hard nipples underneath. I also had no pants on, and my underwear had a huge wet spot on it.

"I see." His eyes ran up and down my body and stopped right in between my legs. He bit his lip, and I could feel my face heating up fast. That alone was enough to make my body tremble.

Stoic put a hand on my knee and started to move it up my leg slowly. "Did you make yourself cum already?"

Oh, god!

"No... I..." I hid my face with my hands.

Why was I answering?

"Do you know how to get yourself off, Emmy?"

Oh, my!

I was about to puke my heart out. I didn't answer. He kept moving his hand up my leg.

He leaned closer to me. "Do you want me to rub your wet pussy until you cum, baby?"

I couldn't breathe! I couldn't fucking breathe! I didn't know what to do. My whole family was here under the same roof, and Stoic wanted to finger me into oblivion.

What if they heard us?

His hand was now on my mid-thigh. "Tell me, Emmerson, use your words."

I didn't know. I wanted it, but it might not be right to do it. It could not be right. Mostly right at that moment. Anyone could discover what we were doing. His eyes were on mine, and I just stayed quiet for a long moment, feeling his hand move.

His hand was already at his target. He pulled on my leg and spread me open for him. He caressed my inner thighs before groping me over my panties. "So fucking wet. You are a horny little vixen, aren't you?" He gave me a soft pat on my pussy that made me jump.

He held my leg with one hand and rubbed circles over my panty-covered wet clit with the other. My clit was hard, and he could see it very defined through the damn fabric. He pinched it softly between his fingers, pulling a gasp out of me. It was so difficult to think. Part of me wanted to stop him, but the other part was just letting him do whatever the fuck he wanted with me. I bit my lip and watched his fingers move on me.

Stoic slid his fingers inside my underwear, immediately finding my rigid sensitive bud, and rubbed slowly with one finger. My hand went to his, and he grabbed it and moved it away while shaking his head no.

"Spread your legs wider for me." His voice was so low I could barely hear him. I didn't know why, but I did it. Stoic put two fingers flat against my pink button and started to move them faster and faster. My cream made them slippery.

Stoic executed the most delicious torture my body had gone through. His hands made a wet sound as he rubbed me without stopping. My legs started to shake hard, and my breathing got ragged.

"Do you like that, baby?" His blue eyes stayed fixed on my pussy.

"Uuhhh! Uuhhh!" I knew they were too loud, but I couldn't control them. Something was building up inside me fast.

"Shh." He put his other hand over my mouth to muffle my moans.

I was close. I was about to reach that place I had never climbed before, and Stoic was the one taking me there.

Stoic pressed his hand over my mouth harder as my nearly silent moans became more desperate. My hips started to buck, and my legs shook violently.

I was cumming. I was cumming hard on Stoic's hand. My toes curled, my back arched, and I dug my nails into his arm. My whole body tensed. Pleasure spread throughout my body. My pussy pulsated hard and fast. My eyes rolled back, and my mouth opened in a silent scream.

I heard steps coming from the hallway, "Emmy?"

Oh no, oh no! No, no, no, no, no!

Stoic covered me fast with my blanket and remained calmly sitting next to me, like nothing at all had happened–like he hadn't just given me my first orgasm.

My body was still convulsing when Kenzo opened the door. "Emmy, Dad said he wants you to go with him to the fields today," Kenzo said, but I just stayed under my blanket, trembling from the aftermath of an earth-shattering orgasm. "Is she OK?" he asked Stoic. He must have seen how my body shook.

"Yeah, just cold," Stoic said, passing his hand over my shoulder up and down as if he was helping me warm up.

"Don't worry. I'll make sure she gets there on time."

How could he be this calm and composed when I was dying of shame?

Kenzo left and closed the door behind him. Stoic kept rubbing my shoulder over the blanket.

"That's my girl." His thumb rubbed my arm. "I don't want you touching yourself, Emmy. That's a job for your husband."

What the fuck? He just fucking did it?

"Go take a shower, baby. Andreas is waiting for you." He took one of my curls in his hands and caressed it between his fingers.

Seriously? How could he act as if nothing had happened?

I didn't get it. I waited for a minute after Stoic left my room. I ran to the bathroom and took a cold shower. Under the freezing water, I held my head, wanting to pull it off!

How did I let that happen?

Things were already complicated enough before that. How was I supposed to face him later? What was he playing at?

After coming out of the bathroom, I noticed Stoic had left with Kenzo. It must be one of those days when they would get lost and not return until the evening.

After working with my father for a few hours, I just hung around the woods by myself. For the rest of the day, I just dragged my feet around, feeling completely ashamed of myself.

Stoic called me a horny vixen. He might think I was a slut.

Did I really look that desperate? What kind of girl did that with a guy that was like her own brother, even closer than her own brother?

He never liked it when girls were too forward with him. He must think I was a freaking pervert.

Why did he do it? Why pleasuring me?

It was clearly something he didn't enjoy. There was nothing there for him. He was serious the whole time. I was so confused.

I thought about it for a long time, and in my mind, there was only one solution. I had to talk to him and clear the air. I was determined. I would take him out after dinner and have this conversation with him.

Dinner time arrived, and our family gathered around the table. While we ate, there were conversations and laughter. Stoic sat next to me, and, as always, he just ate quietly, listening to everyone talk. I waited until everybody looked distracted to try to tell him I wanted to talk to him in private.

The opportunity arose, and I leaned toward him, waiting to quietly talk to him. But before I could say anything, our landline rang, and everyone stopped talking.

"I'll get it," said Kenzo, standing up. It was weird because we didn't usually get phone calls.

"Hello, this is the Silva residence." As soon as Kenzo heard the other person talking, he stood up straight, "Yes, sir."

Stoic's body stiffened up, and his head turned quickly toward Kenzo.

"Yes, sir. Yes, he is here with me." Kenzo looked at Stoic. "Yes, sir. I'll inform him immediately." Kenzo only nodded during the rest of the call. Stoic stood up and walked over to him.

Kenzo hung up the phone and gave all of us a sad look before getting dead serious. "We have to go back. We are taking the first train in the morning. Pack up." Kenzo passed by Stoic and headed to his room.

Stoic curled his fist tightly and left the house, slamming the screen door so hard it almost broke.

"What's happening?" Mom asked. "Kenzo, what's happening?" She followed him into his room.

My eyes landed on Uncle Erik, and he, too, stood up, walking after Stoic.

What was happening?

I stood up, and so did Dad. Then we went to Kenzo's room.

Kenzo was tossing things inside his backpack, getting it ready.

"What happened? Why now? You guys still have two more months of break," my dad asked.

"Something came up, and they need us now." He kept packing, and Dad and Mom just stared at him doing it.

"I want to go and say goodbye to my friends before I leave. The train leaves at four AM. I don't have much time left." I bet he wanted to see Ava. It took him about fifteen minutes to be done, and then he ran out of the door.

Mom sat at the table and cried. I helped her pick up the dishes and clean up. Dad walked out, maybe heading to Uncle Erik's house. I stayed quiet. I was not ready to see them leave so fast.

About half an hour passed before Stoic returned to the house.

"I'm sleeping here tonight," he said to my mom. He had taken a shower, changed his clothes, and was holding his backpack. The one I had made for him. Maybe he wanted to leave from here together with Kenzo like the last time.

"OK, come here." Mom opened her arms, and Stoic hugged her. She kissed his forehead like she kissed us and patted his back. "Go, it's getting late. You should rest."

She pointed to the back of the house, and Stoic took his things and went there.

"You too. Go to sleep." She took the rag I was using to clean off my hands.

She tilted her head toward my room and patted my shoulder, too. "I know they would like you to go with them in the morning, so go."

I hesitated at first but then walked to my room. When I opened my door, Stoic was sitting on my bed with his head in his hands. He looked stressed.

"Stoic?" I was almost afraid to talk.

"Come." He extended his arm to me and pulled me in. Stoic laid us on my bed and spooned me. He held me close to him, wrapping his arms tightly around me.

"Let's sleep, Emmy." That meant he didn't want to talk. So, I didn't. We laid there in silence for a long time. Finally, I turned over and hugged him back, burying my face in his chest. I listened to his heartbeat and his soft breathing for hours. Neither of us fell asleep. We just enjoyed the warm embrace as we held each other.

Sometimes I would run my finger through his hair, and sometimes he would do the same with mine. I softly brushed his eyebrows, and he touched mine. We looked into each other eyes, and he tenderly kissed my forehead. We were very close, but it was not sexual.

Before we knew it, Kenzo knocked on my door. "It's time."

Stoic's face changed. It was like someone had turned a switch on, and he was a different person. He stood up, put his jacket on, and got his backpack. He sat on the bed and started to put his boots on.

I stood and got ready too. Once we were dressed, he took my hand and walked us out of the house. Stoic held my hand all the way there. Both Kenzo and Stoic were quiet, like the dark streets we were walking on.

The train station was deserted, and only a few people were waiting for the train to arrive. At the platform, my mom and dad hugged Kenzo, and Uncle Erik and Auntie Ida hugged Stoic while he still held my hand. It was just like the first time they had left.

This time, though, I was sad. I knew it would be a while before I would see them again. There was so much I wanted to talk to Stoic about. I felt like I had wasted so much time. I should have chased him around, made him pay attention to me, made him stay by my side, pulled his face to mine, and made him look at me and only me for those four months. Stoic pulled me in and hugged me tightly.

"Remember, Emmy..."

"You'll always come back to me," I said, remembering my boomerang, and he held me tighter.

The train arrived, gradually slowing down near us, but Stoic was still hugging me. The train stopped, and Stoic was still not letting me go. Kenzo tapped his shoulder, and Stoic dropped his arms. Before I could see his face, Stoic turned around and got on the train. Once again, not even looking back.

"Take care, Emmy." Kenzo hugged me, kissed me on my head, and got on the train too.

Mom and Auntie Ida stood near me, and both of them threw an arm around me. Dad and Uncle Erik stood behind us.

We all watched as the train started to move, eventually disappearing into the darkness of the morning fog. I put my hand over my heart and squeezed my sweater. Tears began to fall down my cheeks.

"He will always come back to me," I whispered.

TWELVE

EMMERSON

Emmerson 18

They had been gone for more than a year and a half now, and the time for them to come back was getting closer and closer. Any week now, we'd get the notice that they were coming back home. I couldn't wait!

Last year, for my birthday, Stoic left me a really beautiful sundress with Auntie Ida. The fabric was soft, and it flowed perfectly down my body. I was sure it was Mom who sewed it. During the summer, Uncle Erik gave me the usual hoop. They were getting way smaller. I wonder what he would do when he ran out of space. He didn't leave me the fall wooden gift, though. Uncle said he'd give those to me when he came back.

This year's birthday, instead of the usual dress, he mailed me a necklace. It was a bullet on a long chain. It was simple and a bit odd, but I liked it. I wore it all the time. He wrote a cheesy letter to go with it, saying it was a gift from a place near his heart. The more I thought about it, the cuter that silly idiot Stoic started to look to me.

He added a picture of him and Kenzo with friends drinking beers. He had more tattoos, and his beard was longer as well as his hair. Many girls surrounded them, and I could see the hunger in their eyes. They looked at him like a piece of meat. I fucking hated that, so I cut my brothers out and threw the rest of the picture away. I put them on my mirror and threw them a kiss every morning.

I did reply and sent him a picture of myself, smiling in the sundress he gave me. I added a note that said, "from the most beautiful girl you'll ever see," with a kiss print on the side of it. My inner brat would never change.

Ethan was back from his assignment and started going to college. He said he wanted to become a hydroelectric engineer. He and Amelia told everyone about their relationship once Ethan came back. They were both working and getting ready to find their own place to move in together.

None of us were children anymore. We were all grown-ups, and it felt kind of weird. I could tell Mom missed having children in the house. However, that feeling didn't last long because shortly after Kenzo's departure, Ava came by our house saying she was pregnant.

Kenzo missed the whole thing. She gave birth by herself, and Auntie Ida helped her. Mom, Ida, and I tried to help with the baby whenever we could. Kenzo had a beautiful son. She named him Ian and gave him the Silva last name. Mom and Dad were super excited with their grandchild, and I was the crazy aunt, spoiling the hell out of my beautiful baby boy.

We all knew Kenzo would take responsibility for the child, but we didn't think he would marry her. She was a sweet girl, and I hoped she found happiness. We would always be there for her.

My backpacks were a success. People liked them, and I got many orders. Working kept me busy and distracted. I was still dancing with the group and recently started teaching the dance to the younger ones. Since Dad and Uncle Erik were out most of the time, I had gotten really good at speaking Portuguese with my mom. Just like before, I also spent time with Auntie Ida. I already knew many of her recipes by heart. I wanted to pull my own weight around my house, so I did the cooking most of the nights.

Guys never stopped hitting on me. I didn't blame them, as I just kept getting more beautiful by the day. Noah kept chasing after me for a while until he found someone else to pursue. I was glad about that. Other guys asked me out, but I truly never found any of them attractive.

My mind kept running the image of Stoic's hands on my most intimate parts, his face on my neck, and his lips moving on me, telling me he didn't want anyone touching my body. For some reason, I didn't want anyone's hands but his on my body, even when I knew they shouldn't be.

Stoic's demand was confusing because he didn't want anyone touching me, but at the same time, he wanted me to get married. What did he expect my husband to do? Not touch me for the rest of my life? Was I supposed to spend the rest of my life horny and unsatisfied, watching from a distance as Stoic had a family of his own? Having a perfectly normal sex life with his future wife? Fucking Stoic! He was so frustrating and contradictory. After all his fuss, the only one that had actually touched me had been him, no one else.

I had recently gotten curious about my future husband, but Mom always beat around the bush and never gave me a straight answer. She did tell me that once I get married, I would be moving out to a different place not too far away from here. Leaving my family was not in my plans. I was tired of being left in the dark. I was not sure I wanted to go through with this marriage thing.

Since I was eighteen already, a random stranger would come and claim me one day, and I'd have to go with him. I didn't fucking like the sound of that. My hope was that Stoic would talk my parents out of it, but he wanted me to get married, too. I was doomed.

Last time, I didn't have a chance to talk to Stoic and clear things out. No matter how horny I got and how much I wanted it, it was just not okay for me to let him believe he needed to help me get off. That was not good for either of us.

[illegible] got the ideas, and I guess I should do the same. I didn't want to be the reason he failed in his words. I was jealous of her.

Lucky bitch.

It was still hard for me to picture him with another woman. To be honest, it gave me a sour combination of anger and sadness that I hadn't been able to shake off yet.

Once Stoic came back, I would have that conversation with him and completely eliminate any misunderstanding and move on. He had always been a brother, and I wouldn't lose that. I couldn't lose that. I didn't want to completely lose him just because I couldn't get my mind out of the gutters. Oh gosh! That would be one of the most embarrassing conversations in my life. I would have to put my big girl pants on and get it done.

It was going to be hard for me because I still got aroused thinking about him. At random times, he would cross my mind, and I couldn't control the boiling heat that arose all over my body. As he asked me to, I didn't touch myself. I didn't want to fall further into this endless trap where my body desired him and him alone, but my mind recognized he would never be mine. He couldn't be mine.

I spent most of my time during the whole past year repeating to myself over and over that he was my brother and nothing more. I repeated it so many times that it became my mantra.

My overprotective, serious, tall, and handsome brother–nothing more.

THIRTEEN

EMMERSON

Stoic 21

A week ago, we finally got the phone call. Tomorrow was going to be the day Kenzo and Stoic would finally be back home! I'd have my brothers back!

Kenzo would finally meet his beautiful son. I had to say, I loved being an auntie. Ian was so stinking cute. Ava was doing a great job raising Ian, but it must have been so hard to be a single mother.

Since they'd arrive tomorrow, Mom was throwing a big dinner party. She said she would invite the whole family. I knew how Stoic loved to eat fish, so I was trying to catch some for him. I'd make one of the recipes Auntie Ida showed me. He must have missed our homemade food–I would if I were him.

I was so freaking excited about their return. I hadn't seen those two in almost two years. By the picture they sent, I could imagine just how much more different they looked now. I couldn't wait to have my brothers in my arms. I'd hug the farts out of them two.

It was a hot summer day, and since I hadn't caught anything yet, I decided to go for a swim. I took my shirt and pants off and jumped in with only my underwear on. I had the bullet that Stoic sent me hanging low in between my breasts, as I always had ever since I got it.

The water felt great. I floated around and looked at the blue skies and soft clouds above me. It was truly a beautiful day. I let my body sink in the water and held my breath while I swam to the bottom. I could see tiny crayfish crawling by and small little fish that scurried away as I tried to touch them. Resurfacing, I took a much-needed breath of air and started to swim back to the shore.

Suddenly I got self-conscious. My bra was see-through. Oh, well... it should be fine. One, I was completely alone, and two, I had nice tits. If anyone saw me, they would surely enjoy themselves.

I was laughing at my stupid thoughts when I heard a deep voice calling my name from behind me. I turned around, and there he was. Standing on the shore, looking at me, a big smile on his face.

"Stoic!" I swam as fast as I could. I was not thinking about anything else. I just went as fast as I could. I got out of the water and ran to his open arms. His smile dropped, but I didn't care. I jumped up, and he caught me.

Stoic held me tight against his chest. Just like the last time. I was getting his clothes wet, but he didn't complain. My arms and legs snaked around him, and I couldn't believe I finally had him in my arms. His warm hands moved up and down my back as he kept his face on my neck.

"I missed you so much," I said to him, hugging harder.

"I know you did. There's no other like me in this world," he said, and I remembered the last time when I said that to him. We laughed, and he spun me around once.

I was totally consumed with happiness until Stoic's hands moved from my back and grabbed my ass. All of a sudden, I remembered. Holy fuck! I was almost naked! I didn't panic just yet, since it might not be what I thought it was.

Since his face was on my neck, I couldn't see it, so I didn't know for sure.

Was he trying to hold my weight?

When he grabbed my ass harder, squeezed it, and pulled it apart, I knew it. Nah, he was groping me.

My legs fell off his hips, and he slowly put me on my feet but didn't let go of my butt. Stoic pressed me tight against him, and I felt his hardness against my abdomen.

Oh, no. This... this was not good.

"Stoic... I..." He leaned down and kissed me on my jaw. I didn't move. I was too nervous to do so. Stoic sensually kissed my neck, and his hands moved up my back and then back down, over and in between my thighs, caressing me.

My hands went to his chest, and I put a bit of pressure on him, but he didn't stop touching me and kissing my neck. Not knowing what else to do, I stepped back abruptly.

"I... I... was swimming." I pointed at the river. I just needed an excuse to get away from him.

He nodded his head. "I'll swim with you," he said and took his shirt off. I turned myself around and looked away from him.

What could I fucking do?

I could feel his eyes on my body, and it was super uncomfortable. From the corner of my eye, I saw him take his boots off and open his pants.

I looked for an escape, but he was blocking my only way out. All other options required swimming. I didn't want to make things worse, so I turned around with my hands over my chest, covering my breasts, so I could talk to him. This awkward conversation needed to happen right then.

When I turned around, Stoic stood completely naked, a hand moving on his fully erect dick and his eyes on my body.

My eyes locked on his member, and I [illegible] before [illegible] again.

Holy fuck! I just saw Stoic naked.

Behind me, Stoic moved and walked closer to me. I was paralyzed. I should have moved, but I didn't.

Stoic pressed his body against mine from behind and, with both hands, groped my breasts. He pinched and released both of my nipples in between his fingers before he cupped and gently squeezed them in his hands. His mouth was moving on me again, and he kissed up and down my neck and jaw. His hands kept fondling my tender globes until he moved his hands behind me, undid my bra, and let it fall off me. My tits were freed and exposed for him, my nipples hard and sensitive.

His hands went back to my breasts, and I didn't know how to stop him. I wanted to stop this. This was not right. We shouldn't have been doing that. It didn't feel right.

Stoic's hands traveled down over my hips, and he slipped his finger inside my panties, pulling them down with him as his hands traveled south. I was completely exposed. He took my panties completely off, and his hands traveled back up, running over my inner legs and groping my pussy. The only thing I had on me was the bullet that hung low on my chest.

I heard him let out a low growl while he slipped his fingers in between my folds. It was unsettling. I had thought about his fingers on me hundreds of times, night after night, but right now, I was freaking out. I was not ready for it, and I had to stop it.

I opened my mouth to speak, but nothing came out. Stoic walked forward and moved us into the water. There he turned me around, put my legs around his hips, grabbed me by my ass, and walked us deeper into the water. My chest pressed tightly against his.

I stayed there, wide-eyed, looking at him, not knowing how to tell him I didn't want any of this. I could feel his hard cock in between my legs, throbbing.

Stoic took us awfully close to the waterfall and sat me on a rock. He then pulled himself up, stood on the rocks, and pulled me up to standing too. Taking my hand, he led me to the waterfall, where he put his arm around me to shelter me from the heavy weight of the water falling over us. Once we crossed to the other side, we reached a small cave.

The cave was mostly rocky, with a small, round sandy area. There was just enough light to make the whole cave dim. The waterfall fell behind us like a thick curtain that would hide what was about to happen inside this cave. The thunderous sound of the water falling would swallow any sound that might escape my throat. I was scared

Did he plan this?

My body began to shake, and he might have thought I was cold because he immediately hugged me, rubbing my arms up and down.

Stoic lifted me and carried me bridal style, walking deeper into the cave. He laid me down on the damp sand. With both of his hands, he spread my legs apart. It was so humiliating. He could see everything. I didn't want him to see me like that. I tried to cover my pussy, but he slowly moved my hands away and laid them beside me. Not letting me deny him this.

His lips connected with my legs, and his mouth kissed and licked my legs as he slowly moved up. I didn't want it, but I was too frozen to push him off me.

Stoic's lips connected with my pussy, and my body jolted up. My first instinct was to close my legs, but he had both of his hands on my thighs, making sure they stayed open for him. Stoic licked and tasted me. His tongue slid inside my slit and began to savor me. The wet sounds his mouth made against me, and the sound of his fast licking made me feel sick to my stomach. I was not going to lie. I had fantasized about having him like this, in between my legs, pleasing me, but right now that it was all real, I was terrified.

My pussy had a mind of her own, and I started to get very wet, a tingling feeling building up in the pit of my abdomen. Stoic licked me more and used his fingers to flick my clit too. As his fingers went faster, I lost control, and I felt like I was about to cum. I tried not to. My hands grabbed the sand below me, and my body tensed. I refused to look at him doing that to my body. I looked away, but I couldn't escape the feeling between my legs. When I least expected it, my orgasm hit me hard and fast, and I came. I came in Stoic's mouth, and he licked it all up. I bit my lip and refused to moan, as I didn't want him to think I liked it. I was so embarrassed.

I felt Stoic position himself between my legs, and I panicked. I had to talk now. I had to say something. I put my hands on his chest, but before I could say something, I felt it. "Ow!"

Stoic pressed his thick spongy head to my entrance and slipped it inside me.

No! No! Please no!

Stoic pushed a bit harder inside while holding his cock in his hand, inserting more of himself into me. I pushed him harder, digging my nails into him.

"Ow, it hurts. It hurts." I started to cry.

"It's okay," he said without looking at me. He just cared about one thing: taking me. He was going to use me for his pleasure, not giving a fuck about how I was feeling. I cried harder.

Why? Why was this happening to me?

Stoic pushed more of himself inside and moaned, "Uhh! Fuck!" He was enjoying this.

The pain was terrible. I felt like my insides were being ripped apart. I could feel myself tear as he pushed further inside. This was not supposed to happen. I was supposed to wait for my husband.

Stoic's dick got stuck inside me, and he pulled out, then pushed it forward even harder, trying to break through. "AH! OW! OW!" I yelled in pain, more tears falling down my cheeks.

Stoic pushed himself farther inside me and reached my cervix. "Uuhh! Holy fuck, Emmy! Uuhh!"

It was so denigrating. His hips bucked, and he leaned his body over me. He gave me a few shallow thrusts, then stilled. "Uuhhh!" He threw back his head and squeezed my hip with his big hand. He painfully pushed himself hard against me. "Uuhh! Uuhh! Mmm!"

He was taking pleasure in my pain. His eyes were closed, and his body was shuddering. He moved his hands on me, and the warmth I once found comforting now burned me, leaving my skin painfully raw. He gently ran his hands all over my body, including my head, face, and hair.

I looked away. I didn't want to see him. He moved his big wet body over me, crushing me with his weight. He grabbed me by my jaw and made me look into his eyes.

Staring into my eyes, he kissed me, but I didn't kiss him back. Putting his weight on his forearms, he dried my tears away with his thumb and kissed my wet cheeks too. His touch was soft, but instead of soothing me, it made me feel worse. How dare he take me like that and then pretend he was the same loving and caring brother I grew up with. He was buried deep inside me, for fuck's sake.

He put his weight on one of his elbows, spread my legs further open, and started to move inside me.

I was still hurting. The pain was unbearable. I didn't know what to hold on to, so I dug my nails inside the palms of my hands.

"Uhh! Emmerson!" He was pleasuring himself again. I felt so empty. "Uhh! Baby!" He moved faster.

Pain ran from my core to my back and my legs.

Stoic went faster. He pumped into me harder and deeper. Every time he touched the back of my vagina, I felt a painful, stabbing pain.

Please stop!

I wanted to scream, but my voice was trapped inside me. Fear consumed all of my will.

"Ahh! Ahh! Holy fuck! So fucking good!" Stoic moaned next to my ear. His thrusts got even faster and harder. Our wet skin slapped together, making a disgusting sound as it forcefully met. "Fuck, Emmy!"

I was ruined. Stoic just ruined my body.

He pounded away with pure abandon, not giving a fuck about all the pain I was going through. Pleasing himself into oblivion. He made me look at him one more time, and his face was distorted in pleasure. His mouth hung open, his eyes filled with fire and lust, and his hair loose and falling over his face.

He grunted as the rhythm in his hips got irregular, and his breathing became ragged. I laid there with my eyes full of tears, his hands holding my face, making me see how much pleasure he was taking in destroying my body.

Stoic started to make some animalistic sounds and moaned even louder. His solid dick slammed hard inside me. Pain was shooting all through my body. I felt my blood drip down my inner leg to my ass as he violently pounded harder inside me. He took my wrists at each side of me in his hands and held them tight against the sand, immobilizing me. My breasts flapped up and down hard as his thrusts moved my whole body.

Stop! No more. It hurts. Please, no more!

I shook my head, but he just kept going. I should have screamed, said something, anything.

His body was starting to get stiff, and I knew he was near. He dropped his face down and licked my nipples, tugging them into his mouth. First one and then the other. He didn't stop his painful assault. His head landed between my neck and face, and he gave me three extremely hard thrusts and stilled inside me.

"Uuhhh! Uuhhh! Uuhhhh!" His hips bucked as he kissed my neck hard and grasped my wrists harder. His body started convulsing above me, and he lost all strength, falling on top of me. I felt his hot cock pulsating and warmth being poured inside me.

No! No! Please, don't!

There was nothing I could do. It was too late. I was soiled. He soiled me.

Stoic stayed over me, trying to control his breathing. His face raised, and he kissed me again. I didn't kiss him back. I just laid there, crying, feeling used and empty. His eyebrows frowned, and his blues studied me. He looked at my body, observing with his pleasure-filled eyes what he had just destroyed. He got on his knees and started to slowly pull his softening dick out of me.

Stoic's eyes were locked on my pussy, surely enjoying the way his dick slid out of it. He observed with a frown how my pussy expulsed his seed and my blood out of it.

I cried out loud, and he wiped my tears away and kissed me. Once again, I didn't kiss him back. He kissed my neck, and his body fell over me once more.

I wanted to run away from there. I needed to escape and never see his face again. I wanted to fight him, but my body felt weak and lifeless.

Stoic rolled us over to our sides and stayed there, hugging me close to his body. I used to love it when we cuddled, feeling like his arms were a warm and cozy, ever-welcoming home, but at that moment, I couldn't help but hate that feeling.

He rubbed my back and hair, kissing my forehead and the top of my head repeatedly.

After what seemed like forever, Stoic sat up, held me close to him, and picked me up as he stood. He took me back to the river and carefully washed my body. His hands were shaky, and his touch was delicate, but I was already broken. I could tell he was trying not to be sexual about it.

Why did he even bother?

All of this was beyond wrong. I couldn't believe that had just happened to me. I felt so betrayed by him. I thought I would be able to trust in him forever, no matter what. I was so wrong.

Why would he hurt me like this?

He could have had any other woman to please himself.

Why me? Did I lead him on? Was this my fault?

As soon as he was done cleaning me, he hugged me again. I was in tremendous pain, and I could barely stand up by myself. Stoic noticed it, carried me, and walked us back to the shore, where our clothes were laid on the ground.

Once we arrived on the shore, he helped me get dressed first. He put my bra and underwear on me. He walked to the rock where I had left the rest of my clothes and the fishing pole and got them for me. Stoic put on my shirt and pants, then helped me get my shoes on.

Once he was done, he sat me on the ground and turned to get his clothes. As soon as he turned around, I stood up with all the pain I had and took off, leaving him butt naked. I ran as fast as my body permitted me to.

"Emmerson!" he screamed my name, and it echoed in the woods like thunder.

Looking back, I saw him fall on his face trying to put his pants on quickly. I didn't look back again. I ran as fast as I could, and I didn't stop.

"Emmerson, stop!" I heard his angry voice sounding further from me. He must still be trying to untangle his pants.

Pain consumed my body, and I tried to ignore it as much as I could. My core, my legs, my back, my wrists–everything hurt–but I ran faster, getting farther away from him. Tears fell on the ground, and I held onto my abdomen, trying to ease the stabbing pain.

Shame and embarrassment filled me as I got closer to my home. He had cleaned my body, but I still felt incredibly dirty. I could still feel him over me.

I went into my home, leaving my shoes at the entrance, and ran to my room. I was glad Mom didn't see me coming in. I locked myself in my room and fell on the floor, completely exhausted. Not wanting to be anywhere near my door, I grabbed a pillow and crawled with it under my bed, then rolled myself around it. The bed Stoic had made with his own hands was my only shelter from the world.

I wasn't safe anymore. I'd never be safe again.

I put the pillow over my face and screamed my pain. I tried to be silent, not wanting my family to know what had happened to me. I was so fucking hurt, and my heart was as broken as my body. I felt like the old Emmerson had just died behind that waterfall.

I heard someone shake my door handle and then four hard knocks. "Emmerson!"

Stoic! I held onto my pillow tighter.

"Emmerson! Emmerson! Fucking open the door!" Stoic kept knocking on my door repeatedly. He sounded angry. He was angry because I ran from him.

"Open the fucking door, Emmerson." He knocked harder, making the whole door shake. Stoic was furious. He might even break it down.

Stoic stopped knocking for a moment. "Emmy, baby. Open the door, please." His voice was calmer now, but I was not buying it. There was no way in the world I would open that door.

"Baby, open the door. We need to talk."

Never.

"Baby?" He wasn't knocking anymore.

"Emmerson, please. I know you are there, please."

I didn't want to see him ever again. I could have screamed a thousand different things at him, but I just hid under my bed and stayed quiet.

"Emmy, please."

"Emmy?"

"Baby ...."

His voice got softer and softer. He kept calling me like that for a while. After a few more minutes, he left. I heard his steps get further away, and I breathed out the air I didn't know I was holding.

I let my body relax a little. I needed to think of a way I could escape from Stoic without being followed. I knew that as soon as he got a chance, he would try to use me again. I couldn't let that happen. I should have known better. People had told me that this was what he wanted, but I didn't listen. I felt so guilty. I should have done something. Pushed him, fought him, hit him, fucking said something, anything–but I didn't. I let this happen. I let him do this to me.

I hated him. I had been saving myself, and he just forcefully took it all. I was not a virgin anymore.

More pain spread throughout my body, and I doubled over. Still under my bed, I closed my eyes and tried to rest my aching body.

A few hours passed, and I heard my mom knock on the door. "Emmerson, get ready. We're about to serve dinner. Oh, and put something pretty on, OK?"

She sounded excited.

It was going to be hard, but I had to do it. I had to go out there and put a smile on my face for my family. I didn't want any of them suspecting me. After dinner, I could leave and go to Amelia's house and hide. I'd see what to do from there.

I crawled out from under the bed and got dressed. I usually flirted with myself in the mirror, but at that moment, I couldn't stomach looking at my own image. I wore a long-sleeved shirt to cover my bruised wrists and took off the bullet necklace.

Before opening the door, I took a deep breath and wiped away the last of my tears.

I could do this.

FOURTEEN

STOIC

Emmerson 18

Laughter, wine, food, and cheerfulness. Everybody was happy, celebrating, everyone but Emmerson. She looked lifeless. The warm summer breeze entered her house through the front door. This should have been a good evening, one of the most important days in our lives, but instead, she looked like she was thousands of miles away.

The clear skies showed millions of blinking stars, and the moon shone through the windows, making her skin shine like a true goddess. But I knew she wasn't enjoying any of this. Our families were joking, laughing, and telling stories, but Emmerson was just quietly staring at the floor. Even when they spoke to her, she did not talk.

Kenzo and I had finally returned home after a five-year-long deployment to the northern border. Emmerson thought we were celebrating our return, but that was not all we were celebrating tonight. I had been waiting for tonight my whole life.

Glasses were raised, and we all listened to Uncle Andreas's toast. "For this and many other dinners together as one family."

The whole family cheered right after. I raised my cup, but I didn't drink from it. My eyes were fixed on Emmerson. She had yet to move. She was barely breathing.

Our whole family was here, including grandparents and some cousins. This mid-sized dining room was full of cheerful people, but Emmerson's gray, sad image sat in the middle of them all. It was all my fault.

I saw her nails digging into her arms, and there was nothing I wanted more than to hold her in my arms like I just had a few hours ago. Hold her close to my chest, rub her back, and tell her that everything would be fine. She looked exhausted.

Emmerson readjusted on her chair, her face contorting with pain. She hissed, and her hand immediately grabbed her lower abdomen. She was in pain. A lot of pain. It was no one's fault but mine.

Fuck. What had I done?

I let a grunt escape my mouth and leaned forward, trying to see her better. Wanting to reach for her. I wanted to help her. Get her out of here and go somewhere she could rest and recover. I hated myself for this. I was beyond angry with myself.

How did I let it get that far? Fuck me. I was an idiot.

My elbows were on the table, and I ran my hands tightly over my face and mouth, pulling on my beard. My eyes stayed fixed on Emmerson's face. My heart hurt, and I wished she knew how important she was to me.

The dinner continued, and laughter boomed and bounced off the thick wooden walls of her childhood home. Some of my most precious memories were made here, with her. Emmerson hadn't taken a single bite yet. She had been moving her food around the plate but never ate anything. She looked weak, and I was afraid she would be sick. If she did, that would be on me too.

Knowing she was this badly affected made my blood boil with anger. I wanted to punch a wall repeatedly until it crumbled under my fists. Fuck! I had protected her for her whole life, and I ruined it all at the very last moment.

Why couldn't I just keep it in my pants?

She wasn't ready. No matter how much I had wanted it for years, she wasn't ready. I fucking hated myself. I grabbed my fork in my hands and squeezed it hard, keeping myself from storming out of her house and starting to break shit down.

Trying to calm myself, I took a deep breath. I could still feel the warmth of her soft, wet skin in my hands and the sweet smell of her hair. She'd forever be my obsession, the only woman I'd ever desire.

"Emmy, pass the vegetables," Ethan said to my right, waking her up from her daze.

She picked up the bowl and stretched her arm out, waiting for Ethan to grab it when her eyes met mine for a few short seconds. I saw the pain, and it angered me. Those beautiful eyes had always been full of life and happiness. I looked deeper, but to my dismay, pain and sadness were not the only things I saw in them. There was fear. She was afraid of me. I had fucked everything up.

Ethan took the bowl, and she looked away once more. I wanted her to look back into my eyes, but she didn't. My heart sank. I knew I deserved her indifference. I should back away, but I wouldn't. I couldn't. I never had. Even if it took me the rest of my life, I would win her back. I'd do anything. She was my beacon of light, and without her, I was lost.

My mind traveled back to the cave. The way her small body made way for my eager member. How tight her sex felt around me. Her soft body trembling under mine. The feeling of her spread legs on each side of my hips. The wet sounds of our bodies colliding. How I got lost in my passion and pounded her hard against the sand. Her taste. Her smell. The feeling of my hips bucking and euphoric feeling of knowing I was the first and that I would be the only one in her life as she was in mine. Pulling out of her pussy and seeing how my seed and the blood that signaled her purity left her slit and rolled down her tender thighs.

I knew it must have been hard for her to suddenly see me as a man. I had always been a friend, her rock, closer than a brother. I shouldn't have been so much like a brother, although I never saw her as a sister. I should have always kept her safe. I failed.

Andreas stood with a cup of wine in his hands. "Family, the time has come to make an important announcement. As most of you know, this dinner is not only to celebrate the safe return of my brave two sons. Today is so much more, a night that some of us have been talking about and looking forward to for over eighteen years. I have seen my children grow and become men and women during this time. Imany and I believe it is time to finally tell Emmerson who she will be spending the rest of her life with."

Andreas had a sweet smile on his face, and I couldn't help but feel guilty. I clenched my hands into fists and laid them on my lap. My eyes landed on Emmerson's sad ones once more, knowing she wouldn't like what she was about to hear.

"Emmerson," Andreas said with a smile.

"Emmerson, dear," he tried again. This time he signaled with his head to

Imany to get her attention.

Aunt Imany shook Emmy's elbow, and she looked completely disoriented. She wasn't listening at all. Imany slowly pointed at Uncle Andreas, and Emmerson finally noticed him.

"Emmerson, dear, did you hear what I just said?" Andreas said with his eyes full of love. He was a kind man, always caring for his family, always doing the right thing. I was embarrassed. I had failed him too. As soon as he knew what I had done, he would beat my ass down.

"What?" she asked, completely lost.

"As you have known your whole life, your hand in marriage has already been promised, and your mother and I couldn't be happier. After all these years, we have finally decided to tell you who your fiancé is. As we have always told you, your fiancé is an extraordinarily respected man, and no one is more worthy in my eyes of the great honor of becoming your husband. There's no one I'd be happier to call my son."

She was thinking. Her eyes looked unfocused, and she seemed lost again. I wished I could just take her away. Sit her down and have a long talk before she learned we were bound to be married soon. I know she was confused, and she needed to know how I felt. I had never said it to her out loud.

Andreas coughed to get her attention back.

"With that said..." he extended his arm toward me. "We are glad to announce that these two families will soon be officially united. Stoic, my son, the day has finally come when you can claim your wife, and in a month's time, you two will be joined in holy matrimony. I hope you two find all the happiness you deserve and that together you'll have a long and prosperous life. Of course, we'll be expecting to see little devils running in our halls once again, filling all of our houses with laughter like you two did when you were little. Stoic, you have waited a long time for this moment."

Not long enough. I had ruined it.

"To be honest, I first thought you were just being a silly boy playing around. You gave me your word and kept it, Stoic. It's time for me to keep mine. Stoic, my daughter is yours."

I felt like shit. I failed them all.

Imany excitedly shook Emmerson's arm. Cheers from everyone in our family erupted, and I saw Emmerson sink down further in her chair. Realization of the situation she was currently in was written all over her face. She hated it.

Tears started falling from her eyes, and our family mistook them for joy.

They all "awed" and cheered louder. If only they knew, I wouldn't make it out of here alive, let alone in one piece.

I was scared. What if she refused to be mine? What if she decided to leave? I couldn't give her that option. I needed her; I didn't have any choice. A life without Emmerson was a life not worth living.

I stood up and started to take steps toward Emmerson with the heavy weight of my regrets and mistakes over my shoulders, crushing me. I stepped closer to her with my hands in my pockets, searching for the ring I had carried with me for over eleven years.

As soon as I was close enough, I got down on one knee and took her shaking hand in mine, slowly sliding the ring on her finger. When I let her hand go, it fell lifeless and hung beside her. She still refused to look into my eyes. Anger consumed my body once more. I fucking hurt her. I hurt her badly. I had worked so hard my whole life and waited for so long. I knew I messed up, but I couldn't lose her.

I stood up and got close enough to her body, leaning down closer to her ear. [illegible] that only she would hear, I said, "You are mine." I lovingly tucked her hair behind her ear, but before I could finish saying, "and I'm so sorry. I'll make it up to you," Kenzo tapped my shoulder and pulled me in for a hug. I failed him too.

Soon her whole family and mine were around her, congratulating her.

Why the fuck was I so impulsive? Why didn't I wait? How could I help her heal?

I knew I had to tell her family and mine. I wouldn't let her suffer in silence.

How would I make it up to her?

FIFTEEN

EMMERSON

Stoic 23

Aring, my summer gift was an engagement ring.

I was so stupid. Why the fuck didn't I see that coming? That was why he always acted like I was his–I was. I was nothing but a possession to him. A thing he'd use for his pleasure. A bitch for breeding. Bound to give birth to his children, cook, clean, and meet his every need.

He was obsessed with me. How hadn't I seen his possessiveness? What I wanted didn't matter, and it had never mattered. I wasn't free. I was nothing but a small bird trapped right in the middle of his claws. I had always been, but I just hadn't known it. It'd always be his word and his will, and I'd always have to follow and obey. I fucking hated it.

That was not the life I wanted for myself. I couldn't live my life with a cruel man that took pleasure from my suffering. A man that wanted nothing but to control me like a doll. I needed to escape. I'd wait for most of my family to go first, and then I would run for it. I didn't know where to go, though. I didn't care as long as it was not here. As long as he couldn't reach me.

I was alone, and thanks to him, I had lost it all. I'd have to leave everyone and everything I loved behind. I had no idea where to go, but one thing was for sure, I was leaving tonight.

I laid down and tried to rest. I was going to need the energy. Less than half an hour passed before I heard a soft knock on my door.

"Emmy, can I come in?" It was Auntie Ida.

"Yes, one moment." I dried my tears and took a deep breath. I walked with difficulty to the door and unlocked it. I let her in, and she closed the door behind her and locked it.

"Are you okay, darling?"

Lie, Emmerson.

She couldn't find out. No one could find out. It would hurt her, hurt everyone.

"Yes, just ... tired. I might be coming down with a stomach bug or something. I just need some rest."

Please buy it.

"He told me everything. You don't need to lie, Emmerson."

What? He told her what exactly?

"I'm sorry. I don't know what... I... I'm...." I was nervous, so I stepped back. I didn't know what to say. I didn't know what he said to her.

"He hurt you, Emmy. I'm not here to defend him. I'm here for you, to check on you as a nurse. Lay down."

"No! I'm okay, that's not necessary. I...." A stabbing pain spread throughout my body again, and I doubled over, holding my belly.

"My son is an idiot! Emmy, lay down and let me examine you, please." Auntie had teary eyes.

"I–" I was about to refuse her again, but she stopped me.

"Emmerson, I love you. You are more than a daughter-in-law to me. You are like my own daughter. Fuck, Emmerson, I helped Immy deliver you into this world."

She held my face in her warm hands. "Trust me. My heart is broken. That fucking moron doesn't even know what he has done. We'll make him pay for this, but first, we need to make sure you are fine."

"Auntie!" I broke down. I didn't know what to say. I started crying hard. I held on to her as hard as I could.

"I'll help you, Emmy. I know you are hurt, but we'll help you. You are not alone, Emmy. You never were, and you never will be," she said, hugging me.

"Auntie, take me away. I don't want to be here. I don't want to see him. Please, Auntie. I can't be here," I pleaded.

"I think I know a place, and I'll take you there, Emmy." As soon as she said those words, we heard a knock on the door again, and our eyes flew in that direction.

"Ida, Emmy? Open the door. It's me." My mom. My eyes returned to Ida, begging her not to tell Mom. Ida gave me a squeeze on my shoulders, reassuring me it was going to be okay. She went to the door while I dried my tears.

"My baby, how are you?" Mom rushed to me, looking worried and hugging me tightly.

"I'm OK, Ma." I tried to smile at her.

"Are you very hurt? Why didn't you tell us? Why did you keep this to yourself, baby? Don't you trust us, Emmerson?" She touched my abdomen.

What was happening?

"What..." I was afraid to ask.

"I talked to Stoic, and he told me everything. He is talking to your father, his father, and Kenzo now."

What an embarrassment. Everyone now knew I lost my virginity. Holy fuck. Stupid Stoic. I knew he was dumb as a rock, but not this much.

Why would he do that? Was I not denigrated enough? Did he have to make it worse by telling everyone?

This made no sense; this was not good for him.

Fuck him! I hated him so much.

"Mom, I'm... I'm so sorry ... I ...." I started crying. My mom hugged me tighter. She was right. What was I thinking? I should have told her, trusted her.

"It's not your fault, baby. It is not." She rubbed my back and stroked my hair.

"She wants to leave. I know a place we can take her to. The guys don't know where it is. I thought you could distract them, and I could take Emmy there for a couple of days, maybe a week or so, until she heals and settles her mind about all this. After she feels better, we can go from there and think about what we should do next. What do you think, Immy?" Auntie asked.

"That's a good idea. Write the address down for me. No. No, even better, tell me. I'll memorize it. Let's not leave any loose ends." My mom and my aunt were on my side. I had to say, it felt good to have someone on my side now. They were willing to disappear with me, at least for a short while.

We did exactly that. Mom made a ruckus. She screamed and punched Stoic around, and they all followed her. When she had them all on the other side of the house and far away from the entrance, she "fainted." I never knew my mom was such a good actress. Auntie Ida rushed me out, and we took off.

About 20 streets down the road, there was this small house that belonged to Auntie's fellow healthcare worker. This doctor had been deployed to help at the northern border, and she was house-sitting for her. She said her co-worker would understand. The place was nice and cozy.

Ida examined me, and I was so embarrassed. She asked many uncomfortable questions about the rape. She also asked many other health questions, including when was my last period. Ida said I was going to heal, but that she could tell he was too forceful. She said that the soreness might last for about two more days. She gave me some painkillers and put me down to sleep. Ida stayed with me in the room, caressing my hair.

Mom came around three hours later. She brought two days' worth of food with her. I was still embarrassed. I just wanted to be alone, so I pretended to be sleeping. Mom and Ida went to the living room right outside the room and started to talk. Even when they were using very low voices, I could still hear them talking.

"Is she going to be okay?" My mom sounded worried.

"She will. She is strong, Imany," Auntie sounded sad.

"I want to kill your son."

"Me too. What did Andreas say?"

Oh no, my dad. How was I going to face them all now?

"He beat the fuck out of Stoic, and so did Erik. Kenzo got in the way and got his ass beat too. Stoic just stood there and took it. He looks like shit."

What the fuck, Kenzo? Really? He defended Stoic?

"He deserved it." I knew Auntie would have gotten a broom and done some damage as well.

"They asked him to leave. Erik said he didn't want him around Emmy, Andreas agreed. He didn't think Emmy would want to have him anywhere near her. We were two steps ahead, though." Mom gave a sad chuckle. Dad and Uncle were looking out for me too.

"Did they notice you left?" I could hear them moving things in the kitchen.

"No. Andreas and Erik were drinking, Stoic left with Kenzo, and Ethan was a no show. Speaking of Ethan, he left after dinner, so he might not know yet."

"Imany, I... Well ..." Auntie Ida never sounded this nervous.

"What?"

"Stoic didn't use protection, and Emmerson was in her fertile days. I didn't tell her that because I wanted her to rest and not worry about that for now, but I think she might get pregnant."

What the fuck? What the fuck? Oh, no! Oh, fuck no! Fuck, this couldn't be happening. Please say it was not happening.

"Holy fuck." Silence. My mom was in shock, and so was I.

"Do you think he knows?" my mom asked.

"That he might have knocked her up? No, my son is as dense as a fucking rock." Glad to know I wasn't the only one that thought that way. I didn't want this, though. I really didn't want it.

"Well, but she might not get pregnant, right? I mean, it's like fifty-fifty? I mean, we need to wait. Let's not get her worried about that yet." Mom was in denial, like me.

"It's highly likely, Imany. Sorry. I always knew Emmy would make me a grandma one day, but I never thought it would be like this." I could hear her softly crying. This was taking a toll on all of us. This wasn't only about Stoic and me anymore.

"Let her sleep. I'll talk to her tomorrow. She deserves to know. It's gonna be okay. She is a strong woman, and she is not alone. She has us. Let's go and try to rest. There's a ton of shit we need to sort out tomorrow. Emmy will need us." With that, both of them came back into the room.

I hoped they wouldn't notice my tears. They thought I was strong, but I was breaking down. I was terrified. I didn't want to be pregnant. They got into the bed, but I remained quiet. If they noticed me crying, they didn't say anything about it.

Mom laid on my right side, and Auntie laid to my left. They both threw an arm over me, and I felt protected by my two mothers.

If I were unlucky enough to be pregnant, I would soon be a mother too.

Would I be able to love my child as they loved me?

I really didn't know.

SIXTEEN

EMMERSON

Stoic 23

I was pregnant.

It was official. Auntie Ida had given me the test in the morning. Three weeks had passed since the incident, and I missed my period four days ago. We were still living here–Ida and me. Stoic didn't know where I was, and as I learned, he didn't live in his house anymore. Uncle Erik knew I was with Ida, but he didn't know where. Ida was not risking Stoic finding out. Only Mom, Auntie, and I knew about the pregnancy.

Ida had a hard conversation with me alone after the test. She said that if I really didn't want this baby, there were other options. That I didn't have to have it if it was going to be too difficult for me. I knew this conversation hurt her. She wanted her grandchild, but she was willing to respect my wishes.

I didn't have to think too much about it. I couldn't do it. I couldn't give up on my own child. I didn't want to. I knew that if I decided otherwise, she would help me, which would be okay too. This baby was mine first, before it was Stoic's. Now that I knew about it, I didn't have the heart to live my life without him or her. It was not like I would be completely alone, nor would I be the only single mother out there. If Ava could do it, so could I. Also, I knew Stoic was going to want to take some responsibility for this child, too. Be a provider for our child. I was not looking forward to that conversation.

All wedding talks and preparations were called off. Our family had many things going on before the "welcome back" dinner because they knew that was the day they'd make the announcement. I found out my mom already had a dress made for me. Dad had got me beautiful shoes, and Ida had already contacted the officials. Even Ethan and Amelia were working on some decorations. Everything was hidden in Ida's spare room at her house.

If anything, these past three weeks had helped me to reflect on my life. During the countless hours we spent together, Auntie Ida told me hundreds of stories and anecdotes from when I was little. She told me many of the things Stoic had done for me, and it was difficult to believe he ever had good intentions. She said that even when he got angry and lost his temper, he would always think about me first and try to make me happy.

She was trying to make him seem less horrible, but when I thought of him, all I could still see was the monster thrusting inside me. I was not ready to face him yet.

Auntie told me she had a conversation with him. She said he told her that it was his first time as well. That he had zero experience. There were other things, too, but she said it was not her place to tell me. It had to come from him and him alone.

I doubted it. Knowing how much of a man-whore Kenzo was and with Stoic being a minion of him, for all I knew, he might have already slept with half the population of the northern hemisphere. Even when he said before that he wanted to save himself, I didn't believe he really had. Now, I knew he meant to say that he was saving himself for me. Of course, he'd try to say anything that would make him look good in my eyes.

With all the things that Ida said, I really wanted to give him the benefit of the doubt, but I was afraid to. What if she was delusional? He was her own son, after all. Of course, she'd be biased. She still hoped for me to become her daughter-in-law, as she had told me.

Auntie promised me that he was not the monster I thought he was and that I should at least give him the chance to explain himself. Whenever I was ready, of course. She said he must also be hurting, but I doubted it. If she had seen the way his face looked as he came inside me or had heard the way he moaned with pleasure as he ripped me apart, she would doubt it as well.

Up until the rape, I focused hard on seeing Stoic as my brother. I was so adamant about not seeing him as a man that I practically hypnotized myself into believing he wasn't. I repeated to myself that he was only a brother to me, like a mantra. I took all those lustful feelings I had for him and locked them away. I felt guilty for wanting him. Why was I so afraid to desire him? Maybe I was scared to lose him. Either way, look where that led me. I was an idiot.

Remembering what happened, I could see why he might have gotten confused. I didn't push him away, and I never said no. I just cried, paralyzed. Not to mention that I ran naked into his arms. He should have stopped, though. I might have confused him, but he still was a fucking moron.

Moving on from this would become truly awkward. The Dokkens had always been so close to us, so I'd have to see Stoic regularly. Of course, I'd have to see him and talk to him. How else was I expecting to co-parent this child? It was not like I had another choice. I was such a coward, but I should be strong and face him head-on. Someday, I'd muster the courage, but not now. I might write him a letter to let him know about the pregnancy and ask him not to contact me.

All I wanted to do was to talk to Amelia. I wanted to tell her about the baby. I wondered what her reaction would be. She might be happy to become an auntie, or she might want to kill me for keeping it from her. Who knew?

Over these last weeks, I had only seen her twice. We didn't want to risk having Ethan or Kenzo following her. Today I had planned to disguise myself and visit her. She didn't know I was doing it, so I hoped I would find her at home.

After finishing my lunch and cleaning the dishes, I covered myself with an old shawl. Then, making sure the road was clear, I hunched and walked like an old lady to Amelia's home. Once I arrived, I knocked on the door. Landon answered.

"Hey, Emmy. Is that you?" He had to double-check to recognize me. I must have done a good job with my disguise.

"Yes, it's me. Is Amelia home? I sort of want to talk to her." I didn't want to stay out in the open for too long.

"Nope, she just left. Do you want to come in?" Landon had always been so nice to me.

"Nah, it's OK. I'd better go." Before I could turn around, Landon grabbed my arm.

"Are you hiding from Stoic?"

How did he know? Did Amelia tell him?

"How..."

"He comes by asking for you every other day." Oh, I better not stay then.

"Oh, I see. I guess I'll go then." I waved bye, but Landon stopped me again.

"Wait, I'll go with you. It looks like you need someone to talk to." Well... he was not wrong.

"OK." He closed his door behind him and followed me.

Landon and I walked to the park and sat on the bench swing. The park was usually full of children running around, but at that time, all the kids must have been taking their lessons at home.

"So, tell me. What happened?"

Should I tell him?

"I... I'm confused." That wasn't a lie.

"About Stoic? I heard you guys were engaged."

Where? Who told him?

"We were, but I broke it off."

"I see." Landon had a smile on his face.

Was he glad I broke off my engagement with Stoic?

Well, he must hate Stoic's guts after what he did to him all those years ago.

"I've got to tell you, Emmerson. That guy is not good for you. He is violent, and I'm sure he'll hurt you one of these days." Too late, he already did. I wouldn't admit it, though.

"I know." My voice was low and broken.

"He doesn't care about you, Emmy. He never did. Stoic is nothing but a big egotistical moron." Landon hated him. I couldn't blame him.

"His mom told me he does care about me. I... I don't know, though. Landon, what... I mean, how can I tell when a guy really likes me?" Maybe it was better to ask a guy these kinds of questions.

"When a guy really likes a girl, he wants to see her happy, Emmerson. He wouldn't hurt her." Landon moved closer to me.

"If I ever had a chance to be the man of a beautiful, smart, and wonderful young girl like you, I would never hurt her." That made sense. Landon got closer to me and threw his arm over my shoulder like he used to do when we were little.

"Is it possible to hurt someone without noticing it?" I wanted to know.

"Emmerson, people that hurt others do so intentionally."

"Do you think so? I mean, sometimes the circumstances are not completely clear and–"

Landon interrupted me.

"Look at me, Emmy. If Stoic hurt you, it means he doesn't deserve you, period. You are better off far away from him." I felt his arm drop further down my back, and he moved my hair away from my face with his other hand.

"But what if…."

Before I could finish my thought, I felt the swing move. Landon jerked backward, and I heard a loud, horrid crack. Landon screamed, and when my head turned to see him, his arm was twisted horrendously, his bone broken and popping out of his arm.

It was nauseating.

Landon screamed louder, and suddenly, he was pulled up by the neck from behind then thrown hard on the ground.

Stoic. Oh, no! Stoic found me.

He was not looking at me. His eyes were red, full of hate. I knew that there was only one thing on his mind. Kill Landon.

As soon as Landon landed on the ground, Stoic started kicking him violently and stomping his huge foot on him, hurting him [illegible] like a bug being squashed. I stood up with my hands on my mouth, unable to scream. I had to fucking get out of there!

I started running, completely abandoning Landon. I didn't know whether he was still alive or not, but I was gonna save my own ass. Stoic saw me and screamed my name.

"Emmerson, stop!" I didn't. I didn't want to die, so I ran faster.

"Emmerson, fucking stop." I kept running. This time, I knew he was running after me. I was so fucked. Landon was right. Stoic was too violent. He'd always hurt me.

I ran fast, but I was no match for him. Finally, he caught me and held me by my hips.

"Fucking stop, Emmy. Stop, baby." Stoic hugged me from behind. I was not having it. I kicked him and tried with all my strength to break free.

"Let me go! Let me go! Help."

"Fuck, Emmy. Stop, I won't hurt you, baby. Stop, please." I didn't trust him. I continued screaming, hoping someone would hear me and save me.

Stoic hugged me tighter and turned me around, putting my face on his chest. I cried as he kept a hand on my head and the other one on my back. I felt him kiss my head and rock me back and forth. His chest moved up and down, pressing hard against me.

"It's OK, baby!" It sounded like he was soothing himself more than me. "It's OK. It's OK. I found you." He caressed my hair and kept hugging me.

"Let me go, Stoic," I said, crying. I had no more energy left. It was useless, and there was no way I could escape him now.

Stoic picked me up bridal style, held me tight, and started walking. I hid my face in his chest and pulled his shirt over me, not wanting to look into his eyes. All along the way, I cried softly, not wanting to face him. I still felt humiliated.

Stoic said nothing. He just walked. Taking a glance around, I recognized the path he was walking on.

He was taking me home.

SEVENTEEN

STOIC

Stoic 5

~Eighteen years before the dinner~

It was spring, and the sweet smell of flowers was in the air. The weather started feeling warmer with each passing day. It was a calm day, quiet, just how I liked it.

Today, my best friend and his little brother were staying with Dad and me at our house. My mom was helping their mom out. All the adults were very busy, walking up and down with worried looks on their faces. Auntie Imany had been growing a baby in her belly for a while now. She would let me touch her belly, and I loved it when I could feel the baby move inside her. My favorite part was when I tapped the belly, and the baby kicked my hand. Her belly was super big, so I guessed it was time for the baby to come out. I had an idea of how it would come out, but I was not sure.

A little after lunch, Uncle Andreas came over. His face was red, and it looked like he'd been crying. My father walked over to the doorframe where he stood and gave him a big hug. After wiping his tears away, Andreas said the baby was a girl. I heard Kenzo and Ethan complain in disappointment. If you asked me, I didn't care. Even if she was a girl, she could just play along with us.

"You all can come by and meet her, but you will have to clean your hands and faces. She is very delicate, and we want her to be safe."

Ethan and Kenzo rushed to the sink and fought to be the first to wash their hands while I patiently waited behind them. I noticed they needed a stool because they were still too short, so I went to get it for them. Kenzo climbed onto the counter and washed first, and Ethan complained about it. I guess I didn't get the stool fast enough to stop the fight. I didn't need the stool as I reached the sink just fine. Once I was clean, my father took us all to the Silvas' house.

My friends rushed in to see the baby, leaving me behind at the front door. Both of our houses had only one level. Imany and the baby were in bed in the room at the back of the house. By the time I made it there, all the adults and my friends surrounded Auntie Immy and the baby. I couldn't see her at all, so I just put my back against the wall and waited. I heard them talk and laugh. They all said the baby was beautiful, but I hadn't been able to see her yet.

After a long while, Uncle Andreas said, "OK, boys, let's leave the ladies to rest. I'll give you some bread, and then you can all play outside." As everyone started to move out of the room, I caught a quick glance at the tiny baby wrapped in a blanket. Everyone, including my mom, had left, and I stood there, staring at the baby from afar, scratching the side of my fingers with my own nails.

"Stoic, don't you want to meet the baby? Come closer. Don't be afraid." Imany looked tired but happy. I carefully walked over and remembered what Andreas said, "she was very delicate, and we needed to keep her safe."

Imany patted the bed next to her, asking me to sit by her side. I did, and for some reason, my eyes couldn't stop looking at the baby. She was the most beautiful thing I had ever seen in my whole life.

"Do you want to hold her?" Auntie asked, and I nodded my head twice.

"Kenzo and Ethan are... a little careless, but you ... I trust you, Stoic. You're always careful, right?"

Once again, I nodded my head twice.

"Here, hold her head like this... and then put your hand there. Hold her firmly, okay?"

I did as she told me, and I could feel excitement fill my small heart.

"Her name is Emmerson, which means brave. She might look little now, but one day she will give you a run for your money. You'll see." I heard her soft chuckles, but my eyes were fixed on the most precious, most magical thing I had ever held in my arms.

Her eyes were closed, and she looked so peaceful. She had light brown skin, lighter than Kenzo's and Ethan's. Her head had a little bit of very fine curly hair. She looked a little skinny and so soft. I held her tightly to my body, making sure she wouldn't fall. She must have felt I was holding her tight because she squirmed slightly, and her eyes opened. One eyelid and then the other.

Suddenly, I found myself looking into her light brown and green eyes. My eyes widened as she looked back at me, and I felt time stop. I knew there and then that I wanted to look into those eyes for the rest of my life. Her small hand escaped the tightly swathed blanket, and she wrapped all her tiny little fingers around my thumb. She squeezed my thumb as hard as her little hand could, and I smiled, feeling my heart beat faster. She then made the most beautiful little sound and closed her eyes. She felt safe.

"I think she likes you," said Uncle Andreas with a smile. I didn't even notice he was in the room.

"I want her." The words blurted out of my mouth before I could stop them.

"She is a baby, not a toy, Stoic," Andreas said with a chuckle. "But you can see her as much as you want."

I never stopped looking at her, not for a second. I couldn't be more serious. I had never wanted anything so badly.

"I want her, and I'll take care of her. I promise." I held on to her tighter. I really wanted her. I'd always keep her safe.

"Well, she is her own person, you know." I could tell he found all this comical, but not me. I really meant it.

"Can I marry her?" I was desperately trying to find a solution, anything so I could call her mine.

"Well..." Andreas looked at Auntie and scratched his neck. "What do you think, Immy?"

"I think this is too cute," she said with a smile on her face.

"I'll tell you this, Stoic." He placed a hand on my shoulder. "My daughter is very precious to me. When she is old enough to get married, I would like to see her marry a good, responsible person. Can you be a good, responsible person?"

"Yes, sir!" I looked straight into his eyes with no hesitation.

"Being a good person takes a lot of work, Stoic. You will have to work hard for many years and always try to do your best at everything you do, okay?"

"I will, sir." I would be the best at everything and anything. I had to.

"OK then. I guess we can have a conversation with Ida and Erik." He laughed. "I gotta tell you, I was not expecting to have a marriage proposal for my daughter on her literal birthday."

"Promise me that when I become a worthy man, you will give her to me." I was serious. I thought they believed I was not. I needed a real promise. I would hold him to his word later on after I became the best man this village had ever seen.

Andreas smiled. "It's a promise, Stoic." He then pointed a finger at me. "But only if you're worthy, OK?"

"I will be. I give you my word."

"Alright then." He patted my shoulder and threw a wink at Imany.

My eyes traveled back to my baby. She slept peacefully in my arms where she belonged. I knew from that moment on, I would care for her with all my heart. I promised myself I would always be there for her, no matter what. I would keep her safe and provide for her. All the things I'd give her would be earned by my hard work and made by my own hands. I'd earn her fair and square.

I lowered my head and kissed her head, "Sleep, baby.

· · · · · · · · · · ● ● ● ● ● ● ● ● ● ● ● ● ● · · · · ·

Time went by, and Emmerson started growing fast. Ever since the day she was born, I had been spending a lot of time with her. I held her during her naps, helped Auntie burp her after her feedings, and helped Auntie launder her dirty diapers. I walked with Emmerson in the mornings, so she could enjoy some sunshine. You name it, I did it.

I was there for all her firsts. I was lying on the floor next to her, encouraging her, the first time she rolled over. Her big head threw her off balance, and she was so scared, she cried. But I was there to hold her. After she got used to it, we rolled all over the house.

I was also there when she got on her hands and knees for the first time, when she learned how to sit by herself, when she started rocking back and forth, when she started crawling, and when she pulled herself up and stood for the first time. After her first steps, she landed in my open arms. I was so happy that day that I couldn't stop smiling.

Emmy was a picky eater. It took forever to feed her her meals. Once Auntie Imany started giving her chunky food, she didn't want to eat. I thought she was lazy, and she didn't want to chew her food. I started to cut her food smaller, so she could eat it easily.

Even though she was picky, Emmerson got very, very chubby. She had so many rolls her mom called her the "Bakery." I couldn't stop kissing her chubby cheeks. She was so squishy.

When she grew into a toddler, she lost all her cute baby chub, and then the most amazing thing happened. Emmerson started talking. Her first word was "oi." That was what she called me for the longest time. Once Emmerson began to form sentences, there was no stopping her. She would babble for hours. I always listened to everything she had to say. She got very playful, and her giggles would fill her whole home as well as my heart. Her laughter was my favorite sound.

Emmerson loved playing outdoors, and she could spend hours outside. She was happy. It didn't matter if it was mud, dirt, water, or grass. She loved it. I often had to carry her back home crying because she wanted to stay outside.

I admitted it. I spoiled her. She had me wrapped around her tiny fingers, and I would do and go wherever she wanted me to. I would hold on to her tiny hands and let her guide me wherever she wanted to be. She was a free spirit, and I'd make sure she would be free to explore and play outside as much as she wanted. I didn't mind cleaning her up afterward as long as she was safe and happy.

I stayed true to my promise of being the best that I could be. I asked my parents to help me manage my time so that I could spend the most time with Emmy. I would wake up three hours earlier, so I could have my homework and house chores done. After that, I would help my father during the first two hours after they opened the workshop and then go take Emmy out for a morning walk.

I would have my lessons with Kenzo at his house from 10:00 am to 2:00 pm. After the lessons, I would help with Emmerson until her bedtime, and then I would put her to sleep. I liked telling her stories. Myths were our favorites. Emmy liked it when I talked to her. Emmerson was the person I spoke with the most. I always held her hand until she fell asleep and then kissed her goodnight before I left.

I wanted to prove to Andreas that I was worthy and that I could provide for her. For that reason, I always made Emmerson's gifts with my own hands. For her first birthday, I asked Imany to teach me how to sew a doll. Auntie Imany was a tailor. I gave it my best shot, even when I pinched myself hundreds of times in the process. The doll was not the prettiest, but it was what I had made all by myself. When I gave it to Emmerson with my small hands full of bandages, she loved it. It made her laugh. She went to sleep every night with it for a long while.

Three years went by, and all the grownups thought I would have gotten tired of Emmy by now. That I would have forgotten about the promise they made to me, but I never did. As a matter of fact, I often reminded Andreas about the promise. I would bring all my test results to him to show him my good grades. I was learning metalwork with Dad and Uncle Andreas daily, and I excelled in all the sports I was signed up for. I also helped with Emmy daily, more during the weekends, even when she had pooped and was stinky. I was always there for her. I knew I was making my uncle and my father proud.

My father told me that loving and being in love was not the same thing, that I was too young, and that one day I would understand the difference. He said that maybe one day, I'd realize that I loved Emmerson but did not want to marry her. He said that would be okay. Dad couldn't be more wrong. I'd marry my baby and live by her side forever.

Regardless, we all agreed that it was best if Emmerson didn't know I was her potential future husband. We didn't want her to treat me any differently.

On the day Emerson turned three, I had another doll for her. She laughed and giggled when she saw her new doll.

"Just like me." She patted the doll's messy yarn hair.

I nodded and smiled.

"Thank you, Stoic," she said, and her small arms wrapped around my waist. Happiness spread throughout me, and I could feel my cheeks blush.

Before the birthday dinner that Auntie always made for her, Emmerson played outside with other three-year-old kids that Auntie invited from the neighborhood. I watched her play with her friends from a distance. Ethan kept talking to me about this new thing he wanted to build, but my eyes stayed fixed on Emmy.

There were three little girls and five little boys playing around her. In my eyes, she shone like the moon in the middle of a dark sky. She looked so happy that it made me happy.

The kids started playing tag, and Emmy began to run after the boys. She grabbed one by his shirt's neck and pulled him down. At first, I thought, "that's my girl," but as soon as the boy stood up and pulled her hand toward him, my smile fell. I had this awful feeling in the middle of my stomach. I didn't like it. Not even a little.

Emmerson laughed and continued running. I knew she was having fun, but I couldn't help but feel something was wrong. Emmy was mine. I didn't want to see those little shits put their hands on my girl.

I took a deep breath and looked away. Emmy had all the right to choose her friends and have fun. I tried to focus on the silly dance moves Kenzo was making. He looked pathetic. I was looking at my friends laughing at his stupid moves when I decided to glance at what Emmy was doing.

Emmerson was sitting on a boy and tickling him as she did with me.

That did it.

For the first time in my life, I felt darkness and anger. I stood up fast without saying a word and walked over to Emmerson. My hands were forming fists, and I could feel my face getting red. My mind had only one thing in it, destroying that little turd.

When I reached her, I pulled her up by her armpits, lifted her off the ground, and put her behind me. I then grabbed that boy by his collar and pulled him close to my face.

"Don't touch Emmerson." I didn't recognize my own voice. When I dropped him, he ran for his life.

He'd better.

I heard him cry as he ran, and my blood boiled.

"Stoic?" Emmerson's sweet voice. I looked behind me, and there stood Emmerson, completely confused.

had to come up with something. I had to think of something fast. She looked worried.

I got down on my knees, held her by her shoulders, and tried my best to smile. "Emmy, little girls should be playing with other little girls." I didn't want her near boys ever again.

"Why?" Her face told me she knew I was full of it. She was too smart. I had no good reason other than I didn't like it.

"Because I said so," I said in a deep voice that I had no idea where it had come from. And then I saw something I had never seen in Emmerson's eyes before. She was angry with me, furious.

"You're stupid!" Those words left her mouth, and I saw red. We were both furious now. I stood tall and stared down at her. She stood her ground and stared back at me. My hands formed into fists again, and so did hers. I could feel my chest move as I breathed hard, and I could see her face getting red.

"Go home now!" I was about to lose it.

"No!" She dared to challenge me. The tiny little peanut dared to challenge me.

"GO HOME NOW, EMMERSON!" I had never screamed at her before. I took a step closer and said in a low voice, "Or I swear I will drag your butt back home." Emmerson's face changed, and for the second time today, I saw something in her eyes I had never seen before. Fear. I should be ashamed of myself. I didn't like this. It felt awful.

Emmerson's eyes shed some tears, and I felt like the shit I was acting like. She kicked my leg and ran home. I deserved it.

I watched her run and cry, and I knew then that things were about to change.

EIGHTEEN

STOIC

Emmerson 5

After that day, she hated me. I didn't regret it, though.

I had been kicking and tossing around any little dirtbags that got too close to Emmerson. Those little kids were scared shitless of me. I could see it in their eyes. None of them dared to step close to my baby. They all knew me. I would rather have her angry with me than her being pulled, pushed, and touched by those dimwits. I didn't like the way boys played, and I didn't want her to get hurt.

My dad and Andreas had given me many talks about how it was not okay for me to hurt others. They said that what I was feeling was called jealousy. I tried to control myself and hold back, but I couldn't. Jealousy got the best of me every time. Dad and Andreas always told me that Emmy was young and needed friends. I understood that, but I didn't want her with those careless dimwits. If she wanted a friend, she had me. I'd always be there for her.

They told me I needed to control my anger, but to be honest, I only lost it when it came to her. The rest of the time, I was very chill. They suggested I participate more in sports and martial arts to channel my strength and anger into something positive, so they signed me up and Kenzo for kickboxing, rugby, judo, and field hockey. We went swimming too. I was way busier than before.

Lessons had gotten more difficult and serious too. Not too long ago, Kenzo and I learned about sex and reproduction. Boy, was I wrong about how a baby was born. I was absolutely wrong about how the baby got inside the mom in the first place.

Apparently, childbirth was an excruciatingly painful experience for women. I sort of felt bad for Emmy. One day, she'd go through all that pain to bring our children into the world. I would make sure to make it up to her. About the sex, well... I wasn't very interested. I supposed something like that would be very awkward. It was what it was. I was glad I didn't have to think about or even worry about that until Emmy was at her marrying age.

I often gave Emmy gifts. A year and a half ago, I gave Emmy the first thing I made with metal. Dad helped me do it. It turned out funny looking but could stay standing, so I counted it as a victory. I told Emmy it was called "Jeg elsker deg," which meant "I love you" in my mom's ancestors' relatives' language. I wrote it on the metal, so Emmy would never forget it. With the help of Dad, I was making hoops for Emmerson. Andreas told me I could marry Emmerson when she turned eighteen, so I wanted to give her a hoop every year until her eighteenth birthday. That day I'd give her the last hoop when I'd put a ring on her finger. It was like a cool countdown.

Last year for her birthday, I made another doll for her, and she said it was ugly. I knew she said that because she was still angry with me. This year, I did something different. I asked Auntie Imany to teach me how to sew a dress. I picked a nice and shiny green fabric from the market. The green matched her beautiful eyes. The woman at the market took two bags of walnuts as an exchange for the cloth. It took me three full days climbing trees and opening walnuts to fill up those bags.

Since I had no experience sewing, Imany chose a remarkably simple pattern for me. I followed every instruction, and the dress turned out to be pretty decent. It didn't look like I sewed it myself. I was proud.

I couldn't wait to see Emmerson wearing something pretty. She always had worn-down clothes with holes. Not because Imany didn't make anything for her, but because that was how she liked to dress. Emmerson hated dresses and all things girly. The one I made was simple enough, and I really hoped she liked it. At home, I put the dress in a box and set it aside for her birthday tomorrow. Maybe if she dressed like a "girl," the other little girls would want to play with her, and she would finally have some friends.

Today, like every other Friday, I worked at the workshop for about two hours, went to the gym for kickboxing with Kenzo, had lessons at Liam's and

Lucas's house, and went back to Kenzo's home for dinner.

Every evening, I sat next to Emmy, asked her questions to see if she was learning her lessons as she should, and made sure she ate her dinner. After dinner, I made sure she cleaned up. The water came out dark brown after she was done washing her face. I waited patiently for Auntie Imany to be done helping her shower, and then I sat her down and combed her crazy hair. She liked to complain, but I had learned to be careful. I always started with the tips and worked my way up until it was all detangled. When she was ready, I told her a story and put her to bed.

That night, I told her about the time Odin, father of all gods, drank mead from three horns and gained a lot of knowledge. What I wanted Emmerson to take from it was that she should seek wisdom. She only cared about playing and having fun. I didn't think she understood half of the things I said to her. She took everything too literally. I knew she still hated my guts, but I was always going to stay by her side.

I patted her head and left her room. Tomorrow my peanut would turn five

-Day of Emmerson's 5th birthday-

"**D**on't go far, and remember to be back home early." I heard Uncle Andreas scream at Emmerson. We were doing our mandatory weekly farming. I was not done yet, so I was staying behind with him and Dad. I saw Emmerson run full speed into the woods, and I knew exactly where she was heading. She had a favorite spot she would always go to.

I had a bad feeling about it. It rained in the morning, and the trees' bark would be damp. I knew Emmerson would try to climb a tree. She never measured the risks before she jumped in headfirst. She could fall. I quickly wrapped things up and signaled my dad that I was going.

"Where ya going? Lucas asked us to play with him. Come with us." Kenzo hit me harder than necessary on the back.

"Your sister." I pointed at the woods. He knew there would be no convincing me. I often followed her and kept my distance. She didn't even notice I was there. I just needed to know she was safe.

"Oh, OK. Don't be late." He patted me again and went to play with Luca.

I started walking into the forest, and when I got near her favorite spot, I saw Noah, Mason, and Oliver. Those three little shits used to be Emmy's friends. I was sure I beat them out of thinking they could be anywhere near her. Those idiots were laughing their asses off, so they didn't even see me getting closer to them.

"Where the fuck is Emmerson?" My voice boomed. The three turds instantly shat their pants. They tried to run for it, but it was too late. There was no escaping me. Before they could run, I had grabbed one by the neck and the other two by their shirts.

I was angry. I didn't see Emmerson anywhere, and if these three morons had anything to do with it, they'd be in for a whole lot of trouble.

All of a sudden, I heard a high-pitched scream and looked up. Emmerson was way up high in a tree, hanging.

"Emmerson," I could barely speak. I saw my future about to fall into nothingness. My heart stopped, and my hands immediately dropped the kids.

"Don't move. I'll get you. Don't move, Emmerson. Hold on." My hands were shaking. I was scared. I had never been so frightened in my whole life. I ran and climbed that tree as fast as I could, ignoring all the cuts I was getting along the way. They burned and itched, but I didn't stop. I couldn't.

In record time, I was near Emmerson. My hand grabbed her arm tightly.

"Hold on to me, Emmerson." I pulled her toward me, and for the first time in years, she hugged me. She must have been scared. I hugged her so hard that I knew it was hurting her, but I didn't care. She was safe in my arms.

"Hold on," I whispered and put Emmerson on my back, wrapping her little arms around my neck. "Hold on tight." She wrapped her legs around my torso. "Don't be afraid, Emmy," I said, more for me than for her.

I carefully climbed down the tree with Emmy on my back, stopping every now and then to make sure she was still safely holding onto me. As much as I could, I kept a hand under her and supported her weight.

We made it to the ground, where I put her down. I felt like I was about to puke my heart out. Like I had just dodged a bullet. She had her eyes closed but slowly opened them. I stared at my favorite colors, glad that I hadn't lost her.

Quickly, I pulled her arm up and looked at it. I pulled her other arm up and looked at it too. I was looking for any scratches like I had. I dusted her pants and turned her around. She seemed to be fine.

"Are you hurt?" I was angry. I shouldn't have let her go by herself. This was exactly why I didn't want her near them. If I ever got to those little shitbags again, I was going to kill them.

"No," she said softly. Her sweet voice was music to my ears.

"Good." My body relaxed, and I felt a weight get lifted from my shoulders. I exhaled the breath I didn't know I was holding.

I remained silent for a while, getting my thoughts straight. It was her birthday, and I knew she wanted to swim.

I took a deep breath and stood up. I could see her eyes travel to my arms. I didn't want her to feel bad about the scratches, so I just started walking.

"Come," I commanded, and she followed. For once, she didn't fight me or ask any questions.

I walked us to the river. Her face lit up as soon as she realized where we were heading.

I started cleaning my arms in the river, and I noticed she was still standing far from me. I signaled her to come closer, and she did.

After two minutes of silence, she decided to speak. "Don't tell Dad." This girl!

"I won't." It was her birthday. I wanted her to be happy, so I wouldn't ruin this day for her.

"I'll never do it again," she said with her face lowered. At least this situation had knocked some sense into her. I nodded my head and kept cleaning my arms.

From the corner of my eyes, I saw her completely hypnotized by the view and the sound of the waterfall. A smile on her face and her eyes sparkling like a thousand stars. I should get her a house with a view like this one, so I could see that look on her face every day.

We didn't have long, so I grabbed her by her hips and threw her far into the river, where the water was a bit deeper. I was not worried since Emmy was a good swimmer.

"That's what you get for not listening," I said as I saw her gasp for air. She looked happy. She giggled like the silly girl she was and started swimming around.

I sat on a rock. "Don't swim too far." I had to be able to reach her quickly if I needed to.

"What if I do?" Bratty little peanut. She'd be the death of me.

I jumped in the water, making a huge splash. "Swim, Emmy, or I'll get you." I played chase with her a lot. It was hysterical to see her try to escape me and fail miserably. She was so little. She was definitely shorter than average.

I heard her squeal, and she started swimming as fast as she could. I let her gain some distance to make it interesting. Soon enough, I caught her, held her like a football, and walked back to the shore. She kicked and splashed the water all along the way.

"We need to go back." I made her stand on the shore. She was soaked. I tried to squeeze her shirt so that it wouldn't drip that much, and I pulled her hair back off her face.

"Emmy, a hill or a valley?" I wondered if she would rather have our home on a hill with a view of the river or in a valley where she could easily walk to the water and swim.

"A hill?" she replied, and I nodded. A hill it was. I needed to start looking for the perfect spot. I'd ask Kenzo to help me.

I put her on my back and carried her back to her house. I left her there and went to get changed and bring her my gift.

When I got to her house, I put the box down and went to Kenzo.

"Hey, dude. What happened?" Kenzo noticed my scratches. If it meant saving her, I would get a million more.

"Your sister."

"She's gonna kill you one day. What were you two doing?" He was searching my eyes. He never said it out loud, but I knew he didn't fully trust me with her. Kenzo thought I was going to screw up one day.

"Swimming." A half-truth. He gave me a look that said, "I know there's more, but I won't ask. Tell me if you want to."

"You know I worry about you. What if Emmy doesn't want to marry you?"

What a stupid question.

"She will." No doubts.

"What if she doesn't?" Kenzo insisted.

"She will." Don't make me think about that, Kenzo.

"What if Emmy is one of those girls who like other girls? She's still young, you know."

"She is not," I answered quickly. Did I need to be jealous of little girls, too?

Fuck me sideways. Stop talking, Kenzo.

"Nah, just saying. What if she is?"

"Don't know." Kiss my imaginary family with her goodbye. Maybe be a good uncle to her children. I would still build a house for her. I'd do anything for her.

Ah, shit! I didn't fucking wanna think about it.

"I don't fucking wanna think about it," I said, and Kenzo laughed at my misery.

"Dinner is ready!" Imany called us to the table.

Andreas put a candle on a cornbread muffin, and we all started singing "Happy Birthday" to Emmerson.

"Make a wish!" I heard my mom say. She loved Emmy like she was her own daughter.

Emmy closed her eyes and took the wishing thing a bit too seriously. She opened her eyes, and with her cheeks full of air, she spat all over the candle. We all clapped, and Ethan rushed to get her the gifts.

The first was a music box that my parents got for her. She liked it. The second was from her family, a fishing pole. She loved it. I'd make sure to take her fishing every once in a while. The third was mine, the dress. Kenzo's words were spinning in my head.

What if Emmerson likes girls?

She opened the box and immediately made a face. She looked at it as if it was the most disgusting thing she had seen before. She didn't like it.

"I don't want to wear a dress!" she said in her bratty voice.

"Emmerson! Don't be like that. Say thank you." Imany said, giving me a reassuring nod. She knew how hard I had worked on it. I could tell she felt sorry for me.

"I don't want a dress. I want a sword!" Emmerson said, and I would be lying if I didn't say I felt sad. What if Kenzo was right? I needed her to at least try to be a girl, to give it a chance. If that was not what she wanted, then there would be nothing I could do. With all the pain in my heart, I'd have to let her go and only be a brother to her.

"You need to start acting like a girl, Emmerson, not a savage little animal," I said. I felt my eyes get watery, so I looked away into the distance.

"You're stupid," she said, stomping her feet. Her and her temper tantrums.

"Dumb." She didn't fucking understand anything.

"And you're an ugly poop," she screamed. I bet that was the worst insult she could come up with.

"Clueless ignorant," I murmured, keeping my eyes away from her. I knew she was angry, but I didn't want her to see me cry. She never got it, none of my messages. She didn't get shit.

Andreas coughed, "OK, kiddos, let's not fight."

"But I don't want to dress like a girl." Fuck, Emmerson, just let it go, will you? Stuff your face with the cornbread and shut up.

"One day, you'll be a woman, Emmerson, and there are girl things you might want to learn," Andreas said. "Why not give it a try?"

He knew exactly how I felt. He has always had. I knew he asked more for me than anything else. He knew it was not the actual clothes that I cared about.

She thought about it and said, "OK. I'll try, but if I don't like it, I'm not wearing a dress ever again in my life."

"Deal. Except for your wedding, OK?" said Andreas.

"OK," she said, defeated. Andreas gave me a smile and a reassuring look.

I won that time. I might lose it all later.

NINETEEN

STOIC

Stoic 14

Emmerson 8

~Day of Stoic's birthday~

She wore the dress I made for her.

She looked cute in it. I guess it was comfortable enough for her to still be able to play with it on. I was glad about that. I mean, I was not out of deep water yet. She might still like girls. Fuck, she might like guys and not like me. Anything could happen. Regardless of all my worries, there was nothing I could do.

Emmerson was nothing but a cute, silly little girl that loved having fun and being playful. She was nowhere near interested in relationships, and she shouldn't be. I loved that about her. I didn't want her to grow up too fast. Let her enjoy her childhood. I'd wait. I'd stay close by and protect that happiness.

Talking about growing, my body was changing fast. I was so much taller, about six feet, and my back was wider. My voice got deeper, and I was growing hair everywhere. Oh, and my dick got huge too. I must have had like three wet dreams so far. Not really a dream, just that I just woke up with my underwear wet. I didn't usually think about sex. I knew it was weird not to, but I just didn't. I couldn't. Thinking about other girls felt wrong, but thinking about Emmerson was worse, so I didn't think about it at all.

Emmerson said she didn't like my facial hair, so I grew self-conscious about it and started shaving my face. It was a pain in the ass. The things I did for her, so she'd like me.

Kenzo recently became obsessed with girls. He was way more sexual than what I liked to admit. I saw girls as beautiful and cute but had zero interest in anything but friendship. To be honest, some of these girls' persistence sort of grossed me out a bit. Some of them were so forward it was intimidating, so I backed away fast. It looked like I was scared of them, but it was not that. It was just that I wasn't into it. Kenzo knew that, yet he made fun of me all the time. What could I say—I loved Emmy—but she was still too little, so I never saw her in that way. I wouldn't think of her like that at all until she got way, way older.

Emmerson hated when girls talked to her just to get closer to me. She embarrassed them in the worst way. If I didn't know better, I would say she got jealous. I sort of liked that. Who was I kidding? I loved that because it gave me hope.

Kenzo, on the other hand, had lost his virginity already. He was having sex with his girlfriend, Ava. I had to listen to him tell me about all the foreplay they did in corners, the woods, and the shadows before they went all the way. He told me all about it with all the details. Everything from what a vagina looked like, how it felt to the touch, and how it felt to bury your dick in it. He said it was the best feeling and that words couldn't describe the high. I had to admit, orgasms did sound great. I really didn't want to hear about the specifics, though, but I figured being a best friend came with its ups and downs.

Ava was cute and pretty, but I thought Kenzo was using her. When he talked about her, it was always about her body. I told him that was wrong, but he didn't listen. I was sure Kenzo would get himself into a lot of trouble in the future.

Kenzo said I shouldn't wait for Emmerson to grow up. He told me that Emmy wouldn't care whether I was a virgin or not, but it was not about Emmerson. It was about me. I didn't want to be with anyone but her, and since she was nowhere near ready, I just forced myself to not think about sex at all. Was that healthy? I had no idea. I just knew that I wanted to be able to keep her safe always, and that included from me as well.

Kenzo thought that repressing myself would drive me crazy and could lead to a bigger problem later. Also, there was the fact that I wouldn't be experienced enough to please Emmerson once we did start having sex. I meant if we did. I thought about that and took it upon myself to study it as much as I could. I read books on female reproductive organs and how to pleasure women, and I was not afraid to ask my dad later if I needed to. I had a pretty good idea of how to give a girl the big "O."

Meanwhile, I occupied my time with useful things like planning and working for my future with Emmerson and other simple things like studies and sports.

Over the last two years, I had been looking for the perfect spot to build a home for Emmerson, and I thought we found it. Kenzo helped me find it. We biked all over the village and asked around for suggestions about a thousand times. Finally, the baker told me about an abandoned lot, and we went to look for it right away. I was not sure if I'd be able to get the land, though. I hoped so.

The lot was on a hill that overlooked the river. It was quiet and surrounded by trees. It was far from the road and had an 80-yard driveway/dirt road in between the trees. The place was beautiful and spacious. There was an old house there, but I'd tear it down, reuse what I could, and recycle or repurpose the rest. I wanted our home to last long enough for our great-grandchildren to live in it.

I had been talking with my cousin Gabriel since he was an architect. We were coming up with estimations, measurements, and materials. I wrote everything in a small notebook I carried around with me. That way, I'd know what I needed. She kept it a reality. I asked Emmerson questions about the house all the time. She gave me silly answers, but I took them seriously.

Kenzo and I went into military training earlier than other boys usually did. The officials saw us playing rugby and recruited us. We trained with the sixteen-year-olds, and we were kicking ass. We were supposed to start mandatory training next year anyway, so neither of us cared too much about starting early.

Today was my birthday, and there was nothing I liked more than spending time alone with Emmerson. I had been taking her to fish weekly. I knew I messed up her chances to have friends, but I didn't care much. I was here for her. I'd always be there. I was busy, but I always made time for her.

Kenzo must have been somewhere pounding Ava, and Ethan had started spending more time with his own friends. The good thing about being alone with Emmerson was that I could listen to her talk for hours. Sometimes she wouldn't shut up, but I really liked listening to all she had to say. She had some firm ideas about life, its purpose, justice, and about people in general. She didn't even notice it, but I think she'd be an advocate when she grew older.

Today she brought me a gift. She had never gotten me a gift before. It was always the other way around. She put it in a box and wrapped it with a red ribbon. I was super curious about what it could be. Knowing Emmy as well as I did, I thought it would be something she thought I didn't like, like worms or bugs. She told me I could open my gift after we caught our first fish. She sounded fishy, but I wanted to see where all this went. It was the first gift I had received from her, so I was sure I'd like it. No matter if it were a dead cockroach, I'd always keep it.

Sitting next to her, waiting for a fish to take the bait, I remembered I hadn't decided on how many rooms our home should have.

"Emmy, three or four?" She gave me the same look she gave me every time I asked her something. She thought I was full of shit.

"Four and a half." Interesting, the half room could be her workspace. Wonder how much more work that would take. I wrote it down, so I could add it to the estimates. Later, I would sit with my cousin Gabriel and draft the ideas for a floor plan.

The line started shaking, and I stood up to reel in the fish. I put the fish in the bucket and extended my arm toward her, asking for my gift.

"What?" She was acting funny.

"My gift."

"OK, but you gotta sit down. OK?" She walked backward without taking her eyes away from me. She was up to no good.

I slowly sat on a low rock, and my eyes narrowed on her. She knew I knew she was up to no good. She gave me the box and got closer to me. It's like she had no sense of personal space, but that was just how Emmy was. It didn't bother me. It never had. Not with her. I had the box in my hands, but I hesitated to open it. I was sure she put the worst thing she could come up with in it.

"Open it," she sang. She had this cute habit of singing what she said when she was excited. I pulled the ribbons and opened the box, but there was nothing inside.

"It's empty." Was that it? An empty box.

"What? No! Did it fall?" She covered her mouth with her hands and looked at the box. Did she really get me something, and it fell?

"What was it?" If I knew what it was, I could help her find it. I looked around the ground, but knowing Emmy, she might have dropped it on the way here. We might need to look around the trail too.

"Oh, I think I see it!" She got closer. Where did she see it? I didn't see anything.

"Where?" I was still looking for it. I was sure I saw nothing around here.

"Here!" she said and grabbed my face in her little cold hands, squeezed my cheeks, and pulled my face up. My eyes connected with my favorite colors in the whole world, brown with a hint of green in them. Before I could react, Emmerson planted a kiss on me. I felt my heart stop, and then a rush of warm blood spread across my chest. My breath was trapped in my lungs, and my mind went blank. Emmerson had given me my first kiss.

Her lips were wet, and I savored her. She pressed her lips harder on mine, and I could feel she was holding back her laughter. I felt my face heat, and I knew it must be super red. Emmerson just stayed there, kissing me while looking straight into my eyes.

At that moment, I felt it. That feeling I had been trying so hard to repress all this time. The thing I promised myself I wouldn't even think about until she was older. Lust. It hit me hard and fast, and I was not ready for it. I felt my dick get hard, and my mind raised a thousand different things I should have never thought about Emmerson. All of a sudden, all those things I had worked so hard to hold back all this time violently surfaced.

She was getting uncomfortable and started to pull away. Some part of me told me to let her go, while another part of me just reacted. I put one hand behind her head, pulled her jaw down with my other hand, and pressed her harder against me, slipping my tongue inside her mouth. I tasted her soft, warm tongue with mine and gave her a heated kiss full of desire. I had never felt so turned on before. I closed my eyes and continued kissing her, wholly immersed in this addictive feeling. Without noticing it, my hand slowly moved from her face and traveled downward, touching her flat chest and continuing lower. I wanted to hold her by her hips, needing to get her even closer to me.

Without warning, Emmerson kicked me in between my legs, hitting me right on my boner. That woke me the fuck up. I fell to the ground, doubled over, and grunted. I deserved that kick.

Soon, the severity of my actions came crashing down onto me. That was wrong. That was more than wrong. What the fuck had I done?

I started hurting, and it was not from the kick. I was embarrassed and ashamed of myself. I fucking messed up badly. Kenzo was right; I was a ticking bomb. I could have hurt Emmy.

"What the hell, Stoic? Yuck!" I heard her make exaggerated noises and spit on the sand, but I kept my face on the ground where it belonged. I was still hard, and there was no way I could stand up without having Emmerson notice it. What the actual fuck! I rarely got boners, and now this mother fucker wouldn't go away. What could I do? I couldn't let her see me like this. I already did enough damage, and I didn't want to ruin her innocence. I didn't know how I would explain this to my dad and Andreas. She was just a silly girl, and she had no idea of what she had done, of what I had done. Fuck me!

"Are you okay?" It hurt to hear her sweet voice. I couldn't fucking face her. Not now. I needed to hide.

"Turn around, Emmerson." I had never been this embarrassed in my life.

"Why, though?" Because I was fucking hard!

"Because I said so. Just turn the fuck around, Emmerson." I couldn't have her joking around now.

"Make me!" Fucking brat. Emmerson could be a real pain in the ass when she wanted to.

"Emmerson, turn around, or I'll kiss you again." I wouldn't. I really wouldn't, never again. I felt bad enough as it was.

"OK. OK. You're so stupid." That convinced her.

As soon as she turned around. I crawled to the water and got in, making sure my lower body was under the water.

"What are you doing?" Hoping that the river would swallow me whole.

"I'm going for a swim. Go, Emmerson. Take the fish with you. I want to be alone." My hands held onto my head as if it was about to fall off. More like wanting to rip it off. How could I do something as horrible as that?

"No, I want to swim too." She was so fucking clueless.

"Fuckdamnit, Emmerson. Leave!" I yelled at her louder than I needed to. I was afraid she would ignore me and jump in the water with me. I was desperate. I needed her to go, and I needed her to go fast.

"OK, you ogre!" She picked the bucket, and I watched her stomp away. Finally.

The cold water felt good, but it was doing nothing to ease the heat I was feeling. I swam to the other side of the river and sat on the shore. I could still feel her soft lips on mine. I could still taste her. I knew it was wrong, but I couldn't help it. There was no way I was going to make it through the evening with her near me and this feeling inside my pants.

Kenzo said that the best way to get rid of a boner when a guy was very horny was to jerk off. I had never done it. In the woods, right after my first kiss, was not how I thought I would start doing it. I guess I had to do what I had to do. I stood up, walked further into the woods, and full of shame, I pulled my pants down. I faced a tree and started to go at it.

It was awkward, to say the least. I tried to concentrate, but my mind kept wandering back to Emmerson's kiss. I didn't want to think about her when doing this, but I couldn't help it. I closed my eyes and remembered the way that kiss felt, and my hand started to stroke faster. It began to feel really good, and I tightened my fist harder around myself. My mouth hung open. I could feel the pleasure building fast. I used my other hand for support against the tree and went faster, wanting to be done with it.

Just then, my mind wandered into a darker place. I thought about her body. I knew it was wrong, but I couldn't stop it. I was so close. I stroked even faster. "Uuh! Uuh! Uuhhh!" I came. I moaned out loud and came all over the tree. I had my first orgasm. My legs felt weak, and my breathing was ragged.

The pleasure lasted a few seconds, but I immediately started to feel bad for what I had done. I felt more ashamed than before. There was something wrong with me. That was wrong. I should have never done that. How would I face her now? This was a mess.

I swam back to our side of the river, picked up the empty box and the rest of the stuff, and walked back home.

Emmerson must have thought I would hate a kiss, and that was why she did That little box she gave me had more than my first kiss in it. That box was just like Pandora's box to me, releasing all my darkest desires. It would take a lot of hard work to fight back against what she had unleashed.

Once I got home, I took a shower and dressed for dinner. As soon as I saw her arrive with her family, I felt ashamed all over again. There was no undoing what I had done. All I could hope for was to hide it–for now–until I could have a conversation with Dad. He would know what to do.

In the middle of the dinner, I stood up and went inside the house. To be honest, I was about to cry. I felt so guilty. My father must have noticed that I wasn't feeling right because he followed me.

"Stoic? Are you okay, son? I noticed you–" Before he could say anything more, I interrupted him.

"I fucked up." Tears were running down my face. My father walked me further inside the house and gave me a big hug.

"What happened? Are you hurt?" He sounded worried. How could I tell him?

"I did something wrong," I said, trying to keep my voice from cracking.

"Nobody is perfect, Stoic. We are all bound to make mistakes sometimes. It's what makes us humans." He didn't know what I had done yet.

"I... I..." I couldn't even say it out loud.

"It seems like this is a talk that will take a long while. I'll tell you what, let's try to go back, and as soon as the dinner is done, we can sit and have a long talk. OK? I'm here for you, Stoic, and whatever it is, we can find a solution together. OK?" I nodded. I still had some time to find the right words to make it sound less horrible.

We walked back to the dinner, and I tried my best to keep it together. Soon it was time for me to open my gifts. My dad handed me an envelope. When I opened it, I couldn't believe my eyes. My dad had got me the land I wanted to build our house on. He must have sent the application for it right after I first told him about it. The papers were in my name. It was mine; the land was mine.

For a few moments, many different emotions swarmed inside me. I was beyond happy that the house I had dreamt of for Emmerson was getting closer to becoming a reality. On the other hand, I had done a terrible wrong to her, and I felt like I didn't deserve any of it. I gave my dad a tight hug, and he lovingly patted my back.

Uncle Andreas and Auntie Imany must have known about the land because they got me tools, so I could start working there. I was incredibly grateful for all the tools. I supposed Andreas was happy I was about to start building a house for his daughter. I felt horrible, though. It was like I'd stabbed him in the back. I hoped he would trust me after he learned about what happened.

We continued with dinner until it was late. Everyone was having fun, making conversation, and laughing. All I could think about was the talk I was about to have with my dad and the talk I would have to have with Andreas afterward. I was going to tell him myself. I didn't want him to find out from anyone else.

Our family finished eating and started to converse. Somehow Imany brought up the girlfriend topic, and Ethan immediately started making fun of Kenzo about his new girlfriend. Kenzo swung his hand and slapped the back of Ethan's head so hard it echoed throughout the backyard. Everyone laughed at how empty Ethan's head sounded. Imany then said how a girl named Riley was asking for Ethan, and he got embarrassed. My mom, being her silly, funny self, let out a ridiculous sound to bother Ethan even more.

They all laughed except Ethan. He tried to defend himself by saying, "At least I have kissed a girl. Stoic runs away from them as if they have the pest!" Fucking Kenzo chuckled at that comment. Making fun of me day in and day out wasn't enough for him.

Out of nowhere, Emmerson let out a big laugh and said, "Pfft, I kissed Stoic, and he was so embarrassed he rolled over and stayed on the ground, hiding his face for five minutes." Holy fuck! Hoooooly fuck!

Emmerson kept laughing hysterically without noticing all the laughter around her had died. Everyone's eyes landed on me, and I felt my face burn with embarrassment. Holy fuck! This was not how I wanted them to find out.

Emmerson kept laughing to herself, and Imany slapped her on her leg. "Stop it."

"What? It's funny." She had no idea that I was dying inside.

"Emmerson Silva, stop," Imany said in a low voice that everyone heard.

"Stoic, can I have a word with you?" Ah, Fuck! Andreas sounded pissed. I was so fucked. There was nothing else I could do other than face it head-on, like a man. I stood up and walked inside the house. I heard Andreas following me, and soon after, I heard my father's voice.

"I'll join you two." Dad walked behind me. At least he wouldn't let me die alone. Once we were all inside, Dad closed the door, and we sat on the couch.

"It's my fault. It will never happen again," I said before they could say anything.

"She pulled a joke on me, but I took it too far. I'm so sorry." That was vague.

"What do you mean exactly?" I guess I had no other option than to spill the beans.

"She tricked me and kissed me, thinking I was gonna hate it and get grossed out, but instead, I held her and kissed her back, with tongue. I got an erection, and ... I touched her chest. She kicked me in the dick to get me off her, so I dropped to the ground and stayed there, trying to cover myself. It was wrong. I should have never done it. I don't know what the hell I was thinking. I don't know what got into me. I feel super bad about it. Please forgive me." I better leave what I did in the woods right after out of this confession. I was sure Andreas would not want to know what I did thinking about his young daughter.

For a moment, there was silence. Andreas and Dad held a silent conversation with their eyes.

"OK. I'm going to be honest. I don't like this." Uncle Andreas was never going to trust me again, and I didn't blame him. "But I understand it."

What?

"Listen, this can never happen again, at least not until Emmerson is old enough to know what's happening too. She has no idea," Andreas said, and I agreed.

"Stoic, I know you are a good child with good intentions, and to be honest, we were all worried that something like this might happen sooner or later. You have always done the right thing, but it would be unfair of me to expect you to be perfect. We all make mistakes, even more now that you are turning into a horny teenager. We have all been there, so we know how it is. Let this be a lesson, and let's not make this mistake ever again. I know my daughter is dense and does stupid things all the time, but you know better, Stoic. You can never let something like that happen ever again. Maybe it's time for you two to get some space from each other." Andreas was right. I just nodded my head.

"Yes, I think so too. We know you want to see her every day, but what if you spend time with her during dinner time when the whole family is there? That way, you can be with her, but you two won't be completely alone. Huh?" My dad was right too. I could compromise and do that.

"OK. I won't be alone with her anymore." I'd make some excuses, and I'd just keep myself busy.

"It's not that we don't trust you, Stoic. It's that we know how fast things can get out of hand."

Trust me, I knew that. I learned it the wrong way.

"I understand." I really did. I was the last person on this planet who would want to see Emmerson hurt.

"OK, then. It's getting late, so I'll get going. Happy birthday, Stoic." Uncle Andreas patted me on the shoulder and walked away. I heard them say their goodbyes and walk out.

"Was that all you had to say?" My father knew me better. I shook my head no. My mom walked into the house, and Dad gave her a sign to "keep walking, we are talking." Mom got it and just went to her room.

"Do you want to talk here, or do you want to sit outside?" My dad knew Mom was nosy, and she could hear us talk. I didn't want Imany to know this part.

"Outside."

"OK, come." I followed him. We sat on the bench, and I had no idea how to start this conversation.

"So... I... After that, I...." I tried to say the words but couldn't. I scratched my head and avoided my father's eyes.

"You jerked off?"

How did he know?

"How..."

"You said you had a boner, right? What else would a teenager with a boner have done?" Oh fuck, maybe Uncle Andreas knew too.

What an embarrassment!

"Yes."

"And ... you feel guilty? You know, because Emmerson is still too young?"

Bullseye.

"Yes."

There was a long pause.

"Listen, Stoic, I can imagine how you might be feeling." Another long pause.

"I think that as long as things like those stay in your mind and you never, never act on them, they truly aren't the worst that can happen. Sometimes we can't control how we feel. You are young, too, and it is normal to have these feelings at your age."

"But... I... I knew it was wrong, but I couldn't help it. I should have been able to, but I wasn't. It was my first kiss, and the first time I, you know, finished myself. I did it thinking about her. I really feel bad, Dad." I hid my face with my hands.

My dad let out a big sigh. "Don't know what to tell you. What about you starting to imagine an older version of her? I don't know if it might help. I mean, as long as you never stop seeing her as the wonderful person she is, it should be fine. Girls are not objects."

"Yeah, I know." That might work. If everything else failed, that could be my go-to.

"Thanks, Dad."

"Anytime. Go back in and get some rest. Today was a long, fucked-up day."

My dad walked me back home. I got in my bed, but I couldn't help but feel sad about tomorrow. I'd have to start distancing myself from Emmy. It would be difficult for me, but I knew it was the right thing to do.

TWENTY

STOIC

Emmerson 8

Two months had passed since the birthday debacle, and as I promised, I was not spending much time with Emmerson. I missed her. I missed the simple daily things. I still went over to her house at night for dinner. I combed her hair and put her to sleep, too, but that was it. That was the only time I saw her. At least I could still see her daily, for now.

I had gotten busier. Working, cleaning, and clearing the land was a ton of work. On top of that, Kenzo and I were selected to train for a special unit, and as soon as we turned fifteen, we would have to travel to different camps. The officials said we were talented, so they wanted to put our talent to good use. That meant I wouldn't be able to see Emmerson for weeks at a time. I didn't like it, but maybe the distance would help us both grow.

I told her I didn't have time to fish with silly little girls like her, but in reality, that was all I wanted to do. Sit and listen to her talk for hours. There was nothing I wanted more than that.

I had no idea what she was up to these days. I saw her leave her home excited from my window every day. Kenzo said he thought she had a friend. I had been hanging out more with Kenzo and Luca. We spent a lot of time at the main road business just talking. The guys liked to check the girls out as they passed by. They were so stupid sometimes that I felt ashamed to be around them. Kenzo broke up with Ava. He was quite popular with the girls, so he'd been with another two so far. I guess it made sense since he was handsome and a smooth talker. I still thought he was gonna get himself in trouble, though. I knew Andreas had talked to him about it too.

We were not the only group of guys checking girls out there. The other day. I saw this group of fucktards talking about girls in a way that really grossed me out. I heard one of them talking about how he was into his little sister's best friend and how that girl was so ignorant that he could touch her, pretending to be hugged, and she would let him. Fuck, there were so many pieces of trash out there. Being a girl must be a fucking nightmare.

Today was the fall festival. As always, I had made a wooden gift for Emmerson. I would soon be far away from her for long periods of time. I'd be coming back and forth for more than two years, and after that, I would be deployed to the northern border for another three years. I decided to give her a gift with another hidden message. I knew I should fucking just say it, but to be honest, I was too shy.

I made a boomerang for her, so she would know that even when it seemed like I was leaving her, I was doing so having her fixed in my mind, and that my only purpose in life would be to come back to her. I would always come back to her.

I asked Auntie Imany where Emmerson was, and she said that Emmy was already at the fair with a friend. I walked to the fair with Kenzo, holding the boomerang covered in a small fabric. As soon as we walked in, my eyes started to search for her, and in the distance, I saw her dragging along a little girl like her. Kenzo was distracted talking with a girl to our right, so I just stood there, looking at Emmerson run to me, happy to see me.

She stood in front of me with the girl. This must be the friend Kenzo told me about. I looked at the girl and raised an eyebrow. Emmerson immediately knew what I was thinking.

"She's my best friend, Amelia," Emmerson said. She was happy. Emmy finally found a friend. I was glad she wouldn't feel alone anymore. Maybe giving her some space was the best thing to do.

"Is that my gift?" she said, pointing at the bundle under my arm. She was excited. I needed to remember to make her gifts in advance and leave them with Dad, so he could give them to her if I happened to not be around.

I nodded and gave it to her.

She eagerly unwrapped it, and her expression rapidly changed. I could tell that she wasn't expecting something like it at all.

"A boomerang?" she asked me. She looked confused. I thought she liked it but didn't quite get why I was giving something like that to her.

"It will always come back to you." I pointed at my name written on the boomerang, hoping she got the double meaning. By the look on her face, I was sure she fucking didn't.

"Thanks. I love it!" It seemed like she really did. She gave me the most beautiful and sweetest smile, and I couldn't help but smile back like an idiot. This is just what I needed–to see Emmy happy. That alone made my week.

"Emmy!" A guy called her name from not too far away. I looked his way, and my eyes couldn't fucking believe it. That was the same scumbag I heard talking about a younger girl not too long ago. His fucking sister's best friend. *Ooooh, fuck, NO!*

"Emmy, Amelia, I thought you guys were gonna be at the petting zoo," he said, putting his arm over my Emmerson's shoulder and pulling her closer to him. I saw red. I was going to fucking kill this motherfucker. For real!

My hands were forming fists already, and I was contemplating in my mind all the ways I could snap that dickhead's neck like a fucking chicken.

Emmerson noticed I was furious and tried to laugh out loud, maybe to de-escalate the situation, but it sounded super fake. There was no saving this shitbag. Today was his last day.

"We were on our way there when Emmy saw her friend. Look, a boomerang." Emmerson's friend said, completely unaware that her brother was about to die.

"Cool!" he said and took the boomerang from Emmy's hands. Without thinking twice, I took a step forward, getting closer to my target. After I was done with him, not even his mom would recognize him.

"Who's Stoic?" He had the balls to ask. He had no fucking idea what kind of shit he had got himself into. Nobody that knew me would have ever tried in their right mind to touch my Emmerson. This bastard was new here. I'd make sure to rip his balls off, so he wouldn't forget my name ever again.

"Me," I said with my deep voice, anger coming out of every pore and eyes fixed on the turd I was about to step on. If Emmerson thought I was bad before, she hadn't seen anything yet.

As soon as he looked up at me, he flinched like the fucking bitch he was. My hands were still forming fists as I stepped closer, determined to end his life. Fuck it! I was going to finish him, even if it got me in trouble. This was going to be worth it. This I was going to enjoy.

Emmerson pushed his arm off her and stepped between him and me. She put her small hand on my abdomen and said, "Stop. Don't do it. They are my only friends, please!"

I remembered seeing her so happy, playing with her friend. Fuck, she was so innocent. This was not Emmerson's fault nor her friend's. Fuck! I wanted her to be happy. I didn't want to be the reason her friend left her. I'd deal with this motherfucker as soon as she was not looking. There was no way I was leaving Emmy alone with this pervert. I was going to beat the literal crap out of him, rip his dick off, and make him eat it.

Emmerson stood there, nervously looking into my eyes, pleading not to ruin this for her.

I took a deep breath and tried to control my darkest urges to kill him then and there. I stretched my arm over Emmerson and harshly grabbed the boomerang from his hands. I gave it back to Emmerson and said, looking at that mofo's eyes, "It's for you and you only." I then leaned down and kissed the top of her head, still looking at him. If he hadn't gotten it before, he'd better do it fast. Emmerson was mine.

Emmy walked to her friend and locked arms with her again. "Let's go! To the petting zoo!" She was faking it. I knew she was nervous.

They took a few steps, and that cocksucker started following them. Before he could put his arm around Emmy, I grabbed his arm and squeezed it tightly in my hand. I was holding myself back, not wanting Emmerson to see me break his bones right in front of her.

"Don't touch her," I said. It was more like a murderous promise than an order. There was nothing I wanted more in that instant than to painfully and slowly break every bone in his body.

He tried to shake his arm off, but I just held it tighter. If he made the wrong move, he'd be dead meat.

"Stoic! Let him go this instant!" She was talking to me as if she were talking to a fucking dog. Maybe that was what I was, her dog. I knew I should control this. I should be the better person. She was looking up to me. She still had hope that I wouldn't lose it and start raining rapid punches onto his stupid face.

I looked from him to Emmy and said, "He touches you one more time, and I will fucking break his arm." I was not fucking joking. I said that to her, but the message was for him. One more time, and I wouldn't fucking care anymore if

Emmerson saw his bones popping out of his arm.

With that, I dropped his arm. I was going to follow them for the rest of the evening. I was not letting Emmy out of my sight. He tried anything, and he would lose his dick on the spot.

"Hey, what the fuck is wrong with you?" Ah, nah! He fucking didn't. He fucking dared, the piece of shit.

I raised an eyebrow, and I couldn't control the humorless smile on my face. He was done. I got closer, and this time I was not holding the fuck back. There was nothing Emmerson could do to help his ass.

"Who the fuck do you think you are, huh? Acting like Emmerson is yours or something. You creep!" Creep? Me? If loving Emmerson with all my heart made me a creep, then so be it. And I was not acting like it; she was promised to me.

I nodded, "Yes, Emmerson is mine, and I fucking hate it when a piece of shit like you touches her."

Before he could open his disgusting mouth once again, I shut him up for good. I landed one solid punch right on his mouth and knocked the hell out of him.

His body dropped out cold on the ground, unconscious, with his mouth bloody, broken teeth, and his jaw completely busted. I thought of getting on him and making his face look like ground beef, but there was no use. He wasn't awake for me to enjoy his screams.

Emmerson gave one look at her friend and then at me. She was furious. Fuck it! I didn't want to see her around this cunt ever again.

"Fuck you, Stoic! You ruin everything! I hate your ass!" she screamed at me. She started to kick my legs, throwing a tantrum, but it did nothing to me. That just got her angrier.

I said nothing. I took the boomerang, grabbed Emmy by her hips, threw her over my shoulders, and walked away.

"Let me go, you huge asshole!" She could kick and scream all she wanted. I was taking her home. On the outside, I was calm like nothing had happened, but inside I was furious, wanting to destroy that guy. Give him a one-way ticket to see Hel.

Kenzo pulled my arm, trying to stop me, but I just kept walking. Not even Odin himself would dare to get in my way now.

"What the fuck, Stoic? What happened?" Kenzo was looking back at the cunt lying on the floor and the people gathering around him.

"Mother fucker had a death wish."

"Fuck, Stoic, I understand, but you can't keep doing this. We talked about it, dude." Kenzo started walking beside us. I knew we did. Dad and Andreas talked to me about how I shouldn't be so jealous all the time. This was not jealousy. I knew I was supposed to control my anger and think before acting, but not this. This was an exception. I should have fucking done more damage.

"Had to." I just kept walking.

"You're gonna get in trouble for this, man!" Kenzo was nervous. I didn't give a fuck. I should have fucking destroyed him. The kid got off easy.

"Don't give a fuck." I didn't fucking care about anything but Emmerson's safety.

"I hate you! I hate you, I hate you, I hate you." Emmy was crying. I didn't feel bad as this was for her own good. I'd rather have her lose a friend than get molested.

She kept kicking and hitting my back with her fists. I didn't stop. She bit me on the back, and I didn't think twice before spanking her butt hard. "Stop that, Emmerson!" She stopped kicking and hitting, but she kept crying.

Soon we were at her house, and I took her to her room. I dropped her on her bed and pointed at the floor. "Stay!" I meant it. I was not joking around. She decided to try her luck and stood up, full of pride, intending to walk out of her bedroom. *Fuck, no!*

I pulled her up by the armpits and sat her on the bed again. "Stay, Emmerson, or you'll regret it." I was angry, but I would never hurt her. Not her.

She stayed, and I left, closing the door behind me. Kenzo walked toward me, his face full of worry. "Dude, you fucked up. He is still unconscious. What the fuck, Stoic? Why the fuck did you do that? You have to stop it with your jealousy, man."

"It was not that. That motherfucker was touching her," I said, pointing at the door. I hated to even think about it.

"Yes! That's what friends do, you moron." He didn't get it.

"No, he was actually trying to touch her, as in touching her body. Fuck, Kenzo, I should have killed that motherfucker."

"What? What the fuck, Stoic? Where the fuck did you get that from?" He was too busy looking at the girls to notice him and his friends talking the other day.

I got closer to Kenzo and said in a low voice, "I heard him the other day bragging to his friends about touching his sister's best friend, making it look like hugs, and calling her fucking ignorant. Fuck, Kenzo, you were there."

"Who? The new guys at the main road? Was that him? Fuck, Stoic, let's go kill that motherfucker right now." Kenzo was as furious as I was.

Before we could make a move, Andreas walked into the house. "What the fuck have you done now?" He was fuming. "Fuck damn it, Stoic! You fucked up that boy really bad. What the fuck is wrong with you? You can't fucking keep doing this! Where is Emmerson? Leave this house right NOW!" Kenzo stepped in front of me. Andreas was about to grab me by the neck.

"No, Dad, listen. It's not what it looks like." He stood his ground, and I stepped beside him. I was not hiding behind my friend, and I wouldn't apologize for defending Emmerson.

"Nah, it's exactly what it looks like. It's always the same old shit with him." He pointed at me and shook his head. "Get the fuck out!"

"No, Dad. That motherfucker was molesting Emmerson. We heard him brag about it, but we didn't know back then who he was talking about. We swear."

"What?" Andreas was trying to comprehend what Kenzo just said.

"A few days ago, we heard him say he touched his sister's best friend by pretending to be giving her hugs and calling her ignorant. Today we saw him and he happens to be Emmerson's best friend's brother. I fucking let him off easy," I said to him.

Andreas's eyebrows frowned. "Are you two sure of this?" His eyes went from mine to Kenzo's and back to mine again.

We nodded our heads. "I tried to hold myself back for Emmy. I wanted to break every bone of his, but I fucking didn't. I should have fucking done it." I was beyond pissed.

Andreas was furious. He walked in a circle and pulled his beard. He was thinking. "Don't tell Imany and Ida. We will deal with this motherfucker in our own way."

"Won't Emmy need to know?" Kenzo asked.

"No, we're going to keep an eye on him. As soon as we get him alone, we'll make sure to make it clear to him that if he tries to touch her one more time, he won't be this lucky. We're going to keep him in check. We need to tell Ethan, too. I don't want her anywhere near him by herself." That was smart. Imany wouldn't suspect Ethan, and he could keep an eye on her for us. If Kenzo did it, she would know we were up to something.

I nodded my head.

"Let's make sure–" Kenzo started but got interrupted. My mom, Imany, and Dad walked into the house.

"What the fuck have you done?" My father was furious. I looked at Andreas, and he shook his head no. I shouldn't tell Dad in front of Mom or Imany.

"He had it coming." It was all I said.

Hell broke loose, and everyone started to scream at me and argue at the same time. My mom was hitting me hard on the shoulder, and Imany was about to get a broom and beat down my ass too. My dad looked ashamed of me. If I had to, I would do it again a hundred times over.

From across the room, Andreas gave me an approving nod and walked out.

I'd let them believe whatever they wanted for now.

We'd hunt down that fucker later.

TWENTY-ONE

STOIC

Stoic 15

Emmerson 10

I was grounded.

My mom grounded me right on the spot, and all was decided between her, Imany, and Dad before I could talk to him. By the time I told Dad, it was too late. I had to go with it. Imany made an apology dinner for his family. Dad made me give them two free metalwork jobs as compensation, and Mom helped that scumbag with the medical stuff.

If we were to tell Mom and Imany, I was sure they would have beaten down his ass too. I understood why Andreas didn't want us to say anything to them. Just like me, he wanted Emmy to be happy and not have to worry about anything but playing and having fun, even if that meant creating a safety bubble around her. Dealing with this kind of shit was our job.

When things calmed down, Kenzo and I followed Landon from the shadows without him noticing. When we saw him take a turn into a small alley all by himself, we cornered him like a rat. As soon as I grabbed him by the neck and lifted him up with one hand, he got so scared he peed his pants and begged for mercy. I waited until his face got purple before I dropped him in a puddle of his own piss, and Kenzo knocked the air out of his lungs with one hard kick as soon as he hit the ground.

Kenzo took out a knife and pressed it against his dick. "Touch Emmerson again, and we'll make you choke on your own dick. Is that clear?"

He nodded and cried, snot running down his hideous face. Kenzo pushed him hard, and his head bounced against the pavement.

Kenzo stood up. "We're watching you. Always." Kenzo said, and I gave him a dead stare. With my jaw clenched and my hands formed into tight fists, I held myself back from killing this motherfucker.

Kenzo gave me a pat on my abs as if to say, "let's go," before he turned. His shoulder hit mine as he started to walk away. I stared down at Landon for a few more seconds before I turned and followed Kenzo.

This wasn't just about Emmy anymore. We needed to make sure that animal stayed away from all little girls. We gave him the scare of his life, but we were not joking around. If we caught him touching Emmerson again, he was as good as dead meat. If we heard of or even suspected he was molesting other girls as well, he was dead, too.

We told him we had eyes on him, and we did. Ethan was to always be around Emmy and keep an eye on her when she was near him. All of our friends were on our side as well. Many guys in the neighborhood knew about it and would tell us immediately if they saw him try anything.

After being grounded, I picked up a new hobby that soon became a part-time job for me. I started to learn woodworking with an experienced carpenter and worked for him during the weekends. It turned out I was good at it. I always did it to build or make things for Emmy, but now I was doing more complex things like cribs, cabinets, beds, table sets, etc. I had to say that these skills would come in handy when building the house and furnishing it.

For the last two weeks, I had been working on a new bed for Emmerson. It would be her fall gift. She was growing so fast. Emmy didn't know it, but she was getting more beautiful each passing day. Her hair was getting longer, and her face was changing. She was looking less like a tiny silly kiddo and more like a "girl." A really cute one. It seemed like it was just yesterday when I held her in my arms for the first time.

It was Amelia's birthday today. Emmerson was able to keep her friend, and she was super happy about it. Andreas and I always sent Ethan with them to keep an eye on the fucktard. He didn't like it, but he knew how important it was. He must be used to it by now. Ethan could use the time they spent playing in the forest to read near them, as he liked to do. He was actually a very smart guy. He would go places.

Amelia's moms invited the whole Silva family, but Andreas and Kenzo stayed with Dad and me today, working on preparing the foundation for the house. I was glad to have my family with me, making my dreams come true.

After a hard day of work, we all went back for dinner together. After dinner was over and Emmerson had showered, I went to comb Emmerson's hair like I always did.

While combing her hair, my mind wandered back to our house. The plans were mostly done. We just needed some final details. I wanted her to have either a big window or a sliding door in our bedroom that had a view of the river and hills.

"Emmy, a big window or sliding doors?" She turned her head toward me and gave me that look again.

"A glass wall! A big one," she said, spreading her arms wide.

I nodded, and when she turned around, I smiled. That would look beautiful. Why didn't I think about that before? I would wake up every morning for the rest of my life with Emmerson in my arms and the perfect view of the sun rising over the hills and river. Every season would be equally beautiful. Eight more years. I just needed to work hard and wait eight more years.

I couldn't help but think that soon Emmerson would be by herself for most of the time, and I'd be miles away, not even knowing how she was doing. I knew Andreas wanted her to remain oblivious because she was still too young, but I wanted to have this conversation with her. There might be many "Landons" in this world, and she would have to learn to protect herself.

"Emmy, are you OK?" *How could I start that conversation with her?*

"Yep, why?" She sounded disinterested.

"Emmy, there's something I want to talk with you about." I was beating around the bush. I was actually nervous about it.

"Yeah?" Now she sounded impatient.

"It's about... It's something important." I tried to talk while I kept combing her hair.

"Yeah..." she said, extending the 'a' sound. She must have been thinking I was stupid.

I cleared my throat, "I... well... you see. Guys, I mean boys, and girls have some differences."

"Yes..." This time she extended the 's.' Oh fuck, she thought I was stupid.

"And, sometimes, when a boy and a girl get older, they–"

I was about to say that they get interested in one another, like in a relationship kind of way, but before I could finish my thought, she jumped in and said, "Have sex?"

Oh snaps, no. That was not what I wanted to talk about. Backpedal, backpedal fast.

"No! I mean, yeah, but... um...." Nothing was coming out. Fuck, think about something else to say, anything. Damn, there was nothing.

"But what, Stoic?" She turned around to look at me. She knew me–she knew I just dug myself a hole and jumped in it. I could see her wheels turning. I was screwed.

Before she got any more ideas, I said, "Yes, people get interested in sex as they get older. But not everyone is thinking about it the same way." *There, back on track.*

"Are you thinking about it?" *Oh, fuck me sideways! How the fuck did she come up with that?*

"That's... that's not the point I'm trying to make, Emmy." Please drop it. It was a difficult thing already, so don't freaking make it worse.

"So, you're not?" Why was she insisting? Why did she want to know?

"Emmy, I... I'm not talking about me. I'm talking in general." Come on Emm, move on.

"Do you or do you not think about sex? It's a simple question, Stoic." Ah, fuck! She must have known I was getting embarrassed. She could smell that I was nervous. I had to make her think I was not. Give her a mature answer. I was the older one, right?

"Well, sometimes ... Emm, the point is that some guys don't have good intentions, so you need to be careful." *Let's wrap this up.*

"What do you mean?" She looked at me with that cute, childish face of hers. Ah! This clueless little girl will be the end of me.

How could I put this in simple words? "Well, sometimes girls want friendships, but guys are looking for something more..." Her eyes narrowed. She was not going to let me off the hook so easily. What had I gotten myself into?

"What if the girl wants the same thing the boy wants, though?" She said, narrowing her eyes more. What the hell? My thoughts went from zero to a thousand in a matter of seconds. What the fuck was she thinking about?

"Emmy, you are too young!" She better not even think about sex until our wedding.

"Who said we were talking about me? We were talking in general, right?" She got me.

I needed to fix it. "We are not... Well, in part, we are... That's ..." I facepalmed myself and harshly stroked my eyebrows. I was in her small claws now.

"Girls like sex, too, you know..." she muttered and turned around. I really didn't wanna fucking talk about this.

"I know, but that's for older girls only, OK?" She better not be thinking about it. Holy fuck. Was she thinking about it?

"Yeah, I know. I'm so young. There's still so much I don't know ..." She turned to face me again. Her angelic face with those big sparkling browns and greens looking at me. She was so innocent. She was so beautiful. "But it's good I have you to answer any questions for me, right?" Well ... yeah. I guessed. I'd rather have her coming to me than any other guy, Kenzo included. He would give her the worst advice.

"Yeah," I said and kept combing her hair. I was glad she trusted me. She gave her back to me again.

"Great!" she said, a bit too cheerfully. "Now that we're talking about this, and I only ask because I don't know," she paused. *Oh, no! What was she up to?*

"How... big... is... a penis?" She screamed the word penis. *Oh no!* I stopped combing her hair, and I felt like my face was about to fall off. Oh, this was no good! What if she went to Andreas and told him I was talking about penises with her? Oh, this could go super wrong. How the fuck did I get myself into this mess?

"Um ... Emm, I don't think that's...." I paused, coughing, "why...." What the hell. I didn't like that she was thinking that way.

"Because I don't know...." Fuck, she was making that innocent expression again. By now, I didn't know if she was being honest or if she was fucking with me.

I would give her a simple, generic answer, hoping she would buy it. "Everyone is different, Emm," I said, scratching my neck. Please stop already. She was missing the whole point.

She nodded her head. I let out a deep breath. Uff, she took it.

"I see. There's no way you would know. OK then, how big are you? You must know, right? I mean, it's attached to you." She pointed her fingers at my pants. The innocent face was gone. *Emmerson fucking Silva!*

"None of your fucking business!" I said and covered myself with both hands after leaving the comb hanging in her hair. I mean, it was not like she could see it, but she would for sure notice if I started to get hard. Oh fuck. I could get hard.

No, this was not good.

Emmerson was not thinking about penises in general; she was asking about mine. Why? I felt my face get super hot with embarrassment.

"Is it that small that you got so embarrassed?" Wait, what? Small? Me? Fuck, Emm, why would you think a guy like me would be small?

"Emmerson, I'm anything but small." I was still embarrassed but couldn't let her believe I had a small dick. If she was going to talk about it, at least that detail should be clarified.

"But how can you tell? It's not like you know how big everyone else is," she said with an innocent face. She was fucking messing with me!

"Trust me, Emmy. I'm big." And one day, you'd do more than just look at it. Ah, fuck. Nah! Oh no! It's happening. Think about something else, think about something else fast. Ah ... Fuck this. Abort the mission.

"Look, Emmerson, what's important is that you learn to recognize guys that present themselves as friends but instead have bad intentions. You need to be careful, Emmy. Do not let anyone touch you inappropriately, okay? OK!" I stood up fast and ran before she could open that bratty mouth of hers and say another word.

"Go to sleep!" I said from the door before closing it.

I walked fast past everyone without saying anything and went straight back home. I went into my room and closed the door.

I fucking hated this. I hated this so much, but I guess it would be me, my hand, and an older version of Emmy again tonight. I got the tissues ready and laid on my bed.

She really gave me a hard time, and by hard, I mean rock solid.

I'd make sure to make her pay for all of it later. I put my hand around myself and started stroking.

You have no idea what you are doing to me, Emmerson.

TWENTY-TWO

STOIC

Stoic 18

Emmerson 12

Kenzo and I completed the regular training in our village and were sent to a different place where they trained the best candidates. They told us it would be more challenging, but they didn't give us more information on why. We only knew we were the best, and that was why we were chosen.

We took the train and traveled about one hundred and fifty miles west to this new training camp. Everything was different there. As soon as we arrived, we were yelled at and treated like shit. I knew the goal was to make us stronger, but I fucking hated it.

The training was excruciatingly painful, and we were exposed to all kinds of weather and fighting simulations. It turned out that the first two months there were just to test us. Out of the nearly three hundred kids from all nearby villages, only thirty were selected. Kenzo and I included.

Officials held a meeting and then explained their real motives. The northerners were planning on expanding south. They told us about all the barbarities they were doing to their citizens and about all the suffering. They said that we had an opportunity to stop that from happening, to take the fight to them, and to eliminate them. If they succeeded in expanding to the south, our way of life could be in great danger.

They gave us a choice. We could stay and train to be at the front of the battle where we would risk losing our lives but have a chance to defeat our enemies. Or we could go back and serve a regular term moving boxes like every other guy.

I immediately thought about Emmerson. Her big smile as she ran through the woods. Her happiness. The way she loved to swim in the river. Our peace.

Some guys stood up and left. I couldn't. If what they said was true, then I would do anything in my power to stop all of that from getting even close to her. I agreed. It needed to be stopped before it grew.

I looked to my left and found Kenzo's worried face.

"Go back home. I'm staying," I told him, taking a big breath. He stayed quiet for a moment.

"Why the fuck do you think I will let you go alone?" Kenzo's face changed. He was angry.

"One of us has to stay behind to make sure Emmy will be fine." The one who went to the north might not come back. It was better if at least one of us stayed. I wouldn't forgive myself if Kenzo got hurt.

Kenzo shook his head. "Fuck, Stoic! We either stay here together, or we fucking go together." He was not willing to negotiate this, but I had to try.

"Look, Kenzo, this is not a joke. We might not come back, dude. You have to stay."

"That's exactly why we need to stay together. We complement each other, so we hold a better chance if we have each other's back."

"But... Emmerson," I started saying, but Kenzo cut me off.

"Why don't you stay then? Huh? I'll go. Just like you want. One of us stays behind."

"Fuck, Kenzo. You know I won't let you."

"Why not? Our parents have three kids, but yours only have you. As you said, Emmerson will need you. If someone has to stay, it should be you. Fuck, Stoic! You already have a beautiful life planned for my sister, and I can't risk that. All I do is fuck around. Between you and me, the choice is clear. If one of us needs to be at risk, it's me."

"No... No, I won't let you...." I shook my head and fixed my eyes on the floor, entangling my fingers.

"And I won't let you either." He threw an arm around me. I knew he was looking at me, but I avoided his eyes. "We'll do this together! We stay together, we fight together, we keep each other's asses safe, and we return home together."

I didn't like it. I didn't want Kenzo to be in danger.

We stayed in silence for a long while. Even if I hated to admit it, he was right. He and I were amongst the best cadets and fighters, and if they were going to bring the fight to them, they would need us. It was the only way to keep our family safe. To keep Emmerson safe. Fuckdamnit!

That day we agreed not to tell our families until we were closer to our departure date. After that, we kept traveling back and forth from training camp to our village every time we could, which was every other week.

We knew this could be our last years and the last few times we spent at home with our families, so we took the time to do what we wanted the most.

Kenzo just fucked around as much as he could. He must have slept with about thirty-something different girls. He was a manwhore. He spent one day at home with his family and two others fucking. Not me. I always took one day to work, preparing the land for our home, and the other two following Emmerson around.

I wanted to spend as much time as I possibly could with her. I knew she was sometimes annoyed, but I had to. I might not come back, and all I wanted was to be near her. Even if it was just looking at her, listening to her voice, or watching her play with her friend.

I took some of that time to write things down and make estimates. I'd bring my notebook with me and write down every detail I could think of. Sometimes I drew Emmerson. I drew like shit, so I'd never show this to anybody, but I did enjoy it. I got to memorize every detail of her beautiful face, every single one of her curls.

Emmerson's body was changing fast. She was taller and grew small bumps on her chest. I tried hard not to think about it, but it was tough. My mind was constantly in the gutter. More than three years had passed since Emmerson had given me my first kiss, and I could still feel her lips on mine. I thought being far away from her would help, but no, I was doomed.

At the end of each day, I would have dinner with the Silvas, wait for her to shower, comb her hair, tell her stories, and put her to bed. I knew she didn't fucking need me to, but I was holding onto every second I could spend with her.

I was missing a lot of her life. Every time I returned, she was doing or learning something new. Kenzo told me she was dancing and learning another language. Imany told me how well she was sewing, and I moved earth and sky to find her a new sewing machine. It took many nights working outside the camp digging a well for this elderly couple, but I got it. The woman was a tailor, and she was about to retire. Her village had given her that new machine a few months before, but she had barely used it.

I loved the smile on Emmerson's face the day I came back with that sewing machine. It was priceless. She was beyond happy.

At the camp, Kenzo and I started training with weapons. We had already learned how to put together and take apart rifles and all kinds of guns. We had tons of drills and tactics training. We were learning how to work as part of a team and to survive independently, too. They were very hard on us. They expected nothing but the best from us, and we understood why. We woke up at four every morning and ran three miles before we started doing exercises every fucking day.

Kenzo and I got taller, stronger, and faster. I knew we looked intimidating. People stared at us when we walked around town. As we walked, guys moved aside to make way for us, girls looked at us as if they wanted to eat us alive, and children ran. We went for drinks on some weekends and almost every time we headed back home, right before we took the train. We would sleep it off on the way.

I had seen many little shits lingering around Emmy. I still got a bit jealous. I always told Emmy she needed to stay away from boys and take care of her body. I lectured her on how she needed to start thinking about her future husband and that he wouldn't like it if she started hanging around guys. It was stupid to talk about myself in the third person, but I did what I had to. She always looked at me as if I were full of shit. Maybe I was. Nah, she was right. I knew I was. I should just leave her alone.

Winters had been extremely cold. Finally, the weather got so bad that the trains couldn't run, and training was canceled, so Kenzo and I stayed at home for about three weeks. That was the longest we had stayed at home in the last two and a half years.

There was a massive storm two weeks ago with strong winds, snow, and freezing temperatures. A big tree fell over our house and broke part of the roof. Dad was beyond furious since they had just repaired the roof before the winter season.

Andreas invited us to stay in his house until the weather warmed enough for them to make the repairs to the house, and my family accepted. I was beyond happy. Maybe that tree falling was the best thing that could have happened to me. I spent so much time right next to Emmy. Imany gave my parents Emmerson's room, and she stayed with Kenzo, Ethan, and me.

In Kenzo and Ethan's room, there were only two beds. Being the sneaky fast thinker that he was, Kenzo quickly made an excuse and said he should sleep with Ethan, leaving Emmerson with me.

I couldn't hide the smile that spread across my face, and he threw me a wink and mouthed, "You're welcome," without Ethan and Emmy noticing. He narrowed his eyes and pointed at my dick as if to say, "control yourself," but he knew better than anyone that I would never do anything I shouldn't.

For two weeks, I shared a bed with Emmerson. It was the best two weeks of my life. I didn't really sleep much because my mind ran with many thoughts it shouldn't have, but I did my best to push them away. I would never act on those thoughts. I loved every second of it. I placed the thickest pillow I could find between us so she wouldn't feel my boner if I happened to get one while sleeping. I told her that the pillow was for personal space. She thought I was crazy.

I just hugged Emmerson tightly in my arms every night we spent together. She would place her head on my arm, and I would throw my other arm over her

Sometimes she would face me, and sometimes I would spoon her. No matter what, I was always facing her. I could tell she was comfortable in my arms where she belonged–just like the day I met her.

One day, Emmerson woke up early in the morning. Since I didn't really sleep well next to her, I could immediately tell she was awake by how her breathing changed. The sun was barely up, and Kenzo and Ethan were still sleeping. She turned around in my arms and stared at my face for the longest time. I had one of my eyes slightly open, but I was pretending to be sleeping too.

I loved the way she looked at me that day. Something had changed because her eyes were different somehow. I wasn't the annoying, ugly thing that bothered her anymore. Her gaze was pensive and soft. I liked that. I felt her take a couple of deep breaths before she raised her hand and caressed my face.

Her fingers brushed my eyebrows and softly touched my eyelashes. Her eyes ran down to my chest, and I saw them widen. She bit her lip, and I knew she was checking me out. My Emmerson was checking me out. It almost made me laugh.

She moved her hands back to my face and touched my nose, and then slowly ran her small, delicate finger along my jaw. Her browns and greens fixed intensely on me. She bit her lip again, and I couldn't pretend I was sleeping anymore. I took in a deep breath, holding her tighter to my body.

I let out a low grunt and kissed her head. "Sleep, Emmy. It's early," I said with my eyes "closed." She snuggled closer to me and put her head on my chest. She was so close to me that I bet she could hear my heart beating hard.

"Stoic?" she said with an angelic voice.

"Hmm..."

"I'll make you a backpack. Do you want it black or green?" she whispered.

"Surprise me," I whispered back. I put one of her soft curls behind her ear, and she nodded. I'd cherish whatever she made for me with her own hands as my most precious possession.

Soon we'd have to go. I wanted to get everything ready, so when we came back–if we came back–I could start building our home right away. There were very few things I had yet to set.

"Emmy, stone or wood?" I asked, my eyes still closed. It was one of the last things I'd do, but I wanted to have an idea of what kind of countertops I'd need.

"Stones last longer than wood," she whispered her answer, and I nodded, giving her more of the blanket, and kissed her head again.

She closed her eyes and relaxed. I felt her chest breathe softer and softer until she was completely asleep.

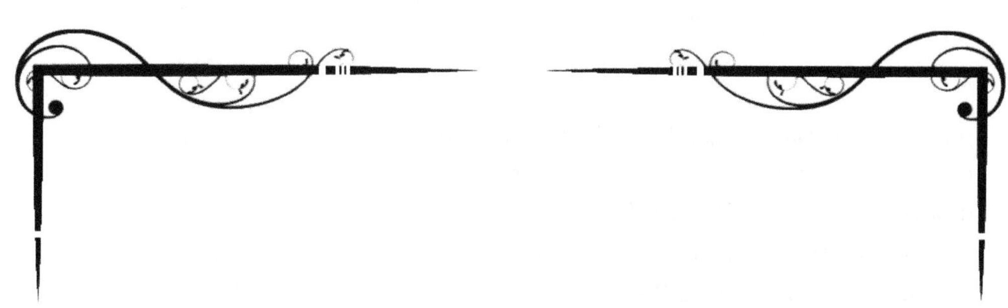

TWENTY-THREE

STOIC

Emmerson 13

Emmerson had her first period.

I didn't really know why, but I was stupidly happy about it. I saw her lying in a corner looking weak, and I got worried about her. At first, I thought she was sick, but she told me what it really was before I carried her and took her to my mom to check on her.

I hugged her for the longest time and told her that it was a special thing, and we should be happy about it. I told her that one day, she'd be able to create a life. I wanted us to have a big family with many little Emmerson's running wild in the woods.

I sat her on my lap, held her tightly in my arms, and hugged her for a long time. I rubbed her aching belly with my hands and watched her relax in my embrace.

More than ever, I felt motivated to work on our home. Thinking that one day my child would be growing in this belly filled me with excitement.

"East or north?" I asked, and she took her time to answer. I wanted to know in what direction the front of the house should face. North was the driveway, and east was the river.

"Northeast," she said while resting her head on my chest. I rubbed her belly until she fell asleep. Then I took her to her room and left her there to rest. Before leaving her room, I stood by her door and looked at her sleeping for a short moment. She was so beautiful.

I closed her door and headed back home. I was in so much trouble. It was getting more and more difficult not to think about her sexually. Like my father said, as long as it always stayed in my head and never, ever came out, it should be fine. I couldn't be too hard on myself, or I'd snap, as Kenzo said.

Her breasts were getting bigger, and she had started to use a bra. Once again, I couldn't keep my mind or my eyes away from them.

What was wrong with me?

Although it was not only her breasts, she had started to get curves too. She looked hella cute. Only Kenzo knew about my struggle. He thought I was stupidly desperate, and I thought he was right. He knew I would never act on it. She was nothing but a little girl. I had many years of waiting ahead of me.

She knew how to get rid of me. Whenever she started to say "my vagina" out loud, my face would get red, and I would disappear. I knew she was not gonna say anything else, but I didn't want to get trapped like the last time. Never again. Learned my lesson.

As the time of our departure neared, Kenzo and I did as we promised. Both of us told our parents we needed to talk with them. We decided to do it together. We told them that there was something important that we needed them to know and that it was important to me that Emmerson didn't learn about it.

They all waited until Emmy went out to play with Amelia, and Ethan followed her as always. We took them to my family's house and sat them in the living room. Kenzo did most of the talking. I just sat quietly and saw how their faces slowly contorted into fear as they eventually understood what Kenzo was saying. I saw all their eyes water and tears start to fall before Kenzo could finish talking.

"I don't get it. Why the fuck do YOU have to go? What the fuck is this, Stoic?" my father screamed. He was furious.

Anger was his first reaction, but Andreas held him back. "Wait, let them finish."

I heard a loud gasp, and my mom held her chest and cried out loud. Fear was hers.

"Why?" Imany cried out. She was trembling.

"We are getting the best training, and we have the best intel. We have the best possible equipment, so we are ready for this. Our team is very professional.

Yes, it's risky, but we got this. We'll stay together. We'll be safe. All we are asking is for you to trust us." Kenzo tried to calm them down.

"Say you won't go. Tell them, call them now!" Imany said while Andreas threw his arms around her.

"This was our choice. There's no backing out. We are in this. We'll go regardless. We just wanted you guys to know. You all deserve to know," Kenzo said.

"But not Emmerson. I don't want Emmerson to be worried. I want her to be happy. Always." I spoke for the first time.

There was an exchange of looks in the room, and Andreas nodded. "We won't tell her."

It took around two hours before they calmed down and stopped crying. After that, we all tried to pretend everything was fine for a couple of weeks.

I talked to my dad and Andreas privately. I asked them to build the house for Emmy if I didn't make it back. I left them all the information in one place where they would easily find it. Both of them promised to do it, and I felt some relief about it. I also left all of Emmerson's gifts with them. Dad had the hoops, Mom had the wooden ones, and I left Imany with some beautiful fabrics, so she could make Emmerson dresses as she grew older.

The day before we had to go, we all had dinner together. It would be three years until I would see those beautiful eyes again–if I returned at all. Everyone's mood was down. We were all sad. Emmerson kept looking at everyone's faces, not understanding why. In the middle of dinner, Emmerson surprised us with gifts. She had made us backpacks as she told me she would. Mine was black, and Kenzo's was green. They were really unique. My heart was filled with happiness and sadness at the same time. It was the first thing she had made for me, but it could also be the last.

We opened the backpacks, and I tried hard not to cry when I saw she put many tags with her name inside. There was a knot in my throat, and tears threatened to fall. On the side of the backpack, we each found a knife. Dad and Andreas had helped her make knives for us. She told us she had designed them herself. I held it in my hands and noticed what the handle said. She had asked them to carve our initials "S&E" on one side, and Dad put "Góðr," her name, on the other. That did it. I lost it. I grabbed everything and rushed out of the house, and then I ran.

I ran fast. My vision blurred, and I didn't know where I was heading, but I ran. I heard the door open again behind me, but I didn't look back. My dad screamed my name, but I didn't stop. I didn't want any of them to see me cry, to think I was weak. I tried to keep running, but my lungs failed me. I doubled over, coughing and crying out loud. My dad reached me, straightened me up, and hugged me tightly. Before I could react, Andreas's arms were around me to my right while Kenzo's were on my left.

They didn't say anything. They just hugged me. There was no judging. They all knew exactly how I felt. They hugged me until I had calmed down and had stopped crying. I knew I had made them cry, too. There were thousands of unspoken words between the four of us. None of us dared to say it out loud, but we were all scared.

We hugged for about half an hour before drying our tears and going back to finish our dinner. I had talked to Andreas previously, and he allowed me to stay with her for one last night. I told Emmy I wanted to leave with Kenzo in the morning as an excuse. Since her bed was bigger, I said I should stay with her, and she bought it. I was glad she didn't fight me. Kenzo got lost. He left the house. Who knows what he was up to.

That night, I didn't sleep at all. I held Emmerson in my arms, thinking it could be the last time I saw her. I should be more positive, but now that I was so close to leaving, I just couldn't. As soon as she fell asleep, I silently cried. I cried most of the night. I caressed her hair, trying to memorize the way it felt in my fingers. I tried to commit to memory the softness of her skin and her sweet smell. With every passing minute, my heart tightened, and it became more and more difficult to breathe.

When Emmerson woke up in the morning, I could see that she was worried about me. I hadn't slept at all. I cried the whole time, and I felt physically sick. I must have looked like crap.

They all walked us to the train station to say their goodbyes. There were many other people around, but all I could focus on was Emmy. Our parents couldn't pretend anymore. They were super sad. I saw Imany and Andreas cry as they hugged Kenzo. My parents were crying as well as they hugged me. My mom begged me to stay safe and to come back. No matter what I did, I needed to come back. Emmerson just stood in a corner, looking confused and watching us cry. Ethan knew as he figured it all out before Kenzo could tell him.

My parents let me go, and Andreas and Imany hugged me next. "Stay safe, son," Andreas told me. I'd miss them all so much. I saw Kenzo hug Ethan and Emmerson and say something to them.

Andreas and Imany let me go, and I pulled Ethan into a hug. "Keep her safe and always care for her. I'm counting on you," I told him, and he nodded. "Thank you!" I said before letting him go.

Ethan stepped away, and I saw everyone else step aside too. I got down on one knee and hugged Emmerson tight. I tried to keep it in, but tears escaped my eyes and rolled down the side of her face.

"There, there. It's going to be okay. Time goes fast, you'll see." She patted my back, trying to console me, and hugged me back. I was so scared of not seeing her again. I was going to miss her so fucking much. I had to be stronger and give myself hope.

"Emmy, do you remember your boomerang?" I took a deep breath and held her small face in my hands, looking straight into her eyes.

"Yeah, why?" she said shyly.

"I'm like that boomerang, Emmy. I'll always come back to you, OK." I made a promise, and I'd do anything to keep it. Her face lit up when she realized the meaning of my gift. She gave me a small smile.

I kissed her hard on her head, stood up, grabbed my backpack with one hand, and walked away. I turned my back to her, not wanting for her to see me lose it, and got on the train without looking back, not even once.

Once inside, I took my seat, covered myself with my jacket, and sobbed as I hugged my backpack.

Kenzo sat next to me, threw his arm around me, and pulled me to him. "We'll be back before you know it," he said, trying to cheer me up.

The train doors closed, and it started moving. My heart sank, and I cried harder.

I had to make it back. We had to make it back.

TWENTY FOUR

STOIC

Stoic 21

Emmerson 16

Hell.

If there was such a thing in this world, I fucking lived in it.

It was the middle of the night, and we had a mission–infiltrate the residence of an enemy general and eliminate the target. We were all dressed in black, fully geared with black balaclavas, a tactical vest, an M4 carbine tricked out with an ACOG and suppressor, and an M17 handgun. Kenzo and I also had Emmerson's knives. I didn't go anywhere without Emmerson's knife.

We jumped the concrete wall surrounding the building. Fifteen of us quietly crossed the front lawn towards the residence's south entrance. There were twelve of us that would enter the main building.

There were about thirty more soldiers spread around the perimeter and ten more blocking all possible exits. We had trapped them like the rats they were.

We used a Halligan bar to break open the door. I entered the room with Kenzo covering my six. We quickly scanned the room. It was empty. I took a right, and Kenzo went left. We checked the room. No curtains, no closets, and only two hallways that led to the west and east.

"Clear." I heard Kenzo say in a very low voice before he signed for the others to proceed.

We divided up. A team of six would go west while Kenzo, four more comrades, and I would take the right. There were three that would guard that entrance.

We started the marching fire and entered the hallway. There was a man with a gun, and I pulled the trigger. Shot to the chest. One down. I got closer to him and shot him in the head.

Confirmed kill.

We continued marching down the hall. Once we reached the end, I heard Kenzo say on the radio, "Hallway clear."

We stopped at the kitchen's entrance. I signed to Kenzo for him to cover my left. I went in. Two males ... guns ... shoot. I took one down, and Kenzo took the other. I walked closer and shot his head.

Confirmed kill.

Kenzo did the same on the other side. We scanned the kitchen, opened the pantry, and found the back door was sealed. Team members were covering the hallway we entered from.

"Kitchen's clear."

We moved further in. There was a smaller hallway, but it was empty.

I walked in with Kenzo on my six. We reached the end.

"Clear."

There was a service room to our left. I checked the door, but it was locked. I kicked it open. I took the right, with Kenzo directly behind me on my left. Woman and child, unarmed.

"Get down! On the floor!" I said, and they did. I kept pointing my weapon at them.

Kenzo opened the closet and scanned the room. "Clear." Another team member walked in and put plastic zip tie cuffs on the woman and the child. Back to the hallway.

We stood in front of the next room. I gestured to Kenzo to hold. I checked the door. It was unlocked. I signaled to let him know we were going in. I entered the room, and Kenzo covered my back. Three girls screamed, all unarmed.

"Quiet! Hands up, get down on the floor. You, too, on the floor!" They lay face down on the floor.

There were three of them in a room that had two bunk beds, and all the beds had blankets on them.

"Where's the fourth one?" I asked them in a low voice.

One of the girls pointed up. Kenzo checked closets and under the beds.

"Clear."

I kept pointing my gun at them. The girls had bruises and were dirty. Those assholes were fucking abusing them. They were all a little over Emmerson's age. Fuck them, I was gonna kill them all.

The teammates came in to handcuff the girls.

"Move on," Kenzo said.

We went back into the hallway, and I signaled to the team that we were taking the stairs up.

I went first and stopped on the first rest, then I signaled to Kenzo. I was covering his back now. He passed by me and stopped at the last step. He signaled me, and I went up. Two more members followed us, and two others covered the bottom of the stairs.

The hallway looked empty. I gave more signals that Kenzo and I would take the room to the right. The other two would take the room to the left. The last team members at the bottom of the stairs walked up and covered the hallway.

When we approached the room, we could hear a girl cry and slapping sounds. He was there with her. He'd use her as a shield, and if I was not careful, I'd have to kill her too.

I signaled Kenzo to hold. I checked the door, and it was unlocked. I cracked open the door. He was on the girl, riding her from behind and hitting her. I took my handgun, outfitted with a silencer, and aimed.

Confirmed target. I had a shot, and I was gonna take it. I shot him, and he fell backward on the bed. I went in, Kenzo right behind me.

"Get down! On the floor," I said to the girl.

I walked to the man and shot him in the head.

Confirmed kill.

Kenzo checked closets, curtains, and the bathroom. "Clear."

I got the blanket and threw it over her naked body. "Stay down."

I heard gunshots from across the room. Those were not ours. The team came to handcuff the girl.

We moved back into the hallway. The other half of our team was on the other side, which meant the west side of the building was clear too. There was only one hallway left. And by the look of it, they knew we were there.

We moved forward. Marching fire. Once we got close to the hallway entrance, I signaled the other team. Hold.

We could hear the clicking sound of someone handling a gun. The other team signaled to us. They would move in, and we'd cover their six. We checked the hallway with a mirror. It was a long hall that led to an open space with no doors, armed men on the other side. One of the other team members threw in an M11 multi-burst grenade as a distraction, and we waited for the three detonations before we proceeded to move in.

They marched in, and we followed, opening fire. I was right behind the one taking the lead. We saw their men dropping down fast. We were gaining territory when a bullet hit the comrade beside me on the side of his head, turning it toward me. His blood splattered my face, and I saw his body fall in slow motion, his head hitting the floor hard and his lifeless eyes staring at me.

My body jumped, and I screamed at the top of my lungs, "NO!"

I was sleeping.

I sat up and pressed my fists together, my body shaking.

This wasn't a nightmare. It was something much worse, a memory. One of the many that haunted me every fucking night.

"Dude, you okay?" Kenzo asked me from across our shared barracks. I had woken him up.

"Yeah." I laid back down on my bed. Kenzo turned around and fell back asleep. I put my hands under my head and tried to relax. We had seen horrors. Things I didn't even dare to talk about. Things that were more fit for nightmares than real life.

It had been three fucking long years, and we were finally going to have a break.

That horrific memory was from the last general that we had a confirmed location on. They had given us six months' break until intel could localize the rest of the targets. I couldn't wait to go back home.

Life without seeing Emmerson's smile was painful. I missed her so much! I couldn't wait to see her. I missed my parents too.

This fight was getting harder and harder every passing day. Whenever I felt my demons pull me down, I thought of Emmerson, and that took me back. Kenzo said the best distraction was a wet pussy and a nice hard pounding. He was a manwhore, though. Kenzo must have fucked half of the base's females already, plus half of the locals. He was handsome and charismatic but was terrified of commitments. That man would never settle, ever. He was affected, too, but tried hard to hide it with jokes and smiles.

He told me that the day before we left that he went to Ava and had raw sex with her. He said that was the best feeling ever. He usually did use a wrapper, but Ava said she wanted to feel him, so he caved.

I wouldn't fucking know. I was still a virgin. I had never even seen a vagina. All I had was my hand, the pillow I pumped, and a made-up image of an older Emmerson. I wondered how she really looked now. I imagined she was still wearing her boyish baggy clothes with her messy hair. Running in the woods barefoot. That image brought a smile to my face.

I beat my meat often, thinking about her older version, and Kenzo knew it. It was awkward as hell, but he was the only one I could talk to about these things. He told me not to make myself blow too fast and practice my hip movements with a pillow in different positions. Kenzo gave me a lot of advice with details, and I took note.

Everything from how much pressure to put on my fingers when I touched her most delicate parts to how to move them inside her, find her g-spot, and make her squirt. I didn't know how he did it. I didn't think I could advise anyone on how to please my little sister. He knew I loved her more than anything else in

Emmerson was sixteen now, but she was still a child. I knew she was too young for sex, so I'd wait longer. I told Kenzo, but he thought I'd snap and fuck her. He said he would rather have me do it the right way and use protection. Even when Kenzo said sixteen-year-olds smash already, I still thought it was too early. It was better for her if we waited. I didn't mind waiting.

Kenzo and I had changed a lot. We got tattoos, and we grew beards. We had to do a ton of exercises, so we were shredded. I got most of my right arm inked with Nordic tattoos of an ax and Odin with knots. I also had two ravens, one on each side. On my left shoulder, I got the triple horn of Odin, and over my heart, I had Góðr written in bold letters. It translated to brave–just like Emmerson's name. Inside my left arm, I had the literal translation of Emmerson's full name. Brave Woods. I was leaving space to put a tattoo of Emmerson's face somewhere around there too. Kenzo's tattoos were primarily women, guns, and skulls.

On the train on our way back home, Kenzo fell asleep with his head resting on the window's glass. I couldn't relax. I was too excited. I'd finally get to see my baby girl again. I couldn't wait to hug her.

Once we arrived, we saw Imany, Andreas, Mom, and Dad waiting for us at the platform.

Where was Emmerson?

My dad pulled me in for a big hug, and I could see he had watery eyes. He was a tough man and tried not to show it, but I knew he had missed me greatly. Mom too. She cried, studied me, gave me a turn, and asked me if I was okay. It must have been difficult for them not to know if I was safe or not.

"I'm OK, Ma." She hugged me tightly.

She let me go, and Imany and Andreas hugged me next. They were my second set of parents. I saw Dad and Mom hugging Kenzo.

"We've missed you so much!" Imany said with tears in her eyes.

"I've missed you, too, Auntie." They released me, and my eyes immediately started wandering around.

Where was she?

"Where's..."

"Emmerson is with Amelia outside. She'll be here soon," Andreas said and patted my back.

She was still playing with Amelia. I was glad she had a friend and wasn't lonely. My eyes were still searching for her as Kenzo stood next to me.

"Don't be looking for a little girl. I bet she has changed a lot," he said.

"She did. She looks so different now, so pretty," Imany said, emphasizing the "pretty" part, but I didn't pay attention to her.

My eyes were still desperately scanning the crowd when I heard it. "Stoic!" My eyes landed on a young woman. A pretty one. That couldn't be her.

She started running toward me, and my brain finally recognized her.

Fuck me, she was gorgeous.

My mind blocked out anything else that wasn't her. For that moment, the world stopped, and I smiled. I was frozen. She ran toward me, bumping into people along the way. My heart was racing, and Kenzo leaned toward me and said, "Told you! You better wrap it, dude. She's too young to get pregnant." I nodded my head without thinking about what he said or looking at him.

Her hairband got loose and fell. Her waves bounced as she ran, and I swear she was glowing like a goddess. She was getting closer, and I saw what she was wearing. I couldn't have been more fucking wrong. She was sexy as fuck. Her body's curves were to die for.

Holy fuck, I was in trouble.

"Stoic! Stoic!" She kept screaming my name, and my heart was about to stop. She got closer, and I dropped my backpack on the floor and opened my arms. She jumped into my arms, and I caught her. Her arms immediately wrapped around my neck and her legs around my waist. I wrapped my arms around her and hugged her tight.

"You're back!" she said and hugged me tighter.

"I'm back, baby." I was back, and I had my Emmerson in my arms. I couldn't believe it. It felt unreal.

She pulled back a little to look at my eyes and smiled. She still had that cute childlike smile. She'd changed a lot. Her face had changed, but her eyes were as beautiful as I always remembered them to be. She had long hair, earrings, long eyelashes, a cute nose, and thick, soft-looking lips.

Fuuuuck.

"Emmy..." I studied her. She had a hypnotizing pair of tits that were the perfect size. Her tight little white shirt wrapped around them perfectly. Her abdomen was flat, and her waist small. Her hips were curvy, and I could feel the beginning of the curve her round butt made at her lower back with my hands. Her short pants showed off her toned, tanned, creamy legs. Holy fuck! She was beyond beautiful. More than anything I could have imagined.

"Stoic!" She woke me up from my daze and gave me another hug. I buried my face in her neck and took a deep breath, smelling the coconut scent that came from her. She smelled delicious.

"Don't worry about your real brother here. I'm fine, by all means... Just hug Stoic. I'm fine," Kenzo said, but we ignored him. He just picked up my backpack and walked away. He fucking knew there was no way in hell that I'd be letting her go now.

"I missed you so much." I heard my own voice say and squeezed her harder.

"I know you did. There's no other like me in this world." Her voice was so sweet. She had no idea how right she was.

I chuckled, "You're right." There'd never be anyone like her for me.

"I don't want to let you go! I'm gonna hang on to you for the rest of the day," she said. If she only fucking knew! I loved this girl more than anything else in this world. I felt so happy that I laughed. I hadn't been this happy in fucking years.

"I could hang on to you for the rest of the month." For the rest of my life! I was not even kidding. We both laughed like idiots.

Without thinking, I moved my hands from her waist to her thighs to help hold her weight, like I used to do. My hands passed by her ass, and as soon as they touched her warm skin, my dick twitched. She was as surprised as I was, and her eyes traveled to my hands. She got goosebumps. When her eyes landed back on me, I was staring into hers. The things I was so sure of a few minutes ago now I was seriously doubting. Kenzo's words running through my mind.

Holy fuck, I wanted her.

I raised my left eyebrow and smirked. I fucking wanted her, but I saw it in her eyes that she wanted this too.

Should I just give in?

We just stood there, looking into each other's eyes for the longest time.

"Do you two want to go back home with us, or are you going somewhere else?" Auntie Imany asked, interrupting us. There was no way I was sharing her now. I wanted her all to myself. I wanted to take her somewhere where we could be alone.

"Go ahead. We'll catch you later," I said quickly, without breaking eye contact with her.

"OK... Dinner is at six. Don't be late," Imany said and walked away.

"See you at home, son." Andreas patted my arm and followed Imany.

"Emmy! I... Oh! I... I gotta go. My moms must be looking for me. Let's talk later, OK?" That was her friend. She didn't even look at her. Her eyes were on me and me only. I felt myself getting hard. If I keep her like this, she'd for sure feel it.

"Do you want to go for a walk?" I asked her once everyone had left. She nodded with a cute smile across her face.

"Come on. Get on my back." I put her down, turned, and got on one knee. She hopped on my back, wrapping her arms around my neck and her legs around my hips like she used to do when we were younger. I held onto her soft legs and started to walk.

I could feel her tender breasts pressed against my back, and the heat of her body spread all over me. She felt perfect.

We walked out of the station and down the road toward the park. Every time I readjusted her, she would hug me tighter. I was trying hard not to think much because I knew exactly where that would take me. I was afraid I'd get too horny and make a mistake, so I walked without saying anything at all.

I got us to the playground and sat her on a swing bench. I sat next to her and pulled her closer to me. I couldn't help touching her hair and tucked a curl behind her ear. Her hair was so soft. Before I knew what I was doing, my body leaned over and kissed her head.

"You have grown a lot. You look so different I barely recognized you." I was not lying. My thumb caressed her face. She was not a baby anymore. She looked more like a woman, but she was still young. Too young. If I wanted to keep to my own words, I'd have to be careful around her. There was no way I could let myself snap around her and risk hurting her, as Kenzo said. She was gorgeous, but I still had to wait. Fuck, it was going to be hard.

"You changed too." She gently touched my beard with her fingers, and my mouth immediately curved into a smile. I guessed she changed the way she felt about my facial hair. She pointed at my tattoos. "When did all this happen," she asked, and I started to think.

How much should I tell her?

"Many of them, I had always wanted to have. I guess the time was right to get them." Having her name on my skin was always something I wanted. A mark to tell the world I was hers.

She put on this naughty expression and lifted and dropped her eyebrows, trying to be funny. "Are you sure it was not to impress the ladies?"

What? Pff! Fuck, nah.

"Nah, there's no one to impress there." I wondered why she was asking.

"So, you're telling me no girls run after you in the North as you have them here?" My eyebrows frowned.

My eyes drifted to hers. I gave her a shy smile and shook my head. "Nah. I mean, yes. There are girls, but...." I patted her head and continued, "I've never been interested in any of them."

They ain't got nothing on you, baby. No one ever will.

"So... are you telling me you don't like girls? I mean, that's okay–"

What?

No, correct that fast. "I fucking like girls, Emmy," I interrupted her.

"Oh, I thought...."

Forget what you thought.

"I'm saving myself for the right one." Her eyes widened, and she smiled. She liked that answer.

"Good! I like that. Keep up the good work!" she said, giving me a thumbs up and a cheeky smile.

I looked at the ground and slowly shook my head, "I don't think I'll be able to for much longer." Not if I stay this close to her, not with how ridiculously beautiful she was. I was starting to lose confidence in my own willpower. Maybe being alone with her was not a fucking good idea.

"What?" she questioned. I didn't want to explain this to her. I didn't want to fucking talk about this.

"Let's go back," I interrupted her before her mind started wandering too far toward the exact place I wanted her to stay far away from.

I stood up fast and kneeled. She hopped on my back again, and I headed home. Yep, it was better if I didn't stay alone with her for too long.

I took the long way back home, and instead of the road, we went through the woods. I missed these woods. The smell of fresh air. The quietness.

I walked quietly for a while. My mind was on all the things I needed to start doing for our home. I'd start working on it first thing tomorrow. I couldn't fucking wait to marry her. I wanted her so badly.

Swinging with her on that bench felt nice. I should put a swinging bench on our porch overlooking the river. We could sit there and relax and cuddle.

"Emmerson, a hammock or a swing bench?" It took her a moment to answer.

"A swinging daybed!" She chuckled, and so did I. That was actually kind of perfect. I could make love to her there and eat her pussy until she came in my mouth. Ah fuck, I had to stop thinking like that.

I remained silent for a few minutes, trying to get my mind out of the gutter. Emmerson couldn't stand it and started talking once again. Some things never changed.

"Stoic, what were you actually doing there?" My body tensed up, and I readjusted her on my back. I couldn't tell her that. I could never tell her. That I had been killing people. That I had been in the middle of fucking hell.

"Not much. Just guarding the fence. It was pretty boring." I lied. It was the best I could do for her. I was afraid of how she would react if she knew.

"I missed it here. I missed this," I said, trying to change the topic. By "this," I meant us. Me carrying her on my back in the woods. Just Emmy, me, and nature —nothing else.

"Is the north as boring as the girls that live there?" She was not dropping the topic. She sounded jealous.

"Emmerson, the girl I like is here, not there." I should be more direct, but I was kind of nervous about confessing my love for her. I didn't want her to think I was a creep.

"Oh! So... you have a secret girlfriend?" She was definitely jealous.

"Sort of. I'm taken if that's what you're asking." She stayed quiet. Her thoughts must be going a hundred miles a second.

She was so cute.

"And so are you, right?" I asked. I couldn't wait for the day I would take her as my wife.

"Yeah..." She tried to not sound depressed but failed. "Do I have to marry him?"

"Yes," I said quickly, no second thoughts. She had to be mine.

"What if I don't like him?"

"You'll learn to." Another fast answer. I was not gonna leave room for an argument here. With the way her eyes ate me up, I could tell she liked me, too.

"What if he doesn't like me?"

Was she fucking kidding me?

"That's not possible. You're drop-dead gorgeous, Emmy." Fact. I wouldn't lie about that.

"Do you think so?"

"Yes." One hundred percent.

"Well... you are not alone there," she said and laughed.

What the fuck did that mean?

"What do you mean?" My voice dropped.

stopped walking. She was right. Why the fuck didn't I think about that before? Guys must be following her, begging on their fucking knees.

Fuck me!

"Are guys hitting on you?" I was pissed.

"Pfft, of course. All the time."

Fuck! I was gonna fucking kill them all.

"Who?"

"Why do you want to know that? So you can go on a murder rampage? Don't be silly, Stoic. You'll have to kill half the village."

That many... Don't tell me...

"Have you dated anyone?" I was angry as fuck. She'd better say no, or I'd have to add some heads to my count.

"Uhm... Let's see... What counts as dating?" She started thinking.

Fucking hell.

There I was rejecting free wet pussy, saving myself for her, and here she was, dating dickheads.

I put her down and turned around. I wanted to murder somebody. She bit her lip and held her laugh back.

Was this funny? Did she think this was a fucking joke?

"Has anyone kissed you?" I felt my hands forming fists. She thought about it again and smiled.

Had she kissed someone? Fuck! More than one?

Nah. Nah. This couldn't be. I was about to lose it. "Has anyone fucking kissed you, Emmerson?" I tried to remain calm, but I could tell I was failing.

"Well... I can't say no to that."

Oh, no! Fuck no!

I cracked my neck and got closer to her. Someone dared to kiss my woman. I was beyond pissed. She could see the fury in my eyes, and she got scared. I didn't fucking care anymore. I walked to her, and she stepped back. I gave one step towards her, and she took one back.

"Are you still a virgin?" I said, looking up and down her body. That pretty little body. I had fucking waited for her for so long. I had fucking jerked myself off thinking about her for years. I had a hundred desperate girls trying to get into my bed, and I'd send them all to hell because I wanted to be Emmerson's and Emmerson's alone.

"That's none of your business, Stoic."

Wrong answer.

That pussy was definitely my business. I took another step, and she backed up again. "It's a yes or no question, Emmerson." I was losing it. I couldn't control where my mind was taking me.

Keep it together, Stoic. Fucking keep it together. Don't fucking snap.

Another step.

"What if I'm not?" My eyes widened. She fucking wouldn't. I was an inch away from losing control. I forgot what Emmerson was capable of doing to me. No one else could make my blood boil as she did.

"Don't fucking joke around, Emmerson. Answer." I was giving her one last chance to rectify this. Another step, and she hit the tree behind her. I refused to think that someone else had already had her body. That couldn't fucking have happened.

"I don't have to tell you shit, Stoic."

Brat! That did it!

I took another step, and my body was so close to her that I could feel her tremble. I looked down on her, put my hand right over her pussy, brushing my thumb over her mound.

"Tell me now, Emmerson, or I'll pull these cute little pants down, spread your legs open, and check it myself." Don't for a second think I was joking. Act like a brat one more time, and I'd do it.

She was frozen in place. Her eyes widened, and her mouth dropped open. Her face blushed, and I knew. If she wasn't a virgin, she wouldn't have reacted this way.

"I... I... am." She sounded scared. I should back away, but instead, I kept brushing my fingers over her. I already knew the answer to my question, but now, now I was getting hungry. I wanted her. I wanted her badly.

I was going to stop... I had to. I just wanted to tease her a little. "You what, Emmy? Use your words." I got my face close to her neck and breathed in her addicting smell. She was so nervous her body was slightly shuddering. I didn't think she had even noticed it.

"I am still a virgin," she said fast and loud, pressing herself further into the tree. I nodded, and my hands slowly moved up her body. I had to stop. I should fucking stop, but I couldn't. I moved the back of my fingers softly, trailing them over her delicious-looking breasts until I reached her neck and jawline.

She was breathing heavily and was more flushed than before. Fuck, she must be getting wet with this. I was rock hard. She looked so innocent right now.

"Have you let anyone touch your body?"

Who was I kidding?

I wanted her. I wanted to undress her, lay her down, and take her. Right on this ground.

"No," she said softly. My dick moved in my pants. I felt a drop of pre-cum dripping down the tip.

"Good girl." She was lying. She was being a brat to bother me. She had never been this close to a guy before.

Fuck, I fell for it.

My hands moved down again, but this time, instead of brushing with my fingers, I let my whole palm caress her. I wanted to grope her but held myself back. When I passed my hands over her tits, I added just a little pressure. And she let out a small gasp. Fuck, she must be so wet. I wanted to spread her lips and eat her sweet pussy.

"I would have fucking hated it if anyone had touched you." I was too far gone. My hand moved further down her body, and I moved it behind her and grabbed her ass. Fuck! Her ass was so fucking firm and tender. I could get my hand full of it. I wanted to spread those cheeks and rub my dick in between them.

"Nobody else can have this body." That was almost a whisper. My voice was full of desire. I was not thinking, just doing. I lowered my hand and snaked it in between her soft thighs, moving it up and getting my fingers under the hem of her pants. She flinched and covered her mouth in surprise. I wanted that pussy. I wanted that cherry pie so fucking bad.

"Have you been a good girl, Emmerson? Hm?" My lips were so close to her neck that I could feel her skin when I moved them. I moved my hand incredibly slowly up her leg. I was giving her time to stop this. If she didn't want this, she had better talk fast. I had to make it clear, and she needed to know what I wanted, what I was after.

"Have you touched yourself, baby?" My hand was sliding higher up her leg. I put my other hand on the tree and caged her in.

Fucking tell me to stop, Emmerson.

She was still quiet. I needed her to say something. "Have you played with this tight little pussy?" My voice was full of desire.

Say something, Emmy, or I'm gonna play with it.

"No," she said with her voice filled with lust. She was driving me crazy. She fucking wanted this. My hands reached her damp underwear, and I lightly brushed it with the back of my fingers. She was soaking wet.

"Are you getting wet, Emmy?" My voice got even lower somehow. I knew the answer to that question, but I wanted her to tell me, to ask me to touch her.

"I... I..." She was too nervous. Fuck, I couldn't take it anymore. I took my hand out from under her pants and put it on her waist over her zipper. I pulled the zipper open and slipped my hand inside her pants and underwear, slowly moving down. She placed her hand on mine as I caressed her. She did nothing else, so I kept going down.

Her eyes were fixed on my hand, her breathing ragged. I was consumed by this hunger, this desire of feeling her. She was all I had ever desired. My hand reached her mound. Fuck, she was shaved. Her pussy was clean and soft. I softly passed my middle and index finger over her. I slide my middle finger right over her slit and my index over her velvety lips. I trailed them slowly from top to bottom.

Once I felt her wetness, my dick leaked more pre-cum. I was going to have a fucking spot on my pants. I knew my finger must have been right at her entrance. I put a little bit of pressure and slipped my middle finger inside her lips. I took a few seconds to feel her tight opening, and then I slowly moved it back up, searching for her clit.

She squeezed my hands hard but didn't stop me. She was soaked. It was so slippery. Her pussy was warm and soft. All I could think of was rubbing my tip in it.

"Fuck, Emmerson, you are so fucking wet." A low groan escaped my mouth, and I pressed my hips to her body. I wanted to hump her like a fucking dog. Emmerson held my hand but said nothing.

I found it, her small clit. I remembered all the things that Kenzo told me and started to gently rub little circles around it.

"Uuhh!" she moaned—she fucking moaned. Her head fell back, and I saw pleasure in her face.

Yes, baby, let me make you feel so good.

I kept rubbing circles, and she held onto my hands as if her life depended on it. I locked my eyes on her, watching her melt on my hands.

"Uuhh! Uuhh! Uuhh!" she moaned softly, her lips trembling. I was getting her off. I was fucking getting her off. I needed to stop. If I saw her cum, I'd snap and take her. I had to stop it.

I stopped rubbing her delicate pearl and slid my fingers up and down her mound, making them wet with her juices. I gave her a soft pat on her pussy that made her jump, and then I mustered all my strength to pull my hand out.

Her eyes, full of desire, saw how I put two fingers in my mouth and tasted her juices.

"Mmm," I said. She tasted so fucking good. My lust-filled eyes were set on hers. She blushed again. I zipped up her pants, pulled her away from the tree, and brushed the dirt off her clothes.

Taking a few steps back, I said, "Little girls shouldn't be walking around with their underwear soaked, Emmerson. Let's go home. You need to wipe yourself clean and change. Everyone is waiting."

Without even noticing, I had started rubbing my dick inside my pants. It was so hard, it almost hurt. I needed to ease it. I was going to have to beat it really hard this time. She saw me, and it took her a second to realize exactly what I was doing. Her face made a surprised expression when she saw how low on my pants my dick hung.

Even though I was fucking enjoying how horny she was getting, I couldn't let her. I fucking couldn't. I turned around since I couldn't let her stare at my dick. It was gonna make me wanna pull it out, and once out, I wouldn't stop until it was inside her.

"Move, Emmerson," I said, turning my back to her. I started to walk away, and she quietly followed me.

I needed to get some distance. That couldn't fucking happen again. It was for her own good.

TWENTY-FIVE

STOIC

Stoic 23

Emmerson 16

Since I felt her wet pussy in my hands about four months ago, I'd been jerking off constantly. I couldn't fucking be in the same room with her without getting hard. I knew exactly how that pussy felt, how wet she could get, and exactly how she liked to be fingered.

I was avoiding her. I watched her from afar sometimes, but I was afraid to get too close, even more, to be alone with her. When I did stay by her, I acted as if nothing had happened. My face might have been calm, but my heart was constantly beating fast as if it was about to jump out of my chest.

I kept myself busy. My father had pre-ordered the materials for our home, and I started working on it right away. Anyone that wanted to build their own home was entitled to a certain quantity of materials to build it. It was about enough to make a two-room home. The only requirement was to serve the community, which I already did, for longer than the average person would. And I wasn't even done serving.

Since I served for longer and Emmerson wanted four-and-a-half bedrooms, I did get more materials than the average person did. I had to work for extra materials and unique things she asked for, like the fucking glass walls she wanted. I made a glass wall in our bedroom and another one in the half room that I planned to use for her working space.

For the first two months, Dad, Kenzo, and Andreas helped me do the heavy lifting and build up the structure of the house. We finished some plumbing, all the electrical, walls, roofing, and the heating system, as well as put up windows, doors, and siding... you name it. Once the big things were done, I spent most of my time at home finishing the things I could do by myself like the floors, tiles, more plumbing, cabinets that I built myself, lights, painting, and so on.

The house was coming along really nicely. At this rate, I'd have it ready before I returned to the North, which was good because if I didn't come back, at least Emmerson would be able to live in the house I built for her. If I came back, I would marry her immediately and move in right away.

Emmerson had a dance performance. I knew she liked to dance, but I hadn't had a chance to see her. I didn't know what I was expecting, but what she danced that day was definitely not it.

She was excited and invited us all. The place was full of people, so I decided to stay in a corner, leaning against a column with Kenzo by my side. By the time she started to dance, I was optimistic. She came out wearing a tight outfit, looking like a complete and absolute queen. My queen.

The dance started, and the music was contagious. Their moves were really well-coordinated and so freaking incredible. She was a badass. Her eyes found mine in the crowd, and for a moment, I felt like she was dancing only for me. Her hips were moving perfectly in rhythm. All I wanted was for her to press that ass hard against me and move her hips like that. I was getting a fucking boner.

I was enjoying the dance until they started to sensually roll their hips. Then the crowd lost it. My smile fell. Guys all over the fucking hall started to whistle and yell out compliments. Some even yelled out Emmerson's name. They were saying things like, "Emmy, you are mine," "You are killing me," and "I want some of that."

Fuck me sideways.

She was not wrong. If I did go on a murder rampage, I'd have to eliminate half the fucking village. She was too beautiful, and her body moved so sensually. She was so fucking perfect.

I was beyond pissed, already thinking of ways to murder them and making it look like an accident, when her eyes drifted to mine once again. Yes, I was angry, but right in front of me was the woman of my dreams, sensually rolling her hips while looking straight into my eyes. I fucking wanted her. I wanted to have her. I wanted to make her cum hard and scream my name loudly, so all those mother fuckers would know who the fuck she belonged to.

She got nervous and lost her steps. She quickly got back into rhythm, but I had seen it. She wanted me, just as much as I wanted her. I started to think that maybe I should do something with her but definitely not go all the fucking way. I needed to have her trembling in my hands. Let her know she was mine.

I stayed there, eating her up with my eyes. I covertly rubbed my hard cock over my pants. Everyone's eyes were on her, so nobody noticed. Nobody but Kenzo.

"Dude, really?"

I stopped.

"My bad." I tried to adjust, but no, it was too hard to hide it.

"Take this." He threw me his bag. "Carry that for me," he said so loud our friends could hear it.

We laughed at our inside joke, and I put the bag right in front of me.

Fuck, what's wrong with me?

my eyes, but she disappeared.

"Hey! We're going down to the river. You should come," Kenzo said, pointing at our old friends.

"Yeah, OK." I needed a distraction.

"Great!" I heard this brunette say, overly excited. She bit her lip and walked closer to me. Perfect! Another horny girl chasing after me. Ever since I had come back, they had all swarmed around me like flies. Every time I went out with Kenzo, it was the same.

"Maybe you and I can catch up," she said.

No thanks.

Kenzo gave me that look. The one that said, 'Not bad at all. Take it, it's free.' I shook my head. I said nothing to her. I turned around and walked out.

Kenzo followed me, and we headed to the river. There were about seven guys and ten girls, including Ava. Ava and Kenzo had started to hook up again. He said it was nothing serious. I knew it was just a matter of time before he fucked up.

As soon as we got to the river, they all stripped and jumped in, in their underwear. Kenzo and I took our shirts off but kept our pants on. I didn't need to give these girls any ideas, and Kenzo already had his designated pussy for the evening.

"Come, I'll race you!" Kenzo jumped in, and I followed him. The water was cold, but we didn't care. It was colder in the North.

"Where to?" I asked.

"There!" He pointed at the furthest rock on the other side.

"OK."

"Ready, set..." And the mother fucker took off. I should have known better than to trust Kenzo.

I tried to catch up with him, but just like Emmerson, he seemed to have been born in the water.

Kenzo reached the rock first and sat on it. "Come on, Grandma. I wanna talk to you."

"You fucking cheated."

"Get over it, dickface. Come." I sat next to him, pulling my loose hair back.

"Tell me. Did something happen?" he said. What and when were better questions.

"What are you talking about?" Maybe if I played dumb, he'd drop it.

"I'm not blind. I saw the way Emmy looked at you while dancing and the way you looked at her. Not to mention that after three years of nonstop talking about her, now you are fucking avoiding her and giving her the fucking cold shoulder. So, start talking."

"Fuuuuuuuuuuuuuck," I said and looked away.

"Fucking talk, Stoic."

"You don't want to fucking hear it. Believe me."

Trust me on this one.

"Stoic, yes, I'm her brother, but I'm your best friend too. And right now, you need me. We're more than friends. We're brothers, and we have each other's six all the time. There's no one I trust more than you, and I know there's no one you trust more than me. Fucking tell me because I know it's eating you."

Ah, fuck! He was right.

"I fingered her." Silence. Kenzo's eyebrows frowned.

There goes my friendship.

"More like rubbed her...." Still silence.

Well... that didn't make it better.

"Not even an hour after arriving here, and I had my hands down her panties." I was ashamed.

"So..." Kenzo said

"So...?" I didn't know where he was going with this.

"Did she like it, or did you screw it up?"

Was he serious?

"I don't know. I started it, and I ended it. It didn't last long. I was afraid to lose it."

"To lose what? Your patience then have sex with her?"

"Yeah."

"And that's bad because...."

"Fuck, Kenzo, you know how I feel. She's too young."

"Stoic, nobody is expecting you to behave like a saint around her. Not my family, not yours, and with the way she looks at you, not even herself. We all know you love her and have waited for her, and you'd do anything for her. You fucking built a badass house for her, dude. Chill." I didn't know. I didn't fucking know. I shook my head and stayed quiet.

"I... I think so. She started to moan... Kenzo, I don't wanna say these things to you."

"So, you are telling me you had the girl of your dreams moaning in your hands, and you fucking left her...?" He raised an eyebrow and gave me a look of disbelief. I looked back at him, and he started to laugh out loud.

"Fuck, Stoic, you're so fucking dumb!" He grabbed his stomach and bent over, laughing more. His laughter echoed. Fucking idiot! And he called this helping. I frowned and tightened my fists. I was about to punch this fucker.

"So, you're telling me you warmed her up and left her. Gosh, she must be horny as fuck!" He kept laughing. I didn't think about it like that.

Did I really leave her horny? Ah, fuck me!

I always fucking screwed things up. It was more than just that, though. "She wasn't talking,"

"What do you mean?" He started to calm his laughter.

"I made advances on her, and she didn't say anything. What if she didn't want it?"

"Are you for real? If she didn't stop it, she freaking liked it, OK? She just was too nervous to say it, but believe me, she wanted it." He might be right.

"Next time, don't leave her hungry and finish the job, OK? If she is nervous and says nothing, just keep going. Sometimes when they're inexperienced like

Emmy, they might even get shy and give a little resistance, but trust me, they want it. If she asks you to fuck off, then you stop." He had more experience, so maybe he was right. I remembered how Emmerson held on to my hand. How nervous and shy she was.

Fuck, I was an idiot.

"Girls are too fucking complicated." How was I supposed to know what she wanted or did not want if she was not fucking talking?

"That's what you've got me for." He gave me a wink. Jerk.

"A race back?" he asked, and I nodded

"Ready..." He started, and I jumped in and left him behind. I was not falling for it again. He still won.

We swam and talked to friends for a long while. I took a break and sat on the rock, wanting to be alone. Those girls were hitting on me hard the whole time, and I was uncomfortable. I took in the view. I only had two more months, and I didn't want to leave.

Kenzo sat next to me. "Dude, I'm gonna take Ava to the other side. Cover my ass OK?"

I laughed. "Dude, you're gonna get yourself in trouble."

"What's the use of having a big purple crayon if I'm not gonna put it to good use?" We laughed. He was a jerk.

"You're gonna dig your grave with that dick." I shook my head.

"Nah! The only thing I'm digging right now is that pussy." He pointed at Ava.

Fucking idiot.

We laughed some more, and then we heard Emmerson's voice. "Kenzo!"

"Don't fuck up again," he told me before patting my back. He stood up and started to walk toward his sister. How could I fix this? Should I finger her again? Should I try to go all the way? No, not that. I should at least get her off; I owed her one. I should definitely have a conversation with her. Fuck, I was a 21-year-old man. I was acting like a boy. I needed to grow a pair.

"Hey..." I heard Emmy say in a low voice, but I continued to stare into the distance. I was going to be honest. She made me nervous, but I had to try to be more direct with her.

"You looked beautiful dancing. Like a fucking goddess. Did you have fun?" I said to her, but I was still not looking her way.

"Yeah, I did. Did you like it?" The dance? I loved it! The fucking crowd of throbbing boners, not so much.

I nodded my head. It was not her fault. She liked dancing, and it made her happy. I was not going to ask her to stop doing something that made her so happy. If I had a problem with it, I'd deal with it myself. I'd better change the topic.

"Dark wood or light wood?" As soon as I finished putting up the floors, I had to stain them.

"Dark, because why the hell not!" she laughed, and I glanced at her and laughed too. Dark wood floors were gonna look really good. I had to go find that stain later.

We saw Kenzo swimming across the river with Ava and disappearing into the woods shortly after. I shook my head. He had no fucking shame.

"These are cool." She pointed at the ax-wrapped with Celtic knots I had on my right arm.

I looked at it and said, "A tool for building or a weapon to destroy."

I leaned forward, resting my weight on my elbow on my thighs. I opened my hands and looked at them before closing them and letting them hang. She had no idea what these hands had done or what they'd keep doing. Good and bad equally. She couldn't fully understand what it meant to me. The things I had built, and the lives I had taken.

"Oh! What about this one?" She pointed at the triple horn of Odin on my left shoulder.

"The triple horn of Odin." I must have told her that story about a hundred times. She might not remember since she was still so little.

"Oh, I remember that one! Wisdom, right?" I'd be damned! She did remember.

"Yes."

Always seek wisdom, Emmy.

"And this? I think I have seen this somewhere else." She pointed to the "Góðr" over my heart and under the wing of one of my ravens. Of course, you've seen it. You guys wrote it on my knife.

"Góðr, it means brave." I patted my chest twice. "Right over my heart where it belongs." Come on, Emmerson, this one is an easy one. It was the meaning of your freaking name, over my heart... It wasn't rocket science.

"Braveheart? I like it. It goes well with you." She gave me a shy smile, and I did a mental facepalm. Fuck me! Did I need to explain it with a little drawing and a dance for her to get it?

I raised my left hand to comb my hair back, and she stopped me. "What does that say?" She pulled my arm to her and read the words.

"Brave woods?" she asked. That one was super obvious. I couldn't believe her. My eyes were fixed on hers, not knowing how she could keep missing it all.

Her hands held my arm, and one of her soft fingers ran over her name. I loved the way her touch felt on my skin. It was so gentle. I was speechless. Just having her this close caressing my arm was enough to make my heart want to stop. I just nodded to her as an answer.

I tilted my head a little, and a curl fell over my face. I had to tie my hair again. I was about to move my hands to my hair when she stopped me.

"Let me do it!" she said, moving behind me. "You combed my hair a thousand times, so it's my turn now." How could I object to that? I enjoyed having her close to me. Touching me. Even if it was just my hair.

She undid my messed-up man bun and started running her fingers through my hair. Her hands gently gathered all my curls in them. I felt her finger brush my scalp. Emmy used her fingers to detangle it. She took way longer than she needed to, but I was okay with it. She was just feeling me. Emmerson twisted my hair and tied it with the band.

"Done!" she said cheerfully.

I was expecting her to come back and sit next to me, but she surprised me. She hugged me from behind. Her face was skin to skin with mine, and her arms were wrapped around my shoulders. She leaned on me with her chest pressed against my back.

Unlike all the other times, this didn't feel sexual. It felt sweet, heartwarming, and calm. Like it should be. My hand went to her arms, gently brushing my thumb over them. The view made me think about this old song, "Misty Mountains," that I used to sing to Emmerson when she was little and couldn't sleep. Without noticing it, I started to hum it softly with my baritone voice.

My heart filled with emotion, knowing that in two months, I'd have to return to hell and risk my life, so I could come back to this–peace in Emmerson's warm arms. If I could come back to this, it would all have been worth it. We stayed like that for the longest time, just feeling each other, taking in the scenery right in front of us. The girls in the water were fuming. I was glad. Now they knew for sure who I belonged to.

I went back to my parent's home and lay on my bed that night, thinking of all the beautiful moments I wanted to create for Emmerson. I wanted her life to be happy and full of joy. I'd work my ass off to make sure of that.

TWENTY-SIX

STOIC

Stoic 22

Emmerson 16

The next morning, I woke up screaming. I had another fucking flashback. They were getting more and more recurrent. Sometimes I had them when I was awake too. Mom ran into the room and hugged me. I was glad she didn't say or ask anything about it. I didn't want to talk.

I had breakfast with her, took a shower, and then went to Emmy's house. Kenzo would come with me to my house and help me finish the porch. Going to the Silva's house was like walking in my own home.

I walked in without knocking.

"Stoic! Morning. Did you have breakfast already?" Imany was always trying to feed me.

"Yeah, with Mom."

"Good! Kenzo is not done with breakfast yet. He's in the dining room."

"OK" I was about to go on my way to the dining room when Imany stopped me.

"Stoic!"

"Yeah?"

"Could you wake Emmy up? She's late, and she hasn't eaten breakfast yet." I smiled.

Sleepyhead. Should I sneak in and scare her?

"Yeah," I answered Imany and walked to Emmerson's room.

I quietly opened Emmerson's room, but I wasn't fucking ready for what I saw.

Emmerson was under her blanket, clearly with her legs open, with a hand in between them. She was touching herself.

Holy, fucking, hell!

"Uuh! Uuh! Uuh!" she was moaning softly, her fingers moving fast. Fuuuuuck! Kenzo was right. I left her horny. That was about to change.

"Emmerson," I said in a low voice, and she jumped and uncovered her face.

She was blushing, completely embarrassed. I just fucking walked in on the girl I had been fantasizing about for my whole life while she pleasured herself. She shouldn't have to do that. That was my job. Pleasing that tight little pussy was my job.

I stepped into her room and closed the door behind me. I had to be quick and quiet if I didn't want her family knowing what I was about to do to her wet slit.

"Stoic..." She was freaking out.

So cute.

"What were you doing, Emmerson?" I said in a low voice.

"Nothing," she said, holding onto her blanket tighter

I walked over and sat next to her. My cock was getting hard inside my pants.

"Nothing?" I asked. I wanted to tease her. See her get nervous and lose control.

"Yeah, nothing!" she replied, trying to pretend everything was fine but failing.

I pulled her blanket back and saw her. She was barely wearing anything. Her irresistible body was exposed to me. Her nipples hard inside that fucking see-through shirt she wore. No pants and a huge fucking wet spot in the middle of her underwear. She must have been creaming the whole fucking night.

"I see," I said, my eyes fixed right between her toned legs. Ah fuck, I wanted to open her legs up and eat her cunt like a fucking savage. I bit my lip at that thought, and I saw her blushing even more.

I put a hand on her knee and started to move it up her leg slowly. "Did you make yourself cum already?" She looked wet as fuck. It didn't really matter. I'd try to make her cum again.

"No... I..." she said shyly and hid her face with her hands. She was so embarrassed. If only she knew the things her silky mound was doing to my mind.

"Do you know how to get yourself off, Emmy?" She was surprised to hear that, but she didn't answer. We were back to this. I was going to follow Kenzo's advice. I kept moving my hand slowly up her leg.

"Do you want me to rub your wet pussy until you cum, baby?" That was as direct as it got. She gasped but didn't answer me. She was not fucking stopping me. I didn't fucking stop then. I wanted her to tell me, though. I wanted to be sure that this was what she wanted. My hand was now on her mid-thigh.

"Tell me, Emmerson, use your words." My eyes were on hers, waiting for a reply, but she just stayed quiet.

After a long silence, my hands reached her wetness. I was not going to stop. I was going to assume she wanted this.

Fucking hell, I wanted this.

I pulled her leg toward me, spreading her open so I could have better access to her dripping core. I caressed her inner thighs and groped her over her soaked panties. "So fucking wet. You are a horny little vixen, aren't you?"

I gave a soft pat over her sensitive pussy that made her jump. Gosh, I wanted to slap her like that with my hot and heavy meat. I wanted to rub my pre-cum all over that pretty slit. Separate her lips with my head and rub myself in her wetness.

With one hand, I held her leg, and with the other one, I rubbed circles over her panties. Her clit was so hard that I could perfectly see it through the wet fabric of her underwear. I pinched it softly between my fingers, pulling another gasp out of her. She was so fucking turned on right now.

She bit her lip and watched my fingers move over her. It was time to stop playing. I slid my fingers inside her underwear, immediately finding her wet sensitive bud, and rubbed it with one finger.

Her hand went to mine, but I brushed it away while shaking my head no. She wanted this. She was soaked and trembling. She must have been thinking about it the whole fucking night. There was no way I was stopping this until she fucking came hard on my hands.

"Spread your legs wider for me." My voice was still low, almost a whisper. She did as I asked. I put two fingers flat against her pink button and started to move them faster and faster on her. She was nice and slippery, her pussy soft and warm. I wanted to slip a finger into that tight hole, but I didn't want to break anything inside her yet. That was for my hard cock to destroy. Slam hard inside her and mark her body as mine.

I could see the pleasure on her face. She was loving this. She was immersed in this feeling that my fingers were delivering to her. As I relentlessly flicked her, my hand made an erotic, wet sound. Her legs started to shake, and her breathing got ragged. She was fucking loving it. Her pleasure-filled eyes were lost in this feeling.

I was incredibly hard. My dick pressed painfully against my pants, twitching with every ragged breath that Emmy took. Begging me to release it. Aching to be near Emmerson's warm entrance.

"Do you like that, baby?" I asked her, my eyes fixed on that pussy. Looking at my finger flicking all her juices around. Seeing how she was making us both shiny with her thick, clear cream. She didn't answer me again.

"Uuhhh! Uuhhh!" Emmerson moaned out loud, not able to control it. I couldn't have that.

"Shh," I hushed her and put a hand over her mouth to muffle her sexy moans. Fuck, my dick was dripping, and I knew I must have a fucking spot on my pants.

She started to lose control over her body. She was so close. She was about to cum hard, and I was the one making her. My whole body was aroused, and my skin had goosebumps, but I didn't fucking stop my fingers. Watching Emmerson cum was so fucking hot.

She started to moan louder and sounded more desperate. I pressed my hand around her mouth harder to muffle them. Her hips began to buck, and her legs shook violently.

She was fucking cumming. My baby girl was cumming undone on my fucking hands. So fucking beautiful. I felt more cum drip out of my tip, but I couldn't stop it. My dick throbbed hard. I had never seen anything that hot and addicting before. I wanted to fucking ram my hard wood inside her and fuck her senseless. Make those perfect tits bounce hard.

Her toes curled, her back arched, and she dug her nails in my arm hard enough to make me bleed. Her whole body tensed, and I could see the pleasure spreading throughout her body in the form of goosebumps. I could feel her pussy pulsate hard and fast on my hands. Her eyes rolled back, and her mouth opened in a silent scream. Holy fuck, yes! Yes, Emmerson!

Oh, no! Fuck! Oh fuck, no!

I was cumming in my pants.

Holy fuck!

I came in my fucking pants.

Fuck damn it!

Emmerson's body started to convulse hard. My fingers were still moving when I heard steps coming from the hallway.

"Emmy?" I heard Kenzo call her. Fuck off, Kenzo. Not fucking now!

I covered her and the wet spot on my pants quickly with her blanket. I remained calm, sitting next to her, acting like nothing at all had happened as if I didn't just fucking come in my pants after giving Emmerson an orgasm for the first time.

Kenzo opened the door without knocking. This motherfucker had the worst timing ever.

"Emmy, Dad said he wants you to go with him to the fields today," Kenzo said, and I gave him a "get lost" glance. He didn't fucking get it.

She was still trembling from the [illegible] how her whole body shook.

"Is she OK?" he asked, pointing at her.

"Yeah, just cold," I said, passing my hand over her shoulder up and down as if I could help her warm up. I gave Kenzo the "what the fuck, dude. Get the fuck out now" look, and he got it this time. He mouthed an *oh,* and then a smirk appeared on his stupid face.

"Don't worry. I'll make sure she gets there on time." I was trying to stay calm. I signaled to the door with my head, and he nodded and gave me a thumbs up. Oh, fuck! He was going to burn me for this later.

Kenzo left and closed the door behind him. I kept rubbing her shoulder over the blanket. Trying to comfort her trembling body.

"That's my girl." My thumb rubbed her arm. "I don't want you touching yourself, Emmy. That's a job for your husband." I wanted to be the one giving her pleasure. Setting her body on fire and watching her convulse in a puddle of her own cum.

"Go take a shower, baby. Andreas is waiting for you." I took one of her curls in my hands, feeling the softness in between my fingers. Every inch of her was perfect. I let her hair go and turned my back to her, not wanting to let her see my pants full of jizz.

I headed out of her room and went straight into Kenzo's.

"Did you... What the fuck!" Kenzo started laughing like the fucking idiot he was. Of course, he was in his room.

"Don't even fucking say it." I locked the door behind me, and I started pulling my pants down. "I need to change."

Kenzo stood up, getting briefs and pants from his drawers and throwing them at me. I wiped myself as much as I could with my underwear and rolled them into a ball.

"Give me a bag or something. I'm taking this with me. I'll wash them at home." What a fucking embarrassment.

Kenzo looked in his closets for a bag while I dressed. "Here." He tossed it to me.

"Thanks." My head hung low. "I'm... I... Fuck!" I facepalmed myself.

"Don't worry, I jizzed my pants, too, when I fingered my first pussy." I took a deep breath.

"Six fucking years ago!" He started to laugh again, and I threw my boot at him. Motherfucker.

I left their house in a rush. I was too ashamed to stay any longer. The image of Emmerson's face as she came, with her eyes rolled back and her mouth opened, permanently stuck in my mind. It was all I could think about. There was no way in hell I'd be able to keep my hands away from her pussy now that I knew how beautiful she looked when she came.

I was gonna have to have a conversation with her. Maybe ask her to be my girlfriend. I didn't know, but I just felt like I should start something with her now. Anything. It must be obvious to her already that we had a thing going on, and I didn't want her to think I was just using her for fun. She needed to know I was serious about her, that I cared for her.

I went to the new home with Kenzo, and we worked for most of the day. Kenzo didn't know if he was going to build or just buy one and move in. He was not in a hurry. I bet he just wanted to stay in Uncle's house where everything was easy for him–his mom cooked for him, and he could just fuck around more. If he ever decided to build his house, I'd be there beside him, helping every step of the way as he was for me.

That evening we went back together to his house like we usually did for dinner. Emmerson looked stunning. I sat next to my girl and quietly enjoyed the evening. I was planning on taking her out after dinner and having a conversation with her about us. Maybe by the end of tonight, we'd be officially dating.

Everybody was joking and talking when all of a sudden the landline rang.

We all stopped talking, and Kenzo went to get it.

"Hello, this is the Silva residence." I heard him say.

"Yes, sir."

Oh no! Oh, fuck no!

My whole body tensed, and I turned to look at him. I had a bad feeling about the call. I tried to search his eyes for anything that would indicate my instincts were wrong, but nothing.

"Yes, sir. Yes, he is here with me." Kenzo looked back at me. *No!*

"Yes, sir. I'll inform him immediately." Kenzo kept nodding, and I stood up, walking toward him. It couldn't be. Not now. Kenzo must have seen how desperate my eyes looked.

Kenzo hung up the phone and gave all of us a sad look. "We have to go back. We're taking the first train in the morning. Pack up," he said to me and headed to his room. Fuck! I pressed my fist tight and left the house, slamming the screen door hard on my way out.

Fuck! Sadness and anger consumed my whole body. I [illegible] ready. My steps went faster. I needed to get ready as fast as I could. I only had hours left, and I wanted to spend every possible second of them in Emmerson's arms.

I entered my house and rushed to my room. I got Emmerson's backpack and started tossing things in it quickly. I put aside an outfit to change into, and then my dad entered the room.

"What's going on?" he asked with a worried look in his eyes.

"I don't fucking know!" I screamed. I was angry. I shouldn't lash out at him. I kept tossing things around, and my dad came closer, held my hands, and pulled me in for a hug.

"It's okay." He hugged me tight, and I started to cry.

"Fuck, Dad, I'm not ready. I'm not fucking ready." Tears fell. I was not ready to leave Emmerson again, to walk my own two feet back into the darkness of Niflheim.

My dad patted my back and cried with me. "You make me proud, Stoic. I love you. You know that, right?"

I nodded, but I didn't say anything. We hugged for a few minutes before he let me go. "I've got to go get your mom."

"I want to be with Emmerson."

"I know. Go shower, and I'll get your mom. You can say your goodbyes and then go back to Emmerson." He left in a hurry.

I did that. After my backpack was ready, I took a quick shower and got ready for the long journey. I gathered all the papers and details I had of the house and all the things I was planning to do and put them all in a bag.

My dad walked into my room again. "She's on her way."

"Dad." I walked to him and gave him the bag.

"What's this?"

"Our house documents. Everything is there–plans, permits, you name it. You know what's left to get done. It's not much. Promise me that if I don't come back, you'll finish it, so Emmy can live in it," I said, pointing at the bag. All my hard work for almost a decade was in his hands.

He shook his head. "Again? No! You do it yourself when you get back." He was in denial. He gave me the bag back.

"Dad."

"No, Stoic! You will come back. Are you listening? You'll do everything in your power to fucking come back to us." He was crying again. "Because I can't lose you."

I hugged him again. "Dad, please. I need a promise. Please!"

"No, Stoic. You have to come back."

"I will, Dad." I patted his back. "It's just in case I don't, but don't think about it, Dad. I will come back."

"OK, then. Leave the fucking bag there."

"Stoic!" My mom walked in.

"Ma." She rushed in and gave me a hug.

"You be safe. You hear me. Don't try to be a hero, just be safe."

"Yes, Mom." I hugged her tight. Her head only reached the middle of my chest. She had started to look so small.

"Mom, keep an eye on Emmerson for me."

"I will, baby, I will. She is a wonderful girl. She'll be fine. You go and don't worry, okay. She'll be safe with us."

I nodded and kissed her head. Dad joined in the hug, and we stayed there hugging in silence for about five more minutes.

"Erik!" That was Andreas.

"I've got to go, Ma," I said to her, giving her one last hug. "I need to go to Emmerson."

"OK." She watched me leave my room.

Dad and I walked outside to where Andreas was standing. As soon as I was close to him, he pulled me in for a hug.

"Stay safe, Stoic. Stay safe." He patted me. He, too, had tears in his eyes.

"Where's Kenzo?" I thought I knew the answer to my question.

"Fucking disappeared. Who knows where to?"

I nodded. "Can I stay the night with Emmerson?"

"Yeah, sure. Go, go, you don't have much time left." I gave him a sad smile, and he gave me a soft push before I left. I walked into Emmy's home and saw Auntie Imany first.

"I'm sleeping here tonight." She understood what I meant.

"OK, come here." Imany opened her arms, and I hugged her. She kissed me and patted my back. "Go, it's getting late. You should rest." She pointed to Emmerson's room, and I just grabbed my things and went there.

I opened the door, put my bag down, sat on the bed, and took my boots off. I [illegible] to make her my girlfriend. There were so many emotions running through my mind right now. I felt that if I started talking about them, I'd break and waste my time crying, so I'd better not.

I was holding onto my head, feeling the weight of all the stress I was going through, crushing me when Emmerson entered her room.

"Stoic?" There was no time to waste. All I wanted was to have her in my arms for as long as I could.

"Come." I extended my arm to her and pulled her in. I lay Emmerson on the bed and spooned her. I pulled her even closer to me and wrapped my arms tight around her.

"Let's sleep, Emmy." That meant I didn't want to talk, and she understood.

We lay there in silence for a long time. She turned over and hugged me back, burying her face in my chest. I enjoyed the soft beating of her heart against my chest, her soft skin, and her sweet smell for hours. Neither of us fell asleep. We just enjoyed the warm embrace we were giving each other.

Sometimes she would run her finger in my hair, and sometimes I would do the same with hers. She softly brushed my eyebrows like she used to do when we were little, and she thought I was still sleeping, and I did the same to her. We looked into each other's eyes, and I softly kissed her forehead.

It was like nothing we had ever had before, and everything combined at the same time. It was new but familiar. It wasn't sexual. I had the most beautiful woman in this world in my arms for the last time in what could be years, and I was not thinking of anything even close to sex. For those hours, we were each other's universe.

This was love. The sweet kind. The kind of love I had always felt for her. A love that shaped my life. The kind of love that would never disappear even if I did. A love that would last long after I was gone.

Time flew by while I was lost in her browns and greens, and before we knew it, Kenzo knocked on the door.

"It's time."

My face hardened. At that moment, I wasn't the Stoic that created and built for her future, but I had to be the Stoic that would fight and defend her safety.

I stood up, put my jacket on, and pulled my backpack closer to me. I sat on the bed and started to put my boots on. She also stood and got ready.

Once she was dressed, I took her hand and walked us out of the house. I held her hand all along the way, not wanting to miss the feeling of her skin, not even for a second.

The train station was deserted, and only a few people were waiting for the train to arrive. At the platform, Dad and Mom hugged me one last time while I still held Emmerson's hand in mine. Imany and Andreas hugged Kenzo too. Everyone here knew what we'd be facing, everyone but Emmerson. I didn't want her to know. Imany and Andreas had agreed to keep it a secret again. It was the best thing I could do for her. I didn't want her to live a life in fear or uncertainty. As I said before, I wanted her to be happy. Always.

I pulled her in and hugged her tight.

"Remember, Emmy..."

"You'll always come back to me." She remembered. I held her tighter, and tears started to fall from my eyes.

The train arrived, gradually slowing down near us, but I was still holding on to her. The train stopped, and I refused to let her go. Just another second. Please.

Kenzo tapped my shoulder, and I had to face reality. I dropped my arms and turned my body before she could see the tears in my eyes. I got on the train without looking back and sat down, covering my face with my hands.

A few moments later, Kenzo sat next to me and threw his arm around me like he had the first time around.

"It's going to be OK. We'll make it. Together, remember?"

I nodded, but that didn't stop the sadness from spreading fast inside my chest.

The train started to move, leaving my life and my whole world behind me, standing right on that platform.

We were headed full speed back to hell.

There was only one thought in my mind. I had to make it back to her.

TWENTY-SEVEN

STOIC

Two months after we arrived, we got a call from home. Ava was pregnant, and she was going to keep it. Kenzo was going to be a father. He was scared as shit. He called Ava and had a long talk with her. Auntie Imany and my mom had told him not to worry, that they would make sure Ava and the baby had everything they needed. Kenzo didn't say it out loud, but I knew he felt like shit. He was still fucking around, but not as much as before. Maybe having a kid would change him for good.

A month after that, we got assigned to a mission that went terribly wrong. Somehow, the enemies knew we were coming, and we were ambushed. We were trapped in an abandoned building, under fire, completely surrounded with no possible way out. There were ten of us, and we fought back and held our ground as much as we could. We used every trick in the books to give us more time, but soon we started to run out of ammunition. Our backup team had arrived, and we could hear the shots going off outside.

Our forces outnumbered them, and many of the enemy forces started to retreat. But some of them were trapped in the building with us, and they decided to hunt us down. Only a few of us still had ammo, so we kept those who ran out in the center. I had only a few rounds left. Kenzo was out.

We crossed fire with two, and I took one down. A teammate to my right took the other one, and we went to get their rifles. I was covering Kenzo, but when he bent over to take the rifle from the body, another two bastards appeared. I shot at them, but my fucking gun jammed. We were sitting ducks. Kenzo was still trying to get the rifle, and I saw them aim at us. I acted before I could think. I threw my body in front of Kenzo to cover him. I felt four shots hit my vest and another one enter between my left shoulder blade and my armpit. It hurt like a motherfucker.

As my body fell on the ground, Kenzo stood with the rifle and took one of them down. From behind them, someone from our side took the other one down.

Everything that happened after that was a blur. I remembered very little of it. I remembered hearing Kenzo screaming my name and shaking me, a brief moment in the car transporting me, and then hospital lights.

I woke up two days later with Kenzo by my side and an awful pain in my back, shoulder, and arm. I grunted, and Kenzo jumped.

"What the... Stoic! Stoic, are you awake?" Kenzo shook my right arm.

"What the actual fuck?" I was disoriented. I tried to sit up, but Kenzo pushed me down.

Kenzo stood and slapped me hard on the head. "Motherfucker!"

"What the fuck! Ow!"

Why was this fucker hitting me?

"You fucking scared the shit out of me, Stoic! Don't you fucking do anything as stupid as that ever again, you fucking idiot!" Kenzo was screaming at me, his hands shaking. He turned and started to walk away.

"The fuck are you going?" I said, my throat dry. Ah! I felt like shit.

"To get the fucking doctor, you fucking asshole!" He walked out and came back with a nurse. A doctor walked in a minute later to check on me.

Kenzo told me I was lucky the bullet missed my heart. I was in a lengthy surgery to remove it. He saved the bullet for me. I stayed in the hospital for three weeks. Since I was bored, I asked Kenzo to get me a chain, and we made a necklace with the bullet.

Once I got discharged from the hospital, Kenzo took me out for a drink. Someone had one of those instant picture cameras, so we took a photo with friends. I sent Emmy the photo with the necklace for her birthday. I wrote to her that it came from a place near my heart.

I knew she wouldn't get the double meaning. Getting back in shape was hard. I had no idea that three weeks laying like a potato could be that damaging.

They put me in therapy for another month to get me back to my previous condition.

Two weeks after I sent her that picture, Emmerson sent me a reply. She sent a photo of herself wearing the sundress made from the fabric I gave her last year as her birthday gift. Imany did a great job. She had the most beautiful smile, and her hair was loose, blowing in the wind. My baby was gorgeous, like a fucking angel. She left a kiss on the picture and added a note that said, "from the most beautiful girl you'll ever see."

Fuck, she wasn't wrong about that.

I loved that picture so much that the week after, I went to get it inked on my left arm. The artist did a great job. It looked perfect.

I jerked off to that picture almost every day after that. I kept it next to my bed and stared at it until I fell asleep. I missed her so much. I wondered if she was as horny for me as I was for her.

I got many other tattoos. I even had them on my hands, torso, and neck. Both arms were full. I was leaving space on my chest for my kids' names. I wanted as many kids as Emmy could give me. I wanted to have her pregnant all the fucking time. What was good about having a big house if we couldn't fill it. Couldn't wait to go back and work on that. Making the kids, I meant, since our home was nearly done.

For some odd reason, we randomly found Ethan in town. He was about to return home. We took him out for drinks. He had grown taller and stronger. He told us he was planning to marry Amelia and wanted to start studying to become an engineer. I told him to continue keeping an eye on Emmy when he got back, and Kenzo asked him to make sure Ava was fine until he returned. It was nice having someone from home here with us, even if it was just for a day.

Kenzo and I went for drinks as often as we could. We usually didn't get drunk, but a few times, we did. One of those times, I regretted terribly. Something horrible happened to me, and I never got drunk again after that.

After a long week of training and a successful mission, we went to celebrate, and I got shit-faced. We drank so much that Kenzo had to help me walk back to our barracks. Kenzo left me on my bed and went to fuck with a girl he had been talking to at the bar. I didn't know how, but a fucking girl snuck into our room. I knew her since she'd been stalking me and asking me out for months, but I had rejected her many times.

I was drunk as fuck and almost passed out. She got on my bed and took her shirt off as well as her bra. I didn't fucking want that disgusting bitch to touch me, but I was so drunk that I couldn't push her away. She started to grope me and grind against me, getting me hard. She had begun to pull my pants off when Kenzo opened the door and found her. Thank goodness he had forgotten his condoms and came back for them. He immediately pulled her away from me and threw her out of our room. I felt so dirty. That was close, too fucking close. I didn't even want to think about it.

Kenzo felt bad for leaving me alone, but I told him it wasn't his fault. Here I was thinking only guys would do that kind of shit. A man my size being abused by a woman was the last thing I thought could happen. I was so wrong. I'd never trust anyone. I was so glad Kenzo had stopped it. I was still a virgin for Emmerson. I wanted her to be my one and only.

A few months after that, Ava gave birth to a boy. She named him Ian. Kenzo was beyond sad. He had missed the whole thing. He did ask for permission to go see his child, but it was denied. That day, I hugged him as he cried. He couldn't wait to see his son. If I was willing to take a bullet for Kenzo before, now I was going to be fucking paranoid. Kenzo was a father, so no matter what happened, I had to make sure he returned home safely.

We were so close to ending this war. The enemies had only one base left, and we knew the location. All higher officials had been eliminated, and the only ones left were their resistance. The plan was to blow that last base up to pieces, but we hadn't figured out how.

They had sent us in teams of five to see if we could identify a weak point for us to strike. We spent weeks observing them. We were in the snow on a nearby hill with sniper rifles, dressed in our winter camouflage. Our team observed their movements and identified a pattern. We reported it back, but it was taking them forever to come up with a plan.

One snowy day, Kenzo and I noticed they had transported explosives and left them all in storage near their vehicles. They had a deep trench surrounding the east side, and one of the idiots had left the gate open. Kenzo didn't think twice. I knew what he was going to do. We looked amongst our things and found TNT and a detonator.

We could set the whole thing up next to their explosives, attach a five-minute timer, and run like hell out of there. He and I could hide in the trench and have our other three comrades cover our asses from a distance. They wouldn't know what hit them.

We told our superiors our plan, and they gave us the go-ahead. It took us an hour to prep before we all descended the hill. Kenzo and I sneaked around the corner, and the other three positioned themselves at a safe distance where they could cover us from every angle.

Kenzo and I moved in, and since it was snowing, most of the enemy soldiers were inside the building. There were around six patrolling that side. As we approached their storage building, our team members took out the guards. Kenzo set the TNT in place, and I covered his back. He set the timer for five minutes, and then we ran for it.

Our teammates noted that the enemy started to come out, so they began shooting in the opposite direction we were running to distract them. A little over four minutes later, Kenzo and I made it to the trench. We got in and covered our heads. Seconds passed, and then the explosions started.

We covered our ears, trying to shield them from the deafening sounds. The explosions were so strong that the earth shook beneath us. I looked up, and it looked like fireworks and fire shooting in all directions. We could feel the heat above us, but luckily, we were safe there in the trench.

After it was all over, we climbed out to find our enemy's last base completely flattened and destroyed. It was over.

[illegible]

We didn't give a fuck about that. All we wanted to do was leave and go back home to our families. There was a big end-of-the-war celebration planned where we were supposed to get promoted to majors, but we skipped it.

Both of us couldn't wait to get home. We were so anxious that we rushed everything up and were on our way back a week earlier than planned. They ended up giving us everything in a small ceremony before we left. As an early payment, they gave us a small truck, and we decided to drive back home in it. Kenzo said I could keep it, that he had no use for it. During the long drive, neither of us could sleep. We took turns driving, so we could make better time. We only stopped to eat and use the restroom. Kenzo was super excited to see his child for the first time, and I was anxious to pick things up with Emmy where we left them.

She was finally old enough. I was not going to hold back anymore. I'd kept my distance before, but now I'd be making my moves. The first thing I'd do would be to seduce her. I wouldn't wait until the wedding day. I'd deflower her right away. It'd been almost ten years since she gave me my first kiss, and I had started to feel this consuming desire for her. Ten fucking years! I couldn't wait to have her.

We arrived home at noon, a day early. We both climbed out of the truck as soon as we parked it. Kenzo ran to Ava's house to see his child, and I ran to

Emmy's. I found Imany first. When she saw me, she screamed, dropped the dish she was cleaning, and ran to hug me. She gave me a bone-crushing hug and studied my face.

"You're here! I can't believe it! I thought you guys were going to be here tomorrow," she said, holding my face.

"We couldn't wait." I smiled.

"Where's Kenzo?" she asked, looking behind me.

"He went to see Ian and Ava," I replied.

"Oh, my! I'll go there!" she squealed.

Before she left, I stopped her. "Where's Emmy? Where's Mom?" I took her hands in mine.

"Your mom will be back in a few hours. Emmy is at the river. She said she wanted to catch a fish for you," Imany said with a smile.

I dropped her hands and ran out of the house. My legs took me quickly through the woods. My heart was beating rapidly in my chest. I got to the river in record time. Once I arrived, I didn't see her. My chest was moving hard as I tried to catch my breath. All I saw were her clothes, a bucket, and the fishing pole on a rock.

My eyes were desperately searching for her. I looked everywhere but nothing. All of a sudden, Emmerson emerged from the water and took a deep breath. She had her back turned to me and started swimming toward the shore.

The sun was hitting the water just right, and there were one thousand small blinding reflections of light all around her. My eyes widened, and I took in how beautiful she looked. It was almost surreal, like a dream. A smile spread wide across my face.

I made it. I had come back to my baby.

TWENTY-EIGHT

STOIC

Emmerson 18

My eyes were fixed on the most beautiful girl in this world.

I heard her laugh, and I couldn't stop the smile that spread over my face. She hadn't noticed me. She was still slowly backstroking toward me.

"Emmerson!" I called out to her, my heart beating fast.

She turned around and smiled. "Stoic!" she screamed before starting to swim faster.

When she reached the shore and started to get out of the water, I opened my arms for her to jump into like last time. As soon as she stood up, my smile dropped. She was almost naked! She ran, and I could see her beautiful breasts perfectly through the very thin fabric of her bra. Her nipples were hard, and her perfect tits were bouncing up and down. Her panties were tiny and see-through too. Fuck me!

She jumped into my arms with a huge smile, and I caught her. I held her tight against my chest, my rough hands feeling her soft skin. Her arms and legs snaked around me. I felt my dick get harder with every rapid beat of my heart. She was cold, but I didn't give a flat fuck about that. Emmerson was naked in my arms.

I moved my hands up and down her back, feeling her silky skin, and buried my face in her neck, taking in her smell.

"I missed you so much," she said, hugging me harder.

"I know you did. There's no other like me in this world," I said, remembering the last time I had her in my arms just like this. We laughed, and I spun her around, my heart filled with pure joy.

This was it, the moment I had waited for almost a decade. I was going to make love to my girl. Finally, bury myself deep inside her body and make her mine as I always dreamed of. I needed her. I needed her so badly.

My hands moved from her back, and I grabbed her round ass. It felt perfect in my hands. My face was still buried in her hair, and I could feel the lust build and bubble up inside my body. It was intoxicating.

I grabbed her ass harder, squeezed it, and pulled it apart, wanting to make space for my hard erection to rub against her. I wanted her to feel how much I needed her.

She squirmed, and her legs fell off my hips. I slowly put her on her feet, but my hands never let go of that delicious ass. I pressed her hard against my body, letting her feel my hardness, wanting to let her know how much she was affecting me. How much I wanted her.

"Stoic... I..." she stuttered, and I leaned down and kissed her jaw. She was nervous, like before. She didn't move. I sensually trailed open-mouthed kisses along her neck, my hands moving up and down her body. I snaked them between her thighs and caressed her over her wet underwear.

Her hands went to my chest, and she put up a bit of resistance toward me. I remembered what Kenzo told me, so I didn't stop. I kissed her neck. I knew she was nervous, but I was nervous too.

She stepped back quickly and out of my arms. I stared at her nervous face with my eyes full of desire. I noticed she was wearing the necklace I had given her. She had no idea how much I loved her. She was my everything.

"I... I... was swimming." She slowly pointed at the river with her shaky hands. She was turning shy. Even when she was this nervous, I wouldn't let her make an excuse to get away from me.

I looked around briefly. We were completely alone there. I had the perfect opportunity to take my clothes off, too. I nodded my head and said, "I'll swim with you."

I took my shirt off quickly, and when she saw my bare chest, she jumped and turned around, giving her back to me. I took my clothes off as fast as possible while looking at her butt cheeks that were entirely out of her panties. Most of the thin material was lost in between her thick, wet cheeks. Her toned legs pressed together. I wanted to open those legs and eat her pussy and make her cream in my mouth.

I got completely naked, and I started to pump my dick slowly while looking at her irresistible body. She shyly turned back to me, covering her breasts with her arm. I shamelessly continued to move my hand on my hard cock. She saw my erect penis, and her eyes widened. I pulled my foreskin all the way back and stared at her eyes while I held onto the base, letting her see it. She let out a loud gasp and turned once more. It was the first time she had seen me. She was so cute.

I walked closer to her. She was so nervous that she seemed to be frozen in place. I pressed my eager body against hers from behind, and with both of my hands, I cupped her tender breasts. I pinched and released both of her hardening nipples in between my fingers before I weighed her tits in my hands. She was perfect.

My mouth moved to her again, and I kissed up and down her delicate neck.

hands behind her to undo her bra. I let it sensually fall off her, freeing her round, firm globes.

My hands went back to her breasts, and I could tell she was sensitive. My fingers moved over her nipples, and she trembled with need. It wasn't enough. I needed her completely exposed to me. Completely naked. I wanted to feel every inch of her soft, cool skin on mine. I needed her to ease this fire that was burning me alive and consuming my mind.

My hands traveled down her hips, and I slipped my fingers inside her panties, pulling them down as my hands traveled south. I took them completely off, and my hands traveled back up, going in between her legs and reaching her clean-shaven pussy. Holy fuck!

Her pussy was soft, warm, and wet for me. I let out a low grunt as I gently slipped my fingers in between her velvety folds. My mind went back to her cumming face as I flicked her clit between my fingers, making her convulse in my hands like the last time I saw her. I needed to have her now.

I walked us forward, getting into the water. I wanted us to have some privacy as I deflowered her, and I knew just the right place for it. Kenzo told me about the cave many years ago. It'd be perfect. I turned Emmy around, put her legs around my hips, grabbed her by her ass, and walked us deeper into the water. I pressed her tightly against me, wanting to feel as much as I could of her skin.

Her eyes were wide, and her breathing ragged. I knew she could feel my hard, throbbing cock between her legs as I got us closer to the waterfall.

I sat Emmerson on a rock and pulled myself up to standing. I then pulled Emmy up, too, and, holding her hand, took her closer to the cave's entrance. Putting my arm around her, I shelter her from the heavy weight of the water falling over us. Once we got into the cave, Emmerson started to shake. I knew part of it was because of the cold, and part was because she was anxious. She must have known by now she was about to lose her virginity. I was about to make her my woman.

I immediately hugged her, rubbing her arms up and down. I wanted to calm her down. The truth was that I was just as nervous as she was. I wanted her to enjoy herself, to make her feel like a princess.

I lifted her and carried her in my arms. I walked deeper into the cave and lay her down on the damp sand. The only thing she had on was my bullet that hung low on her chest. She looked so fucking beautiful.

I used both of my hands to spread her legs open for me. Oh, fuck! She was gorgeous. Her wet pussy glistening, begging for attention. She got shy again and tried to cover herself, but I was not having it. I moved her hands away and laid them beside her. She was absolutely beautiful, and there was no need for her to cover herself from me.

My lips connected with her legs, and my mouth kissed and licked her legs as I slowly moved up her body. She was breathing hard, and her face looked worried. I was sure that once she started feeling pleasure, she would relax more. She was so timid right now.

My lips reached her sweet pussy, and her body jolted up. She tried to close her legs, but I had both of my hands on her thighs, making sure they stayed open for me. I licked and tasted her sweet nectar.

Fuck, she was delicious.

My mouth warmed her slit as I slipped my tongue in between her lips. She was soaked, and my mouth made an erotic wet sound as I licked her pulsing clit faster and faster.

She was enjoying this. She started to get very wet, and her body trembled. I licked her more and used my fingers to flick her sensitive bud. As my fingers moved faster, I saw her starting to lose control. Her hands grabbed the sand beneath her, and her body tensed hard.

She must have still been feeling shy because she looked away while I kept getting her closer and closer to her orgasm. Silly, she didn't have to. I had already seen her cumming before. Her legs shook, and I felt her pussy clenching tightly on my tongue. Yes! She creamed more, and I licked it all up. Emmerson tasted so fucking good. She bit her lip as she rode out the last of her orgasm on my tongue. She was perfect, priceless.

I couldn't wait any longer. I needed to have her. I positioned myself in between her shaking legs and rubbed my swollen head up and down her wet slit. As I found her entrance, she put her hands on my chest, and I pushed my thick spongy tip inside her.

"Ow!" she cried. It hurt her. I knew that was normal. I was popping her cherry. She was so fucking tight. I was stretching her entrance to the maximum. I pushed my hard dick harder inside while holding it in my hand. She was so tight that if I let it go now, it would pop right out. I leaned forward and carefully inserted more of me into her. Holy fuck! I lost my virginity. I lost it to Emmerson as I had always wanted.

She pushed against me harder, digging her nails into my chest. "Ow, it hurts. It hurts." She started to cry, tears running down her cheeks. She was in pain. I was not surprised, as my dick was huge, and I was hurting her so much.

I'm so sorry, baby.

She tried to shrink away from me, but I didn't let her. "It's okay," I said, looking at where our bodies were united.

The pain will pass soon, baby. Please, Emmy, just endure it for another minute.

She cried harder as I continued invading her tiny hole. I pushed myself further in, and a moan escaped my mouth. "Uuhh! Fuck!"

So good, so fucking good.

I knew my dick was leaking pre-cum. I felt her small walls opening, making space for my rod to enter her. My dick got stuck inside her. Not wanting to make this pain last longer for her, I quickly backed out and then pushed it forward even harder, trying to break through.

"AH! OW! OW!" She started yelling in pain, more tears falling down her cheeks.

So fucking sorry, baby. It would all pass soon.

My cock was throbbing hard. I was close. I pushed myself further inside her and hit the back wall of her pussy. Holy shit! I deflowered her completely. She was mine, all mine. Oh fuck, it was too good. I lost control of my body, and I started to feel my orgasm hitting me hard and fast.

"Uuhh! Holy fuck, Emmy! Uuhh!" I started to cum hard. It was the best feeling I had ever felt in my life. My hips buckled, and I lost my strength, leaning my body over her. I tried to make it last by giving her a few shallow thrusts, but I couldn't move, and my body stilled.

"Uuhhh!" I moaned loudly as I threw my head back and squeezed her hips. My body wanted to be deeper inside her, and I pushed myself hard against her.

"Uuhh! Uuhh! Mmm!" I moaned as the last of my jizz ejaculated out of my pulsing sensitive tip right into the deepest parts of her pussy. I came so much. I closed my eyes as my body shuddered in pleasure.

I moved my hands over her trembling body, trying to ease the pain I knew she still felt. My warm hands gently rubbed and caressed her soft skin everywhere. I wanted her to feel how much I loved her, how thankful I was for what she had just given me.

I ran my finger over her head, face, and hair, wanting to make this moment more intimate, but she looked away.

Why wasn't she looking at me?

I put some of my body weight over her as I shifted to reposition myself. I took her jaw in my hands and made her look into my eyes. Her browns and greens didn't have that sparkle they usually had. She looked sad. She might still be hurting. While staring into her eyes, I gave her a passionate kiss, but she didn't kiss me back. Her lips never moved on mine. I didn't... understand what was happening.

Putting my weight on my forearms, I used my thumb to wipe her tears away and kissed her wet cheeks. I touched her gently and softly, trying to soothe her, but she didn't stop crying.

What was happening? I thought it must have hurt her more than it should have. Maybe she'd feel better after I started moving. If she didn't want this, she would have told me or pushed me away, but she hadn't. She might just be sore. It should pass soon.

I put my weight on one of my elbows and spread her legs further open. I started to move inside her softly, not wanting to hurt her. That was a new feeling. I had only put it in and immediately came. The friction between our bodies blurred all my senses. I saw her hands form tight fists as I slowly eased my cock in and out of her.

"Uhh! Emmerson!" It was perfect. I felt my swollen meat melting inside her heat. She was my better half, and without her, I was incomplete.

"Uhh! Baby!" My mind went blank. I felt my hips move faster, chasing after the purest form of pleasure that only Emmerson could give me.

I closed my eyes, and for a fraction of a second, my mind went back to hell. I heard shots and screams. It was as if I could almost feel the debris of an explosion crashing hard behind me. I blinked rapidly, trying to shake it off, but it happened again. No! Fuck, not now. Out of all the times that my mind decided to fail me, it had to be now.

Without thinking, I moved faster in her, trying hard to forget everything. My mind was pulling me away from this moment, and all I wanted was to focus on her, on us. I just wanted to feel her. I wanted to feel human again. I wanted to feel the pleasure that Emmerson was giving me and not the all-consuming fear. I didn't want to see more empty eyes and dead faces. I mindlessly pumped into her harder and deeper, my dick hitting her back wall with every thrust I gave her.

I got lost. I pounded away with abandon. The harder I gave it to her, the further I felt from falling back into my own memories. The fast pace built my pleasure quicker than I was expecting.

"Ahh! Ahh! Holy fuck! Ahh! So fucking good!" I moaned with every thrust next to her ear, no longer able to control my hips anymore. The loud sound of our wet skin slapping as it met drowned the screams of children in my head, the bombs going off. "Fuck, Emmy!" I was close again.

I had been pounding mindlessly into her. It felt so good. For a brief moment, the images in my head had stopped, but just when I thought it was over, it happened again. I didn't know what was triggering it. This time, I could see every hole I put in every one of my confirmed kills.

Fucking hell!

Emmerson–she could pull me back. I made her look at me once more. My hips rocking hard, my cock pistoning inside her. She looked at me with sad eyes, but I couldn't help but have my face distorted in pleasure. My mouth hung open, my eyes were filled with lust, and my hair had gotten loose with the strength in which my body rocked back and forward, falling over my face.

Too good, too good.

I grunted as the rhythm in my hips became irregular, and my breathing grew ragged. I held her face, wanting to look into the eyes I had fallen in love with the very first time I saw them. Wanting to have her light pull me back from the darkness.

I saw her lay there with her eyes full of tears. My body was overstimulated with this addictive feeling, but it didn't seem she was enjoying it. She was still crying.

Was she still hurting?

Pleasure hit me hard, and I started to make some animalistic sounds and moaned even louder as I got closer to my climax. My body felt the desperation of knowing I was reaching my orgasm, and I pounded harder inside her.

I wanted to take her hands in mine and entangle our fingers together to make this more intimate, but her hands were still closed into fists, so I held on hard to her wrists. I was so close. Her firm tits slapped up and down rapidly as her body met my hard thrusts. The sound of bullets hitting the walls getting more and more distant with every thrust. She cried more. She must still feel sore.

A few more seconds. I was so close. So close, baby.

My body was starting to get stiff, and I dropped my face down to her chest and sucked her tender nipples into my mouth. One first and then the other. I didn't stop pounding her. I was about to cum. I was going to cum hard. I laid my head in between her neck and face and gave her three hard thrusts before stilling inside her.

"Uuhhh! Uuhhh! Uuhhh!" My hips bucked vigorously. I grasped her wrists harder, and consumed in this ecstasy, I kissed down her neck. My body started convulsing above hers, and I lost all strength, falling on Emmerson. My hard cock pulsating inside her with every rope of warm cum that escaped me.

Oh, Fuck! I was not using protection. I gave her two full loads without protection. It was our first time. She couldn't get pregnant this easily. There was no way. Right?

I stayed over her body, trying to control my breathing. I raised my head, and I kissed her lips again, very gently. She didn't kiss back.

Why hadn't she kissed me back?

She just lay there crying, her eyes empty. My eyebrows frowned as I studied her. She looked so fucking sad.

What the fuck?

I felt my softening dick easing out of her, and my eyes traveled there. Her pussy's skin was reddish. As I slowly pulled myself out, I saw my thick cum and her blood spilled over her inner thighs and slipping out of her slit.

Was that much blood normal?

Emmerson cried more, and my heart sank. No! I wiped her tears away and kissed her. Once again, she didn't kiss me back. I was scared. Not knowing what to do, I kissed her neck, and my body fell over her once more. What should I do?

Now that I thought about it, she stopped enjoying the moment I put it inside.

What the fuck have I done?

She kept crying, her body weak. I rolled us over to our side and hugged her close to my chest. I was scared, I was so scared. I rubbed her back and hair, kissing her forehead and the top of her head repeatedly. I was desperately trying to comfort her. My heart was aching.

I hurt her. I fucking hurt her.

After a while, she was still crying, so I stood up with her and carried her back to the river. I was hoping she would feel better after I cleaned her. I carefully washed her body with my shaky hands. My heart hurt as I tried to soothe her pain. I tried my best to not make it sexual, wanting her to be comfortable.

Consumed with regret, I hugged her tightly. What an idiot. That was not what I wanted. I never wanted to hurt Emmerson. It was supposed to be special for both of us. I fucking ruined everything. I was so sorry. I was so fucking sorry. I wanted to say it, but I was too nervous to speak. I would take her home and care for her until she felt better.

She was in so much pain that she could barely stand up by herself. I carried her and walked us back to the shore, where our clothes lay on the ground.

Once there, I helped her get dressed first. I didn't want her to feel ashamed any longer. I put on her bra and underwear, regretting terribly having taken them off in the first place. I walked to the rock where she had left the rest of her clothes and brought them to her. I helped her put her shirt, pants, and shoes on. I sat her down on the ground and went to get my own clothes. I wanted to carry her home and see what I could do to help her.

As soon as I turned around, she stood up and took off, leaving me butt naked. My eyes widened as I saw her run, pain evident on her face.

"Emmerson!" I screamed her name, and it echoed through the woods. I rushed to get my pants and briefs on. Trying to get them on as fast as possible, my foot got tangled, and I fell on my face. I lifted my head and saw her run while holding on to her lower abdomen. No! She was hurting herself even more.

Why the fuck was she running away from me? Was she that scared?

I struggled with the fabric that got stuck to my wet legs. "Emmerson, stop!" I screamed again, angry with myself. Why the fuck did I not snap out of it and stop. She fucking cried the whole time. I should have stopped.

I got my pants up and didn't bother to zip them. I put my boots on, leaving the socks behind. After grabbing my shirt off the ground, I took off, putting it on as I ran. I ran fast through the woods, my heavy heart thumping in my chest, wanting nothing more than to have Emmerson back in my arms. To tell her how sorry I was.

What had I done?

I ran faster with my fist closed, wanting to hit myself. Assuming she ran to her house, I headed in that direction. I got there, saw her shoes at the entrance, and rushed inside. I remembered Imany just left to see Kenzo, so there was no one there but us. Hurriedly, I ran to her room and shook her door handle. It was locked. I gave it four hard knocks.

"Emmerson!" I screamed, full of fear.

Please be okay. Please be okay.

"Emmerson! Emmerson! Fucking open the door!" I kept knocking on her door repeatedly. I was desperate and angry. Emmerson was hurt, and it was my fault. I just wanted to help her.

Let me help you, Emmy.

"Open the fucking door, Emmerson." I knocked harder, making the whole door shake. I could break this fucking door down if I wanted to. I remembered her face as she ran from me. She was scared. I didn't want her to be afraid of me.

I stopped knocking and took a deep breath. "Emmy, baby. Open the door, please." I said, trying to sound calm. She didn't answer me.

"Baby, open the door. We need to talk." My heart was breaking. She was fucking terrified. If I broke in, she would just feel worse.

"Baby?" My hands softly touched her door.

Please, Emmy. I never meant to hurt you. I'd never hurt you again.

"Emmerson, please. I know you're there, please." No answer. She didn't want to see me. How could I beg for forgiveness if she doesn't let me talk to her? How could I help her heal if she doesn't let me get closer?

"Emmy, please."

Open the door, baby.

"Emmy?" I was begging.

"Baby..." My voice sounded weaker as a knot formed deep in my throat. I was so sorry.

I kept calling her like that for a while. After a few more minutes, I backed off. With heavy steps, I went to the living room and sat there. I was not going to leave her all alone. I sat with my head between my hands, feeling embarrassed.

After forty minutes passed, Imany returned home. She walked straight into the kitchen, and I sneaked out of the house, not wanting to face her. I went home and found my mom standing in the living room waiting for me. As soon as she saw me, she held me tight. I hugged my mom, and tears escaped my eyes. She must have thought I was so happy seeing her. A few minutes later, my dad walked in and hugged me, too.

I wanted to say something, to tell them, but I was ashamed of myself.

How could I be such an idiot?

Maybe after a couple of hours of rest, she'd feel better, and we could talk. I'd let her rest, and I'd talk to her after dinner.

TWENTY-NINE

STOIC

Stoic 23

Emmerson 18

~After the dinner~

When I arrived at her house for dinner, Andreas stopped me. He gave me a huge hug and told me he would be announcing our engagement. I felt like shit. I had failed them, all of them. I hurt her.

I was determined to get her alone after dinner and have a talk with her, but she rushed inside her room while doubling over. It'd been hours since I took her, and she was still hurting badly. I couldn't let her suffer like this. I needed to come clean.

I waited until our extended family left before telling my mom. She was talking with Imany, but I had no time to wait.

"Mom, I need to talk to you," I said seriously while taking her hand and walking her out of the house.

"What's going on?" She sounded worried.

I never do this.

"I fucked up," I said, my face full of worry.

I don't even know where to start.

"What do you mean? Stoic, look at me. What do you mean?" She pulled my face, making me face her.

"I fucked Emmerson, and she's hurt," I said in a sad tone, a lump in my throat.

"What? Do you mean you had sex with her? What…" She was confused. I needed to be clearer.

"I had sex with Emmerson. I thought she wanted it, but after I was done, I realized I forced her. She is hurting. Mom, she's hurt, and I don't know what to do. I need you to please help her."

"How the fuck didn't you notice she didn't want it?" She couldn't believe it.

"Cuz I'm a fucking idiot. I had zero experience and didn't know what I was doing. Mom, I'll talk to you, but not now. Go to her. She needs help." I turned her around, and she rushed into the house.

Mom rushed past Imany, and Imany walked out of the house and came toward me.

"Is Ida okay? What happened?" She searched my face and saw my red eyes. "Holy shit, Stoic. Are you okay?"

I shook my head. "I'm sorry," I said with a shaky voice.

"What do you mean?" Imany was still looking straight into my eyes.

"I… I hurt Emmerson. I'm so sorry," I said, my eyes glued to the ground. I couldn't look her in the eyes.

"What do you mean?" She started to get nervous.

"I… When I left here, I found her swimming in the river. She barely had anything on, and I got confused… It was my fault. I made a huge mistake." I took in a painful breath.

How to tell her I abused her daughter?

"What mistake?" she asked, but I didn't answer.

"What mistake, Stoic?" she said louder, shaking my arm.

"I… forced her. I thought she wanted it, but I think I forced it." My face was red with embarrassment. She had always trusted me with Emmy. I let her down in the worst way.

"How could you?" She shook her head.

"I was confused. I got confused. I was not thinking. I'm so sorry. I'm sorry, Imany." Before I could say more, I was interrupted. Dad, Andreas, and Kenzo walked toward us. Kenzo threw his arm around me. He was going to joke around, but as soon as he saw my eyes, he stopped.

"Dude, you OK?" he asked worriedly.

"Imany, what happened?" Andreas asked her, and she shook her head.

"Let Stoic tell you himself," she said before walking back inside the house.

Three pairs of eyes landed on me. I felt like the shit I was, but I had to face the consequences of my actions. I took a deep breath.

"I hurt Emmerson." I saw them shift their bodies.

"What did you say?" my dad asked, taking a step forward.

"I fucking hurt Emmerson. I'm sorry," I said, and this time Andreas took the step forward.

"How?" he asked, and I shook my head. The lump in my throat was getting bigger.

"I... for... I forced her." Those words came out with incredible difficulty.

"You did what?" Andrea closed his fist, and Kenzo stepped in front of me.

"Wait, I know it sounds bad, but I know Stoic. He loves Emmerson more than anything in this world. Let him talk," he said, trying to de-escalate the situation.

"Talk," my dad said, fist closed too.

"I... thought she wanted it, but it... it turned out she didn't. I... I wasn't... was confused. I should have stopped," I said, looking at the ground.

"How the fuck didn't you notice?" Andreas asked, grabbing me by my shirt.

"She didn't ask me to stop. She didn't..." I started to say when I heard Kenzo gasp beside me.

"Holy fuck! Dad, no! That was my fault." He tried to get in between us, but it was too late. Andreas landed a solid punch on my face, and I fell backward.

"Motherfucker," he said and launched at me. Kenzo got in the way, and my dad pulled him and tackled him. Andreas got on top of me and landed punch after punch after punch. I didn't even bother to cover my face.

"I fucking trusted you." He kept punching me. Behind us, Kenzo got away from my dad and tackled Andreas, getting him off me.

"Fuck, Dad. Stop. He didn't fucking know what he was doing." Kenzo was trying to defend me. He shouldn't.

"No, Kenzo, I should have fucking known," I said that, and a solid punch landed on my face. This time it was my dad.

"What the fuck have you done?" He kept punching me—my stomach, chest, arms, everywhere.

I could feel the metallic taste of my own blood in my mouth. I saw Kenzo trying to escape Andreas and failing. My left eye was already closing. I fucking deserved this beating. Kenzo finally got away from Andreas and threw his body over mine. He got kicked by Dad and Andreas repeatedly on his ribs and back.

"Fucking move, Kenzo," Andreas screamed at him.

"I'll move when you promise to stop beating the fuck out of him," he said, but I wasn't going to let him take a beating for me. I pushed Kenzo aside and stood my ground.

"I'm sorry, Andreas. I'll make it up to her. I promise," I said, and he launched at me again. We would never get to talk if he just kept punching me. I lifted my fists in a boxing stance and got ready to cover myself. Andreas did the same. I was going to spar with him. Get him tired first, and then talk to him later.

He threw a combination of jabs, hooks, and uppercuts at me. I could barely see, but I avoided them all. I threw a few paws to keep him further away and make him move. I wasn't gonna fucking hit my father-in-law. I moved him around some more. He launched forward again, but I evaded him with my footwork. He kept trying to land one on me, and I kept avoiding most of them for about another four minutes.

"I'm gonna fucking kill you!" Andreas was pissed, but he was getting tired.

"Calm the fuck down. I want to talk to you. Trust me, no one is angrier at me than myself," I said, but he still didn't listen. He threw a cross punch at me and almost got me.

"I love her!" I screamed, my voice breaking. Another hook. I moved away just in time.

"I love your daughter, Andreas. I'll marry her and spend the rest of my life making it up to her. I promise," I roared as I shifted around.

"Promise? You promised you'd always keep her safe, too. I don't fucking trust you anymore, Stoic. Stay the fuck away from my daughter!" Andreas threw a punch at me. I moved my body out of the way and pushed him forward, making him lose his balance. Andreas fell on his knees and stood up, angrier than before. He cracked his neck, getting ready to kill me when Imany rushed out of the house.

She walked straight to me, pushed Andreas away, and punched me on the chest.

"Do you have any idea what you have done to her?" she screamed at me. My heart stopped.

"Is Emmerson OK?" My arms dropped, a worried expression forming on my face.

"Is Emmerson okay? What kind of stupid question is that? You fucked my daughter! Of course, she is not okay!" she screamed at me and pushed me.

"I'm sorry, Imany. I'm so sorry. Please, let me see her. I need to tell her–" Slap!

Imany slapped me across the face. That hurt more than all of Andreas's and Dad's punches combined.

After that, everything seemed to happen in a blurred, slow motion. Imany kept pushing me and screaming at me, but I couldn't hear anything anymore. I saw Kenzo talk to her, and she pushed him too. Dad was screaming at me, Andreas was screaming at me, and Imany was screaming at me and punching me. Kenzo was constantly getting in the way and being pushed around. All I could think of was how badly hurt Emmerson must be.

As I felt my body being pushed around by different people, tears rolled down my face. I looked down to the ground and started to say "I'm sorry" repeatedly.

Imany had moved us further back to the side of the house. She punched me one last time before fainting. Andreas caught her in his arms and lowered her down.

Andreas screamed her name and shook her. I was petrified. Kenzo kneeled and tried to help Andreas pick her up.

"Go get her water!" my father told me, but Imany woke up before I could move.

"Immy, are you okay, baby? Immy, talk to me." Andreas was worried. If something happens to Auntie Imany, it would be on me too. Kenzo helped her sit up, and she started to gag as she was about to puke. Andreas lifted her up and helped her. He rubbed her back as she slowly calmed herself.

My dad's eyes trailed toward me. He was disappointed. I was a failure. He was ashamed of me, and I knew it. I was ashamed of myself, too.

"Get the fuck out, Stoic!" Dad told me.

"I don't want you anywhere near Emmerson, you hear me?" Andreas said, pointing at me.

I nodded. "I'll give her some space." I took off, and Kenzo followed me. I got in the truck, and Kenzo took the driver's seat. Kenzo drove to Lucas' house and parked the truck.

"Wait here," he said before getting out.

I just sat there with my hands shaking, hitting my head softly on the dashboard.

What a fucking mess!

Kenzo came back with two bottles of whisky and drove me home. My home, not my parent's house. We got there, and I opened the door. It was the first time I had been there since we came back from the North. I could tell my dad came by and put some things up and finished others. Fuck, maybe Andreas helped him too. I sat on the empty living room floor, and Kenzo passed me one bottle. All my body ached, but the pain wasn't worse than the regret I was feeling.

"Let's get wasted and go to sleep. We'll figure things out tomorrow," he said before he started drinking. I took my bottle and downed it in one go, ignoring the burning in my throat. I didn't want to be fucking conscious. The effects of the alcohol started to kick in immediately.

"Dude, this is my fault. I'm so sorry. I told you not to stop." I heard Kenzo say softly.

My body started to lean sideways, everything turned black, and I was out before hitting the floor.

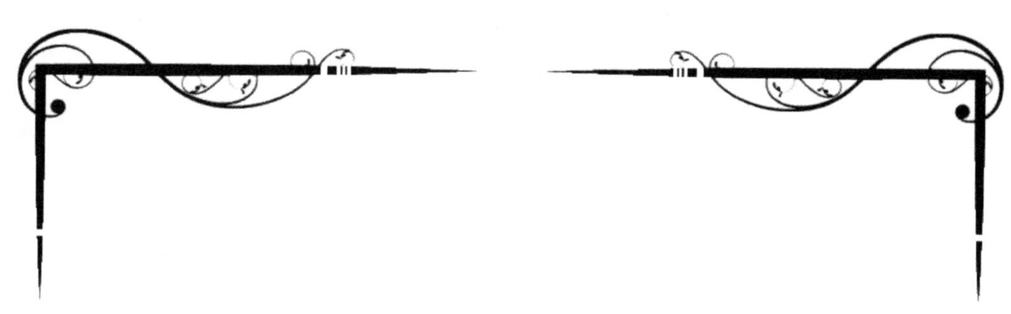

THIRTY

STOIC

Stoic 23
Emmerson 18

I woke up on the floor with a dry throat and a splitting headache that got ten times worse with the morning sunshine. Everything hurt. My hands went to my face, and I found that my left eye was closed shut, my right one was swollen, and my lips were cracked and swollen too.

My stomach growled in protest, and I knew I was about to puke. I stood up and stumbled out of the house. Once outside, I fell on my knees and vomited on the grass.

Ah, fucking hell!

I felt like trash. I tried to stand up straight, but I felt it again. I doubled over and puked some more. It tasted horrible. I was still dizzy and feeling drunk as fuck. I must have looked pathetic. Wiping my mouth with the back of my hand, I looked at the driveway and noticed the truck was gone.

That was it. Kenzo must have gotten sick of my ass and left me, too. I walked back into the house and straight to the kitchen. I turned on the faucet and rinsed my mouth before I drank from the running water. All the cabinets were empty, and there was nothing to eat in this house. I didn't even bother looking.

Sinking onto the kitchen floor, I held my pulsing head, regret hitting me hard. Everything was fucked up. Emmerson was hurt, and all my family hated me. I fucking hated myself, and even Kenzo had left me. I didn't blame him. I fucked his sister. I fucking ruined her. I didn't deserve her, but I was not gonna give up on her, never.

I laid on the floor again and tried to shield the light.

What would I do now? How could I fix all this shit?

I was completely alone.

I'd give Emmerson a week before I showed my stupid face to her again. What an embarrassment. It was going to be hard, but I had to grow a pair of solid balls and fucking do it. I'd make her a nice gift, bring her flowers, get on my knees, and then beg her like the desperate motherfucker I was.

I had to talk to Mom, Dad, Andreas, and Imany too. I might as well start with the easiest conversation first–Kenzo. I knew he was angry with me, but I was sure he'd at least listen without trying to kill me.

I stayed on the floor for another half an hour before standing up and getting to work. I still needed to get this home ready for Emmy. I'd marry her and make her happy. I had to. The showerhead and faucets in our bathroom were not installed yet, so I'd start with that. I got my tools and began to work on them.

Two hours must have passed before I was almost done installing everything and connecting the drainpipes and the trap under the sink. It was hard to see with only one eye as the other was swollen shut. I heard the front door open and went to check it out. Kenzo walked in with bags in his hands.

"Damn, Stoic, you look like shit. Dad really fucked you up. Here, I got you food and medicine. Put this shit on your eye. You're starting to turn four different colors there," he said with a chuckle as he put the bags on the counter and threw me a container.

I caught it. He didn't leave me. He was out getting me food. My brother was still by my side. When everyone had turned their back on me, Kenzo was still there, covering my six.

I gripped the container hard in my hands, and a tear left my eye. I didn't deserve Kenzo. He noticed I was losing it again and pulled me in for a hug.

"It's gonna be OK. We'll get you out of this mess, together. Remember?" he said, and I nodded. He let me go and went back to taking everything out of the bags.

"It took me this long because I went to Ava's house to see Ian, went home to pick up some food, and got to talk to Dad and Erik. I got you good news and bad news. Which one do you want first?" he asked.

"How is Emmerson doing?" Nothing was more important to me than her.

"That's the bad news. We don't know. My mom, your mom, and Emmerson disappeared. Dad thinks they are together, but he has no idea where," he said, passing me some bread.

"What do you mean they don't know?" I just held onto the bread without eating it.

"They don't know. Nobody saw them leave. Apparently, after downing your ass, they went drinking, and Emmy, Mom, and Ida took off," he explained. "By the time Dad came back home at midnight, they were already gone. Don't worry. I'm sure she is safe. They must be together. This is a small village, so we'll find them. Give them some time." I nodded. I was planning on giving her time, anyway.

"What's the good news?" I said as the door opened. In walked Andreas and Dad.

"They want to talk to you. They promise they won't beat you up. I already explained some things to them," Kenzo said, pointing at them.

Ah, fuuuuuuck! I didn't think I was ready for it. I put the bread down and walked closer to them.

What did I have left to lose? My right eye?

"Kenzo told us you took a bullet for him. He said you almost died," Andreas said, and I narrowed the only eye I had open at Kenzo. I told him not to fucking tell anyone about it.

"He said it was dangerously close to your heart and that it took you almost two months to recover. Why didn't you call us? Your mom or I would have gone to the North and helped you," my dad said with sadness on his face.

"I'm OK. I didn't want you guys to worry." My voice was raspy, my throat still hurt.

"You saved my son's life putting your own life at risk." Andreas shook his head. "I wanted to hate you for what you did, but I can't. You have loved Emmerson ever since the first time you saw her. I saw your eyes light up each and every time you saw her, year after year. You took care of her, often forgetting to take time for yourself. With your little hands, you made gifts for my daughter and combed her hair every night before putting her down to sleep. You were always there, helping, keeping your promise, and doing your best. What the fuck happened, Stoic?" Andreas asked, and I didn't know what to say.

"I... I..." Nothing came out.

"Kenzo also told us about what happened between Emmerson and you right after you arrived here for your break and what happened before you left. He told us about the conversation you guys had, too," Dad said, pointing between Kenzo and me. I frowned my eyebrows, narrowing my eye at Kenzo again. Kenzo just shrugged his shoulders.

Fucking Kenzo told Andreas I fingered his daughter. I couldn't believe it! Perfect! Just what I needed to make a painfully awkward conversation worse.

Hey Andreas, I abused your daughter, but only because I fingered her when she was sixteen, and she liked it, so I assumed she would want it again and went for it without thinking.

Yeah, that should do it. Thanks, Kenzo. "I'm so sorry, I should have known better." That was all I could say. What an embarrassing mess I'd gotten myself into. I shook my head and palmed my face.

"Tell us what happened and be specific. We need to understand," my dad demanded.

I took in a deep breath.

Where to start?

"First thing I did when we arrived home was to look for her. Imany told me Emmy was at the river, so I ran there. When I arrived, she was swimming. I called for her, and she swam to me. She got out of the water–basically naked–and jumped into my arms. She was happy to see me and smiling. She fucking jumped naked in my arms. I never thought she was not gonna be into it. It didn't cross my mind. I..." I took a deep breath in.

"I started to... go for it, and she got nervous," I continued. "She has acted like that before, so I just kept going. I... took her to the cave behind the waterfall, and she still didn't say anything. I... I... I gave her oral sex, and... she came. I never thought she didn't want it; I just thought she was nervous. I... deflowered her, and she cried. I thought the pain was going to pass soon, but it didn't.

"It was somewhere around that moment that I lost my mind and was consumed with pleasure. I wasn't thinking, but I was too far gone to stop. She kept crying, and she cried the whole time. It's all my fault. I misread everything. It's all on me. I should have stopped, but I didn't. I'm so sorry. I never wanted to hurt her. That's the last thing I wanted," I added while scratching the inside of my fingers with my nails.

"Knowing what happened before between you two, I do understand you were confused at first. But why the fuck didn't you stop when she was crying?" Andreas asked.

"I wanted... I needed to... feel... normal. I... I have... I have some side effects. It's not what... It should not be an excuse for what I did. I... don't want that to be an excuse. Never mind, I messed up. It's on me. I'll get it under control. Now I know, and I won't let it happen again. Never again," I said, noticing my rambles weren't making too much sense. I fucking hated to admit it, but my mind was fucked up badly.

"What do you mean?" Andreas said, and Dad walked closer to me.

"We got PTSD, Dad," Kenzo answered for me from the kitchen. "Everything is still too recent, so it's quite bad. Anything could trigger it. I have it too. I, too, would fuck girls very hard while my mind wandered, trying to feel anything but... anything but the recoil." Kenzo said, looking into the distance. His eyes looked like mine tended to get from time to time. We made it back, but we were fucked, both of us.

Dad pulled me in for a hug. "I'm so sorry, son. I didn't know. Why didn't you tell me?"

"I'm OK, Dad. I'll figure this out. I'll get it under control." I tried to reassure him,

"Don't worry, Uncle. He is not alone. We went through hell together and will get out of it together, right, Stoic?" Kenzo told him, and I nodded.

He was right. I was so happy to be back that I didn't realize we were still trapped there. We were still trapped in hell. Kenzo patted my dad's back, and Dad pulled him in for a hug.

"You have to stop keeping shit like this to yourself, Stoic. We can't help you if we don't fucking know what's happening." Andreas pulled me in for a hug, too.

"I'm so sorry, Andreas," I told him as he patted my back.

"I'm sorry I beat you down. You look like shit," Andreas chuckled.

"Nah, I deserved it," I said, hugging him tighter.

"Yeah, you did. I still don't want you close to Emmy. Give her time," he said, and I nodded.

· · · · · · · · · · · · ● ● ● ● ● ● ● ● ● · · · · · · ·

-Three weeks later-

Ihadn't seen Emmerson in weeks. I was desperate. I was so worried about her that I could barely sleep. I had only seen my mom once. We had a conversation, and she assured me Emmy was okay. Imany too. She told me Emmerson was safe and well, but they never said where she was. I knew Mom would take good care of my girl, but still, I was concerned. She said Emmerson wasn't ready to face me yet, which meant she was still affected. I understood why she wouldn't want to see me, but it still hurt me.

After that conversation with Dad and Andreas, they started to slowly warm up to me again. They weren't happy with me, but they weren't angry either. Imany, too, wasn't as mad as when I had first told her. She even hugged me. Kenzo telling them I almost died for him somehow got them all to calm down and listen. I didn't like that they found out about it, but I was glad I hadn't lost my family. All I needed now was to apologize to Emmy.

Every day I went to her house, hoping she had returned. I walked around the village for about two hours every day, looking for her before returning home. I went to all the places I knew she liked. I walked to the river, the meeting house, and the park. I walked the streets, and I went everywhere. I went at different times every day but, so far, no luck. I even went to her best friend's house and asked for her every so often. I had even asked fucking Landon. I hated his face.

When I wasn't looking for Emmerson, I was working my ass off trying to get the house ready. Since I couldn't sleep anyway, I worked day and night during the first week. After I finished everything inside, I took one day to clean the whole house thoroughly. I had been working on whatever was left of our furniture, but that was not much. Dad came by and helped me sometimes, although he still didn't talk much with me. Kenzo came by with Ian every once in a while.

Ian was super cute. Kenzo made a handsome child. He had Ava's hair color but with Kenzo's curl. He looked so much like Kenzo. It was difficult to believe he was a dad. Ever since we came back, he hadn't fucked around with anyone, partly because he didn't have any time to. I knew he was staying with Ava most nights. He was changing, and he was truly happy with his kiddo. I loved being an uncle. I was going to spoil that little fella rotten.

I couldn't wait to marry Emmy and start our family. I wanted to help her forget everything and make her happy. It might take some time, but I was sure she'd come around. She had to. I didn't know what I would do without her.

Today, Dad and Uncle Andreas went to pick materials up in a nearby town and took my truck with them. Since I didn't have much left to do at home, I was just going to walk around and stay at my dad's. Dad told me Mom was working today, so that meant Emmy was alone. I didn't want her to feel lonely.

I went to Imany's and talked to her before she headed out. She was on her way to see her parents, who lived near the edge of the village. She told me she left me food and told me to make sure I ate it. Imany knew I was not eating like I used to eat.

Ethan was at home but was heading out as well. He told me he had plans with Amelia. He apparently had a romantic evening planned and told me not to wait up for him. With that, I knew Amelia was not going to be at home. I wouldn't even bother passing by asking for Emmy. Kenzo was with Ava and Ian. He told me I could join them, but I didn't want to interrupt them. They needed time to catch up.

I ate the food Imany left for me and cleaned the dishes for her. Since I was already at it, I swept and dusted the kitchen and the living room. I stood in front of Emmerson's door, and my chest tightened. I missed her so much. I put my hand on the handle but didn't have the strength to open her door, so I left.

For some reason, I went to the train station. I remembered how happy she was to see me the first time I returned. How beautiful she looked when running towards me. Her loose hair flying as she ran. I couldn't even imagine that I could see her running into my arms in a more beautiful way than when I saw her in the river.

She was happy then, too, just like before. I fucking ruined it all. I wouldn't say it was because she was practically running naked towards me, but no, I already had my mind set on seducing her as soon as possible. Thinking about it, I hadn't thought about sex during this whole time. Not once had I jerked off or thought about her sexually. Maybe it was because I was too worried, or maybe it was because I was too ashamed. Either way, I felt as if I lost it, that burning need of wanting to be inside her. That thing she gave me on my birthday in a small empty box.

Wanting to remember that beautiful day, I decided to trace our steps back to the house. I walked to the park with my head low, looking for that bench, our bench. From a distance, I saw there were people already sitting on it. I was about to turn around when I recognized Landon's fucking face. Next to him was a girl with a shawl and curly hair, just like Emmerson's.

No fucking way!

My heart stopped before starting to beat faster. I felt warm blood pumping out of my heart and spreading quickly through my chest. I started walking slowly at first. The closer I got, the clearer it was. That was my Emmerson. I saw Landon get closer to her, and my steps became faster.

Landon threw his arm around her. Fuck no! I ran. I told this motherfucker I would fucking break his arm next time he touched her, and I was not kidding. I was gonna rip his arm off, and I was going to enjoy doing it.

As I got closer to them, I slowed down, so I could sneak behind him. I was not letting this fucker escape alive like last time. I saw him drop his arm further down and move her hair away from her face with his other hand before he started to talk.

"Look at me, Emmy. If Stoic hurt you, that means he doesn't deserve you, period. You are better off far away from him." That motherfucker wanted to take Emmy away from me. Over my dead body.

"But what if–" Emmy started to say something, but I took Landon's arm off her back and snapped it like a toothpick. The bone broke through his skin, blood spurting all over. The fucking cunt screamed like a bitch, and I grabbed him by the neck, lifted him, and threw him hard on the ground like the turd he was.

I knew my Emmy was there, but I didn't look at her. I had to kill this bastard first. Out of all my kills, this was the only one I'd fucking enjoy.

As soon as Landon landed on the ground, I started kicking him violently and stomping on him, wanting to break every bone in his disgusting body. I was squishing him under my feet like the fucking bug he was.

Emmerson started to run away, and I snapped out of it, immediately forgetting Landon. My heart was beating fast, remembering the last time she ran from me. I couldn't let her go.

I screamed her name as I ran to her. "Emmerson, stop!" She didn't; she just ran faster. She looked terrified.

"Emmerson, fucking stop." I kept running after her, getting closer and closer. She ran fast, but she couldn't outrun me. I caught her and held on to her by her hips, pulling her back toward me.

"Fucking stop, Emmy. Stop, baby." I hugged her tightly from behind, and she started thrashing around and screaming. She was kicking me and trying to escape from my arms with all her strength. I held onto her tighter. I was scared she'd hurt herself trying to run as she had last time.

"Let me go! Let me go! Help." Emmerson screamed desperately, and I felt like shit. I was not going to hurt her. I'd never hurt her.

"Fuck, Emmy. Stop. I won't hurt you, baby. Stop, please." I tried to soothe her, but she didn't stop fighting me. I kept hugging her tightly and turned her around, putting her face on my chest.

She cried, and I kept one hand on her head and the other one on her back. I was so sorry, Emmy. I kissed her head and rocked her back and forth to calm her down. My chest moved up and down hard against her with every painful breath I took.

"It's OK, baby!" I wasn't only trying to soothe her. I was comforting myself, too. She was crying. She had no idea how much it hurt me to see her crying.

"It's OK. It's OK. I found you." I caressed her hair and kept hugging her. There was no way I was letting her go.

"Let me go, Stoic," she said, crying with the saddest voice I had ever heard coming from her. It broke my heart. She stopped fighting me. She was tired and weak. I leaned down, took her legs with my right hand, and held her back with my left, picking her up. I held her close to my chest and started walking.

She was still crying when she pushed herself further into my chest and pulled my shirt over her face, not wanting to see me. I didn't mind. I'd let her do whatever made her more comfortable.

I took the short way back to her house. She cried softly all along the way, with her face hidden. I didn't talk. I just walked, wanting to take her to the safety of her home fast.

I had to have this conversation with her. I was ashamed to show my face, but I had to do it. She needed to know how sorry I was. I was going to apologize and hope for the best.

I love you so much, Emmy. Please give me a chance. I'll never let you down again.

THIRTY-ONE

EMMERSON

Emmerson 18

Stoic 23

"We need to talk." Stoic put me down on my room's floor and closed the door behind him. He had walked us to my home as I cried on him all along the way.

The house was empty. Dad and Uncle Erik were in a village to our east to pick up some materials and wouldn't be home until tomorrow. Mom was visiting Grandma on the opposite side of the village that we lived in, and she wouldn't be home until late at night. Ida was catching up with her work after the whole deflowering debacle, and Kenzo was spending the day with his son, Ian. I didn't know where Ethan was, but I guess that he was with Amelia. He was the only one that could come by and save me, but he never came back home early, so it was not likely. I was screwed.

"I don't want to talk to you." I stood tall and faced him. It was time. I needed to be firm with him. He had always acted as if he had authority over me, but that was changing right now. Now that I was facing him, I noticed he still had traces of bruises on his face. Surely from the beating that my father had given him. He well deserved it. I wished I was there to see it.

Stoic shook his head before insisting, "No, Emmy, we need to talk, and we are going to talk, now."

"I said no. I know you don't understand what no means, so I'm going to put it simply for you... When I say NO, you leave me alone! OK?" I made some little hand gestures to make it look more obvious.

"Don't get on my nerves, Emmerson," Stoic said under his breath. He was trying to control the volume of his voice and his breathing.

"Or what? Hmm? Are you gonna force me, Stoic? Again?" Those words left my mouth, and he fell silent. That was a low blow. I saw it in his face. He looked hurt, and his eyes turned glassy. He took a couple of deep breaths.

"Emmerson, I know I hurt you. I know you don't want to see me now, but I can't wait. This conversation can't wait. We need to talk, Emmy. If you don't want to talk, then don't–just listen," he said, trying to remain calm. I could hear it was hard for him to speak. It was like he had a knot making his deep voice crack.

"Not now." I shook my head and looked away from him. I didn't want to face him, not now. It was too soon for me. I wrapped my arms around myself. Stoic fixed his blue eyes on me. His mouth opened and closed multiple times before anything could come out of it.

He walked forward. "I'm sorry, Emmy. Let me..." Stoic tried to take my hand in his, but I pulled away. I didn't want his hands to touch me.

"Emmy," he tried again, and once again, I moved my hand away.

"No! You raped me, Stoic. I trusted you, and you broke me. You fucking broke me," I said with tears in my eyes.

His hand dropped. He was defeated. I had never seen Stoic this affected. The man standing in front of me wasn't the giant angry Stoic I had known my whole life. In a matter of seconds, he became weak and small somehow. You could see the shame and regret in his eyes. His body started to shiver.

"I'm... really sorry, Emmy." Tears, Stoic was crying. I didn't know what to do. These past three weeks, I had wanted him to be hurt. I wanted him to hurt as much as I did, and he was. Now what? I had never seen Stoic cry like this.

"I'm so fucking sorry, Emmy... Please forgive me." He started sobbing. His shoulders shook, and he tried to hold back his tears and failed. I could do nothing but remain quiet. Look at him becoming as destroyed as I was, maybe worse. Ida's words ran through my mind. He was suffering too. We were both suffering.

"I'm angry, Emmy. I'm angry with myself because I hurt you. I swore to myself that I would always protect you, but I lost my mind and hurt you, Emmy." More tears. He was even hyperventilating. I had never seen him this exposed, this vulnerable. I felt bad for him.

He tried to calm himself. "I should have said this a long time ago, Emmy. You should have known long ago, so there was no confusion between us. And no confusion about what you have meant to me, but for whatever stupid reason, I never did." He dried his tears with the back of his hand. He was looking at the floor and not at me. His face and his eyes were almost as red as his hair. His fingernails were scratching the inside of his fingers. He looked like a lost child.

"I have never been good at communicating. Worse if it has to do with feelings or shit like that, but that doesn't mean I don't have them. Fuck, I act like a rock sometimes, and I know that. But I'm not one, Emmerson." He raised his eyes to mine, and I could see the intensity of the storm swarming in his. I could see this was painful for him to do. He must have been fighting himself for a long time now.

"Emmerson, I have always loved you, ever since the day you were born, and I will love you until the moment I take my last breath." I kept looking into his eyes. He wasn't lying. He loved me.

If he loved me, why would he do that to me?

nothing but make my existence miserable, but even with all his flaws, he was always there. He always took care of me. In his weird jealous way, he cared.

"I'm beyond sorry. I will make it up to you even if it's the last thing I do." He was determined. He moved closer, and I stepped back as his hand reached for my face. His hand shook, and I saw more pain in his eyes.

"Please forgive me. I know I'm a fucking idiot, but I've always been your fucking idiot, Emmy," he said in a low voice. Mine? Does he think he's mine? Is that what he meant when he said he was taken? Did he really save himself for me? Did he wait almost a decade for me?

I kept walking back, but I ran out of space, and he took another step forward. My bed was right behind me.

"Please." That was a plea. He was not asking, he was begging.

"I don't think I can, Stoic. You hurt me, and I... I'm..." I was confused. All this was just too much, too fast, too soon. He got closer to me, and I sat on the bed.

"I... I... need space." Literally. He was still getting closer. I started leaning back, and he leaned forward. His hands landed by my side, holding himself over me, and my eyes immediately locked on them. What was he doing?

I felt him getting closer, and when I looked up, his face was super close to mine.

I rested my weight on my elbows, and Stoic paused for a long time, never moving his blue eyes from me. His chest rising and falling fast before slowly calming. He said nothing, and he didn't make a move. He just studied me. His deep blue eyes moved from my eyes to my nose, then to my lips, then to my neck, and back to my eyes again. I took a couple of deep breaths, and for some reason, I didn't feel like I had to run away from him anymore. I was calm, my mind gently floating in a sea of his intense blue spheres. My reflection staring back at me in his pupils. Stillness. He was so close, I could feel the heat coming from his body.

"I love you." Stoic broke the deafening silence. I remained quiet.

"I love you so much," he said again, looking into my eyes. Once again, I didn't respond.

What could I say to that?

"I'm madly in love with you, Emmerson." His eyes traveled to my lips and then back to my eyes.

He leaned in, and I stopped him. I placed a hand on his chest. "You are going too fast," I said before thinking. I realized too late what I had just said. There was no taking it back. He stopped, looked at my hand, and pulled back a little.

"So, as long as I go slower, it's okay?" Stoic asked, his face brightening.

Oh, crap! I gave him hope.

"No, I mean. I... what I said was... I..." He leaned in slowly.

"I'll go slow, Emmy." This idiot doesn't know what I meant to say when I said it was too fast, or he just doesn't fucking care.

He kissed me once, a very soft, light kiss, and looked into my eyes. "I'll give you time."

Stoic took in what looked like a painful breath, pulled back, and sat next to me. "I'll give you time," he said, nodding his head.

He backed up further from me, increasing the space between us. My body immediately missed his heat.

"I'll wait for as long as you need me to. All I'll ask of you are two things. Let me help you heal, and... give me a chance to prove myself to you." He sounded sad. I could tell the biggest beating he got was from himself. He hated himself for what he did.

Stoic set his eyes on the floor. "I'm not going to make any excuses. What I did was wrong, very wrong, and I will regret it for the rest of my life. That's a shame I have to carry, but not you. I want you to be healthy, and I want you to be happy."

I sat up and placed my hands on my lap. We were on opposite corners of my bed. I couldn't help but study his sad figure. He put his hands on his lap and started to fidget with his fingers again. I hadn't realized it before, but that was something he did when he was nervous.

"I don't deserve you, but I don't have the strength to live without you, either. You are a strong, independent woman, Emmerson. You always were. You don't need an asshole like me around you for nothing. Make no mistake, it's me who needs you," Stoic said, still not looking at me. I remained quiet. I did not know what to say. For the first time in our lives, Stoic was the one talking, and I was the one listening.

"Give me a chance to show you just how much I love you, how important you are to me. Even if it's just a small one. I'll take whatever you want to give. We'll take it slow, OK," he said, finally searching my eyes.

I didn't know what to say, so I said nothing. We looked at each other for the longest time in silence. My mind was trying to make sense of all the things that had happened. I started to feel like my reality wasn't *real* anymore. I didn't know what to believe. The Stoic across from me was a different person. For every

this time, we had been living the same but different moments. If what Ida told me was truly as it seemed to be, then I might have misjudged everything ever since the very beginning. I misjudged him.

We stayed quiet for a while longer. My mind was going in a thousand different directions, with all of them leading me to the same place, and that was Stoic's sad figure across from me.

There was a question that kept swarming in my mind. Something that, no matter what I did, didn't make sense to me.

"Why did you tell everyone?" I asked in a low voice, breaking the silence.

One of his brows twitched. "Because there is nothing and no one in this world more important to me than you," he said, looking into my eyes once more.

"You needed help, and I wasn't going to stand by and see you suffer alone. No fucking way," Stoic admitted. "I rather get beat by your dad a thousand times than leave you hurting all by yourself for a fucking minute. Never again," he said, shaking his head and clenching his jaw. His hands fidgeted again.

I don't know why, but that made me smile. Maybe it was the way he said it. The more I looked at him, the more he resembled a child. Thinking back, he never hurt me, even when he got angry at me. He never hesitated to put himself at risk for me. I remembered his bleeding scratches after I climbed that tree. He never really complained about it. He never complained about anything I did, and

I did lots of things to bother him. I nodded.

"Landon?" I asked him.

"I don't wanna fucking talk about him," he said quickly and without hesitation. I bit my lip, trying to hold a smile back, and laughed internally. Oh gosh, I was so evil. Poor Landon must still be screaming on the ground. Stoic's face got serious, and he looked like he wasn't done with him. Landon should leave the continent before Stoic got to him again. I didn't know why I found it so funny when Stoic got angry. Maybe that was why I used to bother him so much.

We stayed there, talking for hours. I would ask some questions, and he would give me short answers. Most of what he said were apologies and promises to never hurt me again. He explained to me that it was all his fault and that he was confused when he hurt me. But he didn't want that to be an excuse, so he was going to own his mistakes.

He asked me about those two times he had touched me before. He wanted to know if I did want that or had he misread me again. I said I did, and he let out a sigh of relief. If I was honest, I did more than just want them. The second time he touched me, I would have begged for it. I didn't tell him, though, because I didn't want to boost his ego.

He asked me if I stopped wanting it as soon as I felt pain when he first put it in me, and I realized he had no clue I didn't want it from the very start. I could tell it pained him when I told him. He rarely looked into my eyes after he learned that.

He swore he would give his life for me and that he would do anything to help me heal. I nodded, but I was not planning on fully trusting him just yet. He asked me if he could visit me and talk to me, and I agreed. I didn't think he wanted to hurt me. It was, in fact, the complete opposite.

During the whole time we talked, our bodies didn't move from where we were sitting, but somehow, I felt like the distance between us slowly closed with each passing minute.

THIRTY-TWO

EMMERSON

Emmerson 18
Stoic 23

I moved back to my parent's house. As we agreed, Stoic came by to visit. He came by to visit every day, twice a day. He would visit in the mornings and the evenings.

During the first week, he brought me wildflowers and pastries every day. He would always sit or stand a short distance away from me and start asking how I was doing before staying quiet for a long time, watching me stuff my face. For some odd reason, he liked watching me eat. If he kept feeding me like that, I'd end up fat like a cow. My belly would show sooner than I was expecting. He still didn't know I was pregnant. I hadn't told him. I told Mom and Ida I wanted to tell him myself, but I hadn't yet.

He always stayed just out of my reach. There was no way I could accidentally touch his hands or bump into him. He always stayed three feet away, sometimes further. Even when I asked him to pass something to me, he would place it near me but never put it directly in my hands. He was avoiding me. I thought I should have been the one avoiding him, not the other way around. I wanted to close the gap between us, but when I stepped forward, he stepped back. The only way for me to get close was to sneak up on him from behind, but as soon as he turned and saw me, he would take three steps back.

After ten days or so of that, I was tired of it. I confronted him and asked him why he always kept his distance, and I could tell my question took him by surprise. He said he didn't want me to be uncomfortable. I found that to be a cute answer, but I told him to stop it. He did. After that, I would sit close to him and watch him get all nervous about it and fidget with his fingers. I didn't know why I had to always find a way to bother him.

A week after that, he had a long talk with me, and he convinced me to speak to a therapist about the rape. I didn't want to, but he practically begged me to. He said he had already talked to Ida and that she had already made an appointment for me. He said we could always cancel it, but he really wanted me to give it a try.

I completed two sessions of psychotherapeutic treatment and then decided that it was not for me. It was helpful, but to be truthful, I went there more for him than me. I was feeling okay, I guess. There wasn't a trauma therapist in our village, so we had to go to a different town.

Stoic took me. To my surprise, Stoic had a small truck. It was comically small and only seated three. He said he was going to need it to move materials for his new work. He never said how he got it.

We brought Ida with us to my appointment. It was a forty-minute drive, and Ida sat between us and talked with me the whole way. I was glad I had someone to talk to along the way since Stoic was so quiet. I got sick and puked halfway there, but I told him I was carsick. That was partially true. I was not used to riding in a car, but the morning sickness was not helping either.

I wanted to keep Ida with me during the session, so she stayed by my side. Stoic waited for us outside. When we were done with the session and left the office, he had cheese danishes for me. That made me laugh. He must know I loved them. I never found out if he brought them with him or if he got them somewhere around the therapist's office.

I took my time to carefully observe him, trying to read him. To trace back every memory I had of him, good and bad. I was still confused by him. It was so difficult to read him. He said he loved me, but he barely cracked a smile around me.

I often found myself distracted with the smallest things, like the way his Adam's apple moved when he talked and the way his hair never stayed where he put it. The more I looked at him, the more handsome he became to me. The more I thought about him, the more I felt myself craving to have him nearby.

I had to laugh. Stoic sucked at dating if that was what he was trying to do. It'd been three weeks, and he was still distant. He was so nervous around me that, most of the time, he just sat quietly next to me. I often would catch him looking at me, and he would quickly turn his head away or look at the floor. I was ready to move on, but he never got close to me. I guess it would have to be me making the moves.

Seeing him like that brought many old forgotten feelings back. She was not completely lost. I still could feel her. I still had her, somewhere deep inside me. She was still there, full of life. I felt her rise and laugh maniacally. Hello, my old friend! My inner brat was back. A big smile spread across my face faster than I could hide it. I was going to bother him.

That afternoon, I made one hundred different excuses to get us alone. I convinced him to take me to his parent's house, knowing well neither of them would be there. Once there, I asked to see his room, so he took me. Once in his room, I said I wanted a nap and that I wanted him to spoon me as he used to do until I fell asleep. He fell for all of it.

Stoic moved his blanket and made space for us to lie down. I sat on his childhood bed and pulled my blanket. Stoic laid next to me and hesitated before throwing his arm around me. I turned in his arms and faced him. I knew he was hesitant, but he didn't attempt to say anything to me. I ran my fingers through his beard, over his brows, and down his nose, just like I had all those years ago. When I got closer and captured his lips with mine, his eyes widened. Much like our first kiss, I pressed my lips to his, and he blushed tomato red. A short moment passed, and he started to kiss me back.

His moist lips moved on mine, and he closed his eyes. Stoic had a hand caressing my jaw, asking for permission. He gently pushed my jaw down and slipped his tongue inside my mouth. He held me pressed to him and moved his tongue inside me, savoring me. My heart was beating fast. Stoic didn't open his eyes. He kept kissing me passionately.

It wasn't a harsh or desperate kiss; it was heated, yet soft. He was trying to be gentle. He slowly slid on top of me, holding his weight on his forearms, and kept kissing me. Both of us were consumed by this heated kiss. His strong hands very gently touched my body. Each hair on my skin stood up at his touch. He moved his hands south and started to open my legs to make space for himself. As soon as he did that, I stopped him.

It was a test. Stoic passed it. He did stop. He was confused, but he didn't complain. Stoic kissed me and backed up. He was even sweet about it and held me in his arms for a nap like I had asked him to. He didn't try anything, nothing at all, then we just napped.

The next day, I did it again. This time I let him open my legs. He ran his warm hands in between my thighs and caressed me softly. I allowed him to pull my skirt up and position himself atop me. When he started to pull down his pants, I stopped him. Once again, he stopped, no questions asked. He fixed our clothes and took me for a walk after. We sat by the river, and he listened to me talk for hours like we used to do when I was little.

The day after that, I repeated my act. He must have had purple balls by then. He had no idea I was messing around with him. This time, I let him take my top off and kiss my breasts. He licked and savored my nipples until they were hard and sensitive. He ground his hardness against my thighs, and my core heated with need. Stoic took his shirt off, and his inked skin on mine felt divine. I almost didn't stop it. It felt so good.

He opened my legs, situated himself between them, and once again, when his pants went down, I stopped it. I bit my lip and held my laugh back. This time he took a deep breath before backing off, but he didn't complain. I almost felt bad about it, but no. I went home and laughed out loud. There was a special place for me in Hel with my name in big, bold letters on it.

After that, he started to get suspicious of me. The next day I tried to do the same thing, but he didn't fall for it. He said he was busy and that he needed to go to work. I had never seen him leave my house faster than that. I sat in my living room and bit my lip. The joke was on me now. I wanted him—desperately.

The next day, I invented a more credible excuse to keep him nearby. I told Stoic I was feeling sick and that I was all alone. It wasn't a complete lie. Mom left early in the morning to spend the day with relatives as she did every so often, and I was also feeling sick, although it wasn't anything I couldn't handle myself. It was just some light morning sickness.

I convinced Stoic to help me and put me to sleep. I had him on my bed with me and started kissing him, trying to lose myself in his arms once more. To taste those addictive lips. He kissed me back, then hesitated.

"Are you OK?" I asked, an innocent look on my face. I knew well what his problem was—me.

"Yeah, are you?" He stroked my hair softly and ran his hand lovingly over my back.

"I'm getting better, but I still don't feel completely well yet," I said with a childish pout, and he kissed my lower lip softly. He looked into my eyes before taking my lip in his once more. This time he softly pulled it in his mouth as he kissed it. He kept doing that, and soon the kiss became heated. Just like I wanted it. He kissed me some more and then stopped.

"I think we need to stop it here, Emmy," he said with his eyes full of lust.

"Why?" I said, pulling him to me once more.

He kissed me again and pulled back. "I can't, Emmy." He shook his head.

"You can't what?" I asked, biting my lip, knowing exactly what he meant. I was driving him crazy.

"I'm afraid I won't be able to stop next time you tell me to. We should leave it here. It's for the best," he said and then started to stand up. I took his hand and pulled him back down.

"Then don't." I kissed him hard. He kissed me once and pulled back, his fiery blue eyes searching mine. I said nothing, just pulled him in again, and kept kissing his delicious lips. I caressed his thick beard as we kissed.

His kiss was sweeter, and I felt myself melting slowly into it. I was getting tingly all over, and my skin was starting to get goosebumps.

I opened my mouth and licked his lower lip. He opened his and let me enter dick pressed against my thighs. Everything was building up, but this time I was not going to stop it.

He trailed kisses down my neck, and his hands started caressing my chest. He was being gentle, the warmth of his hands making my nipples stand at attention. My hands immediately went to his long hair. I undid his bun and ran my fingers through his curls. Our child would have crazy hair for sure. Luckily, Stoic was good at combing hair.

"Emmy?" That was a question. He was asking for permission. He was still kissing my neck. I could tell he was nervous. If I asked him to stop at that moment, he might have had a heart attack.

"Yes." That was my answer. There was no way in the world I could stop now. I might have been hormonal or something, but I felt like there was a fire in me that only he could ease.

Stoic looked into my eyes, searching, questioning if he had heard me correctly. "Em–"

"Ahh! Just fuck me already." There was silence. His eyes were wide, revealing his disbelief. I guess he was not expecting me to be this forward.

Get ready, Stoic, because if you thought you'd have a trembling kitten under you, you're terribly mistaken.

His face changed from surprised to amused, and he gave me the sexiest smirk I had ever seen before swiftly taking my pants and underwear off all in one go. He then took off his shirt with one hand and threw it across the room. There he was, my Nordic god. From then on, that body would be my religion, and I would gladly get on my knees and worship the fuck out of him. The man was perfect. I always knew that even when I called him hideous a thousand times.

My eyes traveled to his abs and lower to his perfect V-shaped lines. *Wow!* He lowered his zipper and pulled his pants and briefs below his hips. His hard dick sprang out and slapped his stomach, the head angry red and his shaft veiny.

Fuck me, he was huge!

It must be almost the size of my forearm, as thick too. No wonder why I was so hurt before. Stoic had curly red hair above it, but not too much. I could see he was trimmed. He was beautiful.

He saw me looking at his massive monster, and he took it in his hand and fisted himself slowly, making it leak pre-cum. My eyes widened.

Ah, fuck! I wanted it.

"Aren't you sick, Emmerson? Maybe we should stop," he said with a grin. My eyes narrowed. He knew I was lying.

Forget what I said. I wanted it now.

I opened my mouth to speak, but he must have known what I wanted because he rapidly grabbed my knees, pulled me to him, and spread my legs open. Blue eyes looked at my dripping wet pussy, and I saw him smirk. He lowered his mouth, heading straight for my soaked slit.

Holy fuck! Yes.

Stoic gave me a long lick from bottom to top with his flattened tongue, and I saw stars. His beard tickled my thighs, but I couldn't care less. He slowly separated my lips and did it again, long and wet, his tongue savoring me like a delicious candy. When he got to the top, he circled his tongue around my clit.

Uff, that felt so good.

"Mmm... So fucking good." I heard him say before his tongue came down on me once more. As he deliciously flicked my clit, my hands grabbed the sheets below me and fisted them tightly.

"Uuhh!" I sounded super horny, maybe because I was. I was melting like ice cream, and Stoic was licking me up.

His mouth closed around my sensitive bud, and he sucked it like a lollipop. "Mmm, fuck," Stoic said under his breath. He was enjoying this. I raised my head to see him, and he had a hand wrapped around his hard cock, jerking himself off nice and slow.

The smacking of his lips on me caught my attention, and all of a sudden, his pace got faster. My hands went to his red curls, and I pulled him closer to me. He was hungrier, more desperate. His tongue invaded my insides, and his fingers started to rub my clit quickly. His wet, meaty tongue was doing wonders inside me. My back arched, and I raised my hips, wanting more of him inside me. "Mmm, gostoso!" I let out a little squeal, "Fuuuuuuuck!" It felt so fucking good.

Stoic slid his tongue out and replaced it with his middle finger, immediately touching a tender and very sensitive spot inside me toward the front of my pussy. Instead of moving his fingers in and out, he started moving as if signaling, "come here."

Oh, I was about to!

"Ahh, fuuuck!" My breath was ragged, my legs were shaking, and my eyes were rolling back in their sockets.

How the fuck was he making me feel this good? Where did he learn that?

He added another finger, and the pressure started to build in my whole body, making it stiffen up. I was trying to breathe in, but I couldn't seem to find any air.

"Don't fight it, just cum, baby." With that, he lowered his face and closed his mouth around my clit, licking and sucking it mercilessly.

I felt my body stiffen. "Oh fuck! Holy fuck, Stoic! Holy... Uhh! Uuhh!" I was cumming hard. Pure pleasure shooting fast all through me, making me throw my head back and open my mouth in a silent scream.

My body was convulsing. I had a hand wrapped in Stoic's hair and the other fisting the sheets above my head. My hips were bucking. Stoic grabbed one of my legs, prying me back open. I didn't even know I was closing them on him. He was still there, flicking and sucking my sensitive clit hard with his tongue and moving his fingers inside me, making that amazing sensation last longer.

"Stoic," I was begging. I pulled him up to me. When his face got close to mine, I kissed him hard, tasting myself on his lips. I still had a hand in his sleek hair. Our tongues once again savored each other.

"I can't wait," Stoic said against my lips, out of breath. He wanted the exact same thing I wanted. I spread my legs wider for him, and he pulled his pants a little further down, not wanting to lose time in taking them completely off. Maybe he didn't want to fall again on his face if I decided to run out. He quickly took my shirt and bra off and eyed my body with hunger.

Stoic took his hard cock in his hand and rubbed it along my wet slit. His thick mushroom head was oozing pre-cum.

"Tell me if it hurts, and I'll stop, OK?" I knew if I asked him to stop, it would take every ounce of willpower he had to actually stop, but he would do it.

I nodded my head, and he started pressing himself against me. As soon as his head entered me, I felt light stinging pain from the stretching, "Ah!"

"Are you OK?" he asked with his face red.

Holy fuck, was he?

He looked worried, so I quickly said, "Yes, don't stop." His warm, spongy wet tip slipped inside me, and I saw Stoic open his mouth in a silent moan and look into my eyes.

"Mmm," I said as I bit my lip. Both of our eyes traveled south and looked at where he entered me.

His mouth hung open while he pushed more of himself inside me, eyebrow frowning as if he was in pain.

His round head got somewhat stuck, but he still pushed in a bit further, "Ouch." I flinched a little. He was stretching me to the maximum.

"Do you want me to stop?" he asked, looking into my eyes. His deep voice this time sounded like he was out of energy. I thought this would hurt me, not him.

"No, it's okay. Just go slow. You are huge." A chuckle. I pulled a chuckle out of him in the middle of an attempt to penetrate me.

He tucked his face between my shoulder and neck and took a deep breath. He started to slowly push himself in me once again. I felt him put a hand over my head to hold me in place, and the other tightly grabbed the sheets beside us and squeezed the living hell out of them.

As his hard pole burrowed deeper inside me, Stoic let out a low groan. My hands went to his back, and I dug my nails into him.

Gosh, he was huge.

"Uhhh!" Stoic let out a moan. He reached the back of my vagina, and I could feel him press against my cervix. He was so big that he still had about three inches out that wouldn't fit in.

"Oh fuck. Oh fuck. Uuhh!" Stoic groaned again, his breathing super ragged. He held me tight and shuddered. He gave me a few short thrusts. His member was throbbing inside me, and I felt warmth being poured inside.

Did he just? Nah... Did he, though?

I looked at him, and his face was tomato red, biting his lip, breathing rapidly.

"Did you just..."

"Hmm?" His face was still next to my neck.

"Did you... Uhmm..."

Should I even ask?

"Huh?" He slowly lifted his head and looked into my eyes.

"Did you just... Did you just cum?" Strange conversation to have with a man that was evidently rock hard deep inside me.

"Yeah," he said with his face red.

"Oh! I... hmm... I..." He must have thought I was stupid and clueless.

He kissed my neck. "Don't worry, next time, I'll let you know."

Next time? Could he keep going?

He wasn't moving yet. It took him a few seconds to regulate his breathing, and then he looked into my eyes and gave me a soft peck on my lips. "I love you, Emmy."

What to say to that?

I mean... I loved him. I always had, always would, but I wasn't actually in love with him. It was all too soon. I always saw him as a brother, and there I was, with his dick buried deep inside me and pregnant with his child.

He must have read the confusion on my face and gave me a small smile. "It's OK. You don't have to say anything, Emmy." Oh, I was glad because that was about to be awkward.

"I... I'm okay. You can move." I wanted to change the conversation and get this thing going. I was super horny.

Stoic nodded. "Give me a second or two." He was red-faced.

Was I hurting him?

We stayed there, looking at each other without talking or moving for about a minute or so. His face never lost its redness that seemed to be from embarrassment. He looked like a naughty child that had just done something he shouldn't have. He was so cute.

"I... I'm going to move now, OK." Finally! I nodded to let him know I was ready. He very slowly pulled back. "Holy fuck, Emmerson, you are so tight," he said, and his dick twitched. I could feel everything, each and every one of his veins rubbing inside me. God, his dick felt great. It was nothing like the last time since there was no pain, only pleasure.

Stoic sat on his knees and slowly pushed himself back in. "Mmmm!" I couldn't hold it back. I bit my lip, and my hands held on to his strong tattooed arms. Those three horns of Odin had never looked so sexy. My eyes traveled down his strong arm, admiring his new tattoos.

Wait, was that me? Did he tattoo my face on his arm?

He held onto my hips tightly, distracting me from my thoughts.

Stoic let out a quiet grunt, then did it again, slowly pulling halfway out, then slowly pushing all the way in. My pussy was so wet, his cock was easily sliding in and out of me. His skin had goosebumps. "Uuhh, fuck. Damn, Emmy." His strong muscles were tensing, and his knuckles were getting white from how hard he was holding my hips. Delicious torture, that was what it felt like. My body was all hot and bothered. I could feel his cum running down my inner thigh as he pushed himself deeper inside me.

Stoic stilled deep inside me and gave me a hard look. His eyebrows frowned, and he looked angry. "What's happ–" He didn't let me finish.

"Fuck it!" he said with a dark voice.

What the hell? Why was he... Oh!

Before I could react, Stoic gave a hard, deep thrust. He gave another one and then another one, over and over, making them faster each time. He soon was wildly pounding into me.

"Holy shit! Ah, ah, ah! Oh, fu–Uuuhh." My eyes rolled back, and I moaned out loud like a crazy woman. Stoic was dicking me so good. Any doubt that he wasn't the man for me was being fucked out of my brain right at that moment. Any thought of him as my brother was immediately and irrevocably pounded out of me.

My tits were flopping up and down rapidly. Stoic took one in his hands and gave one a squeeze. After he let it go, he gave it a soft slap. "Ah!" My eyes were wide, and I saw Stoic biting his lip hard. He was moaning and grunting. He mouthed a hundred different things, but he never said them out loud.

Stoic's hips were moving really fast, pistoning his cock inside me. I had no idea Stoic knew how to move his hips like that. He stood on his knees, held onto my hips tighter, and lifted me up. He jerked my hips hard into him as if I was a weightless ragdoll, then, at the same time, his hips rolled into me uncontrollably. "Stoic! Mmm. Uuhhh! Uhhh!"

"Take that dick, Emmerson," he said in a very low voice, sounding possessed. My eyes widened, more heat rising in my core. He let my hips go and softly put his huge hand on my throat. His lips kept moving.

Was he dirty talking underneath his breath?

Maybe he thought I wouldn't like it, and he was holding back. He couldn't be more wrong. He kept pounding me fast. My heart was beating fast with excitement, his dick sliding wetly in and out of me rapidly. Holy fuck, Stoic liked it rough. Apparently, I did too.

"Uuhh! Uhh! Uhh!" His head fell back, his mouth fell open, and he started to moan louder. My mouth was open, too, but no sound came out of it. It was too good—he was fucking my brains out.

My eyes rolled back in their sockets again, and I felt my pussy getting extremely tight around him. I was about to cum. I was about to cum hard.

Stoic must have felt me getting tighter and demanded, "Eyes on me, baby."

I opened my eyes and tried to focus on the devil's blues. His hips were going faster, and every time he entered me, it sounded super wet, and our skin slapped together hard. I felt his heavy balls hit my ass.

"Cum on it, baby. Cum on my dick." He let go of my neck and cupped both of my breasts, giving them a light squeeze. He flicked his thumbs over my hard nipples.

"I'm cumming!" I said softly. I threw my head back and started convulsing, my body shaking violently as pleasure consumed every cell in my body.

"That's my girl." Stoic put his hand between us and rubbed my clit fast, making my orgasm stronger. My mind went blank, and as my body trembled, all I could feel was pure pleasure. He let me ride my orgasm for a little while longer, and then he gradually slowed down.

"Turn around. I want to see your ass." With one swift movement, he turned me around. I felt him moving and taking the rest of his pants off. I was exhausted and out of breath, and I didn't know how he could keep going.

"On all fours, Emmy." He pulled my hips up and moved me into place.

He pressed on my lower back slightly, making me arch my back, and then slowly thrust inside me. Stoic's hard and long strokes quickly got faster and faster. He went at it with pure abandon, at times with irregular strokes, making both of us moan out loud. He was a beast!

Holy fuck, what had I gotten myself into?

As he fucked me harder, my moans got more erratic. I was super sensitive, and Stoic just kept pounding away without giving me time to breathe or think. His hard thrusts moved me farther up on the bed. His moans got louder and more animalistic. "I don't wanna fucking stop." He wasn't. Stoic kept thrusting hard. He pushed my chest down on the bed and pressed me down, keeping me there with his hand on the back of my neck.

He didn't slow down. He was still pounding my pussy hard. I felt so full of him. The pressure was almost too much to handle.

"Uhh! So good." I was not lying.

Stoic pressed himself harder into me, ran his big hands from my abdomen to my chest, and lifted me up to him. He pressed my back against his chest and snaked a hand in between my breasts. He took my neck and tilted my head towards him, kissing me hard. Stoic devoured my lips at the same time he fondled my tits. They must have felt small in those huge hands.

I was drunk on him—his taste, his smell, his touch.

"Hold on." He put my hands on my bed's headboard while his hands trailed down my body. He gave me long and sensual thrusts.

One of his hands lurked between my legs, and he started rubbing circles around my erect clit.

Oh gosh, it was so good!

Stoic kissed my neck and caressed my tender pair. I loved how he paid attention to every part of my body. My juices and his cum lubricated his shaft perfectly, making it slippery for him to ease in swiftly.

His pace quickened, and so did his hand rubbing between my legs. "Uuh! Uhh! Yes! Yes! Mais forte!"

He started to thrust harder, and our sweaty bodies started making that slapping sound again. Stoic grabbed my neck again, tilted my head, and made me look into his eyes while moving faster with both his cock and his fingers.

He penetrated my mouth with his tongue and gave me a kiss filled with pure desire. He slapped my butt with a calloused hand and muffled my moan with his kiss. Stoic released my lips, and when I opened my eyes, there he was, The Dokken. He had the hottest shade of fire burning in him. I looked deep into his eyes and, with a sexy voice, said, "Monte-me. Monte-me, rápido e forte."

Stoic pummeled his dick hard into my pussy. Once, twice, three times. Faster and harder. His finger rubbing incredibly fast, building my pleasure more quickly than what my body was ready for. He started grunting and moaning. His moans sounded so sensual, and it turned me on even more.

While still holding onto my neck, he pressed my lower back down, making me arch for him. "Ah! Fuck, Stoic! Aah! Mmm!" I was getting close. Once my back was arched, just the way he wanted me, he spat on his fingers and moved them back to my core to deliver torturous touches to my clit. My legs started shaking, and he knew I was close.

"There you go, Emm. Take that thick cock all the way up your pussy like a good girl," he said in a very low voice. His dirty talk was so freaking hot!

Uhh! I was so close.

He was still slamming hard inside me and rubbing my clit.

"Uhh! Uuhh! Stoic! Stoic! I'm... I'm gonna...." My mind was blacking out. My toes were curling, air trapped in my throat.

"Emm, I'm gonna cum, baby. I'm gonna cum." He accelerated his pace, and I was out. That did it. My pussy started pulsing hard, and he let out a loud groan. My body shook, and I shouted his name at the top of my lungs. Knowing he was cumming made it so much sexier. It made me hungrier. Made me want more.

"Uhh! Uhhh! Shit!! Uhh! Fuck, I'm cumming!" His body started to stiffen, and he began to slow down his thrusts.

Oh, fuck no!

I wanted more. He made me addicted. His arms wrapped around my waist, and his face got lost in my hair. He was breathing hard.

"I want it!" I moaned out. I sounded desperate. I started lifting my hips and dropping them on him. I felt him grab me harder.

"Emm," was all he said. I wanted it so much. I let my hips loose like when dancing and started bouncing on his cock as fast as I could, impaling myself on it. "Fuck, Emmy. Uuhh! Uuhh!" I was not stopping. I was so close again.

"Baby, I can't. I can't." I didn't stop. Stoic started moaning out like a wounded animal. He was too sensitive. I'd call that payback. His legs were shaking hard, and he was completely out of breath. I was fucking the life out of him, milking him dry.

"Uuhh! Uuhh! I'm cumming!" There it was again, that addicting high. Pure pleasure. Stoic was my new drug.

"Fuuuuuuuuuuuuck!" I squealed. I was cumming hard. My head dropped back and landed on his chest. He held on with his shaky hands to my ribs and moaned loud, shivering. My pussy was pulsing on him tightly. I knew he could feel it too. I felt him twitch with every wave of my pleasure. His meat throbbed inside me, dripping more of his cum.

"Don't fucking move." He was squeezing me hard.

Oh! He should have known better. I was a brat.

I gave him another hard bounce, and he pulled out fast. He threw me on the bed, and his body dropped, exhausted, next to mine. "Holy shit, Emmerson!"

I couldn't stop it. A smile spread across my face, and I started to chuckle and laugh like a demented person. He glanced at me and bit his lower lip, eyes narrowed, watching me laugh. His chest rising and dropping fast.

"Do you forgive me?"

Yeah, I will. Well... partially.

"Only if you promise to make me cum this hard whenever I want it."

He nodded, "Done." Now he was the one smiling like a madman and laid on his back.

"Will you marry me?" he asked, looking up at the ceiling.

Would I?

I mean... I was already pregnant with his child, addicted to his dick, and used to having him in my face daily.

Did I see myself with anyone other than Stoic?

No, I really didn't. I knew for sure I didn't want to see Stoic anywhere near any other woman.

"Yeah, I guess." I was looking at the ceiling too. I didn't want to sound too interested. He still had a lot of making up to do.

He just nodded. We stayed there, lying by each other's side. I glanced at his softening cock and bit my lip. He noticed me doing it.

"Fuck, nah!" He turned over and covered his dick. He was so fuckling cute. Why hadn't I noticed that before?

"You promised! You liar!" I shook his arm.

"We are not married yet. Fuck, woman, you're gonna fucking kill me." His face was red.

Oh, Stoic, you are so screwed! You made this monster, now you'll have to live pleasing it. Wahahaha.

I'd let him be for the moment. I was not gonna tell him about my pregnancy until way after the wedding. Knowing him, he'd get all weird and protective, and I wanted many more nice and hard poundings like today.

The wedding. I was really marrying Stoic Dokken. I'd be Mrs. Dokken. Emmerson Dokken. Emmerson fucking Dokken. I wouldn't get used to that anytime soon.

Stoic shifted, pulled me to him, and pressed my back to his chest, not letting me turn around. "Rest." He was a cuddler. I remembered how much I enjoyed sleeping with him during that winter. I felt his wet and sticky dick against my thigh. Wait, the pillow, personal space.

Ha! Funny one, Stoic.

He must have truly liked me all this time.

I felt him rub my belly with his thumb like he used to do to help me sleep, but I couldn't rest. I was anxious. I'd soon be married to him. That was going to be sort of a permanent thing. I knew he would be a good husband overall. If he was not, I'd have my family and his, kick his ass for me as they did before. How bad could it be?

"Sleep, Emmerson." Stoic must had known my mind had a million and one things running through it.

"Yes, Daddy," I said. That rock-head wouldn't get the double meaning. I laughed in my head, and he got a shit-eating smirk on his face.

Oh, he liked that.

THIRTY-THREE

EMMERSON

Stoic 24

Two weeks after Stoic and I had that hot mess of a sex session in my room, we got married. Since everything was ready and neither of us saw why we needed to wait, we just did it. That was the original plan, after all. I didn't want to make a big deal out of it. It was sort of embarrassing since our whole family knew exactly what had happened between us. It wasn't only me, but I could tell Stoic was ashamed and uncomfortable too.

The day before we got married, Stoic came by my house and took most of my belongings with him to the new place where we'd be living. He said he wanted the place to be a surprise for me, so I would find out about it after the wedding was over.

We got married on a cool afternoon at the end of summer. The ceremony was simple. Stoic had built a wooden arch, and Amelia and Mom had decorated it with drapes and wildflowers. They set the whole thing in front of a big willow tree. We used many mismatched dining chairs to sit our friends and family members. It was simple but beautiful.

I had a fairly plain dress. It was made out of a beautiful flowing off-white fabric and had crocheted sleeves that fell to my elbows. My long, super curly hair was loose, and I wore a crown of flowers. Stoic dressed simply as well. He wore a button-up white shirt that he rolled up to his elbows, showing off many of his tattoos, and plain black pants. I had never seen Stoic dressed so elegantly before. He even trimmed his beard, and he kept his hair in a neatly done man bun.

Someone came to officiate the marriage, and Stoic and I exchanged our vows. When Stoic was asked to kiss his bride, he gently put his hand on my face and gave me a long, soft kiss. Our family cheered, and I saw Dad cry.

Kenzo helped us take some pictures. We took some in the woods and down by the river before we headed back for dinner. We connected four tables, and we all sat together as one big family. During the dinner, I sat next to Stoic, and he held my hand the entire time. Stoic was acting shy, and he gently rubbed his thumb on the palm of my hand, and every now and then, he would steal glances at me.

My father and Uncle Erik made many toasts. We could tell both of them were tipsy. Stoic didn't drink, and neither did I, for obvious reasons. Mom made sure to give me watered-down apple juice in my cup. The only ones that knew about my pregnancy were Mom, Ida, and Amelia. I had to tell Amelia. She was happy for me. She said she was excited to become an auntie.

I knew I was supposed to call Ida and Erik my parents in law now, but it would take some time to get used to it after a lifetime of having them as my uncle and auntie. I promised to visit them often and spend time with Ida as I used to do. She said she would rather come to me, not wanting me to move around too much with my belly.

After the dinner was done, Stoic helped Dad, Erik, and Kenzo to do the cleanup. They all talked for a while, and I saw them hug each other from afar. I went to my room and packed the rest of my things. I suddenly felt sad to leave the place I had lived my whole life and blindly follow Stoic to somewhere new.

My mom and Ida came into my room, and we hugged for the longest time. They told me their homes' doors would always be open for me and that they would be visiting me often to help me with my pregnancy. Mom encouraged me not to wait too long to tell Stoic. Ida agreed with her. He should know too. I agreed.

Ida insisted on not letting me carry anything heavy, so she put my belongings in the back of Stoic's truck for me. We waited for the guys to be done putting everything away, and when they did, they came over to say goodby to me.

Dad hugged me and cried again. He said I was and always would be his princess. Erik hugged me and told me that I had always been a daughter to him. Kenzo gave me a tight hug and told me that he was sorry for all the misunderstandings. I didn't know what he was talking about, but I didn't have time to clarify it either.

Dad opened the door for me, and I sat in the passenger seat. Stoic got in the driver's seat, and we waved goodbye before he drove away. I saw my family wave goodbye to me until we were far away, and I couldn't see them anymore.

"Are we going far?"

"Not really," he said and held my hand in his.

Stoic was silent the whole way. I didn't know how to start a conversation, so I stayed quiet. After about a twenty-five-minute ride, Stoic took a turn into the woods in the middle of nowhere. It was a narrow, bumpy driveway that had a curve to it, so I couldn't see our destination. After Stoic drove past the turn, I saw it.

In front of me was the most beautiful house I had ever seen. It looked big, bigger than any other I had seen in our village. It was all on one level and had a stone veneer for the entrance's siding. Stoic parked the car, and I immediately let his hand go and opened the door.

Getting out of the truck, the first thing I noticed was the smell. Wildflowers and fresh-cut grass. For some reason, the house was facing in a weird direction instead of the driveway. There were freshly planted flowers near the front lawn and an oversized patio to the left. I looked further to my left and saw it. The river. We were on a hill, and this place had the most beautiful view of the river that I had ever seen.

My eyes widened in surprise, and my hand landed on my chest. I walked closer to the fence and looked over it.

"You might wanna get in from the front door," Stoic said behind me, and I saw him point at the house. My eyes drifted to him, and he extended a fist to me and turned it over. When he opened his hand, there was a set of keys on a wooden key chain that read, "Always."

"Is this real?" I gave him a doubtful glare. This couldn't be it. Our home must be behind this one somewhere.

Stoic said nothing. He just smiled, took my hand in his, and put the key in it. I felt my face light up, and my heart beat faster. I took off and ran to the entrance. Stoic walked after me with his hands in his pockets.

I put the key in the doorknob, and it turned! I stopped to look back at him, and he nodded with a smile. I slowly opened the door, and my jaw dropped. The house was huge. It was rustic, with a high vaulted ceiling, big wooden beams, and huge windows that would let in a ton of sunlight. It looked like it had an open floor concept. I could see the kitchen from where I was standing, and it was big with an island in the center. The floors throughout the house were dark wood. It was beautiful.

I stood utterly still at the entrance. Stoic lifted me up bridal style and entered the house. He stood me up in the middle of the living room and hugged me from behind, resting his head on my shoulder. My eyes scanned with wonder all around. The place already had everything we needed. It was furnished, but it looked empty somehow. I could tell everything was new, and it just needed some decor.

"How big is it? It looks huge. How many rooms does it have?" I said rapidly, still in shock. I couldn't believe it.

How did he?

"Four and a half rooms," he said, hugging me tighter.

What? What the hell?

"What? Why four and a half?" I turned in his arms, my face inches from his chest. My eyes drifted up to his blues.

"I don't know, Emmy. It was you who came up with that number, not me."

What?

I had a "what the actual fuck" look on my face, and he just smiled wider.

What was I missing?

I tried to think hard about what he meant, and then, all of a sudden, I remembered. I gasped out loud and covered my mouth. "The stupid questions?"

"What?" he said with a laugh.

"The stupid questions! Stoic, you asked me so many stupid questions that I just started to give you stupid answers." I couldn't believe it.

Wait a minute. How long had he been planning this for? It couldn't be.

I took a step back and shook my head, but his arms were still wrapped around my body. He'd been asking me questions for as long as I could remember.

My eyes were still on him, and he started to scratch his neck, "Well... I guess I took it all too literal," he said.

It could not be. I left his arms and wandered around the house. In every corner of this home, I could hear the voice of my younger self answering his questions. It was almost like a faint whisper.

"Northeast!" My head turned toward the entrance. No wonder the house was facing a weird direction. I looked at the floor. "Dark wood, because why the hell not!" followed by both of our laughter. I walked to the kitchen and trailed my fingers over the countertop. "Stones last longer than wood."

"A glass wall! A big one." No way! I ran to see the other rooms, and I saw our room's glass wall.

I heard young Stoic's voice. "Emmy, a hill or a valley?"

"A hill?" I could also hear my childish voice as my eyes studied the magnificent view.

He had thought about this for as long as I had been alive. My hands began shaking. He hugged me from behind again, resting his chin on my head. I didn't even notice when he entered the room.

"Do you like it?" His voice was soft.

I did. I did more than just like it. I loved it! I was happy, but for some reason, my heart was hurting me. Stoic had really always loved me. But he never told me.

Why? Why me, though?

I turned and looked into his blue eyes. All the things I was so sure about Stoic were crumbling down fast.

Did I even know who the real Stoic was? What else didn't I know about him?

Stoic leaned down and captured my lips with his. It was soft and passionate. I kissed him back, and he dried the tears I didn't know were running down my cheeks. Stoic held me by the waist and slowly walked me to our bed. He had made the most beautiful rustic bed with thick solid pillars and drapes hanging from it.

Once we were close to the bed, he pulled the zipper on my dress down. He took his time to slowly slide the dress off me while leaving open-mouthed kisses down my neck. The dress dropped and pooled around my feet. Stoic ran his big, warm hands from my hips to my chest, gently cupping my breasts. He took my bra off and kissed me from my neck down to my tender globes. His mouth closed over one of my hardening nipples as he massaged the other one with his hand. His touch was sensual, and his mouth stimulated me to the point of making me tremble.

He unbuttoned the first four buttons of his shirt, took it off, and pressed me against his chest. I felt his warm skin on mine, rubbing my sensitive buds, making me immediately aroused. My core moistened. He took my flowered crown off and tossed it onto a corner of the bed. Stoic threaded his fingers in my hair and softly pulled my head back, angling me perfectly. The fire in his blue eyes was focused on my needy ones. He slowly leaned down and gave me a heated kiss. We closed our eyes, and his tongue invaded my mouth. I savored his delicious taste. My core got wetter, and as his hand dropped to my hip, I felt myself clench with anticipation.

"Lie down," he said in a dark and raspy tone filled with desire. I sat on the bed, moved to the middle, and laid down as he asked me to. My chest was moving up and down harshly, trying to find the air he had taken away from me on that kiss. I felt self-conscious, and my hands went to my breasts and covered my nipples. He said nothing; he just smiled.

Why was I so nervous?

I bit my lip and rubbed my legs together as I watched him take off his pants and underwear. He stood right in front of me in all his naked glory. Holy shit, he was so hot, and he was all mine. Stoic was mine. That just sank in. He had always been mine and forever will be.

Stoic got on the bed, his sudden weight making the mattress squeak. He grabbed me by my hips, hooked his fingers in the only piece of fabric I had left on my body, and sensually pulled my wet panties off, sliding them ever so slowly down and off my legs. He took off both of my shoes and threw them on the floor. His blue hypnotizing eyes focused on mine as he slowly opened my legs. I saw him lick his lips in anticipation, and I knew he was about to eat me out. His eyes promised me an earth-shattering release.

Stoic's hands ran down my thighs, and he sensually lowered his body. I felt like a god was about to worship me.

Did I even deserve this?

Stoic kissed my leg softly and trailed up, leaving soft kisses that made my skin tingle. Our eyes never lost contact, and when he reached my eager folds, he gave me a long lick, sending jolts all over my body.

He spread me open for him with both of his hands and licked me deliciously slow. He took his time to slowly devour me, inserting his meaty tongue inside me, flicking and circling my sensitive clit, then licking, kissing, and sucking all over and around my lips. All the while, Stoic kept his eyes trained on me. In his deep blue eyes, I could see I was the most precious thing in this world to him.

Stoic continued pleasing my most sensitive spot until my legs started to quiver. He inserted one of his long fingers into me, finding that spot that made me see stars the last time he went down on me. He made a come here motion with his fingers, and I could feel the tension building deep inside me. Stoic closed his mouth over me, claiming my yearning pearl while inserting another finger.

I started to lose control. I was holding back my moans, but they escaped my throat loud and needy. I gripped the sheets with one hand, and he took my other one, entangling our fingers together. His eyes were latched onto mine, enjoying the way he was making me melt in his mouth.

I gripped his hand and the sheets harder, and a whimper escaped my mouth. I was so close. Stoic must have felt me clenching hard on his fingers because he moved them faster and harder in me. It only took seconds for me to cum hard on his hand and mouth.

My body shook violently, but I never once closed my eyes or looked away from the man that had just take me into paradise. Stoic kept moving his fingers sensually inside me and licking me up, making my orgasm last.

He pulled away and admired my glistening pussy while licking his moist lips. I saw him lower his hand and stroke his hard meat slowly down and then up, making it drip some pre-cum.

"You are so fucking beautiful," he said with his eyes fixed on my needy, wet entrance. "Taste so fucking good too." He leaned down and gave me one last lick and an open kiss over my sensitive lips. "Mmm," He savored me one last time before he started kissing his way up my body.

Stoic left a trail of hot kisses burning my skin, spreading heat all over my body. He kissed his way over my abdomen to my tender hills and kept going up, all the way to my ear. "I love you so fucking much, baby." His voice was full of a thousand different feelings.

Why didn't I see it before? How stupid of me.

I was melting. Stoic was melting my heart and changing my world, one hot kiss at a time. It was clear to me that Stoic was not trying to fuck me today. He was going to make love to me–slowly and gently, pouring over me all the love he'd been holding back for years. He took my chin in his hands and gave me a passionate kiss. I could feel it. The trembling in his hands. He was nervous too.

Stoic's blues landed on me before he spread my legs open, making space for himself between them. Without taking his lustful eyes from me, he rubbed his rigid member against my slit, making it wet and slippery with my cream. Stoic eased his swollen tip inside me and shoved it as deep as it could go.

I let out a gasp as he growled sexily. He was stretching my walls wonderfully. His veiny rod throbbed inside me. My pussy gripped him hard, and he started to pump in and out of me painfully slow.

He captured my lips in his and thrust deeper inside me. Stoic kept that rhythm, slow all the way out, slow all the way in. I moaned against his lips, and he muffled my pleasure with his tongue.

It was so intimate, so sensual. Stoic took my hands in his and entangled our fingers together. I could feel every bumpy texture rubbing deliciously inside me. His already thick meat expanded even more. Stoic let out a long moan, and this time, I muffled his cries with my lips.

His body started to tremble above me, his breathing got ragged, and his eyes closed, immersed in the intense pleasure our bodies were creating. His lips moved on mine softly. He let my lips go and kissed down my jaw to my neck.

"Uhh! Uhh! Emmerson..." He moaned low, almost a whisper. He let my hands go and put both of his over my head, holding me in place. His back curved in, his knees bent forward, and he tensed his abs hard as he drove his hips into mine. His pace began to pick up. Stoic gave me a peck before lifting himself up and putting all his weight on his knees.

He started pumping his hardness in me. He took my legs, held them by my calves, and spread them apart. He kept holding them up, wide open for him to see how my tight pussy engulfed his eager, angry monster. He threw his head back and rolled his hips on me. "Oh, fuuuuuuck!" he moaned. He must have been close.

My tits were bouncing, so I took them in my hands and played with my sensitive nipples. Stoic saw me, and his hips went faster. "Uhh! Uhh!" I moaned, throwing my head back, my legs already shaking. I was going to cum. Stoic was taking us to that bright place.

Stoic closed my legs and put both of my feet over his right shoulder. His hands held my thighs as his hips slapped against me. He gave me a small kiss on my leg without slowing his pace down. "So fucking tight," he said in between breaths.

"Yes! Yes! Don't stop!" I moaned in a low voice. I was so close. I tried my best to keep my eyes on him, not wanting to stop this beautiful connection between us. Stoic's blue eyes focused on mine. His mouth hung open, and I knew he could feel my walls clenching hard around him.

"Oh!" The air got trapped in my lungs as I felt one strong electric shock strike my body hard. My body tensed hard before convulsing. My pussy pulsated wildly, and my juices drenched Stoic's meat, making it even more slippery for him to ease in and out of me. I gripped the sheets hard and moaned out my pleasure.

"Fuck. Oh fuck, I'm cumming," Stoic said in a low, dark voice. His thrusts were fast and erratic. Stoic's body stilled, and his legs shook. He moaned and grunted as he unloaded his seed against my cervix. His large hands found my breasts, and he cupped them hard. Ecstasy ripped through our bodies, and Stoic continued to give me slow, shallow thrusts, making our orgasms last longer.

Stoic pulled out his glistening cock, drenched in our juices, and fell on the bed next to me. He spooned me tightly and kissed my back. My breath was still ragged, and I was trying to control my fast-beating heart. I could still feel small waves from my orgasm when Stoic bent me further into a fetal position and plunged his still hard cock inside.

I was way too sensitive, and I moaned aloud as he penetrated my still pulsing pussy.

"Uhh! Fuck, Emmerson! I don't wanna stop!" Stoic was sensitive, too, but he still pumped his hard wood into me. His legs and hands were shaky, and his hips bucked.

"Uuhhh!" I moaned. It was too much. Every part of my body was thoroughly aroused. My brain was refusing to work under so much pleasure. "Stoic!" I moaned again, holding onto my sheets for dear life.

"That's it, baby. Keep cumming." He quickened his pace. My pussy kept [illegible]

"Ah fuck! I'm gonna cum again!" Stoic let out an animalistic growl, and I felt him spurting inside me once more. He held me tightly by the hips and slowly swiveled his hips until he could no more. We laid there, convulsing together, connected, feeling each other's orgasms slowly calm.

After a short while, Stoic took me to our bathroom, and we showered together under the cool water. In between sensual kisses, he cleaned my body, and I cleaned his. When we were done, Stoic dried us with a big, fluffy towel.

He took me to bed and laid me down under the thick blanket. We faced the glass wall and hugged each other as daylight disappeared and darkness consumed the horizon. Soon a million stars appeared up high in the clear sky, and I felt Stoic trail kisses over my neck.

While wrapped in his warm arms, I couldn't help but think.

Who was I married to?

This romantic and loving, gentle giant was nothing like the angry Stoic I remembered growing up with.

Why the fuck didn't I ever notice it?

THIRTY-FOUR

EMMERSON

Emmerson 18

Stoic 24

I woke up in Stoic's warm arms. It was early, and he was still sleeping. We were completely naked, and I loved how his skin felt on mine. One of his long legs was in between mine, my head was on one of his arms, and his other arm was tightly wrapped around my waist, like when I was little. I loved it. I really did. I always had. The glass wall let the morning sunlight fill the room, and it was just perfect. Stoic had built a house I could have only dreamed about. It was surreal.

I stayed there, with a smile on my face, looking at the sleeping figure of a man that had loved me more than anything else in his whole life. The father of my child.

Stoic's arm twitched, and he grunted. I raised my head to look at him. He was dreaming. He twitched again. Suddenly his body jumped, and he screamed, "Nooo!" Stoic quickly sat up and held his head. He was breathing heavy, his eyes lost. He'd had a nightmare. A bad one.

"Stoic?" I sat up and touched his elbow, but Stoic flinched away.

What the fuck?

Finally awake, his eyes landed on me, and his whole demeanor changed. "Emmerson," he said softly, and his expression softened. He pulled me to him and held me tight. He kissed my forehead, my cheeks, and then my lips.

"Morning," he said. Like nothing had happened.

"What was...?"

"Nothing. Sorry that I woke you up. Stay in bed, I'll make you breakfast." He stood up and walked out of the room. I stared at his wide back and firm butt as he walked.

Damn, he was hot. Mmm, I wanted that!

I threw the sheets aside, stood up fast, and skipped my naked ass to the kitchen. I found him reaching for the bowls in the higher cabinets when his eyes caught my figure. I stood there, pressing my legs together, making one slide up and down my soft skin with my hand twirling one of my curls and my teeth biting my lower lip.

Stoic raised an eyebrow, eyes looking up and down my body, the bowl he just grabbed about to fall from his hands. He knew what I wanted.

I walked sensually to him, moving my hips and running one finger over my breast. He was frozen in place with his mouth open. My body could stop his world, and I loved that. I looked down at my favorite meat toy and smiled. He was already getting hard.

When I got close to him, he put the bowl on the counter and leaned down. He gave me a little peck on my lips and locked eyes with me. I let my hands touch his strong figure. I slid them up to his chest. While looking into his eyes, I pulled him down to me and kissed his bearded jaw, then his neck, then his pecs, then a nipple. I kept going down without breaking eye contact, and his eyes widened.

My hands were already past his waist, and my kisses were already running over his abs. Stoic looked nervous. I got on my knees, held his hard cock with my hand, and pulled it toward me. My hand moved up and down on him, and I gave him a lick from the base to the slit on his head.

Stoic gasped. He was not expecting that. It was the first time I had ever used my mouth to please him. It was time I returned the favor.

I pulled his foreskin back and sucked the head inside my mouth. I gave it a sloppy suck, closed my lips over him, and licked the sensitive ridges of his cock with the tip of my tongue. Stoic's body stiffened.

If I had learned anything about Stoic, it was that he got too excited too fast and ejaculated prematurely. But the second and third loads were the fun ones.

I put him back in my mouth and sucked him again. "Uuhh!" he moaned, and his hand held my head. I bobbed my head up and down, sucking him harder. I used my hands to jerk the rest of his cock. I had only put about three inches of his long sausage in my mouth, but I wanted to get more of him in. I sucked him, saturating his shaft with my saliva.

His breath got ragged fast, and his legs were shaky. He gathered all my hair in one hand and held it back, so he could see my face as I pleased him. I kept eye contact with him and pressed his hard wood further into the back of my throat, but I gagged on it. He stiffened once more. I continued doing it, again and again, making him release a low growl.

I let my jaw relax and pressed him to me until his mushroom slipped past my uvula and then further down. "Holy fuck, Emmerson!" His hand grabbed my curls tighter, and I gave him a few pumps before pulling him out, gasping for air. I sucked him in again, harder, and stroked him with my hands. His cock twitched in my mouth. He was close.

"Emmy!" I relaxed my jaw again and swallowed all of his hard dick. My lips were pressed against his base, and Stoic's eyes rolled back into his head. His hips bucked, and I pumped my head hard on him. "Uuhhh!" He was about to blow.

Stoic held my head still with both of his [illegible] dick sliding in and out of my throat.

"I'm cumming, baby. I'm cumming! Uhh! Uhh! Uhh!"

His cock was throbbing hard inside me, and his thick cum ran down my throat. Stoic pulled his hard cock out, and I took the breath I desperately needed. I swallowed all of Stoic's thick cum. I licked my lips and made eye contact with Stoic's blue fires.

In one swift motion, Stoic lifted me up, laid me over the island's counter, and spread my legs open.

"You have no idea what you are doing to me, Emmerson," he said while staring at my wet pussy and shaking his head. His mouth closed on my clit, and he sucked on it hard. He spread me open for him and licked my pussy like a starved man. He pressed himself hard against me and shook his head, making his tongue flick faster over my sensitive pearl.

Stoic stood up, flicked my pearl once more with his thumb, and slapped me on my pussy. "Ahh!" My body jumped, and he pushed me down with one hand and grabbed his hard, angry cock with the other.

"Tell me how much you want it." His eyes darkened.

"Fuck, I need it! Give it to me!" I sounded desperate.

"So fucking horny!" He slapped my pussy with his heavy dick and rubbed me with his thumb again. "So fucking wet. Beg for it, baby."

I wanted it! I fucking wanted it, and he was playing with me.

Fuck you, Stoic!

You were not winning this battle. I knew exactly what he wanted.

Dickhead.

I looked into his eyes, bit my lip, and used two fingers to spread my pussy lips open for him. "Knock me up, Daddy!" I said in my sluttiest voice.

That did it. Stoic looked possessed. The Dokken had risen. It took him one second to react and another one to hit home hard.

Holy fuck! Yes!

Stoic released the jackhammer and fucked me senseless. My eyes immediately rolled back, and I creamed as if someone had turned a hose on. Not even two minutes into the pounding, and I was coming undone.

"Call me Daddy again," he demanded, slipping a finger inside my mouth for me to suck on.

My toes curled, my back arched, and I was there. "Ah, fuck! I'm cumming, Daddy!" He fucked me harder and deeper. My legs started shaking. "Uuhh! Uuhh! Uuhh! Uuhh!" Bright lights. I saw the fucking doors of Valhalla open for me.

Fuck yes!

Stoic moaned and groaned hard when I came all over his stiff meat, but he didn't stop. He was a man with a mission. If only he fucking knew his mission had been long accomplished. I'd let him have his fun and work extra hard in getting me knocked up. I'd just enjoy the ride. I let out a small squeal and a chuckle, and he furrowed his eyebrows, completely clueless.

He pounded away, and I was moaning incredibly loud–so was he. I was glad there was no one living near us, or it would have been super embarrassing.

Stoic pulled out, made me stand, turned me around, and bent me over. "Spread those legs." He slapped my inner thighs, and I did as he told me. He spanked my ass hard and slipped his pork sword all the way in, hitting my cervix.

"Uuhh, fuck!" We moaned at the same time. It felt so good.

Stoic put some weight on my hips with his two colossal hands and pistoned his dick into me. He threw his head back and moaned, "Fucking take that dick, you pretty little cum slut!" He gave me a hard spank. My eyes widened.

Holy shit! Fuck yes, Stoic! Talk dirty to me.

"Uhh! Uhh! Uhh! Give it to me harder!" I screamed out. Stoic snaked a hand around my throat and mounted me like a wild beast. Our bodies were slapping hard against each other, sweat starting to form all over him. I was almost there.

"Fuck yes, Emmy! Fuck, Emmy! I'm gonna fucking cum! Uuhh!"

"Yes! Knock me up, Stoic! Knock me the fuck up!" That sent him over the cliff. I was a fucking brat. His thrusts became super irregular, and he moaned loud and hard. His whole body convulsed, and his legs lost all their strength.

"Holy fuck!" he said, out of breath, and grabbed the countertop hard, trying not to fall over. Seeing him cumming this hard and the violent throbbing of his dick deep inside me triggered my orgasm, and I came hard, my pussy walls pulsing hard around him, making him moan more, milking all his seed.

He pressed me to him, lowered us to the floor, and lay us down on the kitchen floor, not wanting to pull his dick from me but not having the strength to stay standing. "Fucking hell, Emmerson. You're gonna kill me!"

We laughed like silly kids on the floor for the longest time, still connected. He must have really wanted to get me pregnant. He was so stinking cute!

After a while, we showered together, ate breakfast, and went to sit on the daybed. It was raining. The day was cool, the breeze damp, and the smell of rain filled the whole place. We could hear the dripping sound of the falling raindrops. Even when it was raining, this place was beautiful. Stoic took the almost empty mug of warm milk he had prepared from my hands and put it on the table. He sat next to me and gave me a sweet smile.

My mind traveled back to this morning and his strange behavior.

What was that about?

"Stoic?" My voice was soft.

"Hmm?"

"What was your nightmare about?" I rested my head on his shoulder while he intertwined our hands.

Stoic took a deep breath. "It wasn't a nightmare. It was something much... worse."

"What was it?" I was worried.

"I don't want to talk about it." He shook his head and looked away from me. His eyes were lost and empty. I moved back further in the daybed, took his arm, and pulled him to me. I laid his head on my lap and ran my fingers through his hair.

"Stoic, if we're going to spend the rest of our lives together, you need to learn how to communicate with me. You need to trust me. I need to know what's going on, so I can help you. I don't want to be useless and–"

He interrupted me.

"You are not useless. You have already helped me. You help me every day, every minute, every second I spend breathing. You are everything I hang on to."

What was he talking about?

"I don't understand." I really didn't. I felt lost. It was like there was a huge piece of information that I was missing. Another thing everyone knew, but nobody told me. He paused for a long while.

"I lied to you."

He lied? When? Why?

"About what?" My eyebrows frowned, and I stopped brushing his hair with my hands. I was scared. He better not say he had another woman or a child or some shit like that.

"I was not at the fence guarding it. I was way past it."

What? Was he talking about the North?

"Far beyond the enemy lines, in the heart of the battle, the fucking front line."

What?

I felt my face drop.

Stoic was in a battle? Did he spend years in action?

My heart stopped. I was in shock. I couldn't speak.

"We weren't holding the border. We were on active duty, bringing the fight to them, working to eliminate the threat. Day in and day out, right in the line of fire." My hand went to my chest, and my eyes got blurry.

"I knew..." he paused, then continued, "when I left you here, I knew I might not come back. So, I held on to you for every possible second. You might have thought I was a fucking creep." He let out a humorless laugh.

"I thought you were sad because you had to go far from us, and you would miss us. I never... It never..." I struggled to put words together.

"That too." Silence.

"Emmerson..." His chest moved up and then down hard. I noticed it was difficult for him to say these things, but he was trying.

"I saw it, Emmerson. I saw the destruction with my own eyes. I saw suffering, and I saw what greed can do to the less fortunate." My hand dropped to my side.

Why? Why did he have to go there? Who made him do this?

"I can still see them–when I close my eyes, I can see them. Hundreds of lifeless faces, all the dead children. I can still hear the explosions, the metallic sound of gunshots. Over and over and over. I can still feel the recoil of every shot I took."

Was he traumatized? My Stoic was traumatized.

How could he still be so calm? How was he talking about all this so calmly?

I felt tears leaking from my eyes, and my chest tightened. He went through so much pain. My heart was hurting for him.

Why him? Why not someone else?

He hadn't looked at my face yet, so he didn't know how affected I was.

"I lied because I wanted you to live a happy life, Emmy. That's the reason I went there in the first place, so you could be free and run in the woods without a single fucking worry. So you would be safe. So you would never have to see or go through something like that, ever. To keep all that far away from you, baby. To destroy it with my own hands and strangle it before it grew and put you in danger." Stoic kept looking into the distance.

"If me fighting there is what it took to keep you safe here, I would do it a hundred times over. But it was hard, it was very... hard."

He did it for me? He fucking thought he had to do that for me? How in the hell did he come up with that fucked up idea?

If I knew, I would have never let him go. I would have never let him suffer like that. I would have trapped him in my short arms and hung on to him, held him tight, and never let him leave my side.

Did Erik and Ida know? Of course, they knew!

They all knew, and they didn't fucking stop him. Kenzo! Kenzo was with him.

Did Kenzo go through that, too?

"Kenzo?" I could barely speak, but he understood what I meant.

"Yes." That's all he said.

I felt sadness surrounding me like a thick, dark blanket. The tears that fell down my cheeks formed long strings of never-ending sorrow. The heaviness of my ignorance fell over me like a boulder. The weight of the happy life I lived without recognizing the high price Stoic was paying for it.

"Do you want to know how you have helped me?" He looked at me, wiped my tears with his thumb, and caressed my hair.

"Every time I felt darkness consuming me, I thought of you, and like a beacon of light, your eyes pulled me away from my demons. You and you alone keep me afloat."

I didn't fucking deserve him.

He kept caressing my hair. "You are my gravity, Emmerson. Without even noticing it, you pull me toward you with a force I wouldn't have the strength to fight even if I wanted to."

I didn't fucking deserve this. I had been a brat to him my whole life. A stupid, clueless child.

"You were and are my everything. You are my everything, baby. Without you, I'm lost."

I started crying loudly. I couldn't help it. Stoic sat up, put me on his lap, and held me tight.

I cried a lot–for a really long time. Not the pretty quiet kind of cry. I was crying out loud, sobbing continuously. It was the ugliest kind of cry you could imagine. Snot running down my nose, hiccups, gagging, my whole face red, my eyes swollen, hyperventilating, my body shaking, and babbling unintelligible nonsense–you name it, I did it. Stoic just sat there and hugged me, telling me that everything would be alright.

What had I done to deserve him?

THIRTY-FIVE

STOIC

Emmerson 18

The day I finally told Emmerson about my PTSD, she cried for hours. That was about four days ago.

I knew she was not gonna like it, but I didn't realize she would fucking be destroyed over it. I didn't even get into details, and I never would. I regretted telling her. She was so affected that she even hyperventilated. By the time she calmed down, her eyes were so puffy and swollen that I thought she couldn't see, so I carried her inside. We skipped lunch, and I laid her down next to me for a long nap. After she fell asleep, I stood up and made her rice and chili for dinner. Before I was done cooking, she woke up, somehow looking worse than when she went to sleep.

I laughed internally at her state, but the truth was I was glad. It meant she loved me. She had never said it out loud, though. She didn't have to. I knew it. After that day, I knew.

"Go back to bed, baby. Dinner is not done yet." She walked to me and hugged me from behind.

"I feel so bad, Stoic. I shouldn't have been such a brat to you all these years." I smiled.

"I love you just the way you are, Emmy, bratty little you included. Never change."

She cried some more and did try to talk me into getting therapy as I did for her, but I refused. I promised that if it ever got out of control, even if just a little, I would.

That day we showered together. I combed her messy hair and put her to sleep after reading a Norse mythology book. It was as if time had gone in reverse, and I had Emmerson the child back in my arms. I cherished it.

Emmerson was quite a character. Now that I was spending all my time with her, I noticed how naughty she could be. She was bratty but in a cute way. She was super confident and full of self-esteem. I was so glad that I hadn't ruined that for her with our first time's fiasco.

Emmerson had strong opinions, and I could tell she had deep thoughts about society and the limits between what was wrong and what was right. She sat me down and lectured me on all the reasons why she thought the war I fought was wrong. Emmy made many points that made me rethink all I had done. She said she didn't think violence was the answer.

She was sad for me and told me she was afraid our system had taken my good intentions and the love I had for her and used me as a tool to their advantage. She pointed out that our leaders said the North wanted to expand to the south, but ultimately, the South had expanded to the north. They said the North wanted to impose their way of living on us, but it was us who ended up forcing them to live our way. They said the North was starving their citizens, but it was us who blocked all trading and starved them all.

She was an idealist. If she were to see what I had seen, then she might not think the same way. She did ultimately agree that Northerners were wrong, but she didn't agree on to what extent it was our right to meddle in their democratic process. She said there were always two sides to a coin. We didn't agree. I didn't want to get into details, and she would never back down from her utopic cloud, so we left it there.

Fuck me! If our kids were anything like her, I'd be in so much trouble. At least I wouldn't get bored. I'd never have a minute of silence, that was for sure.

One of the many interesting things I had learned about Emmerson was that when she was super horny, she moaned in Portuguese. It was stupid sexy and got me hard as fuck even when I had no fucking idea what she was saying. She rarely translated what she said. I had an idea, though. Knowing my Emmerson, she might have been screaming the worst, dirtiest things that came into her mind.

She fucking loved sex. No, it was more like she fucking loved my dick. She was obsessed with it. She liked doing things that would get me extremely horny, knowing I'd blow my load in her fast. It was the 'let's see how fast she could milk me' game. She loved watching me cum. She stared at my head and watched me ejaculate, seeing how my jizz shot out in ropes. It got her off. I made sure she could always hear me moan and that she could see my cum face when I was about to orgasm.

She drove me crazy! She was so fucking beautiful and sexy. I was so fucking lucky.

I remembered being worried about her sexual orientation when she was little. Never would I have ever imagined she was gonna grow up to be this seductive. She preyed on me like a hunting predator. Even when she was sensually crawling to me on her knees and acting submissive, I knew she was about to devour me. I had tried to be dominant, but that petite little vixen overpowered me every single fucking time. It was a game for her, and she never lost. I didn't fucking care because what my baby wanted, my baby got.

pregnant and start a family. I had pounded into her hard and had come deep inside her many times, hoping I would knock her up. I couldn't wait to see her round and beautiful, carrying my child. I couldn't wait to have a little baby Emmerson in my arms once again. I was crossing my fingers, waiting for her to tell me she missed her period.

Every time we had sex, I would get off thinking about getting her pregnant, and she would let me enjoy that fantasy. She would play along, ask me to knock her up, to give her my seed, and to fucking put a baby in there. That made me cum so hard that my legs would fail me. I knew she found it funny, but I didn't care because it felt too fucking perfect. The dirtier the talk, the stronger my orgasm hit me. Emmy had a pretty dirty little mouth, and I enjoyed filling it–all the way down her throat.

Sex got intense. I was glad I had saved myself to enjoy all this with her. She was fucking worth the wait.

"Stoic!" she sang my name.

What the fuck was she up to now?

"Here, babe." I was doing the dishes. Yeah, I was that pussy-whipped. Not ashamed to admit it.

"I got something for you!" she sang again. She stood by the corner with a naughty smile, both of her hands behind her, and she was swaying her body side to side. Cute. I felt a smile spread wide on my face.

"What is it?"

"It's something I hid... somewhere..." she sang once again. She wanted to play. I knew how this would end.

"Where?" I raised an eyebrow.

"Mmm...." She put a finger to her lips, pretended to think, and bit her lip. Yep... she fucking wanted it. She called it *The Dokken*. My father would be ashamed of us if he knew what we used his last name for.

"I'll tell you if...." She didn't have to finish that. I dropped the sponge and rinsed the soap off of my hands.

Let's get to work.

"Come here!" She squealed and jumped into my arms. I caught her, and she snaked her arms around me and kissed me. She nibbled on my lower lip and slipped her tongue inside my mouth. I tasted the sweetness of her kiss, and I could already feel The Dokken awakening.

"Where you want it, baby?" I said while staring at the most beautiful colors I had ever seen.

"Bed," she said and kissed my ear. I walked us to our bedroom, kicked the door open, and set her down on our bed. I took my shirt off, and she got excited –like a child about to unwrap a brand-new toy.

"Too many clothes! Take them off!" she laughed. I took my socks off and opened my jeans.

"What about you, baby?" She was wearing a dress. She had started to wear dresses all the time. I knew why. It gave me easy access. If I wanted some pussy, I just needed to lift her skirt and take it.

"Don't worry about me, Daddy." She was doing it. Teasing me. She knew exactly how to push my buttons. Freaking brat. I took my pants off and then my underwear. My hard cock sprang out and slapped me on the stomach. Her eyes widened when she saw it, and she bit her lip again.

"Lay down." She patted the bed. She was not asking, and I was in trouble. I crawled to the center of the bed and laid down as she wanted me to.

Emmerson took my dick in her soft hand and very sensually jerked it up and down, moving my foreskin back. She put one hand above the other and used both of her hands to jerk me off. Not even with two hands was she able to hold my whole dick. My big mushroom head popped out of her grasp, and she put it in her warm mouth and sucked it.

"Fuck, baby." My hands went to her head, and she immediately stopped me. "No! No touching. Be a good boy and let me milk you dry," she said while maintaining eye contact with me, and then her mouth went back to my dick.

I put my hands behind my head and let her do whatever she wanted. I was fucking spoiling her. She sucked me some more and then stopped. Emmerson sat on her knees and started pulling the loose fabric of her dress up. Slowly showing me that delicious body of hers.

Once the fabric passed her hip, I knew what she was doing. She was wearing the sexiest fucking little piece of underwear I had ever seen. She had on white lace panties that stayed high on her hips, showing that irresistible part where her hips and her legs met that made her curves look fucking perfect when she sat.

She kept pulling her dress up, and I felt my dick leaking pre-cum. Fuck, she was so beautiful. It was all one piece, but it had lace and ribbons all wrapped around her. I could see her nipples getting hard, begging for attention. I would fucking rip it off her, but I knew how much work it took to sew an outfit like that.

touching, remember?" Fuck me, I fell for it. It was torture.

"Sit that pussy on my face." I wanted to eat her up.

"Nope." She popped the 'p' and shook her head.

"This is all about you. I want Daddy to feel really good."

What the fuck was she up to?

Emmerson grabbed my dick and started sucking me again. She made it nice and sloppy, just how I liked it. Her saliva ran down my shaft, and she began to gag on it.

"Uuhh, holy fuck, baby. Go deeper." So fucking good.

Emmerson backed up to breathe and then came back down, taking my whole dick into her mouth. That was my girl! Her lips were pressed hard against my body, and she was gagging, but she kept it there. She pulled back to take a breath and moved back down, bobbing her head on my hard cock. "Holy fuck! Ahh!" If she kept doing that, I wasn't going to last long.

Emmerson pulled me out of her mouth and pumped my shaft with her hands, licking down my dick. While still pumping my dick, she licked lower and lower until she got to my balls and licked them, too. She took one in her mouth and sucked it. I felt my cock twitch. I wanted her.

"Emmy..." I moaned out, and she understood. Emmerson sat up and straddled me. She moved her underwear to the side, took my hard meat stick, and placed it at her entrance. She slid my thick head inside her and dropped slowly on me, filling herself to the hilt.

I enjoyed the way my dick stretched her wet walls. "Uuhh, fuck, Stoic! So big." She looked so sexy. I wanted to touch her body, please her, and play with those sensitive nipples. It was killing me.

Her tits looked perfect from here. I had always wanted to rub oil on them, slide my hard dick in between them, pinch her nipples, and then have her suck my tip.

Once she got used to the size, she gave me a playful smirk. She put a hand on my chest for balance, let her hair loose, and started rolling her hips on me very sensually. "Uh! Mmm!" I began to moan. I was not going to last long.

Emmerson threw her head back and started bouncing on my cock, moving faster and faster. "Uuhh, Emm…" Yep, I was gonna fucking cum.

"Stoic! Eu sou toda tua," she said in the sexiest voice I had ever heard, her fire-filled eyes on mine.

My legs spread open, and I couldn't hold back from lifting my hips to meet her as she slammed down hard on me. Fuck, I wanted to touch her.

Her breasts were bouncing inside that thin fabric, and I could feel my dick starting to throb.

"I'm cumming!" I called out. My hands grabbed the pillow under me hard, and my mouth hung open. Emmerson somehow bounced faster on my meat, and my hips bucked violently. The strength of my pounding made her tits bounce out of her skimpy outfit. She was moaning loudly, and her legs were shaking.

"Uh! Uh! Mmm! Fuck, yes! Holy fuck, yes!" I was cumming. I gave her a hard thrust, and my hands held her hips down on me. My head was kissing the back of her vagina, and I felt my dick throbbing hard inside her, my milk coating her cervix. Yes!

I was sensitive. Emmerson was still on top of me with that look in her eyes and that fucking smile that I already knew too well. Before she started bouncing on my dick again, I moved her off of me. I pulled out and kissed her hard. I just needed a minute or two to recover.

I kissed her hard and passionately. I ran my hands all over her body and kissed her everywhere. When I was ready, I turned her over.

"Ass up, baby." She did. I firmly pressed her chest down on the mattress, and her back made a sexy arch. Her ass was up high, ready for my cock just like I wanted it.

I supported my weight on my left knee, keeping it on the bed, and my other leg was bent, my right foot flat on the mattress. My spongy head penetrated her dripping pussy, and she moaned as soon as she felt me sliding inside her. I was getting my dick in at a delicious angle that helped me go deeper into that tight little pussy of hers.

I first started rolling my hips sensually against her, accelerating my pace gradually. Not long after, I started pounding hard into her dripping wet pussy, one hand holding her hips and my other one supporting my heavy weight on the bed.

Emmerson's silky legs were close together, making her already tight pussy tighter for me.

"Foda me duro," she moaned. I didn't know what that meant, but I was gonna fuck her harder.

My dick easily slid in and out of her creamed pussy. My cum was dripping out of her and running down her thighs. With every hard thrust, more of our combined wetness came pouring out of her.

I kept giving her [illegible] thrusts, and she started to get [illegible].

"Make me come!" she moaned, out of breath. With pleasure. I sped up my pace. Fuck, she felt so good!

"Nossa!" she screamed. I tilted her head toward me, and I saw her eyes rolling back into her head. Fuck, Emmerson! So fucking sexy. She was gonna get me off again.

She lifted herself and put her weight on her arms. She tilted her head back, and her long curly hair brushed her butt as she looked me in the eyes.

"Stoic, você vai ser pai. Estou grávida."

I had no idea what the fuck she was saying, but it sounded super sexy. I grabbed her neck and pulled her closer to me. She kissed my lips softly.

"Mmm, baby, you're so fucking tight!" She was close. So fucking close. Fuck, I was close too.

"Uhh! Stoic! I'm... I'm..." She was going to cum.

"Are you gonna cum, baby? Me too. I'm cumming, Emmy." My voice was low and dark. I fucking loved when we came together. She tensed up, her nails digging into the sheets, and she let out a big gasp.

"I'm pregnant! Oh, fuck! Uh! Uh! I'm pregnant! Stoic, I'm pregnant!"

Her body shook violently as she came hard, and I slowed down, feeling her walls gripping me hard. I could feel her pulsing hard around me, and I couldn't fucking think straight. I was about to cum too.

What the fuck did she mean by that? Was she joking?

"What?" That sounded like a moan. She said nothing, and she was breathing heavily, trying to catch her breath.

Did she really say what I thought she said?

I held her hips tighter and went a bit faster to get me over the edge.

"Uuhh! Emmy!" I was seconds away.

"I'm pregnant!" I blew up. Ropes of hot cum shot fast inside her pussy. "Uhh! Uhh! Uhh!" I gave her a few hard thrusts before my exhausted body dropped onto the bed next to her.

Did I hear her correctly?

"Wha... Wha..." I couldn't speak. My body was trembling.

"I'm pregnant."

"Are you fucking joking?"

She was joking; she had to be.

"No."

"How the fuck do you know?" We hadn't left the house.

"I've known for a long time," she said with a smile.

A long time?

"What?"

What did that mean?

My breathing was still ragged, and so was hers. My heart was beating faster.

Hold the fuck up. This might be real.

"You knocked me up at the waterfall," she said, smiling again.

Holy fuck, no.

My face dropped, and my eyes widened. I stayed quiet.

Out of all the times I had sex with Emmerson, that was the only one I had hoped with all my heart for it not to be the time I got her pregnant. I was actually glad, thinking that she hadn't got pregnant that time. I didn't want that to be the way we created our first child. I was fucking embarrassed. No wonder why she was so upset. I fucking ruined this, too.

My hands went to my head, and I pulled my hair.

"What? Are you not happy?" Emmerson looked at me with worried eyes as she sat up.

"It's not that, baby. I'm happy." I was trying to be cheerful. I knew I was failing.

"Is it because I kept it from you?" She was nervous, and I didn't want to fucking ruin it for her.

"No, baby. No, I'm happy, really." I pulled her to me and kissed her. I laid her down again and held her close to my body. My hands went to her belly, and I caressed her. My chest hurt–my baby was growing right there under my hands.

"I am almost three months," she said softly.

I remained quiet. It was bittersweet. Having my family in my arms was more beautiful than I could have imagined. Knowing I made this out of my biggest regret fucking hurt.

"I forgave you. I know you're sorry. I forgave you long ago. You should forgive yourself too." She knew.

I hugged her tighter. I buried my face in her hair and tried hard not to cry.

"I love you, Stoic. It's my honor to be the mother of your children. I'm the luckiest girl in this world." Her thumb brushed over the hand I had over her belly, and I nodded my head. I felt if I tried to talk, I'd break, so I didn't.

We stayed there, wrapped in each other's arms. That cute little girl was going to give me the greatest gift anyone could ever ask for.

I was going to be a father!

THIRTY-SIX

STOIC

Emmerson 19

She was a brat! Now I knew why she kept calling me "Daddy" so much. No wonder why she was laughing so hard.

I spent my days watching Emmerson dance and sing around the house with her baby bump. She looked so beautiful. She danced while she cooked, danced while she showered, and danced while she was dusting–she was always dancing or singing. I liked it. It meant she was happy.

My baby was happy with me, and she was happy in this house I had built just for her. She was delighted with our child growing inside her. I did nothing but stare at her all day long with a soft smile on my face like a creep. I didn't regret any of it. I didn't regret any single path I took. I didn't care what she said, but this was worth it. She was worth it.

In our free time, Emmerson and I would hold hands and go for long walks in the woods every day. She talked non-stop all the way. I always quietly listened to all she had to say. After we were done with our farming hours each week, we usually walked to the river and swam together. If she got horny, I would take her to the cave behind the waterfall and make love to her.

I started to practice archery with the bow Emmerson had given me. She would sit on the porch eating watermelons and laughing as she watched me missing all the targets. I wanted to tell her she looked like a watermelon, but I was afraid she'd take her shoe off and throw it at me. Life was fun and simple, and I was truly happy with her.

I still woke up screaming most mornings, but Emmerson always hugged me, put my head on her chest, and patted me until I was calm. It slowly got better over time.

Our family was doing well. By the time I told everyone about the baby, I realized my mom had known all along, as well as Imany and Amelia. Kenzo, Andreas, Dad, and Ethan were super happy about the news. Dad cried from the excitement of becoming a grandpa for the first time.

Kenzo had the "great" idea of taking all of us out for drinks to celebrate, and we all got shitfaced. Dad, Andreas, Ethan, Kenzo, and I ended up fucking crawling like animals, laughing and talking nonsense, along the streets on our way back home. Imany and Mom didn't find it funny at all. They gave us all hell for it.

Emmy was at her family's house waiting for me. When she saw me completely wasted with a red face and slurring my words, she just laughed her ass off like a maniac. We slept there that night in Emmerson's old room. There was no way I was going to risk my baby and Emmy by driving like that. When her parents went to sleep, Emmy sucked my drunk cock dry. That was fucking amazing! I hoped Andreas had passed out already because I was loud as hell, and Emmerson didn't care about shutting me the fuck up. Imany must have heard us for sure. Ah, what an embarrassment!

At least Ethan was not living at their home anymore. He had moved in with Amelia. They got married shortly after that, and Emmerson did all she could to help them have a beautiful wedding. She put a lot much more energy into their wedding than what she did for ours. She always loved Amelia like a sister, and now they truly were. Ethan started his studies, and Amelia decided to pursue a career as a biologist, so they ended up relocating to a different village. Emmerson missed them so much.

Kenzo's son, Ian, was growing so fast. Emmy took care of Ian at home sometimes. She was a natural with kids. Kenzo and Ava were on and off in their relationship until it finally became settled. After all his insecurities. Kenzo ended up deciding to get a home for Ava and his child, and he stayed with them. At first, he said he wanted to be close to them and saw himself as a roommate there, but we all knew there was way more than what he was willing to let out.

I told him their furniture was on me, and I started to work on the pieces right away. He stopped fucking around with girls. He was too busy to do so.

Kenzo began to work with Dad and Andreas as a blacksmith. He would take over the business after Dad and Uncle retired. They wanted me to be there with Kenzo, too, but I'd rather work with wood from home, where I could see Emmerson the whole time.

I installed a glass garage door in my workshop that I kept open when the weather was nice, and that gave me a perfect view of the house, especially Emmerson's half-room workspace that had a glass wall as well. Every time I could, I glanced at her. I watched her sew her backpacks for hours.

At times, she would stand, stretch with her big belly, and then continue working while standing. If I saw her yawn multiple times, I'd stop working and make some dumb excuse to make her take a break, like asking for a snack or complain about imaginary back pain, so she would give me a short massage in bed. Once I got her out of her workspace, I hugged her hard and didn't let her go.

She knew I was always watching her. Sometimes she pretended not to notice me and sensually took her clothes off to "get changed," pulled her skirt up and showed me more of her legs, or sensually bent over, showing me her delicious in my loose pants and give her a quick but intense release before going back to work with a shit-eating smirk on my face.

In the evening, Emmerson and I would sit on the porch on our daybed and watch the sky slowly darken and the stars appear. I would rub her belly and sing songs to our child, loving the way our baby moved inside her. I caressed and touched her stomach as much and as often as I could.

I was nervous and extremely cautious with her pregnancy, so when her belly got bigger, I insisted on doing all the cleaning and cooking. Anything to take care of her. I had our baby's room and furniture done long before the birth. I also put the tiny rocking chair I made for Emmerson when she was little in the room. I hoped our child would like it as much as Emmy did. I couldn't wait to hold our child in my arms.

The best thing about her pregnancy was that Emmerson was always horny. When we were alone at home, she always wore a dress with nothing under it. I still remembered the fight we had over dresses when we were little. I shook my head at that thought always.

We fucked two or three times every day. I knew this was the honeymoon period, but something told me Emmerson would always have a big appetite for sex. I hoped I could keep up with her.

I recently received a letter from the councils. They offered me a defense position with a higher rank in the military, but I declined. I hid the letter from Emmerson and burned it when she wasn't looking. The medals I received had been left behind and forgotten somewhere in my parent's house. I was happy living this simple life next to Emmy, and I was not going to change that for anything in this world. I never told Emmerson about the things I had done, for which some deemed me a hero. I never wanted to be seen as one.

In the spring, a week before Emmerson's birthday, on a calm day filled with blooming flowers, our child was born. She gave birth at home, and my mom helped her all along the way. My heart broke, wanting it to be me, the one that had to go through that pain and not her.

I held her hand and kissed her as she screamed in pain. I remained calm on the outside, but on the inside, I was terrified. All I wanted was for Emmy and the baby to be healthy. My mom reassured me she was doing well, but with every strong contraction, I felt my heart stop and the air get harder to breathe.

Emmerson had the child in the bathtub. Mom said it was best for both of them to have the baby be born in water. When the time came, I held both of Emmerson's hands behind her and kissed her neck and cheeks repeatedly. Emmerson was so brave, and I was so proud of her. She gave one last strong push, and our baby came out. Mom examined the baby, making sure he was well and breathing fine before putting him on Emmerson's chest.

It was a boy. I had a son. I was secretly hoping for a girl that looked like Emmerson, but I'd love this little boy with all I had. Mom passed me the scissors, and I cut the cord.

Leaning over the tub, I softly caressed my son's head. My heart was tight in my chest. His silky hair was red like mine and curly like Emmerson's, and his light tan skin was soft and still dirty from birth. His blue eyes barely opened. Emmerson let out a choked laugh that sounded like a cry. Maybe she found our baby's serious expression funny. He looked more like me.

"Welcome to this world, Owen," she said as she kissed him.

Emmy was exhausted, but she couldn't stop smiling. She positioned Owen on her breast, and he started sucking right away. My face was serious. I was thinking about the immense responsibility I had now, on how I would do anything to keep them safe, but inside I was extremely happy. The kind of happiness that terrified you, knowing how precious all of this was and knowing I could lose it at any moment. Emmerson held my hand and smiled while looking into my eyes.

"We are fine. We'll be fine. He is healthy," she said, somehow knowing exactly where my mind was taking me. I didn't know how she did that. I nodded and kissed her forehead.

I stayed there watching her feed our child for a while as my mind was already thinking about all the things I wanted to do for him, with him. Mom took Owen and wiped him off with a cloth, wrapped a blanket tightly around him, and gave him to me.

He looked so small in my big hands, so fragile. My eyes studied him, and I knew in my heart I already loved him.

I was a father.

EPILOGUE

THE DOKKENS

Stoic 88

Emmerson 83

They lived their lives.

Time passed them by like a fast breeze, and amidst laughter, games, and hugs, their long-lived time started to run out.

It was a cool fall day. He could see the many colors of the trees extending into the distance. He had seen the same trees change with every season, year after year. Each season was as beautiful as the last, and each year was filled with love in Emmerson's arms.

Their children–Owen, Ezra, Ivy, Eden, Beau, Leon, and Kiara–were there that day. They all stayed beside him for hours, laughing and remembering all their beautiful memories together with their father. They all sat around him, and he heard them talk, his eyes filled with light and happiness. Many of his nineteen grandchildren were there too. Some of his great-grandchildren climbed onto his bed and kissed his wrinkled cheeks.

His family was big. Stoic always made sure to make handmade gifts for all of their children and grandchildren every year, and he remembered all their birthdays and special days. Just as he had done with Emmerson, he combed their hair, told them myths and stories, took them fishing, and watched them grow into wonderful people. He was always there to help them and support them in anything they wanted and needed. Stoic had built more cribs for his family than he could remember. He worked with wood until his tired body wouldn't permit him to anymore.

He had fallen ill, and his breathing was more difficult with each passing day. No one was to blame but his old age. He knew he wouldn't make it past the night, but he didn't care. He had enjoyed a beautiful life.

Looking back on his life. He only had but one regret. The thing that Emmerson forgave him for, but that he never could forgive himself. He spent the rest of his life making it up to her in a million and one different ways, as he had promised.

During these long years, he had seen many of his loved ones leave this world. His parents, as well as Emmerson's, died when he and Emmerson were in their mid-sixties. Kenzo had died of a heart attack at age seventy-five and was survived by Ava and their three kids and seven grandchildren. He did marry her. She had loved him and cared for him always, and he ended up falling madly in love with the girl that gave him everything and asked for nothing in return. Most of his old friends had passed away, too, and the village he once knew so well was filled with new faces.

Ethan moved far away and didn't return, but he sent him letters from time to time. He and Amelia had two kids and five grandchildren.

He was glad he had the chance to spend his time with Emmerson. Each passing day, she got more and more beautiful, even when she had gray hair and wrinkles. No one was more beautiful in his eyes than her. Stoic used to hold her hand and walk her to the river every week. Like the old times, they sat on a rock, and Emmerson would talk for hours. He would always listen.

Emmerson had started to have problems walking, so she needed a walking stick to get around. For as long as Stoic stayed strong, he had held onto her arm and walked her wherever she wanted to go. But not anymore. Emmerson would have to walk alone from now on.

He was thankful for their simple life. His mind was filled with all their happy memories from their family, the slow dances with Emmerson, all the time they played in the rain, and all the times they swam in the river. He treasured the memory of every one of their kids' births and the kids of their kids' births as well. He remembered all the things they did for each other. The simple things like dinner and breakfast in bed or the jokes she told him while swinging on the daybed.

When night fell, Stoic asked to be left alone with his girl. His children left the room, but some would stay the night, not wanting to leave their mom alone during this time.

Emmerson entered the room and, with difficulty, walked to his slowly fading figure. Happy memories of their youth ran through her mind. Ever since they were children, she had done nothing but fight with him up until Stoic became a man, and then she became mesmerized by his charm. She remembered the way Stoic used to hold the youngest of their children in his arms as he did the laundry, and the older ones would run on and play around them on the patio. The way his long red hair shone under the sun. The beautiful life he had built for her.

She sat on the bed next to him, and he slowly laid over her lap. His body still felt heavy as it always did. His chest was moving with difficulty, and he was getting more tired with every breath he took. She lovingly caressed his now white hair, just like hers. The curls in them were still as soft as she remembered them.

She embraced in her arms the once vibrant, strong man that now was gray [illegible] sweet, loving, but quiet man that lived his life for her. The man she learned to understand, even when his face gave nothing away and his words were scarce. She quickly realized that he had always expressed his love for her, but not with words. His actions were worth a million words, and she learned soon enough that he didn't have to speak for her to know. She could see it in his eyes. The very same eyes she was drowning in, knowing well this might be the last time she saw them.

Stoic never said much, but he would always listen. Even at his old age, he could still remember all the things she said, even the least important ones. Ever since her first words, he had saved them in his mind and treasured the memory of her voice for all these years as his most valuable possession.

He placed his now wrinkled hand on his chest, and she wrapped hers around it. His eyes fixed on the most beautiful colors he'd ever seen, the most precious, most magical thing he had ever held in his arms.

He raised his other hand and gently touched her face. His baby. He never stopped calling her that. He tried to smile, and as his hands started to drop, he pinched her nipple. She laughed and slapped his hand. He tried to laugh and started coughing.

"There, there. Stop laughing, you crazy old fart. You can't even breathe," she told him as she lovingly patted him. Her voice, his favorite sound in the whole world.

Years had filled his once strong face with wrinkles. She loved each and every one of them. It reminded her of all the years she had the blessing of being wrapped in his arms.

She held both of his hands that rested over his chest again, wrapped in her own wrinkled ones. The heat that warmed her life slowly fading.

Stoic tried to say something, but the air got stuck in his lungs once again.

"Don't worry, I know. I know," she said, and he nodded.

They stayed like that, feeling each other's hands. Emmerson talked about their life together, how thankful she was to have him, and all the beautiful memories he had created for her. She kept talking to him and softly sang songs as he quietly passed. She noticed the moment his chest stopped moving but didn't stop talking. His eyes were still fixed on her, and she looked at them from time to time. She could still see the love in them, even after he was gone. Her hands caressed his face. She kept talking the whole night, not wanting to let him go, wanting to have him in her arms for at least a few more minutes.

He had held her in his arms the day she was born, and she held him in hers the day he died.

His ashes were spread in the river. Once a week, she would ask one of her children to take her there. Emmerson sat on a rock and talked to him. She spoke for hours. She knew he was silently listening. He always did.

Acknowledgments

I would like to extend my sincere thanks to all the people that help me make this possible. Thanks to my editor, Darci Heikkinen, for taking my project and polishing it the way she did. She went above and beyond and I will always be thankful for her help and for all I learned from her. Also, to the people that helped me proofread the book, Author L.B. Harpdog, Author Silver Taurus, and Author Gigi Foster. I truly appreciate your help and support and I will always cherish it in my heart.

Also, I want to extend my gratitude to the community of readers and authors who believed in me, supported me during the creation of these books, both in English and Spanish, and promoted and recommended my work. Especially those who supported me from the very beginning, even when I was a new and unknown author and my book had countless mistakes. You all saw the potential and encouraged me to reach far. The beautiful people with whom I had the joy of forming a very beautiful friendship. They will always have a special place in my heart. I can't express with words how thankful I am to you all. Thanks!

Last but not least, I want to thank the people who supported me in my Ko-fi account. Their generosity brought me joy at times when exhaustion overwhelmed me and their words of encouragement helped me continue forward. Thanks!

The people who supported me at Ko-fi:

Lorayna	B_kay	Liudmyla
ToniPluke	Mitz	WendyLandicho
Adeena	Aierodesa	Teaatbeesea
RainbowRenee	Anonymous Ko-fi Supporter	Mel
Eyeronic Editing	El Rivers	Cristina
JIA		Jael Brown